RIDUNA

Diana Jackson is an English, business studies and personal tutor at local college in Bedfordshire. Her passions are social history, gardening, cooking her own produce, travelling and following her husband's Rock and Roll band.

Although her great grandmother, an Alderney girl, has been her inspiration, Diana stresses that her first novel *Riduna* is purely fiction.

Hoping to take the reader to a time before the much documented World War II occupation and evacuation, she chose the name 'Riduna', the Latin name for the island of Alderney, to conjure up the mystery and beauty of an island which holds a special place in her heart.

For news of Diana Jackson's next novel in this series,

Ancasta ~ Guide me Swiftly Home

coming out soon, check out her website, her blog or say hello on Facebook or Twitter:

www.dianamaryjackson.co.uk

www.dianamj.wordpress.com

Riduna on Twitter

Diana Jackson's Author Page on Facebook

Diana Jackson

RIDUNA

EVENTISPRESS

A CIP catalogue record for this title is
available from the British Library.

ISBN 978-0-9572520-4-2 paperback
ISBN 978-0-9572520-3-5 e version

Published by Eventispress in 2012
First Published in 2009 by *Pegasus Elliot MacKenzie Publishers Ltd.*
Printed and bound by CPI Group (UK) Ltd, Croydon, CR0 4YY

Dedication

To my Great Grandmother Harriet Jane Hopkins, daughter of Jane Renier and born on the island of Alderney, my original inspiration.

Acknowledgements

Heartfelt thanks to all the family and friends who have given me so much encouragement, especially my writing partner and true friend Lorna Joy

Chapter 1

1882

IT WAS A crisp morning, one of those spring mornings full of promise just like Harriet Loveridge, whose fresh young face of sixteen years still held the prettiness of a child, tinged with the dreams of future summers. She leaped out of bed, just in time to watch her father through her window, striding out of the gate and along the road towards Harbour Quarry. He looked fit and strong for his thirty-six years. It was nearly six o'clock, when her father was due to begin his day's work.

Since her mother's long bout of pneumonia last winter Harriet had taken on most of the cottage chores. She splashed her face with water from the bowl on her dresser and gave her hands a cursory scrub. They would be clean enough after she had finished the washing, but first she had her mother's breakfast to prepare. She went downstairs to find the stove already lit and a kettle simmering on the side. She poured boiling water into the already brewed pot of tea and cut a couple of thin slices of yesterday's loaf.

'Mama, Mama it's a lovely morning,' she gently called as she put down the tray to kiss her. 'How are you feeling today?'

'Ta, Harriet love.' Harriet's mother sat up in bed and sipped her tea. Um, that's good. I'm feeling a touch stronger, but if you could give your father's old work clothes a scrub this morning before going up the cutting to the dairy, I think I could manage the baking today.'

'That's grand to hear Mama, but shall I go to the baker's for a penny loaf as a treat, to save you the trouble of baking?' Harriet asked. 'After all, father was paid yesterday and I did make the pie last night before coming to bed.

'You're a thoughtful girl,' exclaimed Harriet's mother.

Harriet scrubbed the filthy clothes until her hands felt raw, then she put them through the ringer before hanging them quickly outside in the yard. Next she reached up for the red tin and picked out a few doubles. Grabbing her shawl she flicked back her long auburn hair as she walked into the sunshine, following in her father's footsteps.

'Good morning to you,' she called to Mrs Johnson, her next-door neighbour, who was also putting out her washing.

'Good morning Harriet,' Mrs Johnson replied. 'Do you think Annie will be well enough to join us on Friday night?'

'I do hope so Mrs Johnson. She's feeling much stronger today but I must rush now. I'll call in later on,' Harriet replied as cheerfully as possible. In truth, the reminder of the 'sending off celebration' for her neighbour's son Edward, who was leaving the island to work on a passenger steamer from Sarnia to England, brought a cloud to Harriet's otherwise clear blue day.

She turned up La Valée where the shade of a beautiful wooded glen meandered up towards La Ville and seemed to reflect the perceptive change in her mood. Only five days to go before he left. As she walked, her thoughts focussed on Edward. Three years her senior, he had played the role of big brother for as long as she could remember. Since neither of them had brothers or sisters of their own, which was unusual on the island, Edward had always been there for her. Although he teased her incessantly, he had also protected and defended her fiercely.

Each year Edward had spent six weeks of the summer living with his aunt and uncle on the neighbouring island of Sarnia, initially as an errand boy for their lodging house in St Peter Port, but later supplementing this meagre income by helping the stevedores loading the waiting ships down at the harbour. He always came back with exciting tales of people he had met and places he had visited. Last year was the worst of all when he teased her about all the pretty girls he had seen, with their elegant dresses, decorated with the finest frills and laces, like the picture stories of princesses she had seen at school. He goaded her to extreme jealousy when he described in detail their coy blushes and their beautiful smiles as he had danced with them.

Harriet's quick wit had regained the upper hand when she reminded him of the sore toes he had inflicted on the Riduna girls when he was learning to dance. There was very little that Harriet and Edward could not talk about and, if they ever had an argument, she was aware that he usually let her win, just as her father did with her mother. Harriet smiled. As she turned towards St Anne, emerging into daylight once more at the bottom end of Victoria Street, she daydreamed of wearing a beautiful lemon ball gown with a narrow lace trim, just covering her modesty, and floating in Edward's strong arms. She had longed to surprise him by her skills as a dancer, which she had taken to with the grace of a beautiful swan.

At what moment did her feelings towards him change? Harriet mused. She would always miss him during those weeks apart, but when she was younger it gave her time to bond with her other friends, especially Charlotte and Jane her confidante. It was Charlotte who had opened her eyes as to how handsome Edward had become. As the three girls were sitting up on the Butes one Sunday afternoon, talking together, full of mirth, Edward had walked by with his friends. The lads were at the age where they sometimes pretended to be adults, having serious discussions about the world and their future dreams, but at others they played football, racing about between grassy slopes and sand dunes.

The girls, on the other hand, were practising to be young ladies. They, too, conversed, mainly about their families, the books they had read and the clothes they were making or dreamed that they would make. Sometimes they met together to sew, usually mending well-worn family garments, while they gossiped in one of their parents' front rooms, or if the weather was fair, like it was on that day, they would steal an hour to sit, their heads protected by demure bonnets or shawls, just enjoying the sunshine.

Despite their distance, the young people were shy of the changes. Coy glances and unspoken signals passed between them. On this occasion on the Butes, unfinished sentences hung in the air as both groups were suddenly aware of the others and not quite sure what to do next. After a tangible moment of silence, the lads just said 'good afternoon,' and gave mock bows before walking past and down the slope. Their occasional backward glances were followed by laughter, which was blown away on the sea breeze.

The girls looked at each other and giggled, but it was Charlotte's blush that had set Harriet thinking. She had watched Charlotte's expression with irritable curiosity, as Edward's eyes had lingered momentarily on her friend. Charlotte was a year older and certainly developed more physically, if not mentally. A few years ago there would have been no hesitation. The boys would have settled themselves down beside them and suggested that they all go off on some adventure, or game together. She recalled the favourite activities of their younger days, playing hide and seek in 'Fairy Woods,' or building dens in the hedgerows. On one occasion, when Harriet was about ten years old, she remembered vividly when they were playing chase by the infamous 'Lovers' Chair'.

Legend has it that the rock, which is in the shape of a chair, was a trysting place between a handsome man from Sarnia and a beautiful maiden from Riduna. The story goes that their parents forbade their union and so, in despair at the thought of being torn from each other, they joined hands at that very spot and leaped into the sea below! The legend seems to have left a mystical quality to the area above Telegraph Bay, for all who are aware of it.

Edward, the eldest and certainly the fastest runner, had caught Charlotte, and to the amazement of the others had scooped her up in his arms. He had sat on the rock next to her and, without thinking of the consequences, had planted a kiss on her lips. There was stunned silence as the children watched on in surprised curiosity, wondering what would happen next, but realising that they had witnessed an intimacy which was strictly forbidden.

The islanders had strict rules regarding the behaviour of young men and women and although the influx of 'strangers' over the past two decades had influenced their way of life, traditional values remained deep rooted in the hearts and minds of the elders.

As if watching actors in a play, Harriet looked on as Charlotte stood up, her face a pretty picture of pink, followed by a red faced Edward, who bowed gallantly to her, before setting off at a pace along the cliff path towards the village, Michael and John following close behind him. It was soon after this memorable event that the groups had drifted apart; the girls now only allowed to participate in quieter activities befitting the fairer sex, carrying out responsibilities for the home, or finding work in local hotels or shops. Many of the lads had left school by now, too, and had followed in their fathers' footsteps, either working long hours at the quarry or in their family businesses.

On that sunny afternoon on the Butes, Harriet knew that, if she had been alone, Edward would have had no hesitation in sitting down beside her. Even the most stalwart of islanders had seen them together since they were very young and saw them as brother and sister. Is that how I see us? She mused silently.

At home nothing had changed. He would still call in virtually every night, or she would visit next door, and they would spend an hour together, sharing the eventful moments of their day and some of their future dreams. Edward always had a humorous way of telling a tale over the years and even her mother had laughed at the antics that his classmates had enjoyed at school. It was on one of these moments that Edward had first shared his dreams of going to sea. His trips to his aunt and uncle's each year had given him a taste of travel, and a realisation that there was more on his horizon than following his father to work in the quarry. He told Harriet of the sailors he had met, and of the stories his uncle had shared, and the wonderful places they had seen.

Harriet was brought back to the present when she realised that she had reached the island's dairy. Her churn was filled before she headed towards Victoria Street to buy bread, greeting Charlotte's mother before heading back home. She would just have enough time to finish her chores before racing back up to the schoolhouse in High Street to help Miss Green in the girls' class. Not having little brothers and sisters of her own, she was delighted when Miss Green had suggested that, while she continued her independent studies under her teacher's guidance, she could also earn a little by helping out with the youngest girls each morning.

If the truth were known, Miss Green had a soft spot for Harriet, and could envisage her helper following in her footsteps. Of this notion Harriet was totally unaware.

Chapter 2

MR JACK LOVERIDGE walked at a brisk pace. Leaving the door to close with a jolt behind him, he left their cottage in Platte Saline and he thought fondly of his wife and daughter.

She's turning into a good 'un, he pondered as he passed the track leading to La Vallée. It reminded him of the night back in 1866 when Harriet was born. A night he'd never forget. He used to chuckle at the tales of the old fishermen, at the tavern which his uncle ran, down by the harbour. On many occasions they'd been entertained by stories of ghosts and foreboding, which were all the better for the embellishment of a few brandies.

That night, returning from the Diver's Tavern, with his neighbour Joseph, a little worse for drink, but still with all their major senses intact, he had suddenly stopped and shivered. The next thing he knew he was diving for cover, as a white bull charged towards them. It seemed to fly past them at such a pace, that all they felt was a cold wind, as it disappeared up La Vallée and vanished.

Joseph, who had sat down on a nearby boulder, exclaimed, 'An ill wind to pass us tonight Jack, my old friend. I'm sure no good will come of the sight of that old ghost!'

Jack was barely listening to his friend, since another unusual light stole his attention out in the bay towards Burhou. A glow of smoky orange and yellow illuminated the otherwise dark night sky.

'Come Joseph, look over there!' he exclaimed pointing to the horizon. 'You'd be of more use coming with me to find out what's amiss, than mumbling about those old wives' tales,' he called as he was already haring off along the track towards the flickering lights, the bull long forgotten.

Joseph was about to protest as he dragged himself to his feet, but he was soon catching up with his friend as they raced towards the bay. Once it was obvious that their fears of another ship in trouble had been confirmed, they halted in their tracks.

'Oh, no Jack, it's only a year since the Crispin went down in that very spot. The sea is a devil for claiming lives around these isles but what should we do now?' Joseph turned to his friend as he always did in times of crisis, despite being two years his senior.

'I'll run back to the harbour to alert the lifeboat, although they're sure to be on their way by now, if you run to wake up the doctor. It's too dangerous chancing going out in our boat tonight. The skipper must have been green to attempt these waters at night, even with the weather as calm as it is. I'll meet you back down in the bay.'

While the drama unfolded out at sea, and the lifeboat was mobilised down at the harbour, another drama was unfolding at the little row of cottages above Platte Saline. Annie Loveridge had put her feet up for a few minutes. Oh! How her back ached. Jack's supper was ready and keeping warm on the stove, and with only three weeks to go before the baby was due, she was overwhelmed by tiredness. Her eyelids were just closing when she felt a mighty great pain. She muffled a cry, not wanting to worry Beth, her neighbour and best friend, as she gripped the arms of her chair. She took a few deep breaths and started to relax again.

'Where have you got to Jack!' she groaned aloud.

She was just drifting off to sleep for a second time, when she was engulfed by another stabbing pain. This time she screamed out loud in agony.

Beth was just folding her laundry when she heard the cry. She raced next door and took one look at Annie, before running back outside and along to Old Mother's cottage at the end of the row. There was no time to run up to the village to fetch the doctor and anyway, she reasoned, there was very little that Old Mother didn't know about delivering babies. Old Mother was really a nickname for Miss Thomas. She'd never been a mother herself, and certainly had no medical training, but she had delivered more babies during her long life on the island than the last three doctors put together. She was a familiar and comforting sight, both welcoming the new arrivals into this world and preparing bodies for the next. As it happens, it was also just as well that Beth had made this snap decision, because the doctor and Joseph were already on their way down to Platte Saline in the doctor's horse and cart, which was piled high with blankets and medical supplies. They reckoned that any survivors rescued by the lifeboat would be brought ashore in the bay, to be taken by the quickest route to his surgery, or on to St. Anne's Hall if necessary, to await his medical attention.

By the time Jack and Joseph finally stumbled home in the early hours of the morning they were exhausted, bedraggled and wet through. Their clothes were splattered with blood. As Jack raised the latch on the gate, the bent figure of Old Mother came rushing out of the cottage, muttering under her breath as she flew past them.

'Where've you been?' she snapped. 'You nearly lost yer wife and bairn tonight, but you've found time to go a' squabbling down in the bay, by the looks a' you. Disgraceful I'd say!' she tutted as she sped along to her own cottage.

Jack and Joseph stood there open mouthed. Jack was just about to yell after her, to give her a piece of his mind, when a shrill cry of a baby filled the air. Jack raced inside leaving Joseph motionless behind him, a dark silhouette against the moonlit sky. Inside, he found Beth in the rocking chair cradling a now quietly whimpering baby in her arms. She held the baby up to Jack, who slipped off his wet and mucky overcoat, dropping it on the floor, before gently taking the little bundle. The baby was suddenly quiet and Joseph, who had crept in behind Jack, smiled a warm and gentle smile at his exhausted but relieved wife.

'You can tell she's her father's girl already,' mused a weary Beth.

'I told Annie to try to get some rest, but I expect she's straining herself to keep awake for you, Jack.'

'Well done Jack, my old mate,' said Joseph gruffly, full of emotion. 'That'll be a friend for our little Edward, when the little 'un gets a bit bigger.'

Edward, a little boy of only three years, was snuggled asleep under a blanket in the chair next to Beth, oblivious to the dramas of the night.

Jack crept up the steep staircase to their room. Annie was curled up, but her eyes were open. Jack brushed her damp forehead with his lips, before laying the warm bundle next to her pale and exhausted face. He watched in awe as tears silently fell over her lovely cheeks and she lifted her limp arm to cuddle their first child. Jack knelt beside the bed and stroked her hair.

'Well done my lovely,' he whispered. 'I've two beautiful women in my life now, so why the tears?'

'Old Mother said there'll be no more babies for us Jack,' she sobbed.

'Never mind lass. We're a family now and we have each other,' Jack said comfortingly.

He sat on the edge of the bed stroking her forehead as Annie slipped into a fitful sleep.

Beth came up silently behind them and carefully lifted the little one out of Annie's limp arms. She rocked her to and fro, cooing to her as she laid her gently in the beautiful crib that Jack had so lovingly made.

They crept back downstairs, attempting to miss the couple of creaky stairs on their way. Jack lifted the bottle of brandy and three glasses from the dresser.

'Sit yer down again Beth a while,' he said as he poured three generous measures.

So Beth, Joseph and Jack drank a toast to the new arrival, saying a prayer of thanks that Annie and the babe were alive and well. Beth recounted some of the details of the night's events. Annie had experienced such a difficult and painful delivery that twice Old Mother had been fearful that neither mother nor child would survive. Finally, at the moment when the baby was born, she was blue and as still as death itself. The moment of silence seemed an eternity, until Old Mother scooped her up. As she did so, a wave of colour enveloped the child, as her lungs filled and she let out a loud cry.

At first Annie was too weak to even cuddle her infant and she lay limply, as they washed her and helped her to sit up. It was when she had the child in her arms at last, that Old Mother had said pointedly,

'If you bear another bairn you'll not survive the ordeal Annie. It's a miracle both of you are alive today!'

The elderly lady's abrupt and tactless manner had upset Annie, so Beth had picked up the child and encouraged Annie to try to get some sleep. Beth had thanked Old Mother and they had tidied up, trying to be as quiet as possible. Then Old Mother had taken her leave and scuttled out of the cottage, just as the baby had filled its lungs and bellowed, as if to tell the world she was alive and well and here to stay!

'So that was the moment both of you appeared out of the night. It must've been nigh on three o'clock in the morning!' she reproached her husband Joseph. 'Where've you been all this time, when your wife needed you so badly, Jack? It had better be a good reason to tell your beloved tomorrow.'

Joseph and Jack took turns to tell their tale of the evening's events, of the appearance of the Ghost of the White Bull, the fire on the horizon out at sea and the dramatic rescue of all the crew of the Jules.

Once Jack had met up with the doctor and Joseph down in the bay, they watched as they could make out the shape of the island's lifeboat rushing to the ship's rescue. Its profile was clear in the moonlit sky, as it sped across the bay through the whirling waters. It was not even a stormy or foggy night, but it appears that the Jules had misjudged the tides and ventured too close to the treacherous rocks.

It was a notorious stretch of sea to be avoided, especially at night. Even the experienced, born and bred on these islands, thought twice before attempting that stretch of water in the dark. It had claimed too many lives over the years.

As they stood there, waiting helplessly, gazing out towards the lifeboat, Jack was thinking of the men on board, dear friends every one of them. Each able man on the island volunteered for service one full year in three. It would be Joseph and Jack's turn next year.

Just as the lifeboat was approaching the Jules, the ship was beginning to list, and Jack and Joseph gasped, fearing the worst. Each had visions of the tragic disaster of the Crispin only a year before, when they had also stood helplessly by, as they had watched the ship slide down into the water. Then there had been no survivors.

This time, they stood there saying a private prayer, hoping against hope that they were not witnessing a repeat tragedy.

'Jack. Is that another vessel out there?' Joseph exclaimed.

Just as they were giving up hope, the ghostly shape of a tugboat became visible. As they heard from the captain later, it had been travelling along the same waters that night and had reached the Jules just as the fire had started in the engine room. Since the weather had not been too stormy, it had been able to come along the blind side of the troubled ship. By the time that the island's lifeboat had reached the Jules, some of the crew had already been taken directly on board the tugboat, while the injured had also been lowered into the ship's two lifeboats. The captain had been the last to climb down and had courageously rowed clear, as they watched their ship list and sink into the sea.

The tugboat then continued its journey to where it was to be commissioned on Sarnia, taking the majority of the crew on to the neighbouring island, while the lifeboat had guided the other two boats to shore, before returning to the safety of the harbour. Jack, Joseph, the doctor and some other volunteers had helped to lift the injured on to the waiting cart. It took three journeys, but as they sat with the captain and the remaining crew, wrapping them in blankets and sharing a drop of brandy, the captain shared with them the details of their fortunate rescue.

Both vessels had been stranded for several hours in thick fog and when it had eventually lifted it was already evening. Fortunately for the crew of the Jules, the captain of the Watt had also decided to risk sailing through the straits that night, known by locals as The Swinge. More alert to the dangers of these treacherous waters, he had taken a safer course beyond Burhou Island and so was very quickly on hand to offer assistance to the stricken Jules. All crew had been saved. The captain gratefully acknowledged that, without the appearance of the steam tug Watt, the outcome of the night's events might have been disastrous.

In their excitement to tell their tale and exonerate their tardiness, they were slow in noticing that Beth's eyelids were drooping and that she was nearly asleep. Joseph helped his sleepy wife to her feet, supporting her firmly by his strong arm, as she gathered their sleeping lad in her arms. Joseph winked at Jack as he guided Beth to the door. Jack sat on his own for a few minutes, enjoying the silence of the night before heading upstairs himself.

As if awaking from a familiar dream Jack suddenly realised that he had nearly reached the quarry. His last thoughts were of his wife Annie. Since the birth of Harriet, her health had not been good and during each winter she was prone to catching infections. He hoped that the spring sunshine might give her strength today. He was pleased that Harriet, on the other hand, was blessed with extremely good health and not only that, but that she had such a sweet and endearing nature, albeit a little self-willed and stubborn at times.

As he walked towards the foreman's hut, Samuel Allen came out to meet Jack, giving him the orders for the day's work. The other men greeted him cheerily and the light-hearted banter began as they prepared for work, Jack's memories soon pushed to the back of his mind.

Chapter 3

THE FOLLOWING FRIDAY evening Harriet knew Edward was at the front door, even before she heard the knock. She finished brushing and pinning up her long auburn hair and picked up her locket. She slipped into her parents' room where her mother sat up on the bed sipping tea, following her afternoon nap.

'I'm off now Mama, for a stroll with Edward along the shore. Can you do up the clasp of this locket for me?' Harriet asked.

'I won't detain you now Harriet, my love, but one day I want you to tell me all about how Edward came to be giving you that lovely locket, when all the talk of the island is that he and Charlotte are nigh on betrothed.' Annie paused for a moment before continuing, 'I know you're a lovely girl, and I know that you and Edward are best friends, but please be careful.'

'Oh Mama! Don't fret so, especially tonight. Edward is very special to me, you know that, and always will be. I must go now because he's waiting downstairs.'

The precious silver locket sat beautifully in the well of Harriet's neck. She looked in the mirror and blushed, remembering the May Ball three weeks ago when Edward had given it to her. She was not going to allow her mother's doubt spoil their last evening together. The feelings between them were so very new and fragile, although in some ways they felt as ageless as time itself.

At the May Ball Harriet's card had filled up quickly, to dance with many of the island's young men, but also some of the visitors. It was the latter who had made her a little wary. Their eyes seemed to linger on her figure just a little too long, and their hands held her just a little too firmly, for her liking. She was annoyed with herself for feeling a twinge of jealousy, as she was aware that Edward had danced with her friend Charlotte, not once but twice during the evening. She reassured herself that he had marked her card for the last dance, and she tried not to wish the time away towards that moment. Finally, he was making his way towards her, and she could feel her heart beating faster. She knew Edward so well. He was like family to her. As he reached her side, she was acutely aware that her feelings for him were far more than that of sisterly affection.

'Will I be walking you home as usual?' Edward asked, as casually as possible. Harriet was relieved that she probably was not the only one who had felt twinges of jealousy that night.

'Of course!' she reassured him. 'You know that Papa would meet me if Mama was well, but he does trust you to escort me home safely, especially with so many strangers here.'

The music began and as Edward led her expertly on to the dance floor he whispered,

'I've been waiting for this moment all night.'

Then his hands held her as they glided around the dance floor and were soon lost in a world of their own, two figures melting into one. Neither spoke. Each wished to live for the moment alone, memorising each new sensation to hold on to during the lonely future that faced them.

Once the music ended, Harriet and Edward went their separate ways to say their goodbyes to friends, especially Edward who would not see some of them for six months. Harriet waited for him. Her emotions were swinging between elation and grief. As he returned to her side, she smiled nervously as he took her arm and they walked out into the night. At first they walked in silence and Edward led Harriet down to Braye Common, a detour, but he knew that this was one of Harriet's favourite places on the island. Edward stopped as they were overlooking the bay in the moonlight and he reached into his pocket and brought out a little package.

'Harriet, this is for you,' he said. 'Although I'm excited about my new life at sea, in the last few weeks I've not been able to keep thoughts of you out of my mind. Sometimes you're still like a kid sister to me, but at others you're the young and beautiful woman who stands before me now.'

Overwhelmed, Harriet's hands trembled as she opened the neatly wrapped package.

'Oh, it's lovely!' she exclaimed as she set eyes on the silver locket. 'I'll wear it every evening and think of you.'

Edward undid the clasp and slipped it around her neck. As he secured it, she shivered and he took hold of her hands and gently leaned forward to kiss her on the forehead. Sometimes she looked so fragile that he wanted to protect her, and at others he was aware of stirrings inside him, of feelings and wants beyond his experience. Soon, they walked on through Crabby Village and arrived at the gate of Harriet's cottage. Since they could hear the familiar sound of their parents talking, they stepped inside together.

Harriet smiled at her reflection and glowed with the happy memory. Downstairs she could hear the familiar voices of Edward and her father. She and Edward were to walk down to Newtown where her grandparents lived, then drop into the Braye Tavern so that Harriet could clean the tables as she always did, while Edward said his farewells to Harriet's extended family before heading back home.

'I'll be off now Mama, but remember that we're expected around at Aunt Beth's at 8 o'clock. Don't you go drifting off to sleep again now, and be late? Papa is home from work early, so I'll see you both later.'

Harriet stood up, taking one last glance at her reflection in her mother's full length mirror before gliding downstairs.

Edward looked up at her as she came into view. Their eyes met and for the first time his gaze momentarily embarrassed her. Her father noticed it too, and gave a hearty chuckle.

'My girl's become quite a beauty over the last few months, hasn't she Edward?' he said. 'Now, you bring her back in one piece and don't be tempted to go paddling and spoil your clothes, Harriet my girl.'

'We're not children anymore Papa,' said Harriet crossly, her face reddening.

'He's only teasing you Harriet. You should know that by now. You look lovely and I'm beginning to think that I'm foolish leaving you. After all, what will you do without me to protect you?' Edward asked.

'I'll manage quite well thank you Edward. At least I'll only have one man in my life to tease me incessantly,' Harriet protested.

'Be off the pair of you, or it will be Edward who will be late for his own farewell supper,' said Jack. 'Don't worry about Harriet when you're gone lad. I think it's about time I kept a closer eye on little Harriet here. She's getting a bit too independent for a young girl,' he said as he winked at Edward and ushered them both to the door, before Harriet had a chance to protest again.

They walked through Crabby Village and along towards Braye Beach, which swept in front of them, sheltered by the long breakwater and Fort Albert ahead. After visiting the grandparents and spending an hour at the Braye Tavern, it was only about half an hour to sunset and the scene was coloured with a lovely warm glow. The air was unusually calm, albeit slightly chilly for a spring evening and for a while there was a nervous tension between them.

At last Harriet broke the silence.

'I didn't mean what I said to my father about not needing you Edward. I *will* miss you. You know that, don't you but, whereas you'll be having the adventure of your life, back here Riduna will change very little.'

'Are you sure that you'll miss me Harriet? I was watching you dancing on Saturday night and you were having such a lovely time. We're still so very young to be making promises to each other, but I would go with a happier heart, if I thought that you would be waiting for my return.'

Edward struggled to find the right words to say. The moment seemed so fragile, just like Harriet herself.

Reading his mind Harriet replied,

'I'm not quite as delicate as you all think. I can't imagine life here without you, Edward, but this time I'll just try to think of it as an extra long summer. I'll keep busy and count the days until you come home in December, when you'll be home until after Christmas. It's in the New Year that I'll find it harder to bear, when you'll be going away for two years or more to who knows where.'

They had talked often of Edward's dreams of travelling the world, but it was hard for Harriet to imagine these dreams becoming a reality.

'Will you write to me?' Edward asked. 'Letters from Southampton will only take a week or so?'

'Of course I will, Edward. Writing to you each evening will help to fill the gap in my life, when you have always been there for me.'

Edward stopped and turned towards Harriet, aware that the light was fading and that they should soon return home for the feast, but not wanting this moment to end. Suddenly he was filled with admiration for this girl by his side. She did not whine or moan like some girls might have done. She understood his need to travel, even though she seemed to have no desire to escape with him, happy to listen to the tales of his adventures, but making the most of her simple life on this small island. After all, it was the only life she knew, so secure in the love of her family and friends. Sometimes Harriet's strength of character astounded him and he was more determined than ever not to lose her.

'I wasn't going to show you, in case you thought me silly, but look at *this* Edward,' Harriet said, as she carefully undid the clasp of her locket, revealing auburn and jet black hair, neatly entwined.

'After your mama trimmed your hair yesterday, I collected some and plaited it with a lock of my own, so that each evening when I wear this locket, there will always be a part of you here with me. Now do you think me too soft and sentimental?' she asked looking up at him for reassurance.

As a reply, without thinking, Edward wrapped his arms around her, pulling her gently towards him, sinking his lips into her beautiful hair. They stood for a few minutes, wrapped in each other's warmth and watched the glow of the sun sink below the reddened horizon. Simultaneously, they withdrew from their embrace, and with Edward's arm gently resting over Harriet's shoulder, they started to walk towards home, both lost in thought. Neither noticed the lonely figure standing on the grassy banks above the shore, wretchedly watching their departure.

Edward was relieved that Mr Loveridge was intending to keep a closer eye on Harriet in the coming months. An island like this seemed such a safe place on which to grow up, and the traditional and somewhat archaic unwritten codes of behaviour expected of its young people, although stifling at times, were also comfortingly protective. Although easier travel, with the age of steam, and the influx of 'strangers' had made their mark on the island's ways, nevertheless Edward was grateful that Mr Loveridge trusted him implicitly, but was beginning to feel the burden of that trust. Maybe some time apart would do them both good and give time to test their true feelings. If their growing love (was it love?) survived the next three years, then he would have no hesitation in asking Harriet to marry him, but he was aware that she was still so very young.

They reached Harriet's cottage and parted for a few moments. Harriet went inside to collect her parents and Edward went on into his home to see if his mother needed assistance.

Chapter 4

EDWARD HELPED HIS mother to set the table and then went upstairs to his room to spend a few moments on his own. His excuse was that he wanted to have a final check on his sturdy trunk, but in truth he was in turmoil. The thought of leaving Harriet at this time, when they were both only just becoming aware of their feelings for each other, gave him an agonising pain, which was so real that it astounded him. How did he allow himself to feel like this? He thought back to last spring.

Miss Green had kindly arranged to give the young people on the island dancing lessons and the moment had arrived to have a lesson with the girls. He had called for Harriet, as arranged, and they had walked up to the schoolhouse, laughing as they went. With any other young couple, just walking together would be seen as a sign of betrothal, or still frowned upon by the elders of the island, but Edward and Harriet had always been seen as brother and sister by all who knew them. Once they arrived Miss Green had paired them off with partners. Since Harriet was only fifteen years old and would not be allowed to attend the proposed dances until after her sixteenth birthday, Edward had been given Charlotte, who was more than a year older than Harriet, to be his partner.

At first they were both embarrassed by the prospect, remembering their last close encounter playing 'chase' a few autumns ago. Soon their mutual feelings of discomfort vanished as they attempted to concentrate on the music, their floundering feet and Miss Green's helpful instructions. Harriet had danced with Charlotte's brother, Michael, who was nearer her age. The event had been full of mirth, though occasionally tempers frayed.

The first ever dance on the island had been at the May Ball, a year ago. Even with the aid of the intoxicating punch that afternoon, a special Riduna custom of 'Punch a Day Sunday' when Edward had raced up and down the island's streets to be given a free mix of rum, milk, sugar and egg in the island's hostelries, he mustered enough courage to ask only Charlotte to dance. He danced with her no less than three times during the evening, strangely naive of the gossip it would cause. That night when having his usual conversation with Harriet, telling her in detail about the evening, describing the clothes, the music and the dancing, he could not bring himself to talk about Charlotte. It was the first time that he had held a secret from her and that made him feel uncomfortable. In fact, his friends had teased him every day since, and on the occasion when the lads came across the girls sitting on the Butes that Sunday, he was so embarrassed that he did not know what to do. He also noticed Charlotte blushing and thought how pretty it had made her look. Another secret thought that he withheld from Harriet.

At the Summer Ball last July, just before his annual visit to Sarnia, he was more careful. He had danced with Charlotte twice during the evening and had marked the cards of two other ladies present, but he had also promised to have the last dance with Harriet. She had been very excited at attending her first dance, but also a little nervous, and so she had declared that she would stand and watch until that last dance. When with Charlotte, Edward had been quite tense. Charlotte's sky blue gown matched the colour of her beautiful eyes and she was also wearing the most memorable, delicate perfume. Each of them was acutely aware of the watchful gaze of their friends and neighbours, especially Charlotte's parents, who could not wish for a finer young man than Edward to be betrothed to their daughter,

In contrast, the final dance with Harriet had been a delight. Edward and Harriet knew each other so well, that any slight mistake was treated with good humour. As they danced, they began to relax into the rhythm of the music and their movements flowed gracefully together.

When the dance was over Edward made his way to say goodnight to his friends. Instead of teasing him this time, they praised him for his accomplished dance technique, and made comments as to how pretty Harriet had become. Edward went over to say goodnight to Charlotte, and her parents were obviously pleased when he bowed and kissed Charlotte's hand in the most gallant fashion.

'If you would like, I will come down to wave goodbye to you in the morning, Edward,' she had said.

'I'd like that very much,' Edward had replied, although he was not sure whether he had said it to please her, or whether he had really meant it.

Edward had bowed again, and taking his leave he had collected Harriet to walk her home. They did not stop for a long talk that night because, not only was it quite late, but Edward was catching the ship to Sarnia the next morning.

Early the following morning he awoke to a crystal clear day. As he walked towards the harbour the slim buff funnel of RMS Courier came into view. It was a sturdy ship, capable of coping with severe weather conditions because, although today this was unnecessary, the weather changed uncannily quickly in these islands.

As the ship steamed away there were two young ladies waving goodbye, alongside Edward's parents; both had given him something to take away with him. Harriet gave him an amusing poem about the previous night. She had written it in such beautiful handwriting and had signing herself 'Your dearest friend Harriet.' Charlotte, on the other hand, had slipped a handkerchief into his pocket, which still held the fragrance of the alluring perfume that she had been wearing the night before.

After an uneventful crossing, Edward was met by his cousin Joe. They walked up the little alley to Well Road where his aunt and uncle ran a small guesthouse, talking amiably as they went. He was welcomed with open arms by his aunt, who suggested that he unpack his things while she prepared a light lunch. Edward had stayed with Beth's sister and her family during the busy summer season since he was old enough to be sent on errands, and latterly to meet the waiting ships. He and his cousin would carry cases and trunks for the many travellers, attracted to the island by its breathtaking scenery and balmy climate. If the bookings were low, they would compete with each other in touting for custom as the tourists arrived, only too relieved to secure a bed for the night. Whether it was one of the many regular visitors or a new comer, all were greeted with a cheery smile.

It was his cousin Joe who had found the handkerchief. As Edward begun the task of unpacking, Joe sat on his bed talking and catching up on the news of the last year.

'What's that lovely smell?' he asked as he, despite Edward's protests, had slipped his hand into Edward's jacket pocket. Joe held the handkerchief aloft as a trophy and laughed, then held it to his nose and inhaled the beautiful scent.

'Ummm, it must have been someone special to wear this smell and to give it to you as a token of her affections,' he teased.

'It's not like that at all!' Edward exclaimed. 'We just learnt to dance together.'

'Tell me all about her,' encouraged Joe, laying down on his own bed, in the room they would be sharing over the next six weeks. He propped his head up, resting it in his cupped hands and looked expectantly at Edward.

Edward sat down on his own bed and told his cousin about Charlotte.

'Well, she's a pretty girl of sixteen years. She has a twin brother Michael and they live in the island's bakery, which their parents run together. Michael is a good friend of mine too, but I've only danced with her! It had no meaning.'

Edward could feel himself blushing as he spoke, unaccustomed to talking with Joe about girls.

'But what does she look like Edward. I want to know if she's worthy of you!' Joe encouraged.

'Well,' hesitated Edward, trying to make a picture in his mind. 'She has lovely blue eyes, fair hair and a trim figure. She's quiet but she's a warm-hearted girl.'

'I think you'll have to buy the little lady a special gift before you return home,' Joe said, 'and I know just the place to look, but while you're here we'll go to one or two of our island's dances too. I could introduce you to some beautiful girls to distract you from pining too much for this Charlotte of yours!'

Edward hit Joe with a pillow and they began a pillow fight just like old times, which was only halted by a piercing shout from his aunt downstairs.

Edward always enjoyed his time with Joe, thinking of their house as a second home. Since it was a guesthouse, Edward's aunt and uncle were always busy. During this visit Joe and Edward attended three of the island's dances, which were held in local hotels, and he was aware of the flamboyant style of their clothes and fancy hairstyles compared to his little island home. Joe had also taken him to one of the rougher harbour taverns. Watching the antics in such a place was quite an eye-opener for Edward. Joe claimed it as an essential part of his education, as they staggered home and attempted to enter the guesthouse without stumbling over the furniture.

It was on their last evening, before he returned to Riduna, that Edward had experienced a sudden longing for the closeness and familiarity that he realised he only felt when he was with Harriet.

It was as if Joe had read his mind when he said, 'I expect young Harriet is turning into quite a beauty. Since you have other distractions, I imagine she will be looking for a young man of her own. I'll have to come over on a visit with you when we are on leave next year. What do you think Edward?' Joe asked, looking puzzled at his cousin's expression.

Hearing Joe mention Harriet's name simultaneously with his thoughts had confused Edward. The sudden vision in his mind of Harriet in Joe's arms gave him such a pang of jealousy that he was lost for words. Realising that his cousin was still looking at him, he quickly replied, 'She's a bit young for you yet Joe, and anyway, you don't think I could trust you to behave properly, after watching you last night do you?' He teased Joe in an attempt to cover his confusion.

That night, as he tried to get to sleep, he could not get Joe's words out of his mind. Edward adored looking after Harriet, protecting her, teasing her, laughing and talking with her. He missed his daily times with her when he was away and could not wait to see her again and tell her of his dreams and plans. The thought of losing her to another man, even to Joe, seemed unthinkable and yet... At that point he drifted off to sleep.

When Joe had dragged him, complaining, to a little jeweller's shop the following morning, only hours before his ship set sail, he was thoroughly confused. Six weeks had passed and he had rarely thought of Charlotte. He and Joe had spent most of their spare time planning an exciting future. Both had a desire to see something of the world and neither wanted to follow in their fathers' footsteps. Another alternative would be to enlist in the local Militia but both looked to widen their horizons via less regimented routes. They planned to apply for work with the local passenger and freight company, The Great Western Railway, which sailed regularly from Sarnia to Southampton. If all went well then they would look out for opportunities to join a world shipping company the following year, and maybe travel to India on a tea boat or to South America on a ship collecting coffee, which was fast becoming a popular alternative to tea on Sarnia. The sailors down by the harbour had inspired them to this adventure and assured them that their dreams were possible.

Edward and Joe arrived at the little backstreet jewellers, which sold second hand as well as new items. Edward chose a small silver locket and wondered what tales it had to tell. Although he nodded in agreement when Joe remarked that it was the perfect gift to soften the blow that his future plans might give Charlotte, and help to keep her sweet in his absence, he kept his true thoughts to himself. If it did not seem appropriate to give the locket to Charlotte, he could always give it to his mother, or even Harriet. With these reassuring thoughts, he reluctantly paid over the money and they returned to his cousin's house to collect his trunk, before making his way back down to the docks to catch the steamer home.

The journey homeward was frustrating. At first the weather was misty, but fairly calm. They had reached about half way when the mist lifted and the waters became quite choppy. Edward could make out a distant coastline, which he reasoned was more likely to be France than Riduna. He usually enjoyed the journey, but this time he was restless. The clouds billowed and it was as if a grey blanket was heading towards them. As suddenly as the mists had cleared, a thick fog descended. The funnel sounded its booming note and he could hear the sound of the sailors making the ship secure. The distant eerie bellow of the foghorn of Casquet Lighthouse echoed his feelings of melancholy and uncertainty. Even though the waters were now perfectly still, he knew that they would be travelling no further until the fog had lifted. He swallowed his frustration and went back down below to find a seat and try to pass the time. The ship was delayed by eight hours and the thick fog had left them stranded only five miles from Riduna.

It had lifted as suddenly as it had descended, giving a short window of opportunity for them to dock as the sun was setting. Edward's parents had given up hope of seeing their son that day and Charlotte, who had made several trips to the Butes in the hopes of seeing the ship in the distance through the fog, had returned home each time disappointed. Harriet had been visiting her grandparents, who ran The Braye Tavern, to help them polish the tables before opening time that evening and was just about to set off along the track to her home when her head turned inadvertently, to the glow of pink on the horizon. Like magic, the fog began to disperse and through the misty haze she could pick out the figure of a distant ship on the reddening waters. It was as if it was a summons, an invisible thread drawing her along the jetty. The ship in the distance had doubled in size and Harriet stood there transfixed.

As Edward gazed towards the familiar landscape of his island home he could just make out the figure of Harriet waiting alone for him. As he walked off the ship he dropped his bags and rushed towards her. Without thinking he picked her up, swinging her round him as he had always done in the past. Realising that, although she was laughing, her protests were serious, he put her down and stepped back to look at her. Joe was right. She was now a very beautiful young woman.

As they walked home together he was aware that her moment of embarrassment had passed and that they had fallen into amiable conversation, almost as if he had never been away. He could not help but make occasional sidelong glances at her, admiring her lovely features and her womanly figure. He was unaware, of course, that she was not wearing the fashionable corsets worn by the Sarnia ladies, but he could tell that there was a softness about her. Harriet's modest dress showed a slender waist between her maturing curves. Edward reprimanded himself to concentrate more on what Harriet was saying, but he was taken aback by the feelings welling inside him. In fact, he was so engrossed in the pleasurable sensations of walking beside her, that he failed to notice that Charlotte was waving to them from the Butes.

Now, a year later, Edward was brought back from these memories by a sound downstairs. He was rummaging in his top drawer to check that he had not forgotten anything, when he found the handkerchief. He blushed, even though nobody was there to witness it. It was strange how cool Charlotte had been to him of late, ever since he had told her of his plans to travel.

It was at the Harvest celebration last autumn, on his return from Sarnia, that he had found himself having a long conversation with Charlotte.

'Are you joining your father at the quarry, now you've left school Edward?' she had inquired.

'Only for a short while, Charlotte. I have much more exciting plans for the future.'

'And what might they be?'

'My cousin Joe and I are going to sea. We plan to join the crew on a steamship to England.'

'And why do you wish to do that?' Charlotte had asked.

'We hope to find our sea legs and then join an international shipping company and travel the world. That's our dream anyway.'

Edward was totally unaware that this remark had caused Charlotte to be upset, and so he was surprised when she suddenly took her leave and rushed to her parents' side. Her passing remark as she glided away was,

'It would be better to join the Militia than to go to such dangerous and unheard-of places. Please excuse me Edward, I have a terrible headache!' The island's militia were seen to have a quiet role in island life. They were rarely posted further away than Sarnia, since the defence of these islands was so important to the mainland.

It was a mystery to Edward. He had even attempted to make amends by visiting Charlotte and Michael on a couple of occasions, joining the family for supper, but she always seemed nervous in his presence and he ended up spending most of the time talking to Michael and his father. These were yet more secrets that he had been unwilling to share with Harriet, although he thought that Harriet's knowledge of the fairer sex might have been able to explain Charlotte's strange behaviour.

Edward had settled into a routine of working alongside his father at the quarry, usually joining the men for a drink or two at The Diver's and finishing each day with a restful talk with Harriet. They never seemed to tire of each other's company and felt companionable even when lost for words, which with Harriet was rare.

As the winter had given way to spring, Edward began to take note of Harriet's qualities, as if storing the memories for his lonely moments in the future, when he would be far away. He noted the selfless way in which she looked after her mother when she was ill; the way she ran the household, taking on the major tasks of a mature woman; her optimism for life in general and the way in which she shared his dreams with pleasure. In fact she made him feel so free that he began to question whether he wanted to go away at all. Most of all he found himself drawn to her, longing to caress and kiss her. As he sat with Harriet on one occasion, he had remembered the time out with Joe in a rough tavern in Sarnia. With the excuse that he had already imbibed too much drink, he had tried to imitate the elder men and gently patted a barmaid's backside, in the hopes that she would give him some attention. In fact she'd slapped him lightly in the face, jesting that he should come back when he was a man. Edward's face suddenly reddened with the memory.

'You're not listening to me at all!' Harriet had complained. 'What on earth are you thinking about, Edward, to make you go red like that? I bet you were thinking about Charlotte,' she had said crossly.

As earnestly as possible, without admitting the truth, he had replied, 'I never think of Charlotte when I am with you.'

'I suppose you never think of me when you are with her, either,' she had retorted and had walked out into the kitchen.

At a loss as to what he had said wrong, he tried to make amends by peering round the kitchen door saying mischievously,

'I adore you when you are cross, Harriet. Your temper would scare a ghost away.' Not waiting for the wet dishcloth to reach its target as it flew through the air after him, he just caught the glimpse of a smile, which Harriet was trying so hard to conceal. It lightened an otherwise foreboding expression on her face, which he could feel piercing his back as he escaped out of the back door.

There were no more dances during those winter months and although at first he felt duty bound to attempt some form of reconciliation with Charlotte, he felt relieved when she appeared to rebuff him. By Christmas he was enjoying Harriet's company so much that any confusion he had experienced as to how he felt had vanished. With spring in the air he felt more content than ever and although his excitement for his coming travels was undiminished, he was grateful that Harriet understood his needs unquestioningly and was as sure as he could be that she would wait for him.

Downstairs he could hear Harriet's voice as she arrived with her parents, greeted warmly by his mother. He knew in his heart that he had been right to give the locket to Harriet today. The memory of their warm embrace still lingered with him as he listened to her familiar voice before going downstairs to join them.

Chapter 5

CHARLOTTE SAT ON her chair gazing out of her bedroom window. Her eyes were red through weeping and she was deep in thought. From her attic window above the bakery she could see Victoria Street below.

She had just returned from a visit to her grandmother's cottage down at Newtown, to take her some bread and one of her favourite cakes as a treat from her mother. She knew that Edward was leaving tomorrow and was already mortified that they had not really talked since the autumn dance, when she had behaved so badly. It was the shock of it all. Ever since she had become Edward's dancing partner during those lessons, and possibly before, she was aware that her feelings for him were growing. When she had given him the handkerchief down by the harbour last summer, it was the only way she knew to show him that she would miss him.

Everything started to go wrong on the day of his return at the end of last summer. It was a clear morning and the ship was due to dock at midday. At a quarter to twelve she had walked along to the Butes to look out to see if there were any signs of its arrival. As she stood there, she noticed the grey clouds low on the horizon and by midday the harbour below had disappeared in a blanket of fog. Soon she could hardly see the edge of the grass on which she was standing and by then she knew that it was pointless walking down to the harbour. A fine drizzle dampened her hair, as well as her spirits, as she walked slowly back home, her dress becoming heavy as it swished over the damp grass. She tried to busy herself by helping her mother in the shop, but once an hour she walked back up to the Butes to see if the fog was clearing. She had just given up hope of the ship coming in that night when, glancing out of her bedroom window for the last time, she noticed a pink glow in the sky. Gathering up her shawl, she ran out of the house and back along to the Butes.

Breathlessly, she stood there and looked down into the harbour below, only to find that the Courier had slipped in and that most of the passengers had already disembarked. She could just see the backs of Edward and Harriet below her, heading along the track towards Crabby Bay. She felt the first twinges of jealousy for the ease and closeness they obviously shared.

She had waved frantically, but had not been able to attract their attention, so deep were they in conversation and so far away. Sadly, she had walked home, consoling herself with the thought that the harvest dance was only two weeks away and that surely Edward would call for Michael sometime before then.

It had never occurred to Charlotte that Edward would think of leaving the island to work. Unlike Michael, who had been out fishing with their father, she had never taken more than a rowing boat in the bay. To leave Riduna was unthinkable to her. If she had only been warned, then she might have reacted less childishly. She had hoped to meet him on his own, to try to clear the misunderstanding, and to assure him that she would wait for him, but there was never a time when they were not in company. She had been cross with Michael and Harriet for not warning her, but now she knew the real truth, it hurt so.

The dreaded time had arrived, and Edward would depart for Sarnia and his new life the following morning. Charlotte was just closing her grandmother's gate when she happened to glance over the grassy slopes to the shore. Usually it gave her such pleasure. She loved the sea, especially in the evening when it seemed so romantic, but as she looked over towards the bay, this time, she noticed two familiar figures. She watched open-mouthed as they embraced. At first she couldn't move, but when they turned towards her, she fled up the cutting towards home, weeping her heart out. Luckily she had been able to slip into the shop and up the stairs to the safety of her room without her parents noticing. There she sat, twisting a handkerchief absentmindedly between her damp fingers.

Michael found her a few minutes later. He saw the pained expression on her tearful face and without thinking he took her up in his arms and hugged her. After a few moments he looked down into her eyes and seeing more tears, he gently stroked them away with his fingertips. Instinctively he knew not to speak, but waited until Charlotte was ready to say what was on her mind.

'Oh Mikey! Why didn't you warn me that Edward was sweet on Harriet? You know how I feel. It's been agony for me ever since that dance when he told me he was leaving, and I've hardly had a chance to speak with him since.'

'I thought that you were over Edward, Lotte. Last year you spoke of him incessantly, but recently you've hardly said a word about him. You've been so quiet each time he's visited and anyway, what do you mean about Harriet?' Michael asked.

They sat down on either side of the window seat as Charlotte described the scene she had witnessed of Edward and Harriet embracing down on the beach. When she was silent again, Michael paused in thought before responding. He tried to remember if his friend Edward had said anything to hint that his feelings for Harriet had changed.

Michael had a picture in his mind of them dancing at the last ball. They certainly had looked a stunning couple and it had made him think more seriously about Harriet. She had grown up in the last few months and had become an attractive young woman. 'Harriet and Edward' he thought to himself. They had always been an item, but not in a romantic sense. Mind you, the idea of 'a romantic sense' was still quite new to Michael. In that direction he was very aware that he had a great deal of catching up to do, even with his adorable sister.

'I haven't kept any secrets from you Lotte. Edward hasn't said anything to give me the impression that he thinks any differently towards Harriet, than he has always done. They're as good as brother and sister, the way they've been brought up, *you* know that.'

'But I saw them together Mikey. If you'd seen them you wouldn't doubt me,' she exclaimed.

'Think of it this way, Lotte. If *I* was the one who was leaving in the morning, and we were taking a walk together on the beach, how do you think I would console you, if you got upset like you are tonight?' he asked gently.

Charlotte did not answer at first, but the thought of the hug that Michael had just given her, gave her a glimmer of hope.

'What should I do now, Mikey? Even if I did have a chance to speak with Edward, I wouldn't know what to say.'

'Why don't you write a short note to him, and we will both go down to the harbour to see him off in the morning. Then, if you don't have the courage to give the note to him, I can easily slip it into his pocket for you when I shake his hand. If I'm right, and you have nothing to fear, it may be just the thing he needs to encourage him to write to you,' Michael reasoned.

Charlotte gave Michael another hug and a peck on the cheek. They both laughed and he left her at her writing desk, with hope returned to her heart.

Chapter 6

EARLY THE FOLLOWING morning a small, but select band of people, were gathering on the jetty, as the *Courier* was made ready to depart. The little harbour had been full of activity for well over an hour, loading and unloading supplies and making preparations for the return journey to Sarnia. On many other occasions Edward had woken early and ran down to watch. More recently the sailors had even allowed Edward to give them a hand.

This time it was with very different feelings that he walked beside Harriet towards the waiting ship. She was talking about everyday things to take her mind off her true feelings. Their parents followed, his father pulling Edward's trunk in a barrow. It was as this little procession reached the crossroads above the harbour that they met Charlotte and Michael. Since the road widened at this point they naturally joined Edward and Harriet at the front. Thus Edward walked towards the waiting ship with Harriet on his left and Charlotte on his right. Michael walked in the road next to Charlotte, ready to move out of the way if he heard a cartload on its way to the village from the ship.

Charlotte responded to Harriet's questions but Edward heard very little of the conversation passing over his head. His emotions were churning inside him; a mixture of excitement about the future, sadness at leaving his family and friends, a realisation that he had finally grown up and frustration that he really longed to have the last few minutes alone with Harriet. He was also confused and a little hurt that no one had shown any signs of sadness at his departure. He also noticed, to his dismay, that Harriet was not wearing the locket. Although he knew that she had promised to wear it every evening, its presence this morning would at least have been an unspoken reassurance to him, that her feelings for him were as strong as she had professed on the beach the night before.

The meal the previous evening had been a jovial affair. His parents had teased him almost as much as the men folk usually teased Harriet. He wondered if Harriet had been concerned by his father's remarks, even though she had shown no signs at the time.

'Now I hear all sorts of tales of the behaviour of sailors when they dock, young Edward, and I expect none of that from a son of mine, do you hear?' his father had remarked with a glint in his eye.

'I don't know what you mean Father,' Edward had retorted, feigning innocence.

'Treat the ladies with respect, and that goes for the drink un'all,' replied his father. 'Have some more whisky my friend,' he said, winking at Jack.

'But...' started Edward glancing pleadingly towards Harriet. She had looked away trying to stifle a laugh, not quite sure if Mr Johnson was being serious.

His mother interrupted,

'You just remember how you've been brought up Edward, my lad, and don't let that Cousin Joe of yours, or anyone else for that matter, lead you astray!'

'There's no need for you to laugh Harriet, my girl,' said Jack. 'I've had a serious word with my friend here,' he continued, raising his glass to Joseph, 'and if I'm not able to escort you to these dances that you

so love, then Joseph and Beth, here, have offered to keep a watchful eye on you.'

They all knew that he was referring to the times when Annie was ill, but did not want to mention it to protect her feelings.

'You don't know how pleased that makes me Mr Loveridge,' said Edward, relieved to be out of the spotlight.

'Why?' questioned Jack. 'Is there anything you haven't told us, young Edward?'

Both Edward and Harriet blushed, but Harriet was quick witted enough to divert the conversation by replying,

'You're a one to talk Father. The occasions I've heard you return late from the Diver's, falling all over the furniture. What about the story you've told us many times, of the night I was born?'

Jack and Joseph hooted with laughter.

'What have I done to deserve a daughter like this, who answers me back and has no respect for her elders, Joseph my friend? If she were a few years younger, I'd take her over my knee and spank her.'

'Behave yourselves, all of you!' scolded Annie, who was all too aware that the drink had loosened tongues. 'Tell us about all these places you hope to travel to Edward, so that we can try to picture them in our minds when we hear from you.'

Annie, who rarely visited the other end of the island, let alone another country, was fascinated by Edward's descriptions, and never tired of his stories, gleaned from sailors he had met on Sarnia.

So Edward brought the evening to a natural close, by sharing his hopes and dreams for the next few years and although it was all familiar to Harriet, she stored all these thoughts in her memory to help her in the lonely months ahead. While he spoke, lost in another world, she watched him carefully, observing his changing facial expressions, the movement of his hands, the lighting up of his eyes and the way he sometimes put his fingers through his hair as he spoke. If his eyes caught hers, as they sometimes did, she would smile at him with warmth and encouragement.

It was on one of those moments that he was brought with a jolt back to the present. The secret look she gave him made him want to take her in his arms and kiss her passionately. Sternly, he took control of his emotions and other desires that were tumbling into his mind, and stood up. He thanked his parents for a lovely evening and his mother for a wonderful meal. He shook Jack's hand firmly, hiding the guilt he felt and made Annie giggle by gallantly kissing her hand. When it came to saying goodbye to Harriet, his lips probably lingered on her hand longer than was expected, but she just laughed and reached up to kiss him on the cheek in a sisterly manner and then she was gone.

Beth was the first to say goodbye to her son once they had reached the waiting ship. She looked directly at him with that all too familiar expression, which warned Edward to avoid even a glimmer of a smile.

'Now, just you remember what your father said last night and behave yourself Edward, my lad, and don't forget to write to us. Mr Collins didn't waste all that time on your education for nothing. Take care of yourself now.' With that she gave him a hug, glad to look away to hide the tears she felt threatening to appear.

'Trust me Mother,' Edward replied. 'All I need to do is remember your scolding face whenever I am the slightest bit tempted, and it'll be enough to put the fear of God in me, don't you worry.'

Edward turned to Michael and Charlotte next. He shook Michael firmly by the hand and was aware that his friend tucked something into his pocket. He kissed Charlotte's hand and, not knowing quite what to say, he asked,

'I hope that you will give me the pleasure of dancing with you at the Christmas dance, when I come home on leave.'

'I will look forward to it,' replied a blushing Charlotte, as he turned to Harriet's mother and father.

Annie gave him a hug, for he was like a son to her and said,

'Good luck Edward and come home safely.'

Jack shook him firmly by the hand and exclaimed with a wink,

'With all this advice, don't forget to enjoy yourself. I don't know if I'm not a touch envious of you and I might even join you on the next boat!'

'In your dreams!' exclaimed Annie, slapping her husband on his backside in jest.

Harriet was standing beside her parents, as if in a dream. She thought of her brave words the night before. Edward was only going for three months after all, but how many more goodbyes would there be until they could unite as they had promised. For the first time in her life she was frustrated that she was still so young and more importantly that she was a girl and would never be able to join him on his travels, but there was no way that she was going to be emotional in front of all these people. She would save her tears for later, in the quiet of her bedroom.

As Edward turned to Harriet, she smiled that secret smile, the one which stirred up such new but wonderful sensations inside them both. Harriet reached up to give him one of her sisterly kisses, just as Edward reached to kiss Harriet's hand. They both laughed, which eased the tension and, since neither could think of the right words to say, reluctantly Edward turned, but before his father had a chance to open his mouth Edward warned,

'Now don't you start on at me again, Father! You should be proud of your son, if you'd only stop your nagging.'

'I *am* very proud of you Son, you know that. You've turned into a fine figure of a young man. That's what I'm afraid of,' he said giving Edward a hug, 'but if we don't get you on this ship this minute, you'll be saying goodbye to your dreams as we watch it sail without you.'

With that said, father and son walked aboard the *Courier*. They said a few more words in private before Joseph left his son looking out over the bow of the ship, as he joined his wife on the jetty.

It was only a few minutes later that the ship sounded its mournful note and the men began to unreel the ropes, which held it to the shore. Steam was billowing out of the cream and black funnel as it inched its way towards the open water.

Harriet only just stifled the childish urge to run to the very end of the breakwater, to remain as close to Edward as possible. She stood watching him, and when she could no longer make out the expression on his face, she was grateful that she had such a vivid imagination and could picture his smile in her mind's eye. The thought of it made her shiver with pleasure, which helped to suppress her overwhelming sadness.

Edward waved to everyone and watched them all as they seemed to shrink dwarf-like before his eyes. He stood in silence as he watched the bay, then the coastline and finally the whole island that he loved dwindle into the distance. It was only when Riduna was just a thumb-sized speck on the horizon that he gave a deep and lung-filled sigh, and turned to find a seat below for the remainder of the journey. Although it was a fine day, the sea breeze was quite cool, making Edward shiver as he began to move. Unknown to him, it was at the very same moment that Harriet had shivered, standing on the shore. He couldn't stop thinking about her and tried to remember her lovely smile.

Chapter 7

HARRIET LEFT HER parents talking to Aunt Beth and Uncle Joseph down by the harbour. She had always called them aunt and uncle and could not think of them in any other way. For a time she walked with Charlotte and Michael.

'I can't imagine the dances without Edward, can you Harriet?' Charlotte said, looking carefully for a telltale expression on her friend's face.

'To be honest, I can't imagine life without him at all,' replied Harriet, so deep in her own thoughts, and longing to be on her own, that she failed to notice her friend's pained look. 'The only way I can handle the loneliness is to imagine that Edward has just gone away for the summer and continue with everyday life as usual.'

'You have given me an idea,' said Michael. 'Since tomorrow is Sunday, do you think we could take a picnic over to Corblets Bay, if the weather's still fine? We may even have our first swim of the year!'

'That's a wonderful idea,' Harriet exclaimed, glad to plan life ahead and knowing that if she were on her own she would only resort to melancholy. 'I'm going to visit Jane this afternoon so I'll ask her too. She has her cousins over from England for the week and they might appreciate a guided stroll to some of the special places on the island.'

‘That’s a good idea’ Michael replied. ‘We’re off to check on grandma now.

‘I must say goodbye too, because I’m going to help Miss Green with her Saturday School for the remainder of the morning.’

So Harriet kissed Charlotte on the cheek, as she always did, and turned to walk up towards St Anne, glad for some solitude at last. It was only as she left them that she was aware of the tears brimming in Charlotte’s eyes. As she walked away her feelings were in turmoil. Her own sadness was overshadowed by a mixture of guilt that she was partly to blame for her friend’s pain, jealousy and a realisation that she was not the only one harbouring feelings of love towards her Edward.

‘My Edward!’ she found herself saying out loud and, realising what she had done, she looked quickly about her to check that no one had heard her. Then, pausing at the top of The Butes to gaze out to sea towards the empty horizon she spoke more softly to herself in barely a whisper, ‘He’s always been my Edward and I’ve always been his, for as long as I can remember.’

Harriet stood for some moments. She allowed a few tears to fall silently down her cheeks. Their salty taste seemed to be a reflection of the vast ocean in front of her. She rarely thought about what was beyond it. She had never been interested in travelling, content to listen to Edward’s tales in the same way that she used to listen to her father telling fairy stories at night before she went to bed, when she was young. One adventure was as real to her as the other. She loved her island home. She felt secure and content and could not imagine ever having to leave it. She shivered.

Harriet took one more look out to sea, letting her gaze sweep across from the harbour along the breakwater and out to the horizon. Then her eyes focussed on Fort Albert and skimmed along the sandy bay and back towards the houses on the edge of Newtown settlement. Finally she ambled slowly along towards the schoolhouse, knowing that Miss Green would understand why she was late and gently wiped her damp face as she went.

Perhaps she would ask Miss Green to join them on their picnic the following day. She was more of a friend than a teacher to Harriet and would probably enjoy being included; after all, she must live quite a lonely life apart from her work with the children. With that in mind her pace quickened and she walked with a lighter heart.

When Charlotte and Michael finally reached home, Charlotte ran to her room and burst into inconsolable sobs. Michael knew that it was best not to disturb her for a while and so he walked on up the street towards the Rose and Crown where John lived with his parents. He knew that his father was expecting him back in the bakery to help finish the morning's baking and to clean the floors, but he had so much on his mind that he had to clear his head.

John was in the bar, clearing away the coffee cups following breakfast for their paying guests and making the bar ready for when it would open to the public at lunchtime. John acknowledged his friend as Michael sat on the barstool in the corner and he poured him a coffee left over from one of the breakfast tables.

'I'll join you in a few moments when I've finished,' he said. 'Did the *Courier* sail on time?' This was a rhetorical question and he expected no more than the nod that Michael gave him in reply. Since it was a clear morning, only engine failure or an illness would have prevented their friend from sailing. Edward had talked of little else for months.

Once he had finished to his father's satisfaction, John

poured himself a coffee, too, and gestured to his friend to follow him out into the empty garden courtyard. They sat drinking in silence for a few moments, both thinking about the narrowness of their own lives. Each of them was expected to follow their parents into the family businesses and, until Edward had inspired them with tales of interesting places in the world, they had never questioned their destiny. In fact both young men loved their life on the island. Neither had felt the need to work too hard at school, but had just enjoyed the simplicity of a fairly trouble free youth. Growing up was a little more difficult. The reality of working had hit them, as had the realisation that they were already feeling manly needs, and the local girls, who had once been close companions, were now coy and distant, carefully protected by the watchful gaze of their elders.

There were still a few pretty girls in the community of strangers, whose fathers still worked on completing and maintaining the fortifications of the island, ordered by some official far away in England. The fact that these young ladies even spoke a different language added to their allure, though the presence of their powerfully built fathers was enough to put off all but the most daring. Added to this, the work on the fortifications was all but complete and their numbers had already dwindled. No, it was far easier to look towards their own kind for matchmaking purposes.

With that in mind John reasoned, 'Now that Edward is away, perhaps Harriet might look more favourably your way, Michael.'

'I don't know John, there was a time when I thought we were getting quite close but she seems to have grown up so much in the past year. She seems to have left me behind,'

'You're not talking sense Michael; it's all in your imagination.'

'That's the misfortune of it. It's what's in my

imagination that I'm afraid of!' Michael exclaimed.

'In some ways we have life fairly easy? We know exactly how we will be earning a living for the rest of our lives. We'll end up looking after our parents, God willing, in their old age. It is only finding a wife that's the struggle. They don't give you lessons on that subject at school do they?' John, ever the thinking one, mused.

'Maybe we could save up and travel over to Sarnia in order to widen our horizons,' said Michael.

'Widen our acquaintances more like!' exclaimed John, putting into words what they were both thinking privately. They both laughed.

'I'm perfectly serious. After all, Edward has told us of the wonderful dances he attends on Sarnia and we have both got good prospects to offer.'

And so it was that the two young men devised a plan to save up over the next few months for a trip which would take them off Riduna for the first time in their lives. With that thought to cheer him, Michael mentioned the Sunday picnic and then headed back to the bakery, with a slightly guilty feeling that he had taken over an hour off work and that he had left Charlotte in her misery. As he entered the house he was pleased to see that Charlotte was busy helping their mother in the shop. Although she was a little red-eyed, keeping busy was the best thing for her. He invited Charlotte to join John and himself for a late afternoon stroll, since the weather was so nice, and she willingly agreed, giving Michael one of her watery smiles. She watched him as he hurried to the bake-house at the back of the shop, where he worked even harder than usual for the rest of the morning, singing to himself as he thought of his new plans.

Chapter 8

HARRIET ALWAYS TOOK pleasure in her work with the children. She was enjoying her own studies less and less now, especially as she was working on her own with the books Miss Green allowed her to borrow and she found it increasingly difficult to concentrate. Her mind would wander to her recent memories and to dreams of the future. She imagined getting married to Edward in St. Anne's Church with her mother and father by her side, surrounded by all her friends. Her grandparents would put on refreshments in the hall and they would end the evening with a dance. Edward always looked delicious in his Sunday best and she would float about in the most beautiful dress she had ever possessed. She would daydream that they would dance together, gliding among their smiling family and friends like Cinderella and her Prince. Then what? Where would they live? Where would Edward work? Would he be content to work down the quarry like their fathers before them?

'A thoughtful, far-away young lady!' commented Miss Green, looking quizzically at her young friend. 'You know that you don't have to stay and work today Harriet. It's Saturday afternoon after all!'

'Oh, of course it is,' exclaimed Harriet, a little flustered.

'I'd lost track of the days, what with Edward leaving. It's hard to think of anything else.'

Miss Green sat down next to her friend and paused for a moment, as if weighing her words carefully before she spoke. Harriet waited, knowing that she was about to hear a wise comment, which she would dwell on deeply before moulding it to her own thoughts. That was how it was when Miss Green talked with her about life.

'I can see by your expression that you are devoted to your Edward,' she began, looking carefully at Harriet's expression for confirmation.

Harriet nodded silently, pleased by the words, 'your Edward'.

'From what I know of that young man, he would be a loyal and devoted companion, once he has understood himself and learnt to listen to his own feelings, without being swayed by the feelings of others,' she continued.

Harriet never ceased to be amazed that Miss Green, a spinster, could be so perceptive about matters of the heart and could not help but wonder what experiences she had encountered before choosing to come and teach on an island like this. Was she running away from something or someone perhaps?

'You must remember that he is also a dreamer,' Miss Green continued. 'He has a restless spirit and who knows what journeys and experiences in life will satisfy that enormous need he has to travel. He may never be happy to settle for a quiet life.'

Harriet was taken aback by that. It was as if Miss Green had been reading her very thoughts and had put into words the very ideas that Harriet was reluctant to even allow herself to think. It made her a little angry, as the truth is often painful to hear, because it seemed to violate the fledgling love that she and Edward had experienced over the past few months.

'But I love him Miss Green and he says that he loves me. Surely that's the only important issue.'

Without answering her young friend Miss Green reasoned, 'You are still so very young Harriet. Enjoy those feelings of love by all means, after all love is God-given, but don't forget to live life to the full for yourself and those around you. Someone who pines and sulks is not a joy to be with!'

Harriet agreed with her friend on that point. She thought of Charlotte, who could be a pain sometimes and she was determined not to be like that. She owed it to her mother and father to be cheerful and anyway, it was in her nature to be so.

'Talking of living life to the full, a group of us are arranging the first picnic of the year after church tomorrow morning. It would be a pleasure if you would join us.'

'I don't know Harriet. Sunday afternoon is my time for reflection. I like to think through the following week.'

'Now who's hiding away and not socialising. It's time you became more part of the community and got to know us all a little more. After all, you have been with us for nearly six years, haven't you?'

Miss Green paused for a moment, knowing that Harriet was telling the truth and that she was inclined to hide away in her own little world of 'school'. She felt safe there.

Suddenly she said,

'You're right Harriet. I have no business giving away advice when I show a reluctance to take it myself, but if I'm to accompany you tomorrow then I don't wish to hear anymore of this *Miss Green.* I will be Mary to you out of school from now on, if you have no objection, just as long as you don't forget to call me Miss Green when we are with the infants. Now be off with you. I have to do my shopping and have my thinking time today.'

‘Goodbye for now. I shall see you at church tomorrow, Mary,’ Harriet added with hesitant shyness, as she picked up her shawl and set off towards home. She would share some lunch with her mother before visiting her friend Jane.

When she reached home she was pleased to find that her mother was busy in the kitchen. For the last few days Harriet had watched her mother go from strength to strength and it was a relief that spring and summer spanned ahead of them. The thought brought her back to Edward. She would have to fight the temptation of wishing her time away to next Christmas. The island’s weather was deceptive though. They could be in for a cold spell yet and almost certainly for some sea fog. They descended without warning, even in the height of summer, so that sometimes it could be hard to remember what season it really was. Nevertheless it was the wind that the visitors talked about. Often it could be as balmy as any tropical island in Edward’s dreams, but sometimes the wind whipped up and caught even the islanders unaware. That was why Corblets Bay was such a beautiful haven. It did not have the long sweeping beauty of Braye or Longy, but it consisted of sheltered nooks of sand among the rocky banks, where there was always a spot to find shelter from a sea breeze.

Harriet told her mother about the picnic. ‘That means your father and I can have a quiet romantic time at home on our own then,’ she teased with a twinkle in her eyes.

‘You’re both welcome to come of course,’ Harriet encouraged. ‘You could ask Aunt Beth and Uncle Joseph. It would help them to stop worrying about Edward.’

‘Let’s see if the weather holds tomorrow shall we,’ her mother replied.

She must be feeling better, thought Harriet as she began

to prepare some lunch for them both. She tried to hide her gently blushing face in her activities as she realised what her mother was hinting at.

Just after her fifteenth birthday Annie Loveridge had sat Harriet down in her room and closed the door. It was strange really, because no one was there but the two of them, and so Harriet realised that her mother was about to tell her something important. She had explained the facts of life and talked about her own difficult childbirth. Harriet had heard that part before, but listened carefully as her mother explained that, as her body had healed and when she was feeling well enough, they still had passionate times, because, after all, a man had his needs and they did still love each other so. This had confused Harriet because she wondered why she did not have lots of brothers and sisters, but she was too shy to ask.

Not long after that confusing conversation she was invited to her friend Jane's for tea and she took the opportunity to ask her friend, being the daughter of a doctor and knowing about those things, to explain. Jane explained that her mother had been told that she could never have children again and anyway, you didn't always have a child after being with a man. She had tried to explain to Harriet that it depended on the time of the month and your temperature and many other factors that Harriet could barely remember now.

Harriet blushed again at the thought of this conversation, but it also made her determined to have another talk with Jane about the feelings she was getting when Edward was near her. Surely she should not feel that way until she was married, or at least a bit older. Oh, it was most confusing growing up. She sighed.

'I hope we won't hear incessant sighing young lady,' her mother rebuked. 'I'm not having a sad face living here until

Christmas. Now be off with you and sigh somewhere else, but come back smiling do you hear?'

'Yes Mama!' Harriet called over her shoulder, as she was already half way out of the door. It was funny, but that was the second time she had been thrown out in a matter of hours. She hoped that her dear friend Jane would be more understanding. As she walked up towards the doctor's house in the village she knew that they were both right to encourage her to be cheerful. She also knew that she would not live down her father's teasing, if she as much as showed a glimmer of her true feelings in front of him tonight.

Jane had lived with her father, the doctor, on the island for four years now. He used to be a surgeon for the armed forces and for him their new life had been a form of escape when his wife had died so suddenly of pneumonia. He had applied for the post, thinking that it would be a safe place to bring up his son and daughter on his own, while he continued doing the job he knew and loved. The islanders had so quickly charmed him with their humour and openness that he never regretted the decision.

Since then his son had returned to Southampton to find employment and a livelier social life, leaving him and Jane to live quite contentedly among this friendly community. He was aware that Jane had a longing to follow in his footsteps into medicine, which was less frowned upon in these enlightened days. She not only had a caring and gentle nature with people, but she was also extremely intelligent and interested in his work. He encouraged her to help him out in organising his surgery, as well as taking on the role of housekeeper in the absence of a wife. He did draw the line at cleaning and paid for a local widow, Mrs Doris, to come in each day to keep the place tidy and to cook a meal for them both.

He knew that the locals at The Diver's teased him about Mrs Doris. She obviously had a soft spot for him and had more to offer on her mind than just cleaning and cooking, but he was an honourable man and wanted to protect Jane as well as keep the memories of his devoted wife precious. He had no thoughts of marrying again and certainly could keep control of his baser urges, so long as he kept off the drink.

They lived together in a house just off Victoria Street, where the downstairs was taken with the surgery and a small waiting room, with a large kitchen and dining room at the back. There was a parlour, bathroom and the doctor's bedroom on the second floor, then two quaint bedrooms up under the eaves of the house above.

They also had the pleasure of a terraced garden at the back, which was small and secluded, backing on to the churchyard wall. This was covered with a mass of trailing honeysuckle and clematis, which were in flower at the moment. Jane had been sitting in the garden quietly reading when she heard the knock at the front door.

When Harriet arrived at the doctor's house, Jane was still holding one of her father's medical journals in her hand. The doctor had it sent regularly from England to keep himself up to date.

'I don't know how you could read anything as difficult as that,' Harriet said to her friend. 'Are you really serious about going back to England soon to train to be a nurse?'

'I'm sure I will one day, Harriet, but I'm not ready to leave my father yet, or you for that matter. Follow me upstairs to my room where we can talk,' Jane replied.

So they walked up the two flights of stairs and sat together either side of the window, cosily shadowed by the sloping walls of the eaves of the doctor's townhouse.

'How are you feeling Harriet?' Jane asked, as soon as they

were settled. 'I mean, how you are really feeling?' she repeated, with a meaningful emphasis in her words.

Harriet knew that she could be completely honest with Jane. They were very close and rarely kept secrets from each other.

'I'm so confused, Jane. One moment I'm feeling so much love for Edward that it hurts and I miss him so much, even though he has only just left. At other times when I think of him, I can't help but blush, even in my own company!'

She looked at her friend nervously for reassurance before continuing, 'and sometimes Edward's just the boy next door, the brother he's always been. But the worst times of all are when I put myself in agony by thinking of times like the moment he kissed Charlotte in front of us all when we were still children. Then I feel a mixture of jealousy that he's never kissed me like that, and guilt that I might have hurt a good friend.'

Jane, who was always wise not to give advice about something she knew nothing about, was quite moved by her friend's ramblings. She was interested in human behaviour and often wrote down her thoughts on paper in pictures, words and diagrams. She had a very analytical brain for a seventeen-year-old.

'Come and sit with me at my desk,' she directed, 'and tell me again slowly.'

Glad to be distracted by playing one of Jane's mind games Harriet began once more.

'Sometimes I feel so much in love…' she began.

'Stop there. That's what people call your heart talking,' said Jane, drawing a heart in the centre of a large sheet of paper. 'I'm not sure whether, medically speaking, it has anything to do with your heart at all, but never mind. We'll write it there nevertheless.' So she wrote the words 'LOVE' in the middle of the heart shape.

'What else,' she encouraged.

'Sometimes I feel a sensitivity like the capture of the magical moment of a glorious sunset and I shiver,' Harriet blushed.

'Where do you feel a sensitivity?' asked her friend, as if questioning a patient about a serious pain.

'It seems like my fingers and toes are covered in pins and needles and I shiver, oh! I don't know whether I'm clever enough to put these feelings into words. The whole of my body feels sensitive.'

With that Jane drew a body around the heart, making sure that the heart was carefully positioned on the right. She drew little lines radiating out from the body shape with longer lines coming from the fingers and toes and wrote 'SENSITIVITY' along two or three of the lines.

'And he makes you blush,' she added looking at Harriet and adding rosy cheeks with the word 'BLUSH' on one of them.

'Are you sure that you don't have feelings of sensitivity elsewhere?' Jane quizzed, knowing the medical facts more clearly than she had personally experienced.

Harriet went very red and nodded. 'You know!' she said and they fell about with childish laughter as Jane picked up a red pen and drew lines radiating from that secret dark area between the legs that her mother had told her about. Jane paused before writing, not knowing how to describe it, but wanting to say more. She looked quizzically at the stuffed monkey, perched above her desk, which her brother had bought for her and smiled as she wrote 'ANIMAL INSTINCT'.

'What do you mean by that Jane?'

'It's part of the natural system. Otherwise there would be no baby animals in the world would there?' Jane replied.

'I suppose not, but I thought you explained to me that

those ummm,' Harriet paused, as she grasped for the words which reflected her feelings before continuing, 'those animal instincts do not always make babies,' and she blushed again.

'Yes, that's correct, otherwise this island would be overrun with children, like it is with rabbits!' and they fell about laughing again.

When they had caught their breath, Jane encouraged, 'We aren't yet complete. Go on, Harriet!'

'Then at times I still think of him as the boy next door, or my brother, and I find it inconceivable to imagine us living as man and wife. I'm also not sure that he'll ever want to settle like I do,' Harriet continued. 'I can't imagine where you're going to draw all of that?'

'It's obvious, isn't it? That's when you are *thinking* and not *feeling*. You are using your brain and reasoning ideas rationally.'

'So you're going to draw a brain in my head now. I'm relieved to see it!'

They laughed again as Jane drew a large whirling mass in the middle of the top of the head and wrote 'THINKING' inside it.

'What about the jealousy?' asked Harriet, hoping to defeat her brainy friend.

'Ah, that's easy too,' and she picked up a blue pencil and wrote 'rationally' below the word 'THINKING,' in small blue letters, and then 'irrationally' in green.

'There!' she said, admiring her handiwork. 'What do you think?'

'I don't know what it really means,' said Harriet, feeling a little slow to catch on, 'but it looks impressive.'

'This is your picture of the love you feel at the moment? It seems to consist of three main parts: your head, your heart and those sensitive animal instincts. Maybe we've both learnt a lesson from this, Harriet?' Jane said feeling quite pleased with herself.

Harriet felt a step behind her friend on the learning experience, but nevertheless certain that she was missing something vital in her search for an understanding of life, she continued to look puzzled.

'I may be leaping to conclusions here, so forgive me if I am but, to find the person you truly love and want to marry, maybe each of those elements have to be in place,' Jane reasoned. 'There's one thing that we've forgotten, though. You can't live in isolation. There has to be a place to abide together, which is right for you both and I think you also need other people around you.'

With that thought she completed the picture by drawing a partner for the figure holding hands, a house around them and other stick figures in the background. On each figure she put a smiling face.

Harriet took the pencil from her friend and drew an island below their feet, remembering Miss Green's rules in art. Then she wondered why the thought of the island made her sad momentarily.

They both sat back and admired the sketch.

'That's in an ideal world of course,' Jane said wistfully, looking at the two figures holding hands as she thought of her father and how lonely he must be at times.

'When you're famous, and writing in these journals, I hope that you'll remember me,' Harriet exclaimed. 'You're so clever.'

Harriet looked at her friend's changing expression and felt very selfish. She realised that she had been rambling on about herself and Edward, with no thought of Jane's feelings.

'What about you?' she enquired gently. 'Have you ever had any of these thoughts and feelings? If you have, you've never so much as hinted about them.'

Jane smiled. 'It's strange that you should ask.' She paused. 'I'm reluctant to breathe a word about it to even you, my dearest friend, but it's true. I have experienced certain feelings by which I can truly empathise with you, dear Harriet.'

The young ladies, at first stunned by their admissions, were quiet for a moment, then it was Jane's turn to become a shade of pink as she began to confide in her friend.

'It was at the Easter Dance that I first noticed him. It was on the very first occasion that the men from the garrison had been permitted to attend our island dances. They arrived in full uniform about an hour after the start of the evening. You could have heard a pin drop as they entered the room. All eyes turned towards them. If they felt any embarrassment they certainly hid it well because they walked in, bowed to the ladies nearest the door as they passed and talked amongst themselves unconcerned. The music began moments later. The atmosphere relaxed as the gentlemen in the hall sought out a partner for the next dance. I danced with John that time, but it was as we were dancing that I noticed that the soldiers were still standing watching at the side of the hall. A particular pair of grey eyes met mine momentarily as John waltzed me expertly around the floor, so I was not the least bit surprised when this dashing young gentleman came to ask me for the following dance. I looked at my father for approval before accepting, but he just nodded. Oh Harriet, I felt weak at the knees every time he caught my eyes. His hands held me so firmly, guiding me by the slightest movement, so that I could almost feel the warmth radiating from them through to my very skin beneath my dress and petticoat!'

'So maybe we need to put weak knees on the picture too!' Harriet remarked. 'What happened next, Jane? Have you spoken to him since?'

'They obviously had to leave before the evening was over, even before midnight, so I tried to think no more about it. Then, early one evening last week, I was on my way home from delivering some medicine to old Mrs Barton, who lives in one of those isolated cottages beyond Fort Tourgis on the shore side track towards Fort Clonque, when I heard a voice calling me. As you could imagine, I was rushing home by this time. It was getting dark and I had spent far longer than I had intended with the old lady, since she was so glad of the company. To my fright a man stepped out from the shadow of the fort and I instantly recognised him as the man who had cast a spell over my feelings! I stopped still and must have looked quite a picture, because he instantly reassured me.

'What is a pretty young lady like you doing wandering about, in the nearly dark, all by herself?' he asked.

I relaxed a little by the friendly tone in his voice and explained.

Then he surprised me by saying, 'I would like to escort you safely home, if I may. I was about to enjoy a stroll to the Diver's for an hour, but I can easily make a detour for a pretty lady.'

I was flustered at this offer and declined at first, knowing how the elders frown on such behaviour and jump to such irrational conclusions. My heart was tempted however, so that when he insisted, I accepted. He rebuked me for being out in the dark in those parts, telling me that not everyone would treat me with the respect I deserved. As we walked together I relaxed and in that short distance I found that I had told him all about my father, losing my mother, and also about my brother returning to England. He in turn told me that he had been on the island for three months now and until the dance the other night, had found it such a lifeless backwater that he was longing to finish his time here and return to England. It was a beautiful island, he agreed, but he wished for more excitement and action.

As we parted outside my front door he bowed, taking my hand to kiss it gently. Then, as he began to walk away, he looked back over his shoulder and whispered, in a voice only audible to me, 'I am beginning to think that I might enjoy my time serving on this island after all.' He winked at me and was gone.

'Have you seen him since then?' Harriet asked.

'No, but I have found myself looking out for him every time I see a man in uniform. It's quite distracting.'

'Oh Jane, I'm so pleased that we can share these things. I think I would burst if I had to keep all these thoughts to myself.'

'I must keep my head though, Harriet. I have dreams of my own don't forget and anyway, he may not approach me again.'

Harriet and Jane both looked down at the picture in Jane's hand, deep in their own thoughts. After a few moments Jane put it away with all her other notes and drawings and turned to her friend.

'So what are you going to do with yourself now Edward has gone?' she asked.

'I nearly forgot the true purpose of my visit to you. A group of us are going on a picnic after church tomorrow to Corblets. It's going to be a family affair, so it would be lovely if you could bring your father and cousins. Where are they by the way?'

'They've gone out for a walk. I sent them to look for the 'Lovers' Chair' out at Telegraph. It's such a clear day that the views towards Sarnia and Sark would be beautiful today but they should be back soon.'

'I must be on my way too,' exclaimed Harriet.

‘I’ll see you in the morning Harriet and let you know if we will be joining you. I do hope so.’

‘It wouldn’t be the same without you.’

Harriet kissed her friend on both cheeks at the door, turning to wave and smile as she walked towards Victoria Street.

Jane mused as she closed the door; it was the almost naïve innocence and trusting simplicity of the island’s inhabitants which was so welcomingly refreshing to visitors, who allowed themselves more than a few days’ stay on the island. This trait was unique to Riduna and fiercely protected by the village elders, especially with the influx of so many strangers in recent times to build the fortifications against Napoleon. In fact the changes in attitude and behaviour were discussed at length. Only a few years before, if a young lady and a young man were seen talking to each other, they were considered betrothed, and if they were seen walking together without a chaperone they would have been publicly humiliated. Even now it was the cause of rumours and gossip. She knew that she had to be careful.

Chapter 9

THAT EVENING HARRIET sat at her window daydreaming. At first her mind was a complete blank and she hardly noticed the beautiful sunset over the Swinge. It promised to be another fine day tomorrow. Her hand moved subconsciously to her locket. It was their private symbol of love and only the closest to her would know about it.

On a normal day this would be when she would be listening out for Edward's knock at the door. It had always been their special time together. More recently she would have been checking her hair and looking in the mirror to gain a reassurance. She blushed at her less than modest thoughts as she glanced over her shoulder at the mirror beside the door.

She laughed out loud as she remembered her afternoon with Jane, then thought more seriously about the picture that Jane had drawn. There was no way that she would have thought of love in such a logical manner. Perhaps being a doctor's daughter made you think about human nature differently. Harriet had never thought of herself as an animal before and she bubbled with laughter as she imitated animal faces in the mirror. This was not how she had imagined this evening to be. She believed, a little guiltily, that she should be weeping inconsolably and was grateful to Jane for lightening her mood. She decided that it was a good time to write to Edward but also that she would begin a journal, because, after all, she could hardly write all her thoughts in letters to Edward!

Happy with those decisions, she moved to her desk and reached for some paper. Just the thought of Edward made her heart flutter and she sighed. That's one of Jane's 'conditions of love' met, she thought. Then she took up her pen, dipped it in the ink and began to write.

My dearest Edward,

I can still see your face as your ship sailed away this morning and it has left an emptiness in my life that will be hard to fill. Nevertheless, I am resolved to write to you each evening and, when I receive your letters, I will save them to read at this time. It will be like having our normal evening conversation without the closeness of your company. (Oh how I miss that too, or is it not becoming of a young lady to admit to this?) You will be pleased that I have not allowed myself to be melancholy all day, but have kept myself busy. I spent the afternoon with Jane and we talked about the many facets of love, but I cannot share details of this with you in a letter. How we laughed together.

Tomorrow Michael has suggested that we enjoy this window of fine weather and go for a picnic. The idea is becoming quite a community affair, with whole families participating. I have asked Mother to persuade your parents to join us. Although I know that we will enjoy the occasion, I can assure you that we will miss your presence with us and we will talk of you a great deal.

Oh Edward, how I wish you were here with me now to escort me for a walk along the beach. It has been such a beautiful sunset, which only acts to bring back vivid memories of our last night together. My only consolation is that I am wearing the locket, my most treasured possession, which is comfortingly akin to having a small part of you resting on my neck. This thought makes me blush.

Dearest Edward, I will send this on the Little Courier which will call, weather permitting, on Tuesday, in the hopes that you might receive it after your first voyage to Southampton. I cannot imagine that you are really going there. You will have so much to tell me at Christmas.

Ever yours
Harriet

With her first letter completed, Harriet went downstairs to prepare the picnic. Her mother and father were sitting in their favourite chairs by the fire. Although it was the end of May the evenings were chilly and she was glad to warm herself beside them.

'Have you persuaded Aunt Beth and Uncle Joseph to join us tomorrow, Mother?' she asked as she worked at the kitchen table.

'The men folk aren't full of enthusiasm but, if the weather is still fine, they will visit the Diver's for their usual Sunday lunchtime drink and then catch up with the group later,' Annie replied.

'We've offered to carry the food,' interrupted her papa, trying to redeem himself.

'That will be fine, but you'll have to mention it to Dr Hanwell in the morning at church, otherwise he may be the only old man with us ladies!' Harriet replied with a mischievous smile.

'You'll get the back of my hand miss for your cheek,' said Jack as he attempted to try to catch Harriet around the table. Harriet ran behind her mother.

'Mama, Mama, save me. I'm too old to be treated like a child,' she protested.

'She's right Jack,' scolded Annie. 'We must remember that Harriet is nearly a young lady now.'

Jack stopped in his tracks and winked at his wife, which had the instant effect of melting her expression to a smile, and said, 'Harriet will always be a child to me, my dearest.'

Harriet shivered.

'Come and sit with us by the fire for a while Harriet, love,' Annie encouraged. 'It'll be good to share your company in the evenings.'

Harriet gladly pulled a chair towards the open fire between her parents. They talked for a while before hearing a rustle at the door. No one was the least bit surprised to see Beth and Joseph, who, without knocking had walked through the back door and paused.

'Come and join us. The more the merrier!' exclaimed Jack. Without thinking he reached for the glasses from the top cupboard and poured a measure for the gathered company and a tiny drop for Harriet. He was tempted to suggest that he and Joseph take a walk to the Diver's instead, until he looked up at his wife. One look from Annie was enough to say, don't you dare even think it tonight, Jack my man! Then he was left wondering how in heaven's name she could even read his very thoughts.

They had a light-hearted evening, talking about the events of the day, the plans for tomorrow and most of all about Edward. Beth looked tearful at one point, which was so unlike her, so Annie got up to give her dearest friend a warm embrace. Allowing your only son to leave home was hard enough, but knowing that he was going to be travelling to parts of the world that she did not even know how to dream of, made her feel quite inadequate as a mother. For the first time for years she began to cry.

Annie hugged her friend more tightly but kept quiet, knowing with the instinct of a mother, that any consoling words would show insensitivity and that her pain would only be eased by a soothing companionable silence.

'Maybe I'm at fault for building Edward a wooden toy

ship when he was only four!' Joseph exclaimed, trying to lighten the atmosphere.

Remembering how her son's beautiful eyes had lit up on the morning of his birthday that year, and thinking of how he'd treasured his favourite toy through the years, brought a smile through Beth's tears.

'Oh, I'm so foolish,' she apologised.

'Don't worry dear. We're your neighbours and best friends,' said Jack adding cheekily 'You know you've still got a pretty face smiling through those tears, Beth. It could melt a man's heart!'

Annie glared at her husband, not for the first time today, but was pleased that Beth's tears had ceased and so softened her response.

'Don't go looking at pretty faces, do you hear; the only pretty face you should notice is mine!' she admonished.

'What about mine?' exclaimed Harriet.

With that Jack winked at Harriet, walked around the room and took his wife's hand gallantly in his own and kissed it with a flourish.

Annie tried to push him away, attempting to hide her mirth behind her handkerchief.

'I'm to lose either way,' he said, sinking back down into his favourite chair. 'Do *you* understand women, Joseph, my old friend?'

'I don't even try,' answered his friend, giving his wife an encouraging smile. 'I think it's time we made tracks my dear, especially if we've got a picnic to prepare for tomorrow.'

'I'm pleased to hear you'll be giving me a hand,' Beth replied teasingly. 'Goodnight all. Thank you for your company and your friendship.'

With that Joseph picked up his wife's thick woollen shawl and wrapped it snugly around her. He kept his arm protectively resting over her shoulders as they walked the short distance to their own cottage next door.

Harriet also said goodnight, spending some time writing her journal by candle light before snuffing it out and drifting off into a deep sleep.

Chapter 10

IT WAS THE first day in June and, fortunately for the islanders, it was the warmest day so far that year. There was a gentle breeze, which billowed more coolly in open spaces, but otherwise it was a perfect day for a picnic. In each of the various households, even in the guesthouses and hotels, the families were busy washing and putting on their Sunday best, ready for church. By a quarter to eleven many were heading up the various sloping roads and tracks towards St Anne's Church, like ants scuttling towards a nest. The pace was slow, often stopping to await a neighbour, who joined them from a nearby gate or doorstep which fronted the many winding streets. The conversation meandered between highlights of the passing week, any family ailments or the lovely spell of weather they were all appreciating. Even John and his family from The Rose and Crown and Harriet's grandparents from The Braye Tavern had been busy tidying their establishments early, so that they too could join them. There were even some of the visitors to the island, including a handsome group of men in uniform, walking among the islanders towards the church, which nestled among the houses and trees on the hill at the centre of the town.

Harriet, who was walking with her parents, grandparents, Beth and Joseph, was pleased to meet Jane and her father at the church gate and they walked along the path towards the church together. As they entered the arched door they nodded greetings to the folks who were already seated and like one big family the islanders sat and waited for the service to begin. Harriet noticed that her friend had glanced more than once in the direction of one of the soldiers. She also noticed him return a heart-melting smile, with those appealing grey eyes of his.

'I see what you mean,' she whispered to Jane. There was no time for Jane to respond since a moment of hush had brought the congregation to their feet as the priest walked in. Harriet found it hard to concentrate. She enjoyed the singing and said a silent prayer for Edward's safety, as well as remembering to give thanks for her mother's good health, but when the priest prayed for Queen Victoria and other English events her mind wandered. She wished that Edward was in the pew in front with his mother and father, so that she could watch him.

A few weeks before, he must have felt her gaze and had the nerve to glance quickly over his shoulder and wink at her. She had blushed and looked away, praying that her parents had not noticed. Outside church afterwards she had whispered to him about her embarrassment. This had amused Edward no end. It had encouraged the opposite and made him even more daring and mischievous than ever in the following weeks. Last week, like a naughty schoolboy, he had even passed a bit of paper to her through the gap in the old wooden pews. Harriet had not been able to read it, hiding it promptly in her glove and feeling herself blushing profusely. At home at last, later that morning, she had run to her room and slipped it out of her glove. It had simply said 'I LOVE YOU'.

With no such distractions this week Harriet tried to concentrate. It was Jane's turn to be distracted, though the men from the infantry were sitting out of the way at the back of the church and out of her friend's vision. Harriet fidgeted. She added a prayer for Beth and Joseph to her personal thoughts and also asked if God could bless them with a happy and successful picnic. Just as the priest was saying his final blessing she asked God for guidance in her love for Edward and asked him if he would find time to bless that too, quickly adding Jane and her soldier on the end of her growing list.

Everyone filed out of church in an orderly fashion, in much the same way as they had entered it, stopping to talk with various people on the way. I must remember to ask Jane if she knows his name, Harriet thought as the grey-eyed soldier nodded and smiled to them, as he filed out towards the gate. Several more families had been asked to join the picnic by that time and so, by the time that they finally assembled on the Butes an hour later, there were over twenty people.

The friendly group of companions walked snakelike down the grassy slopes together, until they reached the point where the railway crossed with the harbour road. Here the men parted company and headed for the Diver's down on the quay, while the children began to jump along the railway sleepers. Normally this was strictly forbidden, but since it was Sunday and the little single gauge railway was the shortest, flattest and quickest route to the other end of the island, the women had agreed to walk that way. The spaces between the sleepers were such that the adults were able to keep quite a pace, striding from one to the other. The children on the other hand, had to leap between each sleeper and since their footsteps got into quite a rhythm, they began to sing their favourite songs and nursery rhymes. Miss Green, or Mary as she wanted to be known as today, had to stop herself from joining in and leading the singing as the sound of their voices reached her.

The little railway line was used during the week to

transport rocks from the quarry to reinforce the breakwater. It had been completed about twenty years earlier to give shelter to the harbour and bay and allow naval vessels the protection from the harsh westerly winds. Unfortunately for the planners, the effect of the waves pounding against the structure during heavy storms was underestimated and the engineers soon realised that, without the protection of rocks to break the waves' ferocity, the life span of the structure would be severely shortened. The train was also kept busy transporting rocks to the harbour to be shipped elsewhere. The quarry company was one of the main employers on the island for the locals except for the garrison, whose numbers were somewhat depleted, having been scaled down in recent years to a couple of regiments.

The quarry was only a short distance from Corblets Bay. As soon as the rock face was in sight the children gave a cheer. They waited impatiently at the end of the track for the others, especially the grandmothers, who were trailing far behind. They knew that if they ventured any further ahead they risked clipped ears. It had been drummed into them time and time again that it was dangerous near the quarry, so they waited for their mothers to lead the way to the safety of the shore.

Once at the bay the children rushed ahead and down to play on the sand, while the women laid blankets between the grassy dunes, to protect themselves from the breeze. From their vantage point they could watch the children and also talk between themselves. Apart from the occasional, 'Is it nearly lunchtime?' from the children, the women were left in peace. Their offspring amused themselves quite happily, building sandcastles and paddling in the cool shallow waters.

Charlotte, too, seemed to be more cheerful today. She told Harriet and Jane how John and Michael had taken her out for a walk the afternoon before and that they had met up with Jane's cousins. They had in fact walked along the path to the east of the island from Telegraph to Longy Bay and Charlotte had been pleased to show them the beauty of that side of the island. Harriet was relieved to see little trace of the sadness of the day before, as she watched her friend talking with her newfound friends. Her guilty conscience eased a little and she joined in with their conversation, pleased to be able to fill in with more tales of the island's folklore, such as the Hanging Rock at Longy.

'Legend has it,' she explained, 'That a dignitary on the island called Madame Robilliar had been so inquisitive, that a witch had turned her nose into a landmark to keep her quiet!'

'I don't know any of these tales,' exclaimed Mary.

'I was right when I said that you should come out with us. It's surprising what you might learn,' teased Harriet.

'Maybe you should take walks with us around the island, Mary, to fill you in with the historical background,' said Charlotte, warming to the idea of teaching the teacher.

'I'm all for some of that,' said a deeper but familiar voice behind them.

The doctor had persuaded the other men folk that an hour in the Diver's was long enough. They had reluctantly agreed with him and began their walk along Braye Beach, passing Fort Albert on their way to join the others. The hunger they were beginning to feel, and the weight of their heavy baskets, spurred them on and they were soon in earshot of the ladies.

Realising that it was her father's voice Jane retorted, 'You have no time for leisure as it is, without tiring yourself walking.'

'Jane, my dear, walking is for pleasure and if it were combined with learning more about Riduna, which has become our home, then I think even you would benefit.' He sat himself down without really thinking, until he realised that he was sitting on the end of Mary's rug rather than his daughter's. Embarrassed he made to move.

'Don't worry yourself,' said Mary. 'There's plenty of room for us both on the rug.' Realising that what she had just said could be misinterpreted, and that all eyes were on them both, she tried to control her reddening face and continued, 'After all, you have been kind enough to carry my basket along with your own.'

The doctor's sigh was audible to everyone as he relaxed between his daughter and Miss Green and both ladies plied him with goodies from their baskets. He began to enjoy himself and soon forgot his initial embarrassment.

David, the doctor and Mary talked amiably, like long-lost friends, and hardly noticed the looks which Jane passed to Harriet as they talked quietly, with half an ear on the conversation going on beside them. After eating their fill many began to drift away, ambling across the bay or over the grassy slopes. Charlotte, Michael and John offered to take Jane's cousins over the brow of the hill to look down over Longy Bay, the other long sandy bay on the island. The group had taken a path back to St Anne just short of Longy on the previous day and wished to see it and The Hanging Rock before returning to England the following week. Most of the others chose to have a gentle stroll close by and the more daring paddled alongside the children at the water's edge. Jane and Harriet also went for a stroll, although Harriet was aware that Jane was attempting to keep her father and his new companion in view as they walked. It was impossible to divert her attention so she ventured:

'They make a nice couple, don't they?'

'Umm,' replied Jane.

'That was one of your most carefully reasoned responses,' Harriet continued, trying to tease her friend out of her revelry.

'Pardon, I'm so sorry Harriet. I was miles away. What did you say?'

Not wanting to repeat her previous remark in case she offended Jane, Harriet enquired, 'Does it worry you that your father might meet someone else one day?'

Jane dragged her gaze away and turned so that she could watch the pair no longer and concentrated fully on Harriet.

'Let's sit down again,' she said. 'I suppose I expected it to happen one day and if Miss Green is the one, I mean Mary, then it couldn't be a nicer more suitable person.'

There was silence, for a moment, until Harriet broke it by saying, 'I could hear an unspoken but at the end of your last sentence.'

Jane sighed. 'I don't know. I suppose I'm afraid of a time when my father doesn't need me.'

'And yet that would free you to get on with your own life and fulfil your own dreams Jane?'

'Yes, of course it would, but that frightens me a little, too. It's so safe here. The big world out there can be quite daunting,' Jane replied.

Harriet was suddenly reminded of Edward. She wished that the world were smaller, a lot smaller. She hugged herself for comfort.

'Oh, that was thoughtless of me. You must miss Edward so,' Jane said focussing on her friend.

'I have a feeling that you're going to have to leave Riduna to find a man that reaches all your expectations, don't you? That is, if you abandon your dream to become a nurse,' Harriet said. 'Have you discovered the name of your handsome grey eyed soldier?'

'I think it's Thomas,' Jane whispered to her friend. She could not expand on her statement because her father appeared at that moment and sat down beside them.

'Would you think it correct of me to ask the pleasure of your company Harriet, to escort Jane, Mary and myself on walks to all the special places on the island you talk of?' he asked. 'This has been such a lovely day.'

The girls looked at each other and laughed.

'It would be a pleasure doctor,' replied Harriet.

'Where are your cousins?' Jane's father asked.

'There they are!' Jane exclaimed, pointing to the sand dunes to the right of where they were sitting, just as five figures had appeared. 'Perhaps we should walk to meet them.'

Everyone was beginning to gather up their belongings by this time, and to call the children. As the party began to amble back along the road towards St Anne, the doctor repeated his suggestion of future jaunts. So it was arranged that, one Sunday in every month throughout the summer, a picnic was planned, visiting different spots on the island. Secretly the doctor anticipated these coming events with pleasure and realising that he had not felt this happy for years, hoped against hope that Miss Green might feel the same way.

Chapter 11

OVER THE NEXT few days Harriet began to settle into a new, slightly altered routine. The days were much the same as they had been for the past few months.

She enjoyed her work at school. Since the beginning of the year a law had been passed saying that all children were to attend school until at least the age of ten. Even on the island, where lip service was paid to some of the laws made in England, children below that age were forbidden to work. Most parents sent their children to school until at least that age, if not to thirteen, especially since it was now free. The only exceptions were a few Irish and Italian children, whose fathers were construction workers on the last of the of the island's defences. These children usually stayed at home with their mothers.

Also, during harvest-time, the children from the small subsistence farms helped in the fields. The influx of children at the school in the last few years meant that the teachers were quite stretched, especially with the little ones in the mornings. Hence Harriet's help was invaluable and she not only benefited from being able to supplement the family's income, but it also helped to keep her mind occupied.

At lunchtimes she would usually bring a snack from

home and talk with Mary, or help to supervise the pupils who remained at school for their lunch. In the first few days after the picnic, Harriet had tried to tempt Mary to speak to her about David, the doctor. She was impossibly reticent and would not be drawn into conversation, so that in the end Harriet finally gave up trying, despite Jane's inquisitiveness. It was not the first time that Harriet wondered about Mary's past. She rarely talked about her life in England before moving to Riduna so it was a mystery to Harriet.

In the afternoons Mary would give her books, which she sometimes took home. Although Harriet and Jane had officially left school at thirteen, they were both keen to study and so Mary was very willing to give them some guidance. Charlotte, who had left school a year earlier with Michael and John, was kept too busy in the family business to worry about learning. They had all learnt the basic skills well enough for their needs.

It was during the evenings that Harriet would miss Edward most. The moments on her own would often fill her with a gnawing longing to be with him, or at least a wish to know where he was and what he was doing. Despite this sense of loneliness, these evenings at home also fell into a pattern. First Harriet would tidy herself up before supper and put on her locket. This fulfilment of her promise to him gave her a sense of togetherness with Edward which she did not experience through the day. After supper Harriet would excuse herself to write letters to Edward and to update her journal.

The first time that this routine was disturbed was the following Friday. She had been invited to Jane's house for the evening, since it was the last day before Jane's cousins began their journey back to England. They would first have to travel on the *Courier*, which had transported Edward the week before, to Sarnia. Then they would have half a day on this sister island before catching the larger Southampton mother steamer to England. Harriet could not help but wish to be smuggled into one of their trunks, because it was likely that this was the very ship that Edward would be sailing on.

She had finally persuaded Mary that she was more than welcome to join them for the evening. In fact the doctor had asked her, via Jane, to give her a specific invitation, but Harriet thought it diplomatic not to mention this. Instead she stressed that many people would be there, including Charlotte, Michael and John and that it would be another opportunity to get to know everyone better as friends rather than as pupils. Mary was in her late twenties and thus often fell between the age groups on the island, not having a lot in common with the young mothers and yet more mature than the group of young people. Harriet and Jane were pleased when she agreed to come. David was relieved when they told him, though he tried not to show it.

Life had been less peaceful in the doctor's household that week. After helping her father with morning surgery Jane was determined not to neglect her cousins, especially as she wanted to keep her mind off her thoughts of Thomas. Even so, she found herself suggesting that they go for walks to places where she might just catch sight of him. One afternoon they went back along to Platte Saline and by the fort where he had surprised her the week before. On the next afternoon they walked around Fort Albert, where the men often carried out exercises. She even suggested an evening stroll down by the harbour in the middle of the week, in the hopes that she might catch a glimpse of him on his way to the Diver's. On Thursday it rained all day. She was so downhearted that she half imagined that he must have caught the Wednesday midweek sail to Sarnia, to escape the boredom he professed to feel. Jane tried to put him from her mind. It was on the Friday afternoon, when she was out shopping for the evening gathering, that she heard a man clearing his throat in the baker's queue behind her. She ignored it at first thinking that the person must have a bad cold but after paying Charlotte, who was behind the counter helping her mother at the time, Jane turned around and jumped with surprise to see Thomas's smiling face.

'I don't usually have that effect on people,' he said as he bowed politely. 'Do you have to rush away?' he added. 'I have been hoping to see you for nearly a week now.'

Jane waited for him outside the shop, trying not to look too self-conscious and determined not to look at Charlotte through the window, imagining her quizzical face. As Thomas came out of the door she began to walk on up the street, Thomas falling naturally into step beside her. Jane hoped without success that she would not meet anyone who might take it upon themselves to talk to her father; unlikely in such a small place. At that very moment the doctor walked around the corner and almost bumped into Thomas. Looking a little startled at first, he quickly regained his composure, determined to discuss the matter out of the public gaze.

'Hello young man,' he said looking directly at Thomas. 'So *you* were the gallant soldier who escorted my daughter home the other night. I must say thank you for that. She should never have been out in the dark on her own.'

'You are welcome sir,' replied Thomas determined not to be fazed by this meeting, but caught unawares nevertheless.

'Tonight,' the doctor continued in a fairly abrupt, but not unfriendly manner, 'would you like to join us in a light supper, as a farewell for Jane's cousins who are sailing in the morning? Where are your cousins by the way?' the doctor asked, turning his attention to his flustered daughter, rather than waiting for a reply from Thomas.

Jane brought herself to her senses and replied, 'I left them at home packing Father, while I came out to do some shopping for Mrs Doris.'

'Good, good. Well I must take my leave of you. I have an important visit to make before it gets too late. Don't forget to give Mrs Doris a hand with the food Jane. Good day to you,' he said abruptly turning towards Thomas and touching his hat. 'We will be introduced later when Jane remembers her manners!' And he was gone.

Thomas stood there, obviously highly amused by the exchange. Jane's eyes just followed her father's back as it disappeared up the street and looked indignant and bewildered.

'So your name is Jane. I've wanted to have the opportunity to ask you and I forgot to do so the other night. Did you tell your father about me, then?' he asked.

'It's a mystery to me that he knows,' she said, 'but something I've learned to my cost, since living on this island, is that even walls have ears!'

Thomas laughed. 'Then I shall have to take you somewhere without walls, if we are ever to have a private conversation. Do you know that you look even prettier when you're cross?'

Jane just controlled the urge to rebuke him, and wishing to protect him from further embarrassment she replied, 'You are not obliged to come tonight. I will give your apologies if you've changed your mind.'

'It will be a pleasure. I'm honoured to be asked,' he replied. They had reached Jane's front door by this time and, having no excuse to detain her further, he said 'until tonight then,' in a gallant manner as he bowed and simultaneously caught her hand to kiss it. Then he was gone.

Jane shut the door behind her, glad to feel its coolness on her back. She leaned upon it for a while to steady herself. Her heart was thumping and she felt flushed. She stood there in the shadow of the hallway for some moments until she heard Mrs Doris's voice bellow from the kitchen.

'Have you brought the shopping Jane? Bring it quickly! We haven't got all day.'

Realising that, in her confusion, she had forgotten to go to the butcher's for the cold meat, she walked through to the kitchen, emptied the contents of her basket on the large kitchen table and headed straight back for the door.

'Not there!' exclaimed Mrs Doris. 'I'm putting the prepared dishes on that table.'

Jane quickly moved the shopping to the pantry and, making an excuse that she could not carry all the items at once, she raced out of the house again, glad for some fresh air and a chance to be alone with her thoughts for a little while longer.

Later that evening at Platte Saline Jack Loveridge was standing by the door waiting patiently for Harriet to come down. He was determined to keep his promise and keep a closer eye on his daughter, so that when Harriet eventually came downstairs he was ready and waiting to escort her to the soirée.

'You *do* look lovely,' Annie remarked, as her daughter joined her beside the fire and bent to give her a kiss on the cheek. 'Why are you not wearing your beautiful locket, Harriet?' she asked.

Not really knowing an answer to that, Harriet exclaimed, 'But it's a secret between me and Edward, Mama, and anyway I don't wish to lose it.'

Annie was not really satisfied with this response but, not

wanting to upset her strong-willed daughter, she let the matter drop, but Jack added, smiling at his wife, 'If I bought your mother a pretty thing like that I would want her to show it to the world!'

'But you have not, my man, I should be jealous, but if we don't stop this gossiping Harriet will be late,' said Annie. She realised that her daughter was looking confused and felt a little sorry for her.

'Come here wife and I will give you a big kiss. Will that be sufficient?' Jack teased his wife.

'Be gone with you!' Annie said, pretending to be cross, 'and have a pleasant evening Harriet,' she added. 'Give my regards to Jane and the doctor.'

'You really don't have to escort me, Papa,' said Harriet, who was used to her own independence.

'I said I would protect you, miss, and protect you I will!' said Jack, with such a finality in the tone of his voice that Harriet realised she was beaten.

'Au revoir,' she called to Annie and they set off up the track together, Harriet's arm linked amiably through her father's.

A little while before the first guests arrived the doctor called Jane into his surgery and closed the door firmly behind him.

'I am most disappointed in you, Jane. I do not wish to spoil this evening, but I want you to know that I expected more appropriate behaviour from a daughter of mine. Explain yourself.' The doctor was obviously angry, but he spoke in a quiet voice, so that the rest of the household including Mrs Doris, who was in the nearby kitchen, could not eavesdrop.

'I met Thomas at the last dance Father, and I danced with him on one occasion only, with your permission,' Jane explained.

Not waiting for her to continue the doctor interjected,

'I am not talking of the dance. I am talking of the way in which you met him a few evenings ago and yet again this morning without my knowledge, young lady.'

'Father, I can assure you that, on neither occasion, however sceptical you may be, had I arranged to meet Thomas anywhere. On both times we met purely by chance. How was it brought to your notice that he walked me home the other night?'

'I will give you the benefit of the doubt on this occasion, even though it seems very unlikely. You are aware no doubt that Mrs Doris spends one day per week cleaning for Mrs Leck across the road. It was Mrs Doris who saw you that evening and naturally informed me the next morning. I was hoping against hope that you would tell me about it without being asked, and then on the next occasion I found you parading him along Victoria Street this very morning. I also know that now is not the appropriate time to tell me fully what occurred, but tell me you will young lady. Your very reputation in this small community depends upon it.'

Jane realised clearly that it was not the act that had made her father so angry, but the deceit, and the fact that he had heard the news through gossip, rather than from Jane herself. Jane was mortified that she had unwittingly hurt her father so.

'I am so sorry Father. I did not think of the consequences of my actions. Please forgive me.'

Her father, without responding to her plea continued, 'I have to trust you Jane; without a mother to look after you. Please do not let me down again. Now, let us get ready for our guests. I hope I did the right thing by inviting your young man.'

'Oh yes Father. Thomas is his name. I am sure that you will like him.'

Her father nodded and Jane realised that she was being dismissed. Her father was rarely this formal with her.

As Jane was getting ready she realised that, by inviting Thomas officially, her father had put an end to the local gossip, which could be so damaging to both of them. She was sure that, when she had time to talk to her father more fully, he would understand and forgive her. She resolved to try to be more careful in the future.

Jane's cousins came down to the hall just as she heard the first knock at the door. Jane greeted Harriet warmly and wished that they could have some time to talk alone, but was just able to whisper, 'Thomas is coming,' in her friend's ear, before there was another knock at the door. This time it was Charlotte, Michael and John. She showed them all through to the drawing room.

It was a long room, which took up virtually the length of the ground floor of the house. At one end there was room for the guests to mingle. The young ladies seated on simple but pleasant armchairs while the young gentlemen stood by making conversation. At the other end of the drawing room there was a large oak table which was laid to seat ten people comfortably, with china and cutlery which the doctor had recently imported from France, along with some beautiful crystal glasses.

Jane spent some time with her guests until her father joined them, coincidentally just as Mary arrived at the front door. Her cousins were by this time deep in conversation with Michael and Charlotte. Although Harriet was listening to their discussion, she was also aware of her teacher's shyness, so she excused herself to join Mary at the door and walked in by her side, followed by the doctor and Jane, walking close behind. The three began to discuss the picnic, joined in by John, leaving Jane grateful to be free to go to ensure that Mrs Doris was ready. There was a door at the far end of the drawing room to the left of the beautiful table. Jane looked over her shoulder to be reassured that everyone was at ease and was just able to catch Harriet's attention with a brief smile before heading for the kitchen.

She wondered if Thomas would arrive as she walked along the short connecting corridor to the kitchen. It also gave her a moment to ponder on the assembled company. George and Henrietta, her cousins, were children of a well respected London surgeon. They seemed to be surprisingly relaxed with Charlotte, Michael and John. Mary, on the other hand obviously felt out of place in such a gathering, being more accustomed to her own company these days. She was also at least a decade older than the majority of the guests present. Then there was her father. He was also a few years Mary's senior, although there was obviously quite a spark between them.

'I wonder?' she thought aloud.

Then her mind wandered to the wide range of backgrounds of the assembled company: from a quarryman's daughter, bless her, to a publican's son; a teacher and children of a surgeon! Strange, thought Jane, in England it would be a rare occasion for people from such different walks of life to mingle, let alone share supper together, but here life was so different. Maybe it was a small taste of Utopia. Liking the word she smiled, thinking that she must write down her observations sometime. She was brought back to the present by a firm knock at the door. Forgetting that she was heading in the direction of the kitchen, she took the passage to her left to arrive in the hall at the same time as her father.

'Father, this is Corporal Thomas Chapman,' she said as she reached his side. The men shook hands and nodded politely.

'Welcome to our home,' her father replied. 'Come into

the drawing room and I will introduce you to the other guests. You will have to excuse Jane. She needs to go to the kitchen to see that our cook is ready, but that will give you the opportunity to meet everyone.'

'The pleasure is mine,' exclaimed Thomas.

Feeling dismissed for the second time today Jane said, 'Please excuse me,' and left Thomas with her father.

Back in the kitchen Mrs Doris was a little flustered but assured Jane that everything was under control. Since Mrs Doris was not used to feeding such a gathering and they had no other help for the occasion, she and Jane had cleverly devised a simple but fine meal. There was vegetable soup with delicious crusty bread, fresh from Charlotte and Michael's parents' bakery. This would be followed by an array of cold meats, island-made pickles and potatoes. For dessert there was apple and pear torté, to be served with cream from the dairy. It never ceased to surprise Jane as to how rich, thick and yellow the island cream was. She had never tasted the like in England and although it was nothing new to the islanders, she knew that it was a real treat for her cousins Henrietta and George. It would certainly not be one of the most elaborate meals her cousins had partaken, but it would be wholesome and tasty. They would wash it down with some wine, although she would make sure that there was plenty of water for the younger and less experienced guests, within which category she included herself.

Mrs Doris had offered to serve the soup at the table. Afterwards she would clear away the soup terrines and bring in the meats and potatoes. It would be quite late by then, so the arrangement was that Mrs Doris would leave the torte and the cream on the kitchen table. Jane would serve the dessert when the time came, and the bulk of the clearing up would be done in the morning, when Mrs

Doris's young niece could lend a hand. Primitive arrangements compared to their life in London, but ones that seemed to suit their life on the island.

'Now, I don't want you dashing about in my way Jane,' Mrs Doris stated abruptly. Jane smarted at the remark but realised Mrs Doris was stressed, so let it pass.

'I understand Mrs Doris but, in the event that I do not have time to express my thanks later, we greatly appreciate all that you have done tonight. It is the first time ever that Father has allowed me to arrange a soirée like this, and I would never have achieved it without your expert guidance,' said Jane, kissing the elderly lady on the cheek.

Momentarily flustered by this Mrs Doris exclaimed, 'Off you go then. We'll have none of that now!'

Jane smiled at the woman's response, but could not help but have wistful thoughts of her mother as she sped back to the drawing room.

Just before Jane entered she glanced in the mirror, took a deep breath and smoothed down her pretty maroon dress, remembering at the last moment to whip off her apron and hide it under a chair by the door before going in.

Jane announced that dinner was served and guided everyone to their seats. She sat herself between Thomas and George, opposite her father and Mary. Although she was aware that hardly a word had passed between her and Thomas as yet that night, she was pleased that everyone, including Mary, seemed relaxed and deep in conversation. This came to a momentary halt as Jane rang her little bell to alert Mrs Doris's attention, but soon the relaxed atmosphere was restored as everyone began to enjoy the soup.

The meal went extremely well. Jane was pleased that she was able to talk a little with Thomas, finding out more about his family back in England. She was a good hostess and did not ignore her other guests though, especially her cousins and Harriet, who seemed uncharacteristically quiet at times. Whether she was talking directly with Thomas or not, she was acutely aware of his presence and had a feeling that he was also of her. She did not know whether it was her imagination, but occasionally she would be aware of his hand briefly touching hers, almost as if in a soft caress and it sent shivers down her spine. She had little time to dwell on this thought, since it was time for her to serve the torte.

Gratefully she accepted an offer from Harriet to serve the other end of the table. She could not help but be a little impatient with her father, as she headed from the kitchen for the final time, with two jugs of cream in her hands. She noticed that he was still engrossed in a deep conversation with Mary, oblivious of her efforts and worse, he seemed to be unaware of their other guests. She quickly dismissed her negativity and instead thought of her father fondly, and reminded herself of how difficult his life had been in the last few years since her mother had died.

Soon the meal came to an end and Jane was pleased to see that her father had finally woken up to his responsibilities and suggested that Thomas and George stay with him for a smoke while the ladies retired upstairs to the parlour room. Jane was aware that neither Michael nor John knew whether they should stay downstairs or join the ladies upstairs. She nodded at her father to retrieve the situation and to allay their embarrassment. They were both very young and although they had not admitted to their parents that they had tried smoking, both had experimented with the weed.

'Come and join us,' her father said jovially. 'You don't want to follow the ladies yet since they will only be talking about us.' He winked at Jane.

'Thank you sir,' they said, grateful to be given a clear

direction. They sat back down again and, when they were passed a cigarette, both sat up with pride as if it were a sign that they had come of age at last.

'You flatter yourself Father,' teased Jane as she led the young ladies out of the drawing room and upstairs to the parlour, where they made themselves comfortable.

It was Charlotte who spoke first, full of curiosity, asking,

'Who is this Thomas, Jane? I saw you dancing with him at the May Ball, but how is it that your father has invited him here tonight?'

'It's a long story Charlotte,' said Jane. 'But after the dance I have met him quite by chance on a couple of occasions, and we met my father as we were walking along Victoria Street yesterday. I was so embarrassed, but to my surprise my father invited Thomas to join us today.'

'Has he many more months to serve Jane?' enquired Mary, always thinking practically when affairs of the heart of other people were concerned.

'He's here for another six months. He returns to England just before Christmas,' replied Jane.

'Time to get to know him a little more then,' said Henrietta, to which Jane blushed.

There was a moment of awkward hush and Harriet realised that talking about other relationships in the assembled company was walking on dangerous ground. She could not mention Edward for fear of hurting Charlotte and they could not question Mary about David for fear of embarrassing her too. She rescued the situation by turning to Henrietta and asking if she had enjoyed her stay on Riduna and the ladies spent the next half an hour discussing the pleasures and drawbacks of living on a small island. By the time the men joined them, the discussion was in full flow.

The doctor decided to change the pattern of the evening

by asking if any of the ladies would like to entertain by singing or playing the piano which, to his pride, he had shipped from the mainland. It was his wife's piano and so he found it hard to disguise his emotions when Mary offered to play for them. Finally Henrietta and Jane played a duet which brought the evening to a close. As if on cue, as the clapping faded, there was a knock at the door. Jack's arrival to collect Harriet was taken as a signal for the guests to prepare for departure, with the promise to meet on the quayside the following morning.

Chapter 12

IT WAS THE second Saturday morning in a row that the islanders were gathered down at the harbour to say farewell. Following the success of the evening before, it was the same company who stood talking on the quayside, as the seamen made ready the waiting ship. It was also the same vessel, the *Courier*, which stirred vivid dream-like memories in Harriet as she stood at a short distance from the doctor's family with Mary. As they waited for an appropriate moment to say goodbye to Henrietta and George, the young post boy with his peaked cap and uniform, which looked at least three sizes too big, came whistling off the ship. He walked down the narrow gangway and passed them on his way up the track towards the town post office. He was pulling a trolley on wheels behind him and, with his head held high and a cheesy grin, he looked full of his own importance.

Mary, who recognised him as young Tom from the Watkins smallholding out in the south west of the island, smiled encouragingly. Tom, being the youngest of three, had landed on his feet when the postmaster took pity on him and offered him a job back in the spring. He had long since given up going to school, but would hang about at the post office twice a week, when he knew the boat was in. His hope was, that old Mr Tilbury the postmaster, would give him a double or two for delivering special post to the few gentry on the island. Occasionally, if Tom was really lucky, the gentlemen or women concerned, would also give him a tip on receiving their mail. Mr Tilbury knew that there was no way that Tom's parents could feed his family on the proceeds from their little farm, and there certainly was not enough work at home to keep both Tom and his elder brother busy all year. It was not only compassion that led to this arrangement, but also that he was beginning to feel the aches and pains of old age creeping up on him. Tom's luck grew even further following John Tilbury's fiftieth birthday when he was also glad to offer Tom the job of pulling the mail trolley up the hill from the ship. Tom was overjoyed and so were his hard-working parents. It only showed that Tom's persistence had been rewarded tenfold.

'Hello Tom,' said Mary, smiling at a former pupil of the school.

'Good day to you Miss Green,' replied Tom cheerily. 'The weather's looking as if it could close in at any moment don't it Miss?' he continued.

'Doesn't it Tom!' said Mary, not being able to resist correcting his grammar. 'You do look smart in that uniform of yours.'

Tom blushed. 'Must be on my way then, otherwise there'll be more than one storm brewing if I'm not back at the post office by opening time at nine.'

With that he was off.

'I guess you might be expecting a letter Harriet?' Mary said, turning to her young friend, whose eyes were still focussed wistfully on the postbag, which was fast disappearing up the slope.

'I hope so,' Harriet replied. 'Edward did say that he

would write as soon as he could, but I know that he will be very busy and excited about his new life,' she added, as if to numb the disappointment if she arrived up at the post office at lunchtime to find that there was no letter.

The doctor's family were saying their final goodbyes and Harriet and Jane moved forward to wish them a pleasant crossing. Charlotte and Michael had just joined them and Harriet wondered what sort of emotions were going through her friend's head this morning. One day Harriet felt that she would have to face her friend and talk about Edward. She certainly did not have the courage to do so yet, or even the reassurance that she could trust her own feelings at this stage, let alone Edward's.

The *Courier's* funnel sounded, bringing Harriet back to the present. Everyone waved as the ship moved gracefully away from the quayside. It always amazed Harriet that the ropes, which held the ship fast to the harbour, were coiled and thrown back on board at just the right moment, expertly caught on deck and recoiled neatly in seconds. She had watched Edward helping the waiting seaman carry out this task many a time.

'We must make our way to school now, if I am not going to get in trouble with the school master, Harriet,' Mary reminded her. It was nearly nine o'clock and the children would already be gathering in the yard.

'I'll come to see you later this afternoon, if that's all right,' Harriet called over her shoulder to Jane as she began to follow Mary up the hill.

'Perfect,' said her friend.

Jane, feeling guilty about excluding Charlotte recently, invited her to join them, as they walked towards the town together. She thanked Charlotte and Michael for spending time with Henrietta and George and making them so welcome. Soon they reached the bakery where they parted company and she and the doctor went to see how many were awaiting him for morning surgery.

Jane enjoyed organising this for her father, and she always showed a caring interest in the islanders and their ailments, so much so that some of them felt better from just talking to her! She knew that few of them made the decision to seek medical help lightly, due to the cost involved. Many preferred to go to Old Mother down at Platte Saline for her cheaper alternative treatments, which appeared to be a combination of a drop of folklore, mixed with a good imagination and a concoction of whatever wild plants were growing in that particular season. The thought of Old Mother made Jane smile and yet she knew deep down that so much good seemed to be achieved with a belief in the cure, regardless of the medicine. A lot of illness was in the mind she reasoned and perhaps that accounted for Old Mother's success.

David, meanwhile, was wondering just how he could find an excuse to arrange to see Mary again before their planned walk next month. He would love to see her alone, not for anything underhand, and he reddened at the thought, but to give them time to get to know each other, without prying eyes and, even worse, inquisitive ears; especially my daughter's, he thought. So, like a love-struck teenager, he planned to go out on an imaginary call that afternoon, when he knew his daughter would be busy with her friends. He would walk slowly up the street, passing the schoolhouse at the time that he had recently seen Mary leave for home on a Saturday lunchtime. He would make an excuse to walk in the direction of her home. Pleased with his scheming, he arrived home and was more cheerful than usual with his patients that morning. After surgery he tried to control his impatience as he shared a light lunch with Jane.

Mary was so surprised to see David passing the school

gate as she left for home that lunchtime. She was relieved that Harriet had already disappeared along the street and a little flustered at first when he walked in step beside her without asking her permission.

'Good day Miss Green. It's so good to see you again. I am making a home visit in your direction.'

Good day to you too doctor,' she replied, glancing around her as she walked.

Mary soon forgot her concern as they discussed Mary's work and life on the island, so much so that time passed quickly and Mary was a little disappointed when she realised that they had reached the front door of her little terraced cottage in Newtown.

The doctor bade her farewell, touching his hat and thanking her for being such a lovely companion. Before she knew it, she was letting herself into her empty front room, gazing dreamily through the window up the track after the retreating figure. She wished, in retrospect, that she had asked him to join her for a cup of tea. Annoyed with her lack of thought, she settled down to a lonely afternoon and even the tea could not raise her spirits as it usually did. Restlessly, she faced her usual weekend chores, which she tackled with little of her usual enthusiasm.

Harriet left the school and made a detour to the post office on Victoria Street, before returning home for some lunch. Mr Tilbury was just about to shut up shop, since he only worked half days on Saturdays.

'Good day to you Harriet,' he said. 'I thought that you would call this morning.'

'Good day Mr Tilbury. Have you got a letter for me then?' she asked appealingly.

John Tilbury, a kindly soul, was already rummaging through the wooden pigeonholes on the back wall of his shop.

'Ay, here it is,' he said, handing Harriet a carefully addressed envelope.

Harriet was just about to say thank you, and make her excuses to leave, when he called after her.

'Wait a minute lass! I've got one for your friend Charlotte here too. You don't think you could drop it in to her on your way home, do you, especially since she's a good friend of yours?'

Harriet hesitated a moment looking at the other envelope, as if to touch it would burn her hands, and yet she was full of curiosity too. It was obvious to both of them that the writing on the envelopes was identical.

'That's fine,' she mumbled as she headed for the door, hoping that Mr Tilbury would not notice her confusion.

Harriet walked slowly along the street towards the baker's. She wanted to calm herself before she arrived. As she reached the door of the shop she took a deep breath and put a false smile on her face. She was pleased that Charlotte was alone and was busy sweeping the floor.

'Hello, Charlotte,' she said as brightly as she could, when her friend looked up with her own forced smile.

'I've just been to the post office and Mr Tilbury asked if I could bring this in to you on my way home. Just as well I did otherwise you wouldn't have received it 'til Monday,'

Charlotte's eyes brightened immediately as she reached forward to take the envelope. She recognised the writing from school days and it was obvious that she could not wait for Harriet to go, so that she could open it in private.

'Thank you so much Harriet. It looks like Edward's handwriting. I do miss him so much, don't you?' she asked, not really expecting a reply.

'I'll leave you then,' said Harriet, nodding, although she was still standing there, riveted to the spot, wanting Charlotte to reveal the contents of that envelope.

'I'll see you later at Jane's. It's a long time since the three of us have had some time together so I'm looking forward to it,' Charlotte said as she walked towards the stairs at the back of the shop in order to escape to the privacy of her own room. 'Can you make sure that the door is closed firmly behind you?' she added.

Harriet walked out of the shop. Her heart felt heavy, even though she was carrying Edward's letter. Not only was she disappointed that Edward had also written to Charlotte, but she also felt aggrieved that she was going to have to share Jane with Charlotte for the afternoon. The atmosphere between the two girls was decidedly frosty and Harriet had no inclination at this moment to make amends.

As she walked home she tortured herself by trying to guess what Edward might write to her friend. Had he confessed undying love to her too? Surely the words he had said the other night were genuine. Harriet fretted. Maybe all would be revealed later, she tried to reassure herself.

I don't think that it will be in the least bit easy, was her last thought as she entered her back door and called a greeting to her mother, before going up to the peace of her room.

She placed the letter on the mantelpiece above the small bedroom fire, which they rarely had enough money to light. She would open the letter that evening, when she hoped she would feel calmer and less angry with Edward.

Trying to dispel the longing for Edward to walk in and hold her in his arms and put her mind at rest, she made her way downstairs to help her mother.

The afternoon was not as painful as Harriet had imagined. Both she and Charlotte avoided the controversial subjects of Edward or the offending letters. Jane, too, was sensitive to their feelings and allowed their talk to focus on a possible romance between her and Thomas. They also enjoyed speculating on the blossoming friendship between Mary and Jane's father. They sat comfortably in Jane's room and the initial embarrassment that both Charlotte and Harriet felt soon dispersed.

'I don't think my father would have been so quick thinking as to invite Thomas like that, if it had been me,' Charlotte exclaimed, after Jane had retold her story. 'I expect he would have shouted at the soldier in the street, as like as not, and caused a scene.'

Not wanting to accentuate the differences between their upbringing, Jane replied, 'It surprised me, too. It was not until I had time to think about it later, that I realised how wise he had been. Not only did it stop the gossip, but it also ensured that Father could find out what Thomas was really like?'

'Do you think your father approves then?' asked Harriet.

'Father has forbidden me to meet Thomas, unless I inform him about it and have a chaperone; even then I must be collected from home and escorted back here,' Jane replied.

'Me too! I feel so trapped at times, by my papa trying to protect me. I didn't know how lucky I was to have so much freedom when I was younger,' Harriet sighed.

'When do you think that you might see Thomas again, Jane?' Charlotte asked.

'When Thomas left last night he thanked Father for a pleasant evening and kissed my hand as he left, but he didn't mention meeting again.'

'I expect he was nervous, although he seemed perfectly at ease with us during the evening. The way he looked at you, Jane, made it obvious that he was attracted to you,' Harriet said.

'The amusing thing is that, whatever my father might say, on this island it's impossible not to meet people by accident.

It's so small that you can't help but see each other eventually. Then what excuses do I give my father?' Jane asked.

'I'm sure that you'll be quick-witted to know what's right when the time comes. All your father is asking of you is to be honest with him about what you do,' Harriet replied, 'and be careful to keep those animal instincts at bay.' Jane and Harriet laughed at this, but didn't really know how to explain their mirth to Charlotte.

To change the subject quickly, Jane asked her friends, 'What do you think of my father and Mary. Did you notice how bewitched he was with her last night? I was quite embarrassed about it. He barely noticed the rest of his guests at times.'

'He was certainly very attentive towards her, but you don't think he could be serious, surely? After all, she is fifteen years younger than he is, and she is a well respected teacher who's devoted to her work,' Charlotte replied.

'I don't think that it would deter him. He's certainly been acting very strangely since the picnic and he was so pleased when I informed him that Mary had agreed to come last night. Has she said anything to you this week?' Jane asked Harriet.

'She won't talk of personal matters. (At least not her own, Harriet mused privately.) I've tried to encourage her to speak about your father but it was impossible. Mary kept changing the subject.'

'Would you be pleased for him if he remarried?' Charlotte asked.

'I've got to admit that it would be a shock for me to think of my father with someone new, or that he didn't need me anymore,' she replied honestly. 'On the other hand, I have my own dreams about the future and maybe I should be less selfish. It may be just what I need to give me the encouragement to find my own way in the world.'

'You're such a strong person,' said Charlotte, admiringly. 'I hope life is simpler for me. I don't want much from life but I know that I couldn't cope with the major changes you have to face.'

'What do you want out of life Charlotte?' asked Jane, ignoring Harriet's warning glances.

'I want to be secure. To settle down with someone, with whom I can depend, and have a family here on Riduna,' Charlotte answered.

'You don't want to travel?' asked Jane.

'Never!' exclaimed Charlotte.

'You're going to need to find a husband who loves the island as much as you do,' stated Jane thoughtfully. By this time Harriet was listening intently to every word.

'He would certainly have to settle down,' Charlotte added. 'There's enough to keep anyone happy here I think, without dreaming of strange places far away.'

Suddenly, even with her slower wit, Charlotte realised the implications of her words.

She sat in silence for a moment before trying to retrieve her dignity somewhat by exclaiming, 'People can change can't they?'

Neither Jane nor Harriet felt able to reply at that moment and so there was a lull in the conversation.

Charlotte broke the silence as she got to her feet, 'I think it's time I was on my way. It's been a lovely afternoon Jane,' she said as she bent to kiss Jane on the cheek before turning to kiss Harriet too.

Jane and Harriet followed Charlotte down the stairs and the two of them stood talking at the door for a few minutes as they watched Charlotte walk down the street.

'Do you think that she truly reflected on her own words Harriet?' Jane asked. 'She could never tame Edward's lust for travel. I'm not even sure that it will bring *you* the happiness that you deserve in the end, but at least you have more of an independent spirit. You would cope better with the times apart and be even more determined to enjoy times together to the full.'

'Maybe Jane, I'm not that strong either,' admitted Harriet, thinking of her confused emotions earlier that day. 'Is it possible to trust someone who is so far away? I'm not sure that I do anymore.'

'What's brought on this gloom?' asked Jane.

Harriet told Jane about the two letters.

'I'm sure Edward would be able to explain himself, if he were here.'

'Even if Edward's reasons were just in his own eyes, he's not here, is he?' moaned Harriet. 'That's the whole point, as far as I can see. How many times am I going to have to wait months before I see him again, before he can tell me that everything is as it should be?'

Realising that Harriet would not be easily cheered Jane asked, 'Do you still love him Harriet?'

'Of course I do,' she replied, as if defeated by her very self. 'I do believe I love him more than I love myself!'

With that she hugged her friend and they parted, each deep in thought, wondering how their complicated lives might pan out.

Back at the cottage Harriet went straight to her room. She put on her locket, her nervousness momentarily stilled by its symbolism. Finally, she picked up the letter, holding it in her hand, turning it over many times and examining every detail: the writing, the postmark, the stamp. She was aware of the churning in her stomach. She took a deep breath before carefully breaking the seal and slipping the letter out of the envelope. This she placed gently back on the mantelpiece before seating herself by the window. She took one long look out of the window and gazed far out to sea, as if willing Edward to come home, before focussing on the words before her.

My Dearest Harriet,

There has hardly been a moment when I haven't thought of you. Tomorrow morning I set sail to England for the first time and so Cousin Joe and I have decided to be sensible and have an early night. We were less sensible, I'm afraid, last night and I had more than I should have had to drink. Joe's mother was cross with us this morning, which did little to help my aching head. He is talking to his parents downstairs now, giving me time to be alone to write to you.

I am so excited, Harriet, although I am a little nervous too. I will have so much to tell you when I see you at Christmas. I wish you were here with me now, but please try to remember that, however far away I seem to you, I am with you in my thoughts.

Ever yours,
Edward

Harriet read the letter many times over until she had almost memorised it. She would have continued to sit there in the gathering gloom if her mother had not called her to come down for her supper. The letter gave her some of the comfort but there was no mention of Charlotte to ease her puzzled mind.

Chapter 13

AS THE PASSENGERS were boarding the steamer to Southampton Edward and Joe had little time to think about the journey ahead. They were too occupied loading basket after basket safely aboard the ship. Half of the load was belongings and half was produce to sell in England. Load upon load of juicy ripe tomatoes to be handled with care to ensure they were in perfect condition for the trip, not only across the sea, but also by rail from Southampton docks to the city of London.

Each basket swung above their heads before being caught and brought firmly but carefully down to the deck. Joe and Edward soon slipped into the rhythm of the sailors and as they worked they sang. In fact, they were so occupied, safely storing the precious load, that they barely noticed the steamer slipping away from the quay at St Peter Port. It was only as the passenger steamer was at the entrance to the harbour and about to reach the open sea that Joe looked up to glimpse his home town, before it disappeared from view behind the harbour wall. The anxiety he had felt since he awoke in the early hours of the morning returned with an irrational fear of the journey ahead. Edward, on the other hand whistled happily unaware of his friend's concern.

The journey across was uneventful, since the weather was kind to them. Nevertheless, it was with relief that Joe followed Edward off the ship at Southampton docks. Bill, the coxswain took charge of the new recruits. It was dusk by the time they had unloaded and ensured that all the passengers had disembarked safely so that, as well as dodging the countless carriages and traps speeding along the esplanade, they were dazzled by the sight of lighted gas lamps illuminating their path.

'Keep up lads!' called Bill as Edward paused to watch two smiling ladies observing them from a passing carriage. Bill led them to the Seamen's Mission, a couple of streets from the Eastern Docks. The janitor was friendly enough as they were guided to a room full of bunks with a blanket thrown on each. Joe thought wistfully of the comfort of home as he threw his small bag at the end of the bed he claimed for the night. Edward chose the one above and leapt up the ladder in two agile steps.

''Twill not dent your wages too much,' Bill explained, 'and you'll not find a cheaper more hearty breakfast in the port. Now rest yoursel's a while an' I'll meet you downstairs at six for supper. Then us'll show you the nearest watering hole.'

Edward drifted off in a contented sleep while Joe just lay still, glad to no longer feel the vibration of the ship beneath him and he listened to the banter of the many sailors who were by now overcrowding the room. Joe woke Edward an hour later by shaking his shoulder and at first Edward was disorientated, but soon sat up with excitement, so much so that he bumped his head on the all too close ceiling above him. His language made the other men hoot with laugher, as he slid, with less agility this time, on to the floor, rubbing his sore head.

They enjoyed a wholesome supper before following Bill

and his mates along the bustling streets to a local alehouse, which was along a maze of dark alleyways not far from the Mission. Southampton was no busier than St Peter Port during the tourist season but felt a trifle less friendly and welcoming. Joe and Edward were glad of their guide but as soon as Bill entered the alehouse he was greeted cheerily by a buxom woman with an infectious laugh and soon disappeared upstairs leaving the lads feeling very vulnerable and uncertain. They sat down at a corner table near to the door and a barmaid brought them a couple of ales. Neither Edward nor Joe was ignorant of the meaning of the less than subtle gestures of several ladies who approached their table through the evening. Nevertheless they politely refused their advances and so were left to drink in peace.

Joe, who was a little more worldly-wise and whose tongue was loosened by the alcohol, even joked with one lady who swished her gown close to him and leaned over their table unnecessarily low to fill their empty glasses, leaving little to the imagination. Close up, both lads could see that thick make-up only helped to hide the ravages of time and late nights on the cheerful dame's face.

'You're old enough to be my mother!' Joe teased cheekily.

The lady in question took the joke in good humour and retorted with even more suggestion in her voice, 'Older and wiser, they're the best!' and she winked at Joe as she passed on to a more welcoming table.

Exhausted after their day, and tired of the ceaseless banter, Joe and Edward soon slipped unnoticed from the inn and made their way back to the Mission where they quickly found their bunks. Joe was asleep within minutes but Edward, who always thought of Harriet at this time of day, imagined her fondly as he drifted off to sleep.

Chapter 14

MARY WAS LESS surprised to see David outside the school gates the following Saturday. As the summer progressed and their confidence grew, they would go out for walks. They would often be seen ambling on the various bays or along the network of paths crossing the island. The silhouettes of these respected community figures were observed deep in conversation or admiring the views from the breathtakingly beautiful cliff tops. The school mistress and the doctor shared a mutual sensation that they had been woken from an emotional dark sleep which enabled them to ignore the whispering speculation and the inevitable dilemma to be faced sometime in the future.

Unbeknown to either party the elders of the island had already discussed their plight and summoned the headmaster. The meeting had been quite heated, one elder thumping the table with anger that Miss Green should resign immediately.

'It is a disgrace,' he said.

'Miss Green has a responsibility to set a faultless example to the children,' exclaimed another.

'It's despicable. She must go *now*,' shouted a third.

'You need to talk to Miss Green as soon as possible and report back to us,' said the chairman, bringing the meeting to a close.

Following this difficult encounter, the headmaster had spent several hours of indecision, but he knew now that he had no choice. He must call Miss Green to his office, before she took her leave in the summer. He felt loath to give her notice at this stage. She was such a valued member of the staff and it was difficult enough to recruit suitable teachers who would settle on the island. On the other hand he was aware of the power of the elders and that strict standards must be upheld and a scandal avoided at all cost.

Jane on the other hand was trying her utmost to follow her father's wishes, and it was a few weeks after the soiree that she was able to see Thomas again. He had been invited to join the village picnic, accompanied by a fellow soldier. In fact, her father had been much more relaxed since his friendship with Mary had flourished, so that the day went better than she had expected and her father seemed at ease in Thomas's company. The men folk met for a drink in the Diver's before walking to Longy to meet up with the ladies. Harriet had chosen Longy Bay for today's picnic, since the wind was calmer and they could enjoy the views of the sweeping bay which lead majestically out to causeway to Fort Raz.

There was something about the other soldier, who had accompanied Thomas, so she kept her distance sitting with her's and Edward's parents. She felt even more lonely than usual in such a large gathering, and she realised that she was missing Jane's company as well as Edward's. Occasionally, glancing across to her friend, she was pleased to see Jane visibly relax and enjoy herself and, as for her teacher, Mary seemed a different person since getting to know the doctor.

She looked over towards Charlotte and it reminded her of her last letter to Edward when she had plucked up courage to mention his unfortunate letter to Charlotte.

Dear Edward,

It was lovely to hear from you. Since you will have travelled all the way to England, I cannot wait to hear all about it. I must admit that I envied Henrietta and George when we waved goodbye last Saturday, not because I would like to travel so far, because I would be too afraid, but because they might travel on the same ship as you. I miss you so much.

One thing that puzzles me, Edward, and I am sure that you will be able to explain yourself, but I was given a letter to deliver from you to Charlotte by Mr Tilbury on Saturday. I could hardly refuse, but I must admit that it has unsettled me. I am sure that, if you were here, you would have a good explanation and reassure me. If it is a test of my feelings for you, then I must convince you that they have not changed. Nevertheless, it has caused me many restless nights.

Looking forward to hearing your reply,

Yours as ever,
Harriet.

The words floated through Harriet's head as she sat there, and her eyes could not help but linger for a few moments on Charlotte, as she sat with Michael and John. A heavy heart overwhelmed her for an instance, but it took just a look from her mama to bring a smile back to her face. Since the other soldier was sitting near to Charlotte and Michael, he was joining in with their conversation. He caught Harriet's eye as she gazed towards them and Harriet couldn't help but blush. Most unfortunate, she thought, and afraid that her intentions had been misinterpreted she turned back quickly to her parents and listened to them, as if concentrating on their every word.

After the eating was complete, Harriet took some time

pointing out the various landmarks including The Hanging Rock, Essex Castle, Ile de Raz and the Nunnery. Her teacher and the doctor were especially interested to be informed about places which were soon to leave a lasting impression.

There was one special Saturday towards the end of July that Mary would always remember. She and David were walking above Telegraph Bay, where the cliff tops were more imposing and sheer. They were standing admiring the view, when they decided to take the rough cliff path down to the bay. Once they had negotiated the steep climb and boulders to get to the sand, they sat down in one of the secluded coves, protected from the sea breeze.

Mary sighed. 'It's lovely,' she said. 'I'm beginning to feel so at peace here on Riduna?'

'I know just what you mean,' replied David. 'The island seems to have a magical quality, which leaves the world behind. It would not suit everyone's temperament. My son, for instance; he survived for two months and could not wait to get back to England.'

'Do you think Jane will stay?' Mary asked, not having the courage to ask the other burning questions on her mind. In fact, since the school holidays had nearly arrived, Mary was preparing to travel to her family in England for August. The closer the time came, the more she realised that she was reluctant to leave the island. For the first time she was beginning to feel that home was no longer that big house in Hove where she grew up. Riduna, with all its simple charm felt so safe and secure.

'I'm certain that she will return to England to study fairly soon. She is determined to be a nurse one day; that is if this Thomas doesn't change her mind.' He wanted to add, it's strange what love can do, but thought the better of it.

They sat in silence for a few moments. David was fighting

with mixed emotions as he sat watching the waves roll in. Although he desperately wanted to ask Mary to marry him, he did not want to make her so nervous that she would not want to return to the island. He valued her friendship too much. She had certainly filled a gap in his life and even though he longed to have a physical relationship with her, he could live without that, if he had to. He was just frightened of losing her altogether.

On his side there was nothing that would deter him from marrying Mary. She seemed the perfect companion. Now that Jane was of an age where her independence was growing, and since many years had passed since the death of her mother, he did not feel that his daughter would object. In fact, he secretly dreamed that the relationship had Jane's blessing. Certainly, she had said little to make him believe the contrary. No, it was the effect on Mary's life that might stand in the way of their happiness together. First of all he was fifteen years her senior and, though she had never shown any signs that the age gap worried her, it might. Secondly, he intended to remain on this island refuge for many years to come. He was happy here, and did not miss his life in England. Even if Jane were to marry and live in England, it was not so far away that she could not visit. He knew that his son rarely took the trouble to come over to see them, but surely girls were more responsible towards their parents. There was also the large concern of the importance of Mary's work. He knew that, if she were to marry, she would not be allowed to continue to teach, though her work meant a great deal to her. From what he heard from the families that he visited, she was not only good at her job, but well respected and loved by the islands' children. A trust needed to be earned in a community such as this, and he knew this only too well. No, thought David. I am going to have to be extremely sensitive and careful how I word my proposal.

Much the same thoughts had been going through Mary's mind. She had felt unable to share her concerns with anyone, especially Harriet, who was so close to Jane. She was not sure whether she could rely on her young friend to be completely discreet. It's times like these I miss my family so much, she thought, realising how contradictory her mind was being. She often felt a longing to see them far more than her bi-annual visits during the summer and for the Christmas festivities and even then she only travelled in winter if the weather allowed it. Mary would never allow herself the luxury of any feelings of self-pity and instead was usually quite content with her lot.

David was determined not to let Mary leave without declaring in some way how he felt for her, but he was at a loss as to how to express it. Rashly, knowing the implications for island gossip and that it would make it even harder if he had misread her feelings, he had booked a table to take her to The Scott's Hotel for a meal on the eve of her departure for the summer. He hoped against hope that she would not refuse, knowing that she was a very private person, but he wanted the occasion to be a memorable one for her last night before her journey.

Turning to face Mary, David plucked up the courage and asked, 'Since next Friday is your last day on the island, I have taken the liberty of booking a table for us at Scott's. I will miss you every Saturday while you are away and I wanted to say thank you for being such a good friend. I hope I have not overstepped my position?' David asked, almost afraid that his words had let him down.

Mary coloured and tears were threatening to fill her eyes. She had travelled here to avoid such conflicts in her life, but it was obvious from David's eyes that his feelings were genuine.

'David, that's far too expensive. I'm happy to prepare a

meal for us and we could have a quiet evening together,' she replied, almost too frightened to go to the most exclusive of the island's hotels, let alone coping with the implications.

'It's lovely for you to suggest it, but I couldn't have you cook the very night before you leave. I would not allow it. I booked the evening for my own pleasure too. It's such a long time since I experienced a bit of luxury and it would make me so happy if you would share it with me.' David hoped that this explanation made it easier for Mary to accept and sighed with relief when she finally agreed.

They clambered carefully up the cliff path and, after standing to gaze once more over the bay, they walked back along towards the town. They passed the 'Lovers' Chair,' but neither knew the implications of the smoothly worn rock; otherwise David might have been tempted to sit on it.

They parted company on Victoria Street, David to return home and Mary to do some last minute shopping before the stores closed.

'Until Friday then,' he said, giving a slight bow and taking her hand. 'Thank you for saying yes.'

The doctor was gone before he realised the ambiguity of his parting gesture. In confusion Mary nodded at the couple passing by at the time, as they smiled knowingly at her and said, 'Good day to you Miss Green.'

The following Friday evening arrived all too quickly. Mary fretted about what to wear. She had few decent clothes; in fact she so rarely dressed up to go out that she was not even sure that the two elegant dresses she possessed still fitted her. Feeling very unsure of herself she chose a burgundy silk dress which shimmered in the light. The lace neckline set the gown off beautifully and she added a string of pearls which were a gift from her father. She hoped that they would give her confidence which she certainly did not feel. What shall I say if he asks me to marry him tonight? Mary wondered as she looked in the mirror, trying to give some order to her unruly hair. She hoped for a softer look than her schoolteacher style, but it was being especially stubborn today. Having given no answer to her first question she asked herself another. Am I happy here?

Now, this last question was more fundamental to her well-being, but she knew that she could not answer it without a long self searching debate. A final question posed in her mind just as she heard a knock at the door. Do I love him? She took one more look into her sparkling eyes in the mirror and tried to calm her nerves as she went downstairs to answer the door, throwing her best shawl over her shoulders. There waiting for her was a horse and trap. The paintwork and brasses were shining and polished. Even the horse looked as if he had been extra specially groomed for the occasion.

'You look lovely,' David exclaimed as he held out his hand to help her up to the seat.

'You look quite handsome yourself David,' Mary replied smiling at him.

David walked around to the other side of the trap and seated himself, careful not to sit on her full and billowing skirts. Usually they would walk everywhere but this was a special occasion. They discussed the week's events and Mary talked of her preparations for her trip to England. She avoided mentioning the painful summons to her headmaster's office and the difficult, but not unexpected, challenges he faced her with. She was only grateful that her position had been spared, albeit on a temporary basis, giving her precious time to think.

Soon they arrived at the hotel and were greeted by the footman, who helped Mary to alight. The stable boy led the trap away and David took Mary's arm to guide her up the sweeping steps past the doorman and into the ornate lobby.

Her shawl was taken and they were led into the restaurant, where a pianist was playing some gentle music on a grand piano in the corner. They smiled at various couples as they were guided to their table. Most were holidaymakers from the mainland, but they recognised a few of the island's gentry as they passed by.

They enjoyed freshly caught crab, amongst other delightful dishes and soon relaxed in each other's company. For dessert Mary chose a strawberry meringue gateaux, which boasted of locally picked strawberries and was embellished with the notoriously rich island's cream. It was during dessert that David decided to bring up the subject that Mary had simultaneously both longed for and dreaded. He had practised his little speech many a time in front of his little bedroom mirror with his door firmly shut.

'Mary, you must have guessed how I feel about you, but I am not going to ask you to marry me. I value your friendship far too much for that.'

David was quick to notice Mary's crestfallen expression and wondered if he had misread the situation completely. Within seconds she was smiling again making him uncertain as to whether he had imagined it. He continued.

'What I meant to say is that I would like very much to ask you to marry me, but I want to be fair to you and give you the chance to think over the implications during your holiday. Above all, I hope to remain your friend, and wish to do nothing to spoil that friendship. The Saturday afternoons that we have shared recently have been some of the happiest times in my life since…' David did not try to finish his sentence realising that to mention his wife would not be appropriate.

Coming to his rescue Mary reasoned, 'Yes David, I do

have some thinking to do, but I want you to know that I am very fond of you. I love this island, but as you know I also enjoy being a teacher. I had planned to return to England after a few years to find a position nearer my parents. I always imagined remaining alone after…' Now it was Mary's turn to stumble with her words, realising, to her dismay, that she had been about to talk about the life that she had long since left behind. She suddenly realised how little they really knew about each other, about their past lives, or their future dreams.

'Perhaps when I return it will be time for me to tell you my reasons for coming to Riduna in the first place and maybe you could tell me a little about your wife. I think both of us have done some escaping over here, isn't that so?'

David nodded thoughtfully for a moment before saying, 'Whatever we decide about the future I want to give you this little gift to say thank you,' as he reached across the table for Mary's hand with one of his and he searched in his pocket for the tiny box with the other.

Mary left her hand in his for a moment or two, and then she slid it away to open the beautifully wrapped little gift. She was determined not to let herself down at this point and continued to smile, her fingers trembling nervously. It reminded her so much of a situation she had run away from all those years before, when she had been faced with the most brilliant diamond ring. How she had turned down the offer she never knew. Mary just remembered being panic stricken with the knowledge that it just wasn't right. She had fled, not only from the restaurant, but also from the country, much to her parents' dismay.

Mary came to her senses just as her fingers revealed a lovely gold brooch shaped as a crab. It was unusual and quite delicate. She sighed with relief and smiled a genuinely grateful smile across the table at David. She watched his shoulders visibly relax as he returned her smile with equal warmth.

'It's lovely David. It will not only remind me of this meal, this island but in particular it will remind me of our friendship.' She paused for a moment before adding, 'shall we have tea at my little cottage rather than coffee here? It's such a beautiful night that I would like to see the evening light over the bay one last time before I leave.'

'Yes of course,' David replied, not really knowing if he could trust himself to be alone with Mary at this time, but longing to be all the same.

'Thank you for a wonderful meal and a delightful evening David,' Mary said as they walked out into the lobby and he carefully placed her shawl around her shoulders. His hands rested on them just a moment longer than they should have done and Mary shivered, not with cold but with a feeling that she had never felt in her life before.

The horse and trap was brought out for them and David helped Mary up into the seat. He placed a blanket over her lap and set the horse in motion. There was a mixture of nervous excitement as he wistfully wondered if it would be anything like this on their wedding day. It is such a perfect night. If only it was our honeymoon, he thought. But I must keep my feelings under control, he added to himself and with that he gave the horse a slap with the whip and they sped along the lane towards Newtown.

Mary was wrestling with her own thoughts. If David had asked me to marry him I probably would have run a mile, so why am I feeling so drawn to him tonight. It must be the wine. I must keep my wits about me, she resolved, as the trap suddenly gained speed.

As they were nearing her cottage David slowed down to a walk and then to a standstill just outside the tiny front door. He could just make out the curtains of the neighbours' cottage twitching as they stepped down and Mary opened the door. He had to stoop a little to enter the room and he sat down in one of the two armchairs while Mary busied herself with the kettle on the stove and made the teapot ready. They drank tea sitting opposite each other in matching albeit ageing armchairs. David stoked the stove absentmindedly.

'I wish I was coming with you in some ways,' he said to break the silence.

'In many ways I wish I was staying,' she replied with a faraway look, 'but I think that you were right in saying that we need time to think. This island has a certain indescribable quality, a power hard to understand, and so I'm sure we will benefit from some space to know if our feelings are real,' Mary smiled.

David was encouraged by the words 'our feelings'. 'Let's go and enjoy the evening sky over Braye and let Riduna weave a little more magic on you, just to make sure you return to me,' he teased.

They both laughed as they stood up, and Mary reached for her shawl; the tension of the last twenty minutes having vanished into thin air. He took it from her and gently draped it around her shoulders. She looked up into his eyes and smiled.

They walked down to Braye Beach. Mary could not resist slipping off her shoes to feel the sand between her toes and David, feeling slightly foolish did likewise. They strolled along the sand with his arm draped naturally over her shoulder. Part way along the bay they stopped and gazed out towards the multicoloured horizon, both lost in thought. Without hesitating this time he gently turned Mary towards him and lifted her chin so that he was looking down into her lovely eyes and he almost kissed her. Instead he took her hands in his and stole his gaze back to the dreamy horizon. Perfection, he thought.

They walked slowly back to her cottage.

'I'll come to wave goodbye in the morning if you would like me to?'

'I would like that very much,' Mary replied.

'I'd better not come in,' David said regretfully as they reached her little front door.

'What makes you think you would be invited?' replied Mary, and they both laughed as he untied his horse and climbed up into the trap.

''Til tomorrow then,' he called over his shoulder and he winked at her as he nodded in the direction of the neighbour's window. They laughed again as he set off up the road towards the town, Mary waving from her front door.

Mary was grateful that only David came to the quay in the morning. Their friends had diplomatically stayed away. She was also pleased that there were only a few minutes before she would have to board.

'What are you going to do this afternoon?' she asked.

'Pine for the girl who walked out of my life this morning, I suppose,' replied David teasingly.

'Seriously though, you will be coming back in September won't you? I hope you will not walk out on me forever but, don't forget that, above all else I want to remain your friend.'

'Do you treat all your female friends the way you treated me last night?' exclaimed Mary in mock protest. They laughed.

The last of the passengers were walking up the gangway on to the waiting ship and so Mary turned to say goodbye.

David gallantly bowed in a sweeping gesture and gently raised her hand to his lips.

'I hope that I will have the pleasure to treat you like that again on your return,' he whispered. She smiled up at him and just avoided the temptation to reach up to kiss him on his cheek before she was gone.

Chapter 15

THE SUMMER WAS always the liveliest time on the island, with all the visitors, and Harriet was kept busy helping out at the Braye Tavern since the school was closed for the holidays. Her grandparents were grateful for the help, although they banished her from the place during opening hours, since they said it was not a place for a young lady.

Riduna Week, which was organised by the islanders and The Royal Agricultural Society at the beginning of August, was an exciting time for all, giving neither Harriet nor David much time to pine the absence of their loved ones, or Charlotte for that matter. Every business decorated a float with flowers and streamers, and the Militia lead the procession from the harbour up to St Anne's Church for the climax of the week. Flags were waved and many dressed in fancy dress costume, or their Sunday best.

It amused Harriet that every year she would overhear the older islanders reminiscing of the similar occasion back in 1847 when the island celebrated the 'Laying of the Foundation Stone' of the breakwater and the beginning of the construction of the new harbour. Like today, the Militia had fired a salute and led a procession, which preceded an evening of fireworks and festivities. Or she would also overhear comparisons to the exciting visit of Queen Victoria and Prince Albert ten years later to survey the amazing structures near completion. It amused Harriet that their captive audience must have been mainly young children who would have no conception of the Queen in their narrow lives.

On this occasion the island's festivities would finish with a dance at the Town Hall. Although Edward would not be there Harriet was still excited at the prospect, since there were always many willing partners to sign her card. She was also pleased for her friend that Thomas was likely to be attending. Harriet pushed through the people hoping to catch sight of Jane amongst the crowd. She had just seen Charlotte go by on a float. She had been chosen to be the Riduna Queen for the Year and was wearing a pretty pink gown with a mock tiara sitting on her curly fair hair. Harriet had to admit that she looked lovely and was obviously appreciated by the crowd. A sudden memory of the other letter flitted into Harriet's mind and she wondered what it had said.

'Penny for them,' said a familiar voice coming up behind her. 'I've been looking for you everywhere. Why the frown Harriet?' asked Jane as she squeezed through the crowd to reach her friend.

'Oh nothing important! Just a spot of jealousy creeping in,' replied Harriet.

Thinking that Harriet meant all the attention that Charlotte was getting she was puzzled. It was unlike Harriet to be nothing but pleased for others who celebrated success.

Seeing Jane's expression and the path of her gaze, Harriet quickly explained, 'You misunderstand me Jane. I can't explain here. Did you catch sight of Thomas a moment ago? He was near the front of the Militia as they headed up towards the town.'

'I have only just arrived,' replied Jane with a touch of

disappointment in her voice. 'It was so busy at the surgery this morning that I've only just this minute escaped!'

'Don't fret Jane; you're sure to see him tonight.'

'I'm sure they'll be allowed to stay to the church fete for a little while this afternoon too,' said Jane.

The girls were running a stall of toys and games at the fete. Some had been donated by children who no longer played with them and were quite old, but some were newly knitted or sewn by the elderly ladies of the parish. Harriet had encouraged the children to donate at least one of their toys to the stall at the end of the school term and had been moved to tears as they brought them in one by one. Many of the children had few toys and the majority were hand-made and well loved, but as Harriet saw to it that, for a double or two, they could buy a different toy, thus circulating the enjoyment and stimulating their imagination, all won in the end. She made it clear that the gesture was voluntary, but that the money raised would be going to good causes like the people in need on the island and the upkeep of the church.

It was a happy affair and Harriet and Jane were kept busy for a couple of hours. Thomas did visit their stall with his friends, who made an attempt to talk to Harriet while Jane excused herself to have a private conversation with Thomas.

'This island is a bit quiet for a beautiful girl like you,' the young soldier teased.

Harriet was irritated by this, and a little flustered, as she negotiated giving the correct change to a little lad who had picked up a toy soldier and was looking up at this young man with obvious admiration. At the same time she was trying to think of a suitable but inoffensive reply. There was a lull in her trade and so she turned to the handsome young man.

'I love Riduna, sir. I've lived here all my life and my family are here.'

'Don't you ever wonder about the world over the sea?'

the man pressed on, gesturing towards the hidden horizon.

'Of course I wonder about it sometimes, but it's so beautiful here, don't you think so? This is my whole world!' she added with emphasis.

Just at that moment Jane came back to join them and Harriet was glad that both of the gentlemen bade them farewell.

'Until tonight then,' said Thomas and they disappeared into the crowd.

Harriet was curious to hear what had transpired between Jane and Thomas but it was nearly four o'clock and she knew that she would be missed down at the Braye Tavern on such a busy day.

'Do you mind if I leave you to tidy up?' she asked. 'My grandparents will be hard pressed to clear away the lunch things this afternoon before opening time.'

'Of course Harriet; I'll see you later,' Jane replied.

Although she missed Edward, the evening was successful. In fact there were more visitors than islanders attending the dance that night and she was grateful for the watchful eye of her parents. She was pleased to see that Jane was happy, but she could not help but wonder if Thomas and Jane were really suited. Jane was so intelligent. Surely she would not settle and abandon her dreams. I must have a serious talk with her one of these days, she thought.

Charlotte joined her on a couple of occasions during the evening, only to be whisked off again a few moments later. She seems happy too, Harriet thought. Maybe we had better have a serious and honest talk one day as well. Resolved to put the world to rights, or at least her little part of it, she was confused by the approach of the young soldier who had spoken to her earlier in the day. She was too polite, though, to refuse him a dance, in fact she quite enjoyed the experience. The remainder of the evening sped by, finishing with a dance with Michael, who still harboured hopes that Harriet might eventually think of him as more than a good friend.

Soon her parents were hinting that it was time to go home. Glad to have some time to reread her letter from Edward, and begin to pen her reply, Harriet agreed and said farewell to Jane, Charlotte, Michael and John. Jane took her to one side for a moment and explained that she had agreed to meet Thomas with his friend, whose name was Frederick the following afternoon. Harriet was annoyed that Jane had agreed on her behalf but knowing that Jane's father would forbid her to meet Thomas on her own, Harriet agreed on condition that Jane invited Charlotte, Michael and John to join the group. Harriet did not feel that she could refuse her best friend but dreaded the encounter herself. There was something about Corporal Frederick Eaves that she found quite unnerving and Thomas too for that matter. Still, there is safety in numbers, she thought.

She walked home arm in arm with both of her parents and her mama, despite being tired, would not stop talking about how lovely the evening had been. Harriet had noticed her parents dance together on a couple of occasions and was proud that they still looked a handsome couple.

'Next time we must suggest that Beth and Joseph join us. They would have enjoyed tonight,' she mused.

'It must be lonely for them now that Edward is away Mama,' replied Harriet, feeling a touch guilty that she had called to see them very little since Edward's departure.

'Since Harriet will be wishing us to attend every dance, it would be good company for us too, Annie,' added Jack.

'You don't need to escort me to each dance,' Harriet started to say, but realising that she was outvoted by the knowing looks that both parents gave her, she continued, 'but I think that you are right. Edward's parents would enjoy the evening as well as your company.'

With that Harriet resolved to call on her neighbours in the morning. After all, she was sure that they would have received a letter too.

My dearest Harriet,

I am so sorry if I've caused you any hurt or embarrassment over the matter of the letter to Charlotte. When I left you all at the quayside, Michael put something into my pocket as he said farewell. I looked at it later and I realised that it was a note from Charlotte. It was only a polite little note wishing me a safe journey and so I felt duty bound to respond in a similar fashion. I am much grieved if you think that Charlotte might be harbouring any secret feelings for me. In my mind we were dancing partners and nothing more.

How can I convince you from so far away that it is you I love and no one else? I promise with all my heart that I will never write to her again and if you feel that it is in your heart to talk with Charlotte about this matter, you go with my blessing.

As to my new life, I am really enjoying it. You can't imagine what it is like to sail across the ocean like this and as for Southampton: I thought that Sarnia was bustling and busy, but here it is so much more exciting and I long to tell you all about it. I am writing this letter on my bunk in the Seamen's Mission in Southampton. We set sail at first light so I must get some sleep.

Ever yours and only yours
Edward

That night she had a very restless sleep and woke up in the morning feeling tired and irritable. Is it today that is worrying me so much or is it Edward, she thought, as she got herself dressed for church. As it happened the day was very different to Harriet's imagination. She called in to see Beth and Joseph before church. Beth was so pleased to see her and keen to hear her news of Edward as well as an account of the previous night.

'Come in lass, have you heard from my wayward son?' she asked. 'My letter here just says he is well, but so excited. He's a bit of a dreamer, my lad, but he does mention you, too.'

Harriet felt reassured by this but not wanting to pry she agreed, 'He does seem to be living in a different world Aunt Beth.'

'Let's see here. He says he misses us, that's his ma and pa,' Beth explained unnecessarily, 'but he also says he misses you and could we keep an eye on you and cheer you up if you're feeling a bit sad.'

Harriet did not reply immediately and Beth looked at her closely. 'You're looking a bit pale today I must say. Is there anything the matter?'

'I'm so confused,' Harriet replied honestly and, without intending to, she found herself telling Aunt Beth all about the two letters.

'Come here lass,' soothed Beth, giving Harriet a hug. 'It's a shame our Edward is not here to speak up for himself my dear, but I know he cares for you. It's just that men don't think of the consequences of their actions sometimes. You'll learn not to take what they do too seriously by the by.'

'What do you mean by that?' exclaimed Joseph, who had just come in the back door to take his wife to church.

'Just women's talk,' said Beth, winking over her shoulder at her husband, so she was relieved that he did not pursue the matter.

'Do I have a pretty lady on each arm to escort to church this morning?' he grinned.

After church and lunch with her mama and papa, Harriet

spent an hour helping out at the Braye Tavern and Jane came down to meet her outside the tavern. Although it was closed she would not venture inside. This made Harriet laugh sometimes, because in other ways Jane seemed so worldly wise. It was not long before they saw Thomas and his friend Frederick walking towards them.

They shared a pleasant afternoon walking through Crabby Village to Saline Bay and Fort Tourgis and on towards Fort Clonque, where the shore line was more wild with restless waves swirling through craggy outcrops. Charlotte, Michael and John had joined them so, although Jane spent the time with Thomas almost to the exclusion of her friends, Harriet was content to mingle with the others.

By the end of the afternoon she had to admit that Thomas and Frederick had been true gentlemen and there appeared nothing in their behaviour to fear. Since they were also the first to take their leave to return to the garrison, there was also no fear of being left alone in their company.

That evening Harriet's mama quizzed her closely about the day.

'You hear such stories,' her mama warned her, 'of the soldiers getting local girls into trouble. The families cover it up, so we rarely hear the full story!' she added with scorn.

'Oh Mama,' Harriet exclaimed in mock exasperation. 'We had our good friends with us and surely you trust them don't you?'

'Yes, that may be, but I'm only asking you to be careful of your reputation my girl,' she said.

'I will, Mama, I promise.'

Harriet escaped to her room to write a reply to Edward's difficult letter, but attempted to be as light in her response as possible.

My dearest Edward,

I have read your letter many times and wish you were here to reassure me in person. Christmas seems such a long time to wait but nevertheless life continues as it always has.

Riduna Week has been as successful and enjoyable as ever. The dance was especially appreciated by all. John was kind enough to take me for the last dance. He does not have your skill as a dancer and it goes without saying that I longed to be in your arms again.

We have also enjoyed a walk today in the company of our usual friends as well as two soldiers from the Riduna Militia. One of the men, Thomas, is sweet on Jane, but I do not personally think that they are suited. He is a handsome enough lad in his uniform, but do not fear; it would take more than a uniform to turn my head.

I miss you so much Edward but I wish you safe travels.

Yours truly,
Harriet

With that task complete Harriet tried to sleep, but her rest was interrupted by a dream about soldiers. Sometimes the men had smiling kindly faces and at others their expressions were almost frightening. At one point she was calm and happy and the next moment she was tossing and turning, dreaming that she was running as fast as she could. When she woke up with a start, she remembered the dream, and tried to decipher its meaning as Old Mother had taught them. She reasoned that she seemed to be running away from something that scared her, but also that she was urging herself on to reach help before it was too late. Too late for what, she wondered as she drifted back to sleep.

Chapter 16

IT WAS A hot August Sunday, almost too nice to be spending the morning in church and Harriet felt strangely uneasy. Jane had arranged for them to join Thomas, Frederick, Charlotte, Michael and John for an afternoon stroll to Telegraph Bay. Unfortunately John and the twins sent messages that there was too much work during one of the busiest times on the island. Jane was explaining this change of plan as they walked out of church and Harriet misunderstood at first.

'It really doesn't matter if we can't go out today,' she reassured Jane. 'I would like to spend some time with Edward's parents, since they get quite lonely.'

'But *we* are still going out Harriet. I have arranged to meet Thomas and Frederick on the Butes after lunch at two.'

'Oh Jane, but we can't go out without the others,' Harriet exclaimed.

'Why ever not? After all, we know them well enough now and my father has given me permission if you are with me. We can be each other's chaperone. What do you say?' Jane implored.

Jane looked so excited and she would be so disappointed if Harriet refused her. and yet she still felt very uncertain.

'I'm not sure that this is right Jane. I hardly know

Frederick, even though you know Thomas well by now. I'm not sure that I even like him and whatever will people think?' Once she had finished speaking Harriet regretted hurting her friend.

'I must meet them nevertheless, because I have no way of getting a message to them. At least help me and accompany me to the Butes?' Jane asked in a quieter voice, no longer wishing to plead.

Harriet looked at Jane's face and knew that she was beaten. She knew that she could not refuse her and would just have to trust Jane's instincts rather than her own. 'I'll come just this once, and only for a couple of hours Jane, but you must agree to two conditions.'

'What do you mean Harriet?' asked Jane.

'I must be home at four, by the latest, and I also want you to promise that you will not arrange any other assignations like this without asking me first,' Harriet replied.

'Of course Harriet! You're a great friend. I'll make it up to you, I promise.' With that said, Jane kissed Harriet on the cheek and rushed off towards home before her companion had the chance to change her mind.

Harriet watched her for a moment and shook her head. She resolved to have a serious talk with Jane at the next possible moment. She would leave it no longer. She could see that her usually level-headed friend was so besotted with her beau that she was no longer seeing reason. She waited while her parents finished their conversation and walked home alongside them, deep in her own thoughts.

Over lunch Annie became tired with her daughter's unusually gloomy countenance. She looked over at Jack for support as she collected the plates together and he shrugged his shoulders as if to say, I'm dammed if I know what's wrong with the girl.

'Harriet lass, wake up and help your mama to clear away the dishes,' he encouraged.

'Oh yes. I'm sorry,' Harriet stammered.

Realising that her parents were giving her quizzical looks and determined not to worry them, she took the dirty dishes from her mama and then put on a brighter face as she came back in, carrying the deliciously smelling gooseberry pie.

'This smells so good,' she said. 'It's a summer treat I always look forward to!' she exclaimed, a little too brightly.

'What are your plans for this afternoon?' enquired Annie, hoping that it would shed light on her daughter's strange behaviour.

'Oh, just a stroll with the others across the island,' replied Harriet, as casually as she could muster in the hopes that she would not alarm them.

'And what beauty spot are you heading to today,' asked Jack, relieved that her daughter seemed to be acting normally again.

'We're heading south west to Telegraph Bay, since it's such a lovely day and not too windy,' Harriet explained keeping her voice as light as she could.

As Annie watched her daughter put on her shawl and leave the house, she was still concerned, and even more so when she noticed that Harriet was wearing her locket. She settled down and tried to concentrate on some sewing, but nothing Annie could do would shift her unease. She listened to the sound of Jack washing the heavy pans as he always did on a Sunday.

Harriet walked slowly up the path towards the town. Why didn't I tell the whole truth? She thought. Perhaps Papa would have joined us if I had done so but then Jane might have been angry with me, she reasoned. Jane was already waiting at the top of the slope, looking very pretty, with her flushed cheeks matching her rose pink dress. Harriet's blue grey frock was no less becoming, but it seemed to reflect their contrasting moods. They hugged and both gazed down towards the harbour, noticing the two red and white specks of uniform which were making their way ant-like up the track towards them.

'Good day to you ladies,' they called as they reached the base of the grassy slope below them, their smiles clearly visible by this time.

They bowed as they reached the girls and Thomas asked, 'And how are you both today?'

'Well thank you,' replied Jane, unaware that she was answering for both of them.

'What delightful part of the island are you leading us to today Harriet,' asked Frederick. Harriet was immediately flustered that he had emphasised that it was her choice and in her heart she wanted to shout back her denial and run. Inadvertently she grasped her locket, whether for courage or protection she did not know. It appeared to give her the strength of a good idea nevertheless.

'We are walking to Telegraph Bay on the far side of the island but to make it a more interesting walk we will head across to see L'Etaq island and walk the coastal path to the bay,' she explained.

'It sounds delightful,' exclaimed Thomas. 'We'll follow your lead then,' he encouraged.

As they walked Harriet remained quiet for a while. They were talking about places in England and events that Harriet was ignorant of. She was not concerned because this gave her time to think. She planned a route which skirted the town, thus avoiding meeting too many people. She also reasoned that taking a longer route might deter them from taking the precipitous walk down into the bay along the fisherman's path which clung to the cliffs. She had walked down there many a time with Edward and they had played in that idyllic bay happily for hours over the years. The fact that they would be walking along their favourite cliff path and would pass the notorious 'Lovers' Chair' could not be avoided. She hoped that Jane had forgotten its significance and she certainly would not mention it.

In fact it was along this path that she began to relax. Harriet was drawn into their easy-going conversation. Once they had reached the cliffs overlooking Telegraph she stood back from the edge to admire the bay and the Sister Rocks which were little islands adding to the charm and protection of the secluded bays. Her reasons for this were two fold. Firstly the cliffs were imposingly high and secondly it obscured the way down to the bay.

'If we walk on just a little further we will see the 'Garden Rocks,' just in sight of Fort Clonque which is already familiar to you. Then we shall head on back to the town,' she reasoned as she began to turn in the direction she had suggested. Frederick by this time had walked to the edge of the cliff to take one more look at this stunning view before joining the others. His genuine cry of amazement brought Thomas back to his side. From their vantage point the bay looked even more beautiful.

'Look, here's a path,' Frederick exclaimed. 'Wouldn't it be excellent to go down into the bay?'

'It does seem too lovely to miss,' appealed Thomas to Jane. 'What do you think?'

By this time Frederick was already on his way down but Thomas, being more thoughtful turned to Harriet and asked, 'Is it too steep for you girls? Have you been down here Harriet?'

Harriet could not tell a lie. She had been brought up too well for that.

'It's mainly used by fishermen but we came here many times when we were children,' she replied.

Taking that as encouragement Thomas started off down the path, waiting at intervals to check that both girls could find their footings and steadying them with a hand on occasions. Jane obviously needed more help than Harriet, since it was second nature to Harriet to be nimble footed, but she was grateful that Thomas made a point of waiting for them. He was so much a gentleman and handsome at that. She did not wonder that Jane was so taken with him.

When they were nearing the base of the cliffs they had to leave the grassy path and scramble over some enormous boulders and across smaller pebbles before reaching the small sandy cove. Quite out of breath the three sat down on the beach, listening to the waves roll in and brush along the shore. They watched Frederick skimming stones across the water. On one occasion the pebble bounce three times and Thomas shouted 'bravo!'

'Tell us about your childhood Harriet,' encouraged Jane and so Harriet spent the next ten minutes talking about her life growing up on the island mentioning Edward on many occasions.

'Well Harriet, your island is even beginning to weave some of its magic on me too?'Thomas said.

Frederick, who had listened intently to Harriet, observing her with an unnerving stare exclaimed, 'that's Edward you have in your pretty locket, isn't it?'

Harriet's blush was enough to affirm his guess and she quickly looked away. Inside she was relieved that she had been given the foresight to wear it and she smiled as it reminded her of Old Mother's advice on the powers of garlic. She ignored the remark.

'I think it's time we were heading home,' she replied.

With that, they stood up and made their way over the beach. This time Harriet went before Jane, reasoning that it would be better for Thomas to follow at the rear. He fell in immediately assessing the situation as a good soldier would and always kept an arm out to support Jane as she needed it. Frederick was far ahead by now and so it was left to Harriet to turn from time to time to hold out her hand to guide Jane to the flattest safest rocks. Even so, Jane was very uncertain and she began to tremble. She was just making a large stride towards Harriet's outstretched hand to join her friend on a large boulder when her foot slipped. Although Thomas was quick and leaned forward to grasp her trailing hand it did not prevent Jane's foot from slipping between the rocks. Thomas, without thinking of the improper nature of his actions, grabbed Jane firmly by the waist and lifted her back on to the rock on which he was standing. Jane clung to him for a moment and gasped in pain as she tried to put her foot down.

'Sit down here to catch your breath,' Thomas ordered as he held her under her arm to lower Jane down.

Harriet rushed back to her friend calling to Frederick, who was far ahead by now and unaware of the drama behind him.

'Let me have a look at your ankle,' gestured Thomas who reached out towards the bottom of Jane's skirts who flinched as she moved the leg out of his grasp.

'You can't do that. It's improper,' she exclaimed, surprising even Harriet, who thought it was the first time Jane had shown any sense since setting eyes on Thomas.

'He is first aid trained!' remarked Frederick firmly. He had reached them by now and was peering down at them.

Ignoring his comment, Harriet stood by Jane and suggested, 'If you are a little rested, how about standing you up to see if your foot will support you.' She reached for Jane's arm on one side and Thomas obliged by steadying her on the other.'

'It's no good,' Jane exclaimed in agony as the pain shot up her leg. 'I'm unable to walk on it.'

They helped her to sit down again and she looked up at Harriet with unspoken questions.

Before either Thomas or Frederick could speak Harriet took control with as much authority as she could muster in the circumstances. 'As far as I can see there are two choices of action. Either we go to fetch the doctor, who can bring bandages and a stretcher or between you gentlemen you can carry Jane gently to safety…' Without answering all eyes simultaneously stared up towards the steep cliff path, more foreboding now than it had been on their descent.

'Or…?' questioned Thomas, his expression giving away his feelings of doubt as to the safety of that option.

'Or one of us fetches the doctor and another rushes to the harbour to alert a rescue launch by sea,' Harriet finished.

This time their gaze turned to the ocean and its beautiful view, which only a few moments before had charmed them.

'There's no other way?' asked a despondent Frederick who scanned the cove obviously hoping for an alternative route to miraculously appear.

'Whatever we do we need to act now,' said Thomas decisively looking at Jane's pale face. 'I suggest the sea option is the only one that guarantees no more casualties. Just as well there are several hours before sun down because it will take a good while for a boat to reach us, won't it Harriet?'

'Probably an hour,' Harriet replied.

'I suggest you go as quickly as you can to the harbour, since you know all the short cuts, Harriet. Frederick will help me carry Jane gently down to the safety of the shore and then he will run to fetch the doctor in the town,' Thomas ordered.

Harriet hesitated a moment, not wanting to leave her friend alone with the two men after their promise to the doctor, but realising she had no option she bent over to hug her friend before rushing quickly but carefully back up the path. As she reached the top she paused to look back to see that they had reached the shore safely and that Frederick was on his way over the stony shoreline to the path.

She turned and ran.

Left alone, sitting in the sandy cove Jane and Thomas gazed out towards the 'Sister Rocks'. They sat in silence for a few moments.

'It is beautiful here; if it wasn't for the unfortunate circumstances I'd say I was the luckiest man!' Thomas mused.

'What do you mean by that?' laughed Jane, softened by his remarks.

Thomas turned towards Jane and paused before continuing, 'I'm sitting here in breathtaking surroundings with the most beautiful lady by my side. What more could I wish for?'

Jane giggled but her mirth was soon suppressed as he reached over and kissed her on the lips.

Jane gasped, but this time in surprise rather than pain. Realising by her expression that his advances had been appreciated rather than rebuked he put his arm gently around her shoulders, pulling her towards him as he kissed her again. He was so gentle, determined not to spoil the magic of the moment by frightening her.

After that second kiss they sat for a while in companionable silence. Jane rested her head on his shoulder and sighed. She was aware of wonderful sensations arousing deep within her and yet she also felt an overwhelming contentment.

'I will always remember this day,' Thomas said as he lifted her chin gently towards him to kiss her again. Mesmerised by his words Jane melted in his arms. As they kissed she could feel a feather light touch of his fingers gently stroking her bodice. She tingled all over shivering with a longing she never knew existed. They kissed again, this time it was Jane who stroked Thomas's face and encouraged him to lower his lips to hers. Thomas, stirred on by her positive response, gently reached for her skirt and began to stroke her leg.

Suddenly Jane was brought to her senses. She pushed him away with such a force that it startled him and he fell back on the sand.

'Do you think I am a peasant's daughter that doesn't know what you are trying to do,' she cried as she smoothed down her skirts and lifted her knees up to hide even her feet from his gaze.

'But I thought…' began Thomas.

'You thought that you could take advantage of me since we are alone, didn't you? Please remember that I am a doctor's daughter,' Jane barked, interrupting any attempt on his part to explain before she burst into tears.

This was so uncharacteristic that Thomas was at a loss as to know what to do. He stood up and looked down on her, knowing that, if he tried to comfort her she would call out for help. Fortunately he was too much of a gentleman to force his advances on her as some might have done. He handed her his clean handkerchief.

'I'm so sorry Jane. I didn't want to harm you, please believe me,' he pleaded.

At that moment they heard a noise behind them. Jane was so relieved but puzzled to see Harriet carefully finding her footings down the steep cliff path for the second time that day. She sat down next to Jane out of breath yet again. Thomas continued to stand looking a little awkwardly as the girls ignored him and Harriet explained their change of plan.

'As I was racing along the shortest path to the town I

met my parents coming the other way,' Harriet began to explain. Annie had actually been so concerned about her daughter, that she had persuaded Jack to walk with her to meet them on their return. 'As I explained what had happened Frederick caught up with us and so Papa rushed off towards the harbour leaving my mother to fetch your father. They felt that he would be less angry with my papa than he would be with Frederick. I'm sure you agree Jane?' She noticed Jane's drawn expression but put it down to the worry of the incident.

Jane nodded in reply, showing obvious relief.

'What happened to Frederick?' asked Thomas, looking back up the cliff walk as if hoping that moral support would appear.

'My papa suggested that he return to the barracks and explain to your Commanding Officer why you are late,' answered Harriet.

Thomas groaned, disappointed that he had been left alone. The girls ignored him as Harriet fussed over Jane. Was she warm enough? Was she comfortable? Has she taken her shoe off?

In the end Jane became exasperated. 'Stop fussing Harriet and sit down beside me. You don't know how glad I am to see you!'

Harriet settled beside her leaving Thomas pacing up and down the beach, occasionally kicking a stray pebble into the water with the side of his foot. Although Harriet thought his behaviour odd she did not remark on it.

Within half an hour they heard another sound from the top of the cliff face, not from the seaward direction as they might have hoped. This time it was the doctor who had appeared, laden with two bags, one containing medical equipment and the other holding some food and drink, quickly mustered by Mrs Doris and thrust into his free hand as he left the house. Thomas, glad to be of use, ran up the cliff path to greet him as if he were a mountain goat.

'Good man, good man,' was all the doctor could manage as he gingerly followed Thomas back down the path. Thomas had taken the heaviest bag and even then he stopped frequently to check that the doctor could find the path. It took a while for them to reach the rocks where Thomas relieved him of his second bag in order to clamber in an undignified fashion over the boulders to the relative safety of the bay. Just as he reached his daughter's side there was little time to talk since the rescue boat appeared around the headland and they watched the men rowing with all their might to reach them.

'Jane, let me have a look at your ankle and treat it before rescue arrives,' he ordered, 'and strap it up as best we can.'

Jane stared at Thomas, who politely excused himself and walked to the other side of the cove staring out to sea and then Harriet helped her to slip off her stocking. Her foot was a wonderful shade of purple and she flinched as her father smoothed ointment on it and then wrapped it expertly in a bandage. By the time he had finished the boat was in the bay and Jack was running up towards them.

He looked down at Jane and asked, 'Do you mind me carrying you to the boat lass? T'would be quickest and least painful for you.'

Jane looked up at her father who exclaimed 'Fine, fine, let's get aboard then!'

Jack lifted Jane carefully and carried her to the boat followed by the doctor and Harriet. Neither of whom felt that they had the energy to climb back up the cliff path. This just left Thomas standing alone on the bay. He paddled into the water to help to launch them away from the sandy shallows and then watched as the men rowed the small rescue boat away from the shore. Jane just caught sight of him lifting his hand to wave as they disappeared around the headland.

She could not help but wonder, wistfully, if she would ever speak to him again.

Chapter 17

IT WAS THE last weekend in August that Mary was due to return to the island in time for the start of the new school year. David had arranged to meet her off the *Courier* and he nervously waited on the quayside with his horse and trap. It appeared to him like a scene from a novel, the sight of the *Courier* gracefully making its way towards the harbour passing Fort Albert and sailing into the protection of the sweeping breakwater. The billowing clouds and gusty winds of today only added to the drama as the ship reached this haven of safety. He smiled wryly at his poetic thoughts. Is this really me, he mused.

Mary was less poetic as she stumbled ashore, more relieved at this point to stand on firm ground rather than any romantic notion, if the truth were known. All summer she had fretted and puzzled over her dilemma and she was no nearer making a decision.

David helped her into the trap and walked around to climb in beside her. 'I can see that it wasn't a very pleasant journey Mary.'

'I'm so sorry David, but I just need to get home and sit quietly for a while and then I will be fine,' she stammered.

David made a note of her grey complexion and smiled encouragingly at her, 'It's good to have you back Mary.'

Then he proceeded, as carefully as he could, along the short distance to her little cottage in Newtown above Braye.

He helped her in with her bags and seated her by the range. It was already warm since he had called in earlier that morning. He put the kettle on and while it was heating up he went out to retrieve his medical bag to find a drop of something to settle Mary's stomach. He did not sit down himself but made the tea and stood by her chair, resting his hand on one of the wings.

'I'll leave you to settle in,' he said quietly.

Mary looked gratefully up at him and smiled for the first time, a little weakly, but a smile nevertheless. David's heart seemed to miss a beat at the sight of it and he went red with the thought. Realising his discomfort she rested her hand over his.

'Thank you David. I can see that someone has been in here to prepare for my return. Please don't worry about me. I just need to settle and have a good night's sleep. Thank you so much for the lovely flowers.'

'Mrs Doris and Jane came by yesterday to air the place for you and they brought the flowers from our little garden. I'll leave you now but would you like to join us for Sunday lunch tomorrow? Mrs Doris has left you some things for tonight and a drop of milk for your tea. You can just rest now.'

He had hoped to see her later that day but realising that Mary needed quiet and some space he was relieved when she agreed.

'You are all so kind. Thank you. I would like that very much. I'll not look so frightful tomorrow I hope!' Mary replied.

'You look lovely enough to me,' he said as he bent down to kiss her on the top of her head. 'I'll leave you in peace.' He walked reluctantly to the door.

'David,' Mary called, appealing for him to turn back a moment. Shakily she struggled to her feet and walked towards him, reaching her arms out to him and they embraced.

'It's so good to be back,' she whispered as they parted and they stood at arm's length for a while, just looking at each other.

'Until the morning then,' he said as he reached for the door once more, this time smiling warmly back at her. She watched the back of his trap disappear up the street towards the town and sank gratefully into her comfortable chair and fell asleep.

Harriet was impatient for lunchtime when she would finish her chores at the Braye Tavern and head for the post office to see if there was a letter from Edward. She enjoyed the sense of freedom it gave her as she left her grandparents and headed up the cutting towards St Anne. It was one of the rare occasions since the accident over at Telegraph that her father would allow her to walk on her own. He was being impossible and Harriet felt trapped in a world where she had once felt so free and happy. In some ways she was so grateful to her parents for being wise and easing a difficult situation but she was aggrieved that she had lost their trust. As she walked, she anticipated the letter from Edward. She shuddered to think as to what Edward would make of her expedition down to the bay with two men she hardly knew. She wondered how she had agreed to go in the first place and was glad that she and Jane would have the afternoon to themselves to discuss it.

She stopped by at the dairy to pick up some fresh milk and then called in at the bakery for a loaf for Sunday. Her mama had been baking bread regularly throughout the summer but it was nice for her to have a rest at the weekend, especially since her long walk to Telegraph last weekend had left her a little breathless, as did the ripening crops at this time of year. Harriet was full of remorse. She would never forgive herself if her mama became seriously ill following their selfish escapade. Charlotte served her in the bakery and gave her a knowing look when she saw Harriet's gloomy demeanour. That made Harriet even crosser so that when she reached the post office and found it closed by a couple of minutes she stamped her foot in sheer frustration.

'Temper, temper,' came a voice from behind her, which startled her even more. She turned to see Thomas standing there, looking as dashing as ever. She glanced over his shoulder and was relieved that Frederick was not in sight.

'I'm so glad to see you. I've been hoping to talk to Jane but I imagine that she is still housebound with her ankle. Do you think you could give her this note?' he asked.

'I might,' answered Harriet cautiously. She had not had the chance to speak to Jane since the accident and could see no reason to refuse.

'I'm so grateful to you,' replied Thomas as he thrust a small sealed envelope into her hand, bowed and walked quickly away.

She watched him, puzzled that he felt that he could not deliver it himself. She shrugged her shoulders and hid the letter carefully in her pocket just as old Mr Tilbury the postmaster, came out of his shop beside her.

'Hello Harriet. You've just missed opening hours,' he said with a wink as he went back inside. Harriet waited outside. He emerged a few minutes later and she was relieved to see that he only had one, rather thick letter in his hand.

'Oh, thank you so much,' she said, smiling at him as she relieved him of the envelope.

'It was worth it to see your pretty smile lass,' he replied as he winked again in a conspiratorial manner.

She waved to him as she walked down the street towards home.

Once inside she prepared a light lunch for her parents before calling upstairs to see if her mama was awake. Annie had been resting for an hour and so she came slowly down the steep narrow staircase when she heard Harriet's voice. She arrived at the bottom at the very moment that Jack appeared at the door from his Saturday morning shift at the quarry.

'That was well timed Papa,' Harriet said cheerily.

'How is my gentle wife,' he asked Annie as he walked through to the scullery to shed himself of his dusty work clothes and give his face and hands a splash of water from the waiting bowl.

'I feel a touch better after a rest Jack,' Annie replied smiling at him as he came back into the room. 'It's just that I feel so breathless at times.' Jack and Harriet passed worried looks across the table.

'Don't you go worrying your heads about me. I'll be back to myself again in a couple of days, you'll see.' Annie tried to reassure them as they sat around the table. Jack gave the usual brief blessing before tucking into cheese, crusty bread and home-made apple chutney.

'Have you heard from Edward, Harriet?' Annie asked.

'I have a letter from him in my pocket, but I've not had a chance to read it yet.'

'What are you doing this afternoon lass?' asked Jack.

'I am going to spend the afternoon with Jane Papa.'

'I'll meet you at the doctor's at four then,' Jack said in a firm voice and Harriet knew that there was no point in arguing. She could only be grateful that he was allowing her to walk there on her own.

'There's no need to scowl lass,' Jack rebuked. 'You know that you brought it upon yourself. You are lucky that I allow you out at all. Anything could have happened last week.'

'Hush, Jack!' exclaimed Annie, coming to Harriet's defence. 'I think we have said enough on the matter. I hope that Harriet has learned her lesson.'

'I only hope so,' said Jack, reluctant to let the matter drop.

Harriet excused herself and rushed upstairs to be on her own for a while. She hated being at odds with her parents but she also disliked losing her freedom. She lay on her bed, leaning on her elbows and she carefully slit open her letter.

My Dearest Harriet,

I hope you and your parents are well and that you are not still angry with me. I have much to tell you of my new life and I am excited to share it with you.

Since I last wrote to you I have been to Southampton on three occasions. It was so strange arriving in such a large city. There are trams racing along the streets and gas lights, which is a sight to see when docking at night. The lights glow like orange stars in the darkness. Bill the coxswain is looking after us. He took us to the Mission for Seamen near the docks, where we were given a bed for the night, one of many bunks in a long room. Everyone is very friendly. He took us to a local tavern, a few minutes' walk from the Mission. This was just as well because we had a few too many for our first night and were glad that we were not sailing until the following afternoon.

Harriet, I love being at sea. I cannot describe how it makes me feel on paper but will try to explain when I see you at Christmas. Only three months to go and I will see you again! Cousin Joe does not like the work at sea at all and he thinks that he will give notice at Christmas. He says that he prefers to be on dry land and misses Sarnia when he is away.

Harriet, my feelings for you have grown since I have been away. I miss you so much. It will be wonderful to hold you in my arms again when I see you.

I hope and pray that you have found it in your heart to forgive me.

Yours
Edward

Harriet folded the letter carefully and placed it back in its envelope. She felt reassured that his love was genuine. As she put the letter back in her pocket she felt the other letter to Jane and realising that the afternoon was quickly passing, she stood up, brushed down her skirt and checked her hair before going down the stairs. Her parents were sitting drinking a cup of tea. She wished them a quick farewell and left the house, plucking her shawl from the peg on the door as she went.

'Don't you think we are being too strict?' Annie tentatively asked Jack.

'She has to learn Annie,' replied Jack and Annie knew that it was best not to say anything else.

Within minutes Harriet was sitting with Jane in her upstairs bedroom. Mrs Doris had let her in since it was still painful for Jane to struggle up and down two flights of stairs. Once inside with the door closed Harriet looked about her. Harriet loved Jane's room with its large bed and pale pink bed cover. There was a carved oak dresser with an ornate mirror, several little ornaments and a vase of flowers on a small round table by the window at the point where the eves of the house met the floor. It was there they both sat, in the seats either side of the window. Harriet had tried to put flowers in her little attic room but it still looked drab to her in comparison. Mind you, she was lucky to have a room to herself, albeit a small one. She knew many a family on the island where the children slept in a corner of their parents' room, curtained off with some sacking and several where the whole family had to sleep in the only living area that they possessed.

'My parents are being impossible,' Harriet exclaimed no sooner than they had settled. 'How did your father take it?'

'It's very strange Harriet,' Jane replied. 'He has every reason to be extremely angry and the least I expected was for him to confine me to the house for a period of time, but he has hardly said a thing. Of course I can't go very far at the moment anyway so maybe he feels that's punishment enough, but he hasn't said anything.'

'Oh, I nearly forgot,' said Harriet as she retrieved the letter from her pocket. 'I met Thomas by the post office at noon today and he asked me to give you this.'

Jane did not reach for the letter straight away but looked down at it as if struggling to make a decision. Harriet, puzzled by her friend's uncertainty, put the letter on the little table between them. They were silent for a moment and then Harriet asked quietly, 'Do you want to talk about it?'

Jane sighed and replied with a barely audible voice,

'He tried to touch me Harriet.' Then, uncharacteristically, she burst into tears.

Harriet rushed over to put her arm around Jane's shoulders and waited until the sobs subsided almost dreading what she might reveal next. After a few moments Jane, in a faltering voice told Harriet what had happened on the beach. Much relieved that her account was far less disastrous than Harriet's vivid imagination and that she had arrived on the scene in time to give Jane some protection she reached for the letter and was about to put it back in her pocket when Jane stopped her.

'No, I'll read it,' she said resolutely and she tore it open and read it quietly, her cheeks becoming enflamed as she did so.

Dear Jane,

I am so sorry. We were enjoying such a lovely afternoon on Sunday. It was so unfortunate that you slipped and hurt yourself otherwise the time would have been perfect. I must admit that I was glad to have you to myself for a few moments and I will never regret kissing you and I hope you do not think me too impertinent in saying that I believe in your heart you returned that kiss.

I do regret with all my heart what happened next, especially if it means that I may never speak to you again. I stood on the beach watching the boat disappear around the headland, feeling wretched, longing for you to forgive me and to give me another chance. You are wrong in thinking that I forget that you are a lady. I never forget that. Am I so wrong to desire you so much? I promise that, if you see me again, I will always treat you with the utmost respect.

Your faithful soldier friend,
Thomas

Jane looked up at Harriet at this point to see her expression and was relieved to see compassion and warmth in her friend's eyes and not the shock or anger that she felt she deserved. Just then there was a tap at the door. Jane's father entered the room just as Harriet, who had quick-thinkingly snatched the letter from Jane, put it back in the envelope as if it was her own. To Jane's relief her father did not seem to notice. He was too preoccupied with his news.

'Please excuse me Harriet. I just wished to tell you that Mary has arrived home safely and has agreed to come to

Sunday lunch tomorrow.' David spoke quickly, in that excited voice of his which made both girls sneak a smile to each other. 'I also met your young Thomas today, who enquired as to how you were. I hope I made the right decision but I invited him to join us for lunch too,' David continued without waiting for an answer, not aware of the change in expression passing between the two friends.

'Now, Mrs Doris has made tea and a special cake, expecting Mary to join us this afternoon. Unfortunately the journey has been tiresome and Mary needs to rest today. I hope that you will both come down and join me in the parlour, if not to please me, to thank Mrs Doris for all her effort.'

'Of course we will come down Father. Harriet will help me in a few minutes,' Jane replied, amused to get a word in edgeways at last and determined to hide her reservations about his news of Thomas.

'I'm afraid that my papa is coming at four to meet me, doctor,' said Harriet politely.

'Good, good. He can join us too,' replied the doctor, as he was already heading out of the room.

'What am I going to do now?' Jane was just able to whisper to her friend as they followed the doctor down the stairs.

'It will be fine, you'll see. After all, he has promised to be restrained in future,' whispered Harriet. As she supported Jane on her slow descent she slipped the letter into her friend's pocket. Jane smiled and Harriet was relieved that she was back to her cheerful self.

It was not long before Jack joined them and he happily stayed a while to enjoy tea and cakes.

Chapter 18

RIDUNA GRADUALLY RETURNED to tranquillity as September progressed and only a trickle of visitors continued to arrive. The island's children attended school once more and life returned to its winter routine. David met Mary regularly from school on Saturdays and they spent many happy afternoons together. The governors had called Mary to a meeting to ask if she was to resign but she was relieved that they had reluctantly given her more time.

By the end of the month David had made up his mind that it was time to ask Mary if she would be his wife. Surely if she still had doubts she would have brought the relationship to a close by now, he thought as he tidied after Saturday morning surgery. He decided to approach her before the Harvest Ball, which would be an appropriate occasion to make their relationship official. With that decision made he walked to meet her, full of the excitement of a schoolboy on his first date. Jane watched him go and smiled. Her father was certainly a changed man.

Jane's relationship had been very different since her accident. Her foot finally recovered and she had begun to venture out again. The last time she saw Thomas was the Sunday lunch after Mary's return when he seemed his normal attentive self, apart from a slight nervousness initially. In fact he seemed to bond with her father and since then her father had mentioned seeing Thomas at the Diver's of an evening and that he had sent his regards. He made no more attempts to see her and she was beginning to wonder if she had been too stern with him. At times she was cross with herself that she could not put Thomas from her mind. Harriet had arranged one last picnic; this time heading in the direction of the Garden Rocks passed Fort Clonque. It was too close to Telegraph Bay for Jane's liking but nevertheless she would quite like Thomas to be there. In her heart she had forgiven him. Since she would not be meeting Harriet that afternoon she decided to take a short stroll down Victoria Street to sit on the Butes for a while. She was rewarded by the sight of the Militia moving towards the harbour. She strained to see if she could make out the figure of Thomas. It looked as if the men were moving some equipment to Fort Groznez but as they reached their destination they must have been dismissed because several groups were ambling in different directions. One group disappeared from view for a while and a few minutes later appeared heading up the grassy slopes towards her. She could see Thomas before he caught sight of her and her heart began to beat faster. Once he saw her, his face broke into a warm smile of pleasure that melted any remaining reserve that she might have. He excused himself from the group and came over to her.

'Would it be impertinent of me to ask if I could sit down,' he asked, a little hesitantly.

'You may for a few minutes Thomas, and then I must get back,' replied Jane, struggling to remain a little distant. If Thomas was disappointed he failed to show it.

He sat down close enough to her so that they would not be overheard but far enough away to avoid impropriety and said quietly, 'Have I been forgiven?'

His eyes bore into her and if they had been on their own she would have sunk into his arms at that point without a shadow of doubt. It was his air of confident certainty that brought Jane to her senses. She looked quickly away from his gaze out to sea and ignored his question.

He tried another. 'Is your ankle recovered?'

'Thank you for asking. Yes, apart from the occasional twinge, I am fully recovered.'

There was a short silence before Jane continued, still not daring to return his gaze, 'Harriet has arranged the last village picnic of the year, which will take place, weather permitting, this Sunday. You are welcome to join us if you are free.'

If she had but turned at that point she would have seen the glimmer of a grin appear momentarily on Thomas's face.

'Shall I meet your father in the Diver's then Jane?' he asked.

'No, not this time,' Jane replied, risking to look back at him. 'Since we are walking to the other end of the island the men are meeting in the Rose and Crown; until Sunday then.'

Jane made the first move to rise to her feet and walk away but Thomas was quickly up beside her. Although tempted, he did not reach for her hand this time but bowed politely as they parted company and he went back to join his friends, who were waiting a short distance away and one of the soldiers slapped Thomas on the back and Jane could hear stifled laughter as they walked away, the brass buttons on their shoulders shining in the sunshine.

Jane made her way back home and sat in the seclusion of the courtyard garden for a while to gather her confused thoughts.

Harriet had finally arranged to see Charlotte at a time when they could speak. There was more privacy in Charlotte's room above the shop so Harriet had suggested that she call in that Saturday afternoon and Jane, realising her friend's motives, had made her excuses. Harriet tried to hide her nervousness as she followed Charlotte upstairs. Once inside, with the door firmly shut, Charlotte gave Harriet no time to think before asking,

'What has happened between Jane and Thomas, Harriet. I have heard rumours. Please tell me!'

Harriet was taken aback by this abrupt question but was quick to realise the danger she and her friend's reputation was in. She knew that if she told Charlotte anything, then Michael and John would get to know and there would be no stopping the rumours. She formed her reply carefully,

'Jane has been confined to the house because of her ankle, Charlotte; nothing more than that.'

Seeing Charlotte's disappointment she added,

'I know that she intends to ask Thomas to the picnic if she sees him, so as far as I know there is nothing amiss.'

Charlotte was obviously disappointed at the lack of material for a good gossip but not to be deterred she asked more directly,

'So nothing untoward happened at Telegraph Bay then?'

'Certainly not, Charlotte! How could you say such a thing about Jane?' Harriet exclaimed with realistic indignation.

'But...' began Charlotte.

'No buts,' interrupted Harriet. 'Fortunately my parents were close by and I was only away from Jane for a few moments to fetch help.' 'Oh,' was all a disappointed Charlotte could manage before changing the subject. 'Would you like some tea?'

'That would be very nice,' Harriet replied, glad to have a moment to herself while Charlotte went to make the tea.

When Charlotte came back she had composed herself and was ready to launch into the next difficult subject. She decided to be as direct as possible without being unkind.

'Charlotte, I have come to talk to you about Edward,' she began.

Charlotte bristled with obvious resentment as she replied questioningly, 'Edward?' Her eyes stared a challenge at Harriet.

Harriet took a deep breath before continuing, 'I have received several letters from Edward and in his last letter he asked me if I would come to talk to you.'

'How dare he suggest that,' Charlotte exclaimed angrily. 'Edward never seems to be able to explain himself, does he?'

In her heart Harriet agreed with Charlotte. She too had felt angry with his request.

'I quite agree Charlotte. He's so far away at the moment but I know how hard this is for both of us,' she said quietly.

Charlotte relaxed a little, seeing her friend's discomfort and replied in an equally soft voice,

'I love him, Harriet, or at least I think I do, and I thought he had feelings for me until…' She paused for a moment, unable to talk of her agony of that evening before he sailed.

Harriet filled the silence, grateful that Charlotte was beginning to open up to her.

'We have been friends a long time Charlotte and we are still. I would hate to think of us becoming enemies over Edward.'

Charlotte took a deep breath and taking the initiative she asked directly,

'I would be grateful if you could tell me what really happened between you and Edward when he was last home. You owe me at least to be honest.'

So Harriet began to explain how her feelings seemed to

change from sisterly affection to some kind of love and that to her surprise, Edward's feelings seemed to mirror her own. When she was about to talk of the last night on the beach, Charlotte interrupted her by saying quietly,

'I know Harriet, I saw you both on Braye Beach that night. I tried to ignore what I had seen and make believe that Edward still cared for me but in my heart I knew.'

Harriet was stunned to silence at first before saying,

'I have no idea what the future will bring. Edward seems so keen to travel the world and to me it seems so overwhelming. I would like to think I could wait for him but…'

'I understand just how you feel,' Charlotte said. 'It was when he informed me of his plans that we had such a row and it was never the same between us again. Are you sure you are strong enough to let him go, time and time again Harriet? I have thought about this often enough and, though my feelings for him are unchanged, I don't think I have that kind of strength.'

Harriet hesitated and then ventured tentatively,

'So will you forgive me then, if I try to make him happy?'

There was a short pause as Charlotte carefully chose her words.

'I don't think that I envy you anymore,' she replied at last.

Harriet was puzzled for a moment and could not help but ask,

'I don't understand why you were so angry with me, if you had already made that decision.'

Charlotte looked at her friend with misty eyes and replied with an honesty that surprised even her.

'I suppose I was still coming to terms with losing Edward and I was jealous.'

Harriet was grateful for Charlotte's brave honesty. She

knew that it had taken a lot of courage to respond like that and she warmed to her friend for the first time in a long while. They changed the subject for a while, discussing Mary and the doctor and trying to predict the outcome of that liaison. They also talked of Michael and John's plans to travel to Sarnia, which was no longer a secret. Not long after that they heard the loud knock at the door and Jack's voice downstairs. Charlotte and Harriet gave each other a hug before Harriet's father took her arm and they walked home; Harriet far more contented than she had been for a while. She could not wait to write to tell Edward all about it.

Chapter 19

EACH VISIT TO Southampton up until Christmas held the same pattern for Edward and Joe. In fact with each voyage Edward became more excited about journeys to come and had long conversations with well-travelled sailors to help to decide which shipping company he wished to sign up for after Christmas. On the other hand Joe became more and more convinced that it was not the life for him. The seasickness he felt during the slightest turbulence lessened little and he began to dread each new trip.

On land it was Joe who showed the greater confidence. So relieved he was to be on dry land. They were now recognised as they entered the alehouse and for several visits they were left alone. It was early in October. Edward was not in good humour since he had just received a letter from Harriet regarding Charlotte, but he was unwilling to confide in his friend but just sat sulkily by Joe's side. The very same lady who had joked with Joe on their first night brought two young girls, who could be no more than fifteen years old, over to their table. Both looked timid as Joe, who thought his friend could do with a bit of a distraction, gestured for them to sit down at their table. Edward, not wishing for company, ignored the conversation as Joe sweet-talked the older of the two girls, who had soon softened Joe's reserve and he was not unwillingly led upstairs. Edward, not wanting to cause offence but wishing to be left alone, asked the young frightened girl to leave him.

To his surprise she whispered,

'I cannot sir. I have my orders. If I do not go with you tonight I will lose my job.'

Then she added quietly with a plea in her voice,

'It's my last chance?'

Edward was filled with compassion for the girl and so allowed himself to be led up to a small bare room at the end of a long corridor at the top of the winding staircase. They passed many closed doors with various unfamiliar sounds carrying through the thin walls.

Once inside the room, to his dismay the girl started undoing her bodice with fingers shaking so much that she could hardly manage the act.

'Stop that, do you hear!' barked Edward in a firm albeit whispering voice. 'Come and sit by me and tell me why in heaven's name you lower yourself to work in a place like this,' he continued more kindly.

'What is your name child?' he asked when the girl did not respond and looked more confused than scared.

Edward tried to put on an act of an older and wiser person than his twenty-one years made him feel. He took a deep breath to dispel the mixed emotions of nervousness and excitement.

'My name is Marie,' the girl replied in a gentle more relaxed voice. 'I am from a family of seven children who live nearby. Me ma died of consumption just a year ago and me Da turned to drink. He sent me here to make a living to keep the family. I have no choice sir,' and she began to undo the ribbon on her bodice for the second time.

'Please stop and relax. I'm not going to harm you,' Edward reassured her. Looking more startled than ever, but Edward was dismayed when Marie started heading for the door.

'Where are you going now Marie?' he asked.

'I have no choice sir. If you dunna want my services and you're displeased with me I have to find another. If I refuse tonight I'll be thrown out. I have no choice, sir,' Marie repeated her plea.

Edward put out an arm to catch her hand but she turned like a frightened rabbit with wide eyes staring back at him.

'Unhand me sir, let me go,' she cried as she struggled to free herself from his grasp.

'Please accept my apologies but I implore you to come back,' whispered Edward, aware that if she caused a scene it would be he who would be thrown out.

'Here.' He held out money in his hand, believing it to be enough for at least two such encounters and it was certainly more than Marie had ever earned.

She relaxed a little, came back into the room and sat beside him as he gestured her to do, although still nervous as to what he might wish from her.

'Why don't you go into more suitable employment, Marie?' he asked when she had settled.

'Me da would beat me,' she replied all too honestly as Edward winced at her words. 'He has a 'greement with the landlord see, for his ale and … yer know.'

Edward paused, taking in her claims and realising, not for the first time, how fortunate he was to have experienced such a pleasant upbringing, and saddened by the hopelessness of her situation. He could murder a man like that if he ever had the misfortune to meet him.

'And don't go thinking anything rash sir,' Marie exclaimed as if reading his very thoughts.

There was quiet between them as Edward paused to look at the young girl seated next to him. Her innocence took his breath away and he realised for the first time just how pretty she was. It was the way she spoke that puzzled him most. Sometimes she would be quite well spoken and yet when agitated she would speak from the 'gutter', which was obviously where she came from, if his knowledge of the alleyways of residential slums was anything to go by.

'Have you always lived there?' he asked.

Marie was surprised that this man was interested in her and was also so perceptive.

'Well, you're right sir. When me ma was alive I worked for a time at a manor house across the water. I used to go there each day with me ma, and for a time I lived there. The squire used to let me join his children at school, and I was taught to speak proper,' Marie explained in such an eloquent way that Edward was quite charmed.

'Properly,' Edward corrected with gentle laughter in his voice.

Marie lowered her gaze and stared at her hands, not knowing what to do next.

A feeling stirred in Edward which he tried to repress by thoughts of Harriet waiting for him. So lost was he in his thoughts for a while that he did not realise that Marie was weeping silently beside him.

'I have to go sir, don't you see?'

Puzzled out of his revelries he said quietly,

'No I don't see at all…'

Marie interrupted him.

'It's me life sir. It's what I'm destined for. But I'm so scared. You might think you've saved me and that makes you feel good but if it's not with you it'll be with some drunken old man urgggg.' They simultaneously shuddered at the thoughts her words provoked.

'I think…' He hesitated, reluctant yet compelled to express his thoughts.

'What you are saying is that you... have never...' his words trailed to a standstill.

'Yes sir, you are correct, I have never and...' Marie paused again.

"You're scared;' Edward finished the sentence for her. There were a few more moments of silence as each revelation became an understanding.

'Would it help you Marie if I said....' Edward was about to change his mind and lose his nerve but he quickly continued, 'I've never ...either.'

Then all Marie did was smile a very watery smile up at Edward and his resolve melted into the sultry air. He found himself gently untying the ribbon on her bodice and entering a world so new to him that it was almost other worldly.

'You took your time,' exclaimed Joe, more than a little irritated by the long wait for his friend to rejoin him.

'Let's go,' was all Edward would say and he was no more responsive to Joe's many questions than he was earlier in the evening, though Joe sensed that his mood was less sultry and more satisfied and content.

Now, each time his ship docked in Southampton, Edward felt a growing excitement knowing that Marie would be there for him. He blanked out thoughts of what she did in his absence and like many men before him allowed no more than an occasional twinge of guilt. After all, he reasoned, his feelings for her were more related to compassion than love, were they not? They filled a mutual need as they taught each other the ways of love.

As Christmas approached and Edward was to return to Riduna for the first time, he was glad of a few days on Sarnia to gather his thoughts together. He found himself longing for a time when he could show Harriet in a gentle way how beautiful making love could be. He felt doubly blessed.

Chapter 20

IT WAS A chilly December day. The gusty winds seemed to reach every nook and cranny and the grey clouds billowed overhead. Harriet stood at the quayside wrapped up in her thick winter cloak; her hands below snuggled in warm mittens.

She stood silently as she watched the *Courier* sail past the imposing fort and into the relative protection of the breakwater. Today the purpose of its lengthy structure was blatantly clear to the greatest of doubters as waves thundered in with such a force that they sprayed many feet in the air before gushing down on the quayside of the breakwater like a majestic waterfall.

Harriet felt butterflies in her stomach and her excitement grew. Questions raced through her mind. She wondered how he would greet her and whether his experiences had changed him. At last she could make out the familiar shape of Edward standing on deck braving the weather with a few other hardy passengers. He raised an arm to her and waved. The wait seemed endless and Harriet was glad to have Edward's parents as company. Finally the ship was tied to the quay, the gangway was lowered and the passengers began to disembark.

As Edward came towards them Harriet felt almost faint

with nerves. He looked so handsome and relaxed with his bag slung casually over his shoulder. He hugged his ma and pa and then appeared to be overcome with an uncharacteristic shyness as he faced Harriet. Rather than giving her a long awaited hug he looked into her eyes as if searching for an answer, took hold of her hand and in one sweeping movement he gently kissed it as he gave a polite bow. All the time he looked into her eyes with a mixture of adoration and uncertainty.

Harriet broke the silence between them as she reached forward to give Edward a sisterly peck on the cheek exclaiming, 'Welcome home Edward!'

They all laughed and Joseph interrupted their private moment by asking, 'It's not so pleasant travelling in weather like this son, is it?'

'I'm used to it Father. A few waves don't bother me, in fact I love it. A good storm just adds to the excitement,' Edward replied.

Harriet and Beth shivered at the thought. 'Rather you than me, Son,' exclaimed Beth. 'You wouldn't catch me on any sort of a boat in weather like this. Now let's get home before the rain comes again.'

They walked along, talking about the weather and the trip but as they reached the crossroads where the lane veered towards St Anne Harriet took leave of them.

'I must say goodbye now and go on up to school for the morning, Edward,' she said. Edward hesitated, wondering if he should walk with her. Sensing his dilemma Harriet reassured him,

'I shall be home just after noon.'

'May I walk to meet you at the school gate, Harriet?' Edward asked.

'That would be lovely,' she replied as she turned and set off cheerfully walking up the hill.

True to his word Edward spent the morning with his parents and just before noon he walked up to the village to meet Harriet. He was surprised to see the doctor already waiting outside the gate and they greeted each other and talked as they waited. Harriet came out a few minutes later and they wished David good day and began to walk home. Harriet was given little chance to explain about the romance between Mary and David because many folks stopped them to wish Edward well. Their progress was slow so that when they finally reached the end of Victoria Street, Harriet was surprised when Edward turned right instead of choosing the most direct road home.

'Shall we take the quieter route down the cutting?' he said, more as a statement rather than a question. Edward, although pleased to be given such a warm welcome by the islanders, longed to have a moment alone with Harriet. They backtracked behind the church and, passing the lavoir, she followed him down the path towards the Mill. As soon as he could see that they were alone he reached back to hold her hand as they walked down the familiar path. As soon as he was certain that they were unlikely to be disturbed he turned and wrapped his arms around Harriet and sank his lips into her hair. They stood there motionless for a moment, drinking each other's warmth. He longed to kiss her but did not want to frighten her.

'I've thought of you every single day Harriet,' he said quietly. 'It is so lovely to be with you again.'

'It's wonderful to have you home,' replied Harriet. 'The island never seems the same place without you.'

Suddenly Harriet felt a little nervous, a feeling which she was unaccustomed to in his presence.

'I think we should be heading home now. My papa has been very protective of me recently and rarely lets me out of his sight,' explained Harriet.

Edward laughed, reluctantly letting her go. 'I'm glad to hear it,' he replied emphatically.

'He will be happy to hear that you are meeting me but he doesn't seem to trust anyone these days, maybe even you,' Harriet continued.

'Especially me!' exclaimed Edward laughing. 'We'd better not dally.'

They walked on quickly, Harriet lifting her skirts to avoid some large puddles, until they came to the track at the bottom into Crabby Village. Harriet relaxed once they were out in the open again and they began to talk more freely, Harriet listening to some of Edward's sea tales and Edward attentive to hearing the latest of the island's gossip. Once they had reached Harriet's cottage Edward asked,

'Can I see you later just as we used to?'

'Of course Edward, but I think that we should spend the evening at home with my parents, just to get my papa accustomed to having you home?' she replied.

'Until this evening then,' he said as he raised his hand in farewell as he walked on to his own gate next door. He hid his disappointment, realising the wisdom in her suggestion.

Harriet and Edward made every effort to be sociable in the next few evenings, spending pleasant times with their parents and sometimes with friends. It was a busy time, being the week before Christmas and they rarely had more than a stolen moment on their own. The Christmas festivities came and went and the whole island waited in anticipation for the wedding of the year on New Year's Eve.

It was on the Sunday afternoon between Christmas and New Year that Edward finally persuaded Harriet to go out for a walk with him. By that time Jack had become accustomed to having Edward around and to some extent had gratefully relinquished the task of protecting Harriet.

In his own private moments Edward felt the burden of that trust, which he felt to be misplaced at times. Each time Harriet smiled across the room at him, or when they inadvertently touched each other he wondered at their self-control. At times he was tempted to forego his plans to travel and ask Harriet to marry him, but he was realistic enough to realise that, after the initial euphoria of taking Harriet to be his wife, he would long to return to his travelling days. He would hate to regret a hasty decision and have to spend a life frustrated by unfulfilled dreams, even at the risk of losing her. He shivered at the thought.

'If you are that cold while sitting by our fire young Edward, I don't know why you're going to venture out?' Jack asked.

Harriet, who had just come downstairs, rescued Edward.

'Oh Papa, we've been cooped up like cattle in a barn since Christmas. Edward and I just need a bit of fresh air and exercise. A bit of wind hurts no-one,' answered Harriet.

They wrapped up warmly and headed towards their favourite cliff path on the far side of the island. Although it was windy there were occasional bright moments between the grey. Now and then a darker cloud threatened but was soon blown clear of the island. They laughed and talked until it was hard to imagine that Edward had been away and even more difficult to imagine him leaving so soon.

'Why the sad face?' asked Edward, surprised by the sudden change in Harriet's mood. He stopped and lifted her down turned face to meet his gaze. Although it was cold they were both aware of a sudden warmth radiating between them. He was about to wrap his arms around her when the heavens seemed to open up and it started to rain. Edward grabbed Harriet's hand and they ran laughing and stumbling towards the town. As Edward ran he noticed Farmer James' barn to the left of the path. He pulled her towards it and they ran inside, falling on the hay laughing and gasping for breath.

Edward looked down at Harriet's rosy cheeks and mass of ruffled damp hair. He bent over her giggling face and their eyes met. As they kissed for the first time it was as if the world stopped still and the storms of turmoil from within were silenced. In that moment of stillness both were aware of the depth of feeling between them.

The tide of passion that swept over them was overwhelming. As they kissed Harriet could feel Edwards's hands gently caressing her waist, her neck, her shoulders and her bodice. She was overwhelmed by emotion and silent tears began to flow uncontrollably from her beautiful eyes. Edward, controlling himself with a sensitivity he found hard to sustain, looked at her lovingly stroking her cheek and gently kissed away her tears.

'Don't cry for me Harriet my love,' he said softly. 'Will you try and wait for me?'

He shifted himself to kneel beside her and asked gently,

'Will you marry me one day and bear my children? I love you. You know that I hope.'

Harriet tried to reply but could not find the words.

Edward continued looking away in anguish,

'I know that you're still so very young and that it's unfair of me to ask you to promise to wait. I'll be away for at least a year and I'll think of you every day but when I return I'll ask you once more. Do you think you will think of me, too?'

This final plea cut through Harriet's reserve and though she still could find no comforting words for either Edward or herself she stretched out her hands towards him. Her cupped hands gently drew his face towards her and she returned his kiss, which answered Edward in a way that no words could express. Again Edward fought with his desire and drew away from Harriet and fell back on the hay. She fell back beside him and he laughed at the memory it gave him.

'Do you remember the time when we were very young, you were about five I think, when I made you a little den in the bushes?' he asked. 'I told you that one day I would marry you and build you a proper house.'

'You even made a table and a seat out of grass and I pretended to make you tea and cake,' Harriet replied.

'Not forgetting the bed Harriet,' Edward added and Harriet giggled. 'And do you remember what we did on the bed young Harriet?'

'We romped about and you used to tickle me mercilessly!' Harriet replied.

'Well, are you going to answer me this time, or am I going to have to resort to tickling you again,' he laughed, catching her as she tried to struggle away. With that Edward began to tickle Harriet until she laughed out loud and cried for him to stop.

'You prefer this then,' and their lips met and he kissed her with such a passion that it took her breath away. This time he could control himself no longer and Harriet felt his hands untie her bodice and his hands caress her young breasts. He kissed them gently as his hands began to explore beneath the layers of her petticoat. Momentarily he felt Harriet's hand over his and he paused looking at her with pleading eyes. There was a moment of stillness as if the world were waiting to see if that invisible line would be crossed. Then he took her to him as if it was the most natural experience since the world began.

Afterwards they lay back holding hands listening to the rain beat upon the barn roof, more gently now. They spoke no words for a while. Edward gently stroked Harriet's hair and she rested her head on his chest. After a while they could hear that the rain had ceased and they reluctantly broke the spell between them.

Edward stood up first and helped Harriet to her feet and to tie up her bodice and straighten her dress and hair. He lovingly combed it with his fingers, pausing to massage her lovely shoulders and when she was tidy Harriet returned the compliment as if they were continuing their love making in their own private ritual of care and respect. Finally Edward wrapped Harriet's cloak tightly around her and before they reluctantly ventured outside Edward hugged her and exclaimed fiercely, 'You're mine Harriet and don't you forget it.'

That evening their families shared supper together in honour of Edward's brief return. Harriet tried to be her usual talkative self but occasionally, as she felt Edward's gaze burn into her across the table, she felt herself glow with their shared secret. He even risked winking at her making Harriet giggle out loud. Jack and Joseph, who had been deep in conversation at the time about the state of the quarry, looked around puzzled.

'Share the joke with us young Harriet. It would be good to lighten the load of our conversation here,' Joseph encouraged.

Edward rescued her by replying and then expertly changing the subject,

'It's so good to see Harriet looking happy Pa. I was telling her this afternoon about Cousin Joe and his seasickness. Maybe he would be interested in a job at the quarry for a while, now he has given up the sea. He could keep you company in my absence Ma. What do you think?' asked Edward.

'I wish you'd caught your cousin's seasickness. That's all I can say,' moaned Beth, looking crossly at her son. 'Then we wouldn't have to lose you for a year. Why you have to travel so far away I shall never understand.'

'Hush, Beth my love. We've been through all that and no amount of your nagging will get our son to change his mind now. It would take a miracle or a good woman. Now there's a thought. Couldn't you work your woman's wiles on him young Harriet,' Joseph teased in jest.

'Now it's your turn to hush Joseph. Look. You've embarrassed the poor girl,' rebuked Beth at the sight of Harriet's blushing face.

'Yes, that was out of order my friend,' said Jack, coming to Harriet's defence. 'My Harriet here is a good girl.'

'I'm just going up to see if Mama would like anything else to eat,' exclaimed Harriet as she escaped from their gaze. There was a time when she would have thought of an instant answer to their teasing but this time she was so overwhelmed by her feelings for Edward and the memories of their afternoon together.

Edward on the other hand was cross with their parents for embarrassing Harriet. When she was out of earshot he said,

'Now look what you have done. Harriet looked so happy until your thoughtless remarks.'

'Sorry son,' said a contrite Joseph. 'It was only in jest. Do you think Cousin Joe might want to live over here then?'

With that, Beth, Joseph and Edward discussed the merits of the idea while Jack, realising that his daughter would be a little while, cleared the plates away and suggested that they retire to the fire for a night cap. While he busied himself he thought of his wife ill in bed and his daughter growing up before his very eyes. He glanced at Edward, so sure of himself and his dreams that he wondered seriously for the first time whether his daughter fitted into those dreams. He knew that there had always been a close bond between the young people but how close were they now? A sudden surge of protective fatherly love washed over him as her watched Harriet walk back downstairs and he was unnerved to witness a secret signal pass between them as Harriet's eyes met Edward's. In fact it was so subtle that he wondered afterwards if he had imagined it. How he longed to have Annie beside him now. She was far more perceptive in these matters.

'Thank you Papa,' said Harriet. 'I will finish clearing away while you pour the drinks?'

'I'll go up to see Annie before she goes to sleep,' said Beth, leaving her chair for Jack to sit beside Joseph.

The evening came to a close not long after Beth had rejoined them. Aware that their parents were watching them Edward's gesture of farewell to Harriet was brief and brotherly. Jack relaxed visibly and shook Edward's hand heartily.

Harriet made her excuses to retire as soon as they had left. She was afraid of interrogation by her papa. Once alone Jack poured himself another drink and pondered on the evening. His mind was aware of a nagging worry but the drink had softened his memory by now, so that he found it difficult to concentrate. He raked the few smouldering embers to cool the fire and headed for bed where he snuggled up to his wife and fell into a deep sleep.

Harriet was less fortunate. She tossed and turned as her mind dwelt on the events of the day. She wished that Edward was here to comfort her but the thought of Edward with her in her bedroom only added to her confusion. One moment she was filled with a desire to feel him inside her again, kissing and caressing her and the next moment she was filled with an unaccountable fear. What she was afraid of she could not fathom and it was with that thought that she fell into a dream filled restless sleep.

Harriet dreamed that she was a mermaid sunning herself on a rock. She sang a haunting melody for a while before slipping soundlessly into the sea. She danced for a while with the fishes until she was aware of the bows of a ship above her. She swam along-side it for a while, returning the waves from the sailors as they prepared to drop anchor. She smiled up at one of them, not surprised to recognise Edward's familiar face.

By nightfall the wind had whipped up a storm and Harriet dived down to the depths of her ocean home where her father was watching out for her, and scolded her for being so late. The ship's anchor held fast to rocks just outside the entrance to their cave and they could hear it scraping on the rocks as the sea swirled around it. In fact the sound sent Harriet off to sleep, only to be awakened by a crash, as the stone which the anchor had clung to broke away, and came crashing down at the entrance of their cave.

It took all the might of both father and daughter to shift it to make enough room for them to slide through. The light of dawn was seeping through the waters as Harriet swam to the surface, but she was dismayed by the sight that greeted her. Flotsam and jetsam were strewn across the surface of the water. She swam towards her rock and pulled herself up. The sight of the destruction of the sea and storm brought tears to her eyes and she began to sing a mournful ballad about the loss of the ship and its crew.

Harriet did not stir until she heard the sound of her papa downstairs stoking the fire the following morning. Grateful that there was still no school today she gave herself the luxury of a few more minutes before getting up. She went in to check her mama was comfortable before going downstairs to face the dishes of the night before.

Chapter 21

THE FOLLOWING DAY Edward's cousin Joe arrived from Sarnia. Harriet saw little of Edward that day apart from a brief introduction mid morning. It was years since they last met and Joe was rather taken by Harriet from the moment he set eyes on her. He was unaware of the deep relationship between Harriet and Edward, since he believed that Edward was still courting Charlotte, although Edward had mentioned that their relationship had cooled a little due to Edward's determination to travel. For some reason Edward had never explained his true feelings and the confusion that he had caused, perhaps to avoid the incessant teasing on the ship or at the Mission. Whatever the reason, Joe was so taken by Harriet that he decided to take up his uncle and aunt's offer of a home and accepted employment at the quarry. He longed to make the break from home and since he had given up on the idea of going to sea he had been at a loss as to what to do.

Harriet was pleased to have some time to herself. She was putting the finishing touches to a new dress she was hoping to complete in time for Mary and David's wedding and since her mama was feeling well enough to come downstairs, they sat comfortably by the fire and talked. It was in the evening, when she was on her own, that she missed Edward's company most. She was restless at first but decided to go to her room and write in her journal. Her unsteady hands reflected her emotional turmoil as she was careful to write the detail in a coded message, that only she could decipher, but even so the contents made her blush as she reread them. When she had finished her fingers were numb with cold, even though she was snuggled under her blanket, and her candle was getting low. She was tired after the restless night of the evening before and she shivered, overwhelmed by a sense of unreality, before she drifted off to sleep.

The following day was New Year's Eve. Harriet was up early, bright and refreshed. She helped her mama to get up and after ensuring that she was comfortable Harriet raced down to Mary's cottage in Newtown. Mary was so nervous. Although she had returned to the island the previous Saturday her parents had only just arrived on the midweek ship. She and David had taken them to The Scott's Hotel where they had shared a wonderful meal before leaving them to stay in relative luxury. She was not intending for them to see her little cottage but was expecting them to visit her new home with David and Jane after the wedding.

'This is so lovely,' exclaimed Harriet noticing Mary's wedding dress hanging on the back of the door. 'I've never seen anything so exquisite.'

'I was fortunate that my sister is much the same height and build as me, and was able to go for the preliminary fittings. In fact, since she can't be here for the wedding, it's extra special that she chose it for me.'

The dress was ivory silk with a delicate lace from the ornate bodice to the neck. The sleeves were long for a winter wedding with similar trim at the wrists. Over the shoulders loosely hung a cream woollen wrap, softer than anything Harriet had ever felt.

'Look at this Harriet,' said Mary reaching for a small leather pouch on her dresser.

'Ah,' gasped Harriet as Jane opened the pouch to reveal a gem-studded tiara of emeralds set in silver.

'It's very old,' Mary explained. 'It was given to my grandmother on her wedding day. My mother and my sister wore it when they were married and now it's my turn.'

'It's just the colour of your eyes Mary. I thought the other day that it was a pity that there are no flowers at this time of year to decorate your hair but you will not need them.'

'I'm so glad you're here. I had to be diplomatic when my mother wanted to come to be with me this morning, but the last thing I wanted was for her to fuss around me in this little room, complaining about the lack of space. Would you help me with my hair if I get dressed now?'

Harriet looked around the little cottage. It was all in the one room, her bed on the far side with a small table under the window and a washstand. The dresser was on one side of the range, with two comfortable old chairs in front. At the other end of the room were the table, two chairs and some cupboards and a door to a small pantry.

Harriet changed into her new dress while Mary was getting ready. Her dress was made of a beautiful sky blue cloth, the best quality that Harriet could afford with her meagre savings. Nevertheless the stunning colour and simple bodice hugging design enhanced her natural beauty. No sooner had they put the finishing touches to their hair than David's horse and trap arrived to take them to the church. It was sparklingly clean with new blankets to sit on. Once more Harriet wished for some flowers to decorate the carriage but otherwise Mary looked beautiful sitting regally, with the folds of her dress flowing out from the side of the carriage, and covering her dainty feet. Harriet climbed in beside her friend and teacher and gave her a hug.

'You look beautiful,' she said reassuringly. 'Everything will be fine, you'll see.'

And it was. To the islanders it was the perfect wedding. The two much respected members of the community, although not islanders themselves, had soon been accepted among them. Their only regret was the loss of Mary in teaching their young children at school. Most of the islanders came out of their homes to wave to them as they went past. Some of the young families with children in Mary's class even attended at the church and all the dignitaries were there. If Mary's parents had any doubts about the union or Riduna itself, they were soon comforted by the class of many of the people who attended the wedding.

The sight of Edward in his best suit took Harriet's breath away as she walked beside him into the church.

'I wish it was us getting married today,' he whispered as they sat down in a pew amongst family and friends. The service was very moving and Harriet could feel her eyes welling up. She wondered how Jane felt. At the very point when Mary said 'I do', Harriet felt Edward clasp her hand and squeeze it tightly. She dared a brief glance at him and their eyes met momentarily. Harriet could not tell whether it was adoration, love or sheer desire looking down at her. Whichever it was the effect was a mixture of overwhelming pleasure and utter confusion. She looked away and focussed her attention on the bride and groom and the words of the minister until the beat of her heart had settled once more. Neither had been given an opportunity to talk about the afternoon in the barn and yet there was now an invisible thread binding them together so that they walked out of the church feeling as if they had just exchanged vows themselves.

The day continued like a dream for Harriet. She could

not remember ever feeling so happy and contented. She felt as if she was floating on a cloud, especially at the ball that night. Mary and David led the dancing. Harriet saw very little of Jane, since her brother and his wife were there also and Thomas was being his usual attentive self. Harriet did not mind because she not only had Edward to dance with but when he was elsewhere his cousin Joe seemed to take over his caring role. Harriet felt a moment of jealousy when she watched Edward dancing with Charlotte, but she was soon whisked on to the dance floor again, this time by Frederick, who seemed quite pleasant and less threatening with Edward there to protect her.

David decided to leave with his new wife just after eleven. He felt that it would be more romantic to see the New Year in with Mary in their room at The Scott's Hotel. He had ordered champagne which he hoped would help both of them to ease their nervousness about the coming night. He was so proud to escort Mary out to their waiting trap among close family, friends and many islanders who were now so familiar to them both. The people waved and cheered as they left. He wrapped a blanket over them for the short ride and held his arm over her shoulders protectively. Mary smiled shyly up at him.

'Are you happy my dear,' he asked gently.

'Yes David. I am very happy.'

He kissed her on the forehead and hugged her close to him to keep away the cold of the dark winter's night. Although it was cold and frosty, the sky was clear and the stars shone almost as brightly as the new moon.

Back at the Town Hall Jane finally found a moment to speak to Harriet now that her father had left.

'How are you Jane?' Harriet asked, concerned for her friend and wondering how she would feel under the same circumstances.

'I'm fine,' Jane replied. 'I've not had time to feel lonely as yet. It's a little strange though?'

'And Thomas?' Harriet questioned.

'If I said fine to that question I don't think that I would be telling the truth. We are still friends at least and he is still very attentive. It's just that we have lost that feeling of trust between us.'

'And you and Edward?' asked Jane, whispering behind her fan.

'Wonderful!' exclaimed Harriet, unable to hide her happiness.

'His cousin Joe seems very attentive too,' remarked Jane, just as Joe came over with some refreshments in his hands for the ladies. 'They are quite different in temperament aren't they?'

'What do you mean by that?' asked Harriet.

'You know them far better than I. What do you think?' asked Jane, interested to see if her friend had considered the matter.

Harriet was quiet for a moment, glancing occasionally in the direction of the two handsome young men.

'Well, Edward is certainly a dreamer, but he is determined to make dreams come true and live life to the full,' she replied thoughtfully, her eyes misting over.

'And Cousin Joe?' prompted Jane, bringing her friend back to the present.

'Ah, Cousin Joe is more practical and home loving. I could imagine him settling down with a wife and having a contented life with his family,' replied Harriet.

'A commendable quality don't you think?' exclaimed Jane as Joe headed back towards them to see if they required anything or wished to dance. They thanked him but refused, enjoying the short rest and each other's brief company. He reluctantly left them, returning to Edward who was by this time in a deep conversation with Michael and Charlotte.

Harriet turned away, not wanting to be seen to be watching them but burning with curiosity as to what they were talking about so earnestly. Jane looked carefully at Harriet's face.

'Something has changed about you and I can't quite work out what it is,' Jane remarked.

Harriet blushed but did not deny it, glad that her face was turned away from Edward at that moment.

'I long to have a chance to talk with you Jane, on our own, but what with Edward and Joe here and your house full of guests we don't seem to have a moment.'

'You're welcome to come to see me tomorrow Harriet,' suggested Jane, burning with curiosity. 'Now that my father is away for two days life will be quieter for a while. We could spend some time together and then have tea with my family. That's if you don't mind being away from Edward for a while.'

'That would be lovely,' replied Harriet quickly as she and Jane were whisked to the dance floor yet again, this time by John and Michael. 'Until tomorrow then,' she called over her shoulder.

After that dance Harriet was claimed by Edward who danced with her as the clock rang twelve.

'We'd better make tracks soon before your papa comes after us,' teased Edward as the music came to an end.

'Or my dress will turn to rags and you might be left holding a glass slipper,' joked Harriet. They laughed. Harriet walked home with Joe on one arm and Edward on the other. She felt so safe and warm by their presence that she slept soundly that night.

The following morning Harriet readied herself for church before helping her mama downstairs. Annie was feeling a touch better that day and Beth had promised to keep her company while the remainder of the two families went to church. Harriet couldn't wait to see Jane. She felt like a child with a big secret, desperate to share it but hugging it to herself. She also longed to have some time alone with Edward again and knowing that he felt the same did not make it any easier. The church service went by in a blur and afterwards she watched the men walk off together knowing that they were heading to the Diver's Inn. She linked arms with Jane as she emerged from the church with her brother and family. Harriet joined the family for a lovely lunch, after which the girls excused themselves for a while and retired to Jane's room.

'I love my brother dearly but I will be glad when they are on their way home,' moaned Jane.

'What's the matter?' asked Harriet, 'I'm surprised to hear such a comment from you Jane.'

'He never ceases to complain about what a dreary place he thinks Riduna is and that Father could do much better for himself back in England,' Jane explained.

'Do you think he is right?' asked Harriet thoughtfully.

Not answering Harriet directly Jane replied, 'I wish he could admit that Father is happier here than he has been for a long while. It's so obvious that he has gained the respect of the community. Money and prestige are not everything in life.'

'Your father's been accepted by everyone in the community. Not an easy accomplishment on any account. I don't think I have ever heard any words said against him and that's surely something to be proud of in a close knit island such as ours,' added Harriet. 'He looked so happy yesterday with Mary at his side. Surely your brother can see that.'

'Let's not talk about the matter any longer. Come and sit down and tell me all about you,' said Jane.

Since there had never been any secrets between the friends Harriet told Jane everything. When she had finished she was stunned by Jane's silence.

'Oh no, Harriet! Do you know what you have done?' she exclaimed after a moment.

'But it was lovely Jane. Edward was so loving and gentle and he says he wants to marry me,' Harriet said trying desperately to justify her actions. 'We are virtually engaged.'

'But when is he prepared to marry you Harriet?' Jane asked, although she already knew the answer.

'I've explained already,' said Harriet impatiently. 'He hopes to join a ship to travel to America and then maybe on to China. The voyage will take over a year and then he will marry me when he returns.'

'But what happens if you are with child Harriet,' Jane asked as if talking to a child.

'We can't have children until we are married of course,' said Harriet crossly.

'Oh no!' exclaimed Jane angrily, more directed at her own stupidity than her friend's ignorance.

'Harriet. Look at me and listen carefully to what I am saying. I know that I said that you don't always have a baby when a man does that to you,' she struggled to find the right words. 'What you and Edward have done together, but it can make you with child if it's God's will, at any time.'

'You're saying that I could have a baby *now*, even though I'm not married,' said Harriet slowly, as if she was beginning to understand the possible consequences of her actions for the first time. She began to look worried and tears crept in the corner of her eyes.

Jane continued, 'Think carefully before answering me Harriet. Do you think Edward would abandon his travels for a while and stay here to marry you if you *are* pregnant?'

Harriet was silent.

'And I'm not saying that you are,' Jane added in a softer tone, aware of her friend's distress.

Harriet put her head into her hands for a few moments. She tried to imagine Edward letting go of his dream and to picture him standing beside her with a baby in his arms. Then she tried to imagine herself with a baby standing alone. She shuddered at the thought. The humiliation she would have to bear in the community.

'I just don't know,' she said slowly.

'Then you must find some time alone with him to talk,' suggested Jane. 'When was your last flux?' she continued practically.

Harriet thought for a moment. 'Just before Edward's return ten days ago,' she replied.

Jane counted carefully.

That means he will have left the island before you know for sure,' Jane replied. 'You must discuss with him what he would do. A year is a long time before you'll see him again, especially if you have the misfortune of having a baby in your arms.'

Harriet began to weep.

'Hopefully it may never come to that,' said Jane trying to comfort Harriet. 'Whatever happens, don't forget that I am your friend.'

Harriet tried to smile. The friends hugged as they parted company and Harriet returned home via the Butes to spend some time alone and regain her composure. Her mind went blank as she gazed out to sea. As she breathed in deeply she was suddenly filled with a sense of calm. Wrapping her cloak more tightly around her against the cool wind she turned and was surprised to see her father walking towards her.

'I've just been to the doctor's to meet you. You should have waited for me lass, and not wandered off on your own,' he complained, but noticing the pained expression on his daughter's face he put his arm gently over her shoulder and guided her home, Harriet's head resting on his chest.

Mistaking Edward's impending departure as the only reason for her sadness he reasoned softly,

'If it's meant to be lass, then it will all work out for the best. You'll see.'

Harriet hoped upon hope that he was right.

The next few days passed by in a blur for Harriet. There was never a moment when she was able to speak to Edward on his own and since he was leaving in only two days' time she was beginning to despair. Edward felt the same frustration for other reasons. He longed to be alone with Harriet again so that he could hold her in his arms and show her how much he loved her. The memories of their encounter in the barn filled him with secret delight and kept him awake at night. He was also concerned that he had upset Harriet in some way. She seemed so quiet and distant at times. Since the beginning of the week she had returned to working in the mornings at the school. He could think of no reason why his cousin Joe should not accompany him to meet Harriet at lunchtimes but it only added to his frustration. In fact she seemed more relaxed and able to talk to Joe than she was with himself.

Women were a complete mystery. The more he thought he knew them, the less he seemed to understand. It was therefore with some relief that Joe decided to stay at the cottage to complete his packing on the Friday lunchtime. He also said that he had to meet someone in the Diver's but did not want to talk about it yet. Edward left home early just in case Joe changed his mind. He had a drink in the Rose and Crown along the street from the school, to pass the time away and to calm his nerves. The time passed quickly enough as John confided in him about his plans to travel to Sarnia with Michael in the next couple of months. Soon he was walking back up the cobbled street towards the school gate.

The sight of Harriet's relieved smile melted away any gnawing fears that he had been harbouring as she whispered,

'Oh Edward! How glad I am that you are on your own today. I thought I would never get a chance to really talk with you before you left. Don't misunderstand me, I'm very fond of your cousin; he's sweet, but it's not the same as being on our own.'

Edward wanted to hug her on the spot, but he kept a polite distance from her as his excitement grew.

'Time has gone so quickly Harriet and I'm going to miss you.'

They nodded politely at two elderly islanders and Edward could see two old school friends along the street in front of them.

'Let's go this way,' he whispered, as surreptitiously as he could, as he guiding Harriet through the churchyard to the quieter road behind.

'Would you like to make a detour through 'Fairy Woods' and take the back path down to Crabby? Then we can be alone for a short while.'

Harriet nodded as she walked beside him.

'We have many happy memories of times in these woods,' she said trying to sound more cheerful and to break the tension between them.

'Do you remember the times we used to play hide and seek and pretend we were looking for the fairies and elves,' Edward added as they reached the edge of the woods.

'Do you remember when Charlotte and I put out a little picnic for them, on that tree stump which looks like a table?' Harriet asked.

'Yes, I do. You made cups out of acorns and filled them with stream water, and plates out of leaves and put sweets on them, and then you hid behind the bushes and giggled as you waited,' he reminisced.

'Then you and Michael made us run for fright as you covered your faces with mud and leaves and leapt out into the clearing pretending to be elves,' Harriet laughed, relaxing a little.

They had to walk in single file as Edward pushed aside twigs and branches of trees that overhung the path. Both could hear the stream gurgling long before they set eyes on it, swelled by the winter's rain. Harriet was just able to tiptoe across the two stepping stones without getting her feet wet. Edward leapt the short distance to the bank and turned to hold out his hand to help Harriet safely across. As she leapt towards him it seemed the most natural thing in the world to pull her towards him, wrap his arms around her and kiss her. It was light and gentle at first, the tentative kiss of an inexperienced lover. The familiar protection of Edward's arms and the soft embrace, which seeped into her very being, threw Harriet completely off guard and she responded to his kisses.

Edward was so reassured by this that he became more passionate and before long his hands were gently caressing her once more. It was as Harriet was aware that he was beginning to unlace her bodice that she came to her senses. Not wanting to anger him or spoil their last few minutes together by a tantrum she placed her hand gently over his. He paused and looked down into her eyes questioningly. Confused and suddenly insecure by this response he dropped his hand and turned his gaze from her, desperate to gain control of his feelings.

Harriet felt a sudden despair and tears began to trickle down her cheeks.

'Don't be angry with me Edward, on our last day together,' she exclaimed.

Edward's expression softened as he turned back to her. He longed to kiss away those tears from her cheeks and neck but he stood there motionless. Harriet held out her hand to him and led him to the log in the clearing, that magical place of their childhood. As they sat down she sighed.

'Won't you be mine this one last time, Harriet?' Edward asked. 'It would mean so much to me when I am so far away. One day we will be married and laugh about this time when we were so young.'

'It's not that I don't love you, Edward, but what would I do if I was carrying our baby? How would I manage without you for over a year? Think of the shame!' she exclaimed.

Edward looked away from her. He had felt so much freedom with Marie that he had just never thought of the possible consequences of their actions. All he knew was that he felt complete when he was with Harriet. He dropped Harriet's hand as the full implications of her words began to sink in. He thought of his dreams to travel. He thought of his plans for the year ahead and then he tried to imagine Harriet holding a baby in her arms.

His silence frightened Harriet. She expected him to wrap his arms around her once more and reassure her that he would always be there for her when she needed it. She began to shiver with cold and fear.

As Edward turned back towards her he was filled with remorse. His heart ached at the pain he had caused her as he looked once more into those frightened eyes.

'I'm so sorry, my love. I didn't mean to hurt you. How could I have been so selfish?' He put his arm over her shivering shoulders and gently kissed her hair. Harriet rested her head against his chest and began to relax.

'Just being with you fills me with desire. I know it's wrong before we are wed, but can you forgive me?' he asked. 'You don't really think you are with child, do you?'

'I don't know Edward, I really don't!' exclaimed Harriet.

'How soon will you know for sure?' Edward asked gently.

'By the end of the week after you've left,' Harriet replied in a helpless voice, reluctant to mention the words.

'Will you write to me as soon as you can?' Edward continued. 'You could send the letter to the Seamen's Mission in Southampton. I will be staying there for a couple of weeks, while I sort out my employment papers, before I finally set sail. If you send me word that you are going to have a baby then I promise you that I'll abandon my plans, for a while, and return to Riduna as soon as I can, so that we can be wed.

Once Harriet heard those words she relaxed in his arms and placed her arms around Edward's neck and kissed his cheek.

'I knew that you wouldn't let me down,' she sighed.

'Don't sound so surprised,' Edward remarked. 'Surely you didn't think that I would abandon you?'

After a few minutes Harriet stood up, determined to be strong for him once more.

'And if I'm not with child then you may travel with my blessing. So long as you come back to claim me again in a year's time, if you can wait that long,' she teased. 'We must go home now. Our parents will be wondering what we are doing!'

Edward laughed, pleased to see Harriet more cheerful again. He pulled her to him once more and kissed her with a fierce urgency, knowing it may be their last for many months. He would have taken her again. Claimed her as his very own in that familiar place that they had shared since they were children, but he refrained this time, leading her gently back across the stream and through the woods towards home.

The next day, before even a glimmer of daybreak, Harriet made her way down to the harbour yet again, this time with Edward, Edward's parents and Joe. As Edward walked away from her this time she found it impossible to conceal her sadness. He wiped a silent tear from her cheek as his lips brushed against it.

'Be brave for me Harriet,' he whispered.

It was such a windy and cold day that Edward and Joe only stayed on deck a few minutes after the *Courier* had set sail, before retreating to the relative warmth below. Harriet and Beth gave each other a hug, both feeling the acuteness of their loss.

'Come on wife,' Joseph suggested. 'Let's get back to the warmth of our fireside.'

They turned their backs on the *Courier*, which was still in the bay and walked slowly up the track. Harriet parted company with them at the crossroads, making her way up to the grassy slopes of the Butes. There she stood; with her coat wrapped tightly around her, and watched the *Courier*, as it slipped passed the breakwater and disappeared from view. By this time tears fell freely and she stood motionless, as if in a state of disbelief.

She did not realise quite how cold she had become until she finally turned, her teeth chattering and her whole body shivering. It was with relief that she saw her papa striding towards her like a guardian angel. Without saying a word he wrapped his arms around her shoulder and led her gently home. He stroked her hair as she sobbed into his shoulder, so relieved of his presence but full of guilt and fearful of what she might be holding inside her and the pain she might cause him.

Chapter 22

THE NEXT FEW days were a blur for Harriet. She had caught a chill and spent a couple of days huddled at home feeling miserable. Even her mama, who was feeling well and strong, became irritated by her daughter's state of mind. Harriet was short tempered and prone to floods of tears, spending hours shut up in her bedroom under a mountain of blankets and her winter shawl to keep out the cold. Even Jane's rare visit on Saturday afternoon did little to lift Harriet's mood. Her mama lit a fire in her room for the afternoon to give the girls some privacy, a luxury they could barely afford. She was grateful that Jane had been willing to take her place at school that week, but made very little effort to listen to her friend, who had troubles of her own.

'It's not that I don't like Mary,' she explained. 'You know that I am very fond of her. It's just that I am beginning to feel a stranger in my own home, especially now that Mary has taken over my role in the surgery.'

Jane paused for a moment before continuing,

'I'm even thinking seriously that it is about time I travelled to England and did something about my plans to study to be a nurse.' She stopped again and glancing down at the glazed expression on Harriet's face she added mischievously, 'Or I could always get married.'

Harriet sat up at this comment and focussed on her friend.

'Oh Jane, I know you will think carefully and follow your head and not just your heart on an impulse. Promise me that we'll talk this over when I'm feeling more myself,' she pleaded.

Jane kissed Harriet on the forehead.

'Don't fret over my situation Harriet. As for yourself, I'm sure that if you keep calm all will be well. Come to visit me soon.' With that said Jane left Harriet to rest.

By Sunday Harriet's mood was at last beginning to lift. It was partly the routine of going to church, accompanied on this rare occasion by both of her parents, which helped to cheer her up. There was a christening at the end of the service and if Harriet was honest, the thought that a baby could bring Edward home and standing by her side where he belonged lifted her spirits. She almost regretted not succumbing to temptation that last day in the woods to make another attempt at sealing their fate. These thoughts made Harriet flush as she realised that she was still in church and she tried to concentrate on the reverend's final prayers, adding a few quick pleas of her own. She nearly added a prayer for her unborn child and she inadvertently put her hand down over her stomach as she kneeled, trying to focus on the final blessing.

In fact, by the time she was walking to school on the Monday morning she was resolved to put all her difficulties out of her mind for a while. She was ready to face whatever the future held. Within a day or so she should know and according to Jane, the less she fretted about it the better. The winds and rain had also passed at the weekend and the crisp winter mornings of bright white sunshine had returned. The whole of the island responded cheerily to that change. By Tuesday her mama was up singing away before her papa left the cottage for work. He winked at her and then returned to give her another hug before leaving.

'You look as lovely this morning Annie?' he remarked.

She responded positively to his hug and kissed him on the mouth just as Harriet was emerging down the stairs.

'Let's have none of that,' Harriet joked, pleased to see her parents so happy.

'I'll kiss your mama where and when I like, you insolent little lady. If you were a few years younger I'd take you over my knee and spank you,' he teased, although he was relieved to see some spark in his daughter's eyes again.

To prove a point, he bent over to give Annie one more kiss. Then pretending to pick her up in his arms, he joked,

'If I were not so late for work I'd take you straight back to bed wi'me now,' and with that he made a growling noise which made Annie laugh.

She began to hit him playfully with the teaspoon she held in her hand.

'Put me down you animal and get off to work before we starve to death.'

'You just wait until I come home,' Jack said, chuckling as he left for work.

Annie smiled at her daughter and Harriet was tempted to tell her mama all about her fears, but resisted the temptation of unburdening herself. They chatted companionably together until it was time for Harriet to go to school. Annie assured her that she would be fine to do the housework that day, if Harriet could pick up some groceries on her way home. Everyone smiled as she walked along Victoria Street and the morning went quickly enough. The children seemed so pleased to see her back after the short break, the little ones running to the gate to meet her. She told them to run along and play before the school bell rang.

It was during that morning that Harriet's body finally let

her know that she was not carrying a child. The initial relief that swept through her was tinged with a slight regret and she could not help but place her hand on her stomach one last time and think of Edward's child that never was. That evening as she wrote to him she allowed the tears to fall yet again and could feel the tension of the last two weeks flow out of her.

My Dearest Edward,

I wanted to let you know as soon as I was able that I am not carrying your child. In some ways this saddens me because there is nothing I would wish for more in the world than having you beside me and bringing up your children.

Nevertheless, as you can imagine I am relieved that we will not be bringing shame on our families. We love our parents too much to want to hurt them.

This means that you are now free, my love, to follow your dreams and travel the world. I would like you to be assured that you go with my blessing and that, even though I long to be with you, I am setting you free. Try to think of me Edward and try not to forget me when you are so far away and visiting such exciting places.

Your own Harriet.

The following morning Harriet made a detour to take the letter to the post-master in order to catch the morning's sailing. She also called in to see Jane briefly to put her mind at rest. They hugged but had little time to talk for fear of Harriet being late. After that Harriet made her way to the schoolhouse. It was so different without Mary. She had come to love working alongside Mary. They had become friends and she missed her.

It's strange how events have changed all our lives, including Jane's, Harriet thought. I wonder how Mary is adjusting to her new life at the doctor's.

Since a new schoolmistress had been appointed, Harriet felt less and less needed at the school, at least by the staff. The youngest pupils, missing their favourite teacher, clung to Harriet all the more and she was aware that the new mistress did not like it very much. In class it was different. They kept a respectful distance, putting up their chubby hands and replying with dignified politeness, 'Yes miss. No miss.' A few of them liked to sit with her at lunchtime. Milk flowed like water on these islands and so the youngsters, even the poorest ones looked fairly well nourished.

Harriet had been sitting dreamily trying to concentrate on a history book about Queen Elizabeth I. Her mind kept wandering to thoughts of Edward, especially when there was talk of the Armada or Sir Walter Raleigh bringing back his Queen gifts of potatoes from far off America.

Funny to think of life without potatoes or tea, Harriet thought. How will I manage a year without Edward and will he bring any exciting gifts back for me? She mused.

Through the door came the Headmaster followed by a young lad Harriet recognised, who had just started to work at the quarry with her papa. The children rose to their feet respectfully at the sight of the headmaster. He ignored them and looking directly at Harriet he said, 'Miss Loveridge, I have a message for you. Please follow me to my office.'

Turning to the group of children he instructed them to pick up their things and to eat the rest of their lunch in the next room with Miss Quinn and to be quick about it. They scrambled out of the door with their heads bowed, followed by Harriet, who walked in front of the Headmaster down the long corridor to his office.

'Wait there,' he instructed the young boy as he opened

the door for Harriet to pass through and closed it firmly behind him. 'Sit down Miss Loveridge. I am afraid I have some very bad news for you.'

Harriet reluctantly obeyed. The colour had drained from her cheeks and her hands were trembling in her lap.

'There has been a serious accident at the quarry,' Mr Collins continued in a quiet voice.

Harriet made to stand up. If her papa was hurt she should be rushing to his side.

'Sit down Harriet,' he said firmly and then, as Harriet seated herself, he continued in a softer voice, 'I'm afraid that it's too late. Your father has been killed in the accident and Joseph Johnson has been seriously injured.'

Harriet was numb with shock, at first too stunned to shed a tear.

Mr Collins had a quiet word with the lad outside, who responded quickly by rushing off to the doctor's house, then he opened a cupboard by his desk and poured out two drinks.

'Drink this,' he instructed as he handed Harriet the small glass. Harriet almost spluttered it out as the liquid burned her throat.

'Drink it up lass. It will help with the shock,' Mr Collins continued softly, resting his arm briefly on her shoulder in a fatherly manner. He had no words of comfort. What could you say to a girl who had lost her father so tragically? Who could fathom the will of God in this life? It defeated him at times and this was one of those times. He was relieved when he heard a knock at the door. Mary and Jane entered the room quietly. On seeing them Harriet rushed into Jane's arms and began to sob in uncontrollable gasps.

Mr Collins quietly let himself out of the room followed by Mary. They agreed that Harriet should be taken to the doctor's house as soon as possible, especially since it was nearby. Although she would want to be with her mother she needed time to calm down. They sent the lad with messages for Annie and for the doctor, who was by this time just reaching the quarry, to let them know where Harriet would be. The young lad rushed out of the school gates yet again, this time with a few pence in his pocket for his trouble.

Jane guided Harriet to sit down and she sat with her head in her hands weeping. There was nothing that Jane could say or do to ease Harriet's pain but hold her comfortingly. Memories came flooding back to her as she stood there in silence of when she had lost her own mother after her long illness. Even though it had been expected at the time and in some ways the end had been a relief, she still had vivid memories of the shock she had felt. This was so different. Jack Loveridge was a fit man, full of health and a will to live life cheerfully and to the full. Maybe after nearly losing Annie through childbirth it had made him value life all the more. Mary came back into the room and sat on Harriet's other side taking her hand.

'Mama,' exclaimed Harriet, looking up at her and trying to struggle to her feet.

Mary stood up with her and said reassuringly, 'One of the men has taken your mother to your grandparents at the Braye Tavern. She had wanted to go to the quarry with Beth but there was nothing she could do there. Your grandparents will look after her.'

'My father has instructed that she be given a sedative, so I expect that she is sound asleep by now. We will take you there in a little while,' Jane explained. She omitted to mention that her father had been so worried about the effect on Annie's health that the sedative had been a strong one to ensure she would be in oblivion by now. She nodded at Mary and they made their way to the door. Mary went to find Harriet's coat and to tell Mr Collins that they were going now and they slowly made their way the short distance around the corner to the doctor's house. Jane took Harriet up to her room and persuaded her to lie down on her bed and sip some liquid that her father had left. Just as Harriet drifted into a fretful sleep she whispered to Jane, 'Should I write to Edward again?'

'Don't worry about that,' Jane replied, as she watched her friend drift off to sleep.

'What do you think she means?' asked Mary quietly as they settled in the chairs by the window.

'Perhaps we should write to Edward and try to persuade him to postpone his trip for a while,' suggested Jane. 'It won't just be Harriet who would be grateful of his support but also his mother and father.'

She fetched her writing things from her desk.

'We've missed the *Courier* this morning and there won't be another sailing until Saturday Jane. Surely then it will be too late,' reasoned Mary.

'There's bound to be someone sailing today who could take an urgent message to Sarnia, if not directly to the mainland,' argued Jane. She realised that it was too late to prevent Harriet's letter from reaching Edward first, but felt that they should at least try to contact him. They sat and composed a letter together while Harriet slept.

Dear Edward,

We are writing on Harriet's behalf and regret to inform you of some very bad news. There has been a serious accident at the quarry and unfortunately Harriet's father has been killed and your father has been injured. We are not certain at this stage as to how serious those injuries are and can assure you that the doctor is with him right now.

We hope to find a willing bearer of this letter, so that it may reach you before you sail to foreign parts. This being the case we hope that you will see fit to delay your plans to travel and return to Riduna as soon as possible.

In the mean time Harriet is sleeping and we know that she would wish us to send you her regards. Since time is of the essence we will send this letter immediately, rather than await further news of your father.

Yours sincerely
Mary and Jane

'If you stay with Harriet, I will run to the harbour to try to find a boat willing to take it,' Jane suggested as she grabbed her coat and was already heading for the door.

Chapter 23

WHEN DAVID FIRST arrived on the scene of the accident there was pandemonium. Men were rushing about with tools and ropes, some attempting to shift fallen rocks from the injured, others shouting orders at random and a few standing by watching helplessly. The foreman was doing his best to tend to the injured and to give orders simultaneously. The doctor's presence among them seemed to breathe some calm into the proceedings and soon the rocks were dragged clear to reveal several injured. The foreman busied himself with those with minor cuts and bruises while David turned to the two men who had obviously sustained the most serious injuries. It was clear from the moment he bent over Jack that it was too late to save him and so the doctor turned to assess Joseph's injuries. A blanket was gently placed over Jack's face and mutilated body.

The doctor instructed that word should be sent to Annie, Beth and Harriet. He was careful to send them separately. David had the foresight to send one messenger to Annie's parents at the Braye Tavern first, who then travelled on to Annie's cottage with the lad, so that Annie would not be alone when she was given the news. He suggested that she should not be brought to the quarry but taken back to the inn and given a sedative. The last thing he wanted was for Annie's health to suffer any more than it had to. The second messenger went to Beth who could be brought to be with her husband and the third was sent to Harriet.

Next the foreman assisted David to administer first aid to Joseph at the sight of the accident. He was groaning and his face was covered in blood. They were relieved to find that Joseph had sustained no internal injuries but had broken a leg and his left hand was badly damaged. The scratches on his face, although deep, had done no lasting damage. They bound his injuries and he was placed carefully on a stretcher. They gently lifted him into the waiting cart, where Beth, who had just arrived, sat beside him to hold him and keep him steady for the rough ride home.

'You go on Beth. With these strong men to help, you should be able to make Joseph comfortable at home by making up a bed downstairs. I will be along as soon as I have seen to Jack,' David instructed before turning to a much more arduous task.

He waited until Beth was out of sight before turning back to this man whom he considered to be a friend. He had certainly admired Jack's resilience over the years and had a great respect for the way he took on all the household chores as Harriet grew up, when his wife was too ill to manage. Yet he always gave time for others, making them smile at his jokes and giving them the benefit of his warm nature. Living among these island folk had certainly been an eye opener for David. Although he came across hardship in England, it was only in his working life. Their social life had always revolved around the well-off community and so the lives of common people barely touched him. Now he cared deeply about his patients, making times like these even more painful to bear.

David was thankful that Jack's face was barely scratched.

He felt that it was a small comfort to those bereft and that it always seemed easier to grieve for someone whom they could still recognise and say goodbye to. One of the men helped the doctor to move Jack on to another waiting cart. David knew the procedure. Old Mother would be called to bathe the body and prepare it for the funeral. Not only was she the first to be called to see a new life into the world but she was also one of the last to care for a person who was already on its way to its maker. Once Jack was safely installed in the cart the doctor reluctantly recovered Jack's face and asked the man to give him a few minutes before following his trap towards Platte Saline. The doctor took a few moments to check that there were no more injuries that needed his immediate attention before making his way to Joseph and Beth's cottage. Sure enough, when they passed the gate of Jack's cottage Old Mother was there waiting for them. They nodded to each other in respect of each other's skills before Old Mother bowed her head in reverence of the dead. She helped the man to carry Jack's body inside and then was left to her work in peace.

The doctor made his way in to see Joseph and was pleased to see that Beth had already made him comfortable by the fire. He gave something to ease Joseph's pain, although he had not heard the man mutter a single complaint and said that he would be back later that afternoon. The doctor had strapped Joseph's leg as tightly as he could to splints to keep it straight but it would be pointless to attempt any more by candlelight.

'I'll return in the morning to check it over,' he said casting Beth a sympathetic look as he took his leave. In the silence they could hear Old Mother humming softly as she worked, as if she was bathing a baby on its first day into the world. Beth could not help but give the doctor a watery smile.

When he had left she returned to Joseph's side.

'I wish Edward were here,' she exclaimed.

'Write to him Beth. If he knew of our troubles perhaps he would come home, love. If not only for us but to comfort Harriet too,' he suggested.

'But the *Courier* left this morning,' Beth replied with emotion.

'There's a cargo boat in the harbour on its way to Sarnia in the morning. You should also write a note to your sister,' he said.

Beth sat down with a heavy heart. She wrote two short notes. Although she longed for the reassuring presence of her one and only son, she also knew how much this trip meant to him and how disappointed he would be to have to return so soon.

And so there were three urgent letters leaving Riduna. The first for Edward was carried on a sailing boat bound for Portsmouth. It left the island in the middle of the afternoon, with the intention of clearing the dangerous waters of the Race before nightfall. The other letters were bound for Sarnia the following morning and hopefully the one to Edward would catch the steamer the following day.

When David arrived home exhausted and despondent he had one more task before he began to relax. He took Harriet, who had only just woken, to her family at the Braye Tavern. Harriet was understandably very quiet during the short journey. He was relieved to see mother and daughter united and he suggested that they be given some more sedative to help them to sleep that night. He left the family to grieve in private and assured them that there was no need to return to their cottage tonight and that Jack had been taken care of. In fact neither mother nor daughter could face returning home that night and so Jack lay at peace in the cottage that had been his home for so long, all alone.

Chapter 24

EARLY THE FOLLOWING morning Annie and Harriet could put the moment off no longer and so they walked slowly, arm in arm, to their cottage. Both felt guilty at leaving Jack alone. Annie opened the back door quietly as if frightened to wake him and Harriet followed behind her as if she was walking in one of her vivid dreams. Annie lit the candles which Old Mother had placed at his feet and then they knelt in silence beside the table on which he lay. He was wearing his Sunday best but the sight of her still handsome husband gave little comfort to Annie. Neither spoke although Harriet could see her mama's lips move as she said a silent prayer. Harriet tried to concentrate and say a prayer too, but as she gazed at her papa he appeared to her to be in a deep sleep. His death seemed inconceivable, so much so that she wished she could shake him to wake him up and scold him for playing such a trick on them all.

For Annie the place seemed so cold. It was as if life had drained not only from her husband beside her but also from the cottage. Harriet went to comfort her mama and they hugged, though neither of the women cried that day, so deep was their grief. With the funeral on Saturday Harriet and Annie had too much to do to dwell on their feelings, let alone what it meant for their future. All Annie knew was that the quarry company would give them one month's free rent in the cottage and Annie would be given a small widow's pension.

Neither Annie nor Harriet could face staying at the cottage so they packed a few clothes and closed the door quietly behind them. They visited Beth and Joseph for just a few moments before returning to the Braye Tavern where they turned two of the empty guest rooms into a temporary home.

Saturday morning arrived. Annie and Harriet followed the coffin passing the cottages and up La Valée towards St Anne's Church. They walked side by side with quiet dignity; both were still numb with an emptiness which filled their very being. Harriet did not notice Joe, Edward's cousin join the neighbours following behind them. Many of the islanders who would not be attending the service stood at their doorways as a sign of respect. Others joined the procession snaking towards the church. Jack had been a popular man and the church was soon full. The minister thanked God for Jack's life. He reasoned that everyone had tragedies in their lives and the temptation was to ask God why? Why, was the question that God never answered, because life itself was a mystery. If it was not so then life itself would have little meaning. Harriet tried to concentrate on his words. She attempted to make some sense of them but decided that the only truth was that life did not make any sense at all.

As she was walking out of the church and moving as if in a wave of people towards the awaiting empty grave, Cousin Joe touched her arm to offer his sympathy. Harriet's eyes glimmered momentarily followed by a look of disappointment when she realised it was Joe and not Edward.

'Thank you for coming all this way,' she remembered to

say as she moved on to be beside her mama at the graveside.

Later as friends gathered at the Braye Tavern for refreshments Joe plucked up the courage to talk with Harriet again. She was playing the role of the perfect hostess, handing out sandwiches and making polite conversation although the strain of the day was etched all over her pretty face.

'I have decided to stay on with Aunt Beth and Uncle Joseph,' he remarked.

Trying not to show her disappointment yet again that Edward would probably not return she replied, 'That will be a comfort for them with Edward so far away and his father recovering from the accident.' On mentioning the event that had so tragically claimed her father Harriet began to break down in tears.

'Please excuse me Joe,' she stuttered as she escaped upstairs for a while to calm herself. She did not want to let her mama down but she wished that they would all go home now. The doctor, sensing her need, decided that it was time to take their leave. Jane followed Harriet upstairs while Mary and David said their goodbyes. She spent a few minutes with Harriet comforting her friend. They came back down together, Harriet determined to support her mama and yet relieved that everyone was leaving at last. As if on cue, the other mourners began to disperse, saying a quiet word to Annie as they left. Beth was the last to go and although she offered to stay to help, Annie ushered her away to return to her husband's side.

When they were on their own at last Harriet hugged her mama and they sat down exhausted, staring into the fire with their private thoughts of the man they both loved so much.

Over the next couple of weeks Annie and Harriet frequently returned to their cottage to sort out their belongings but neither wished to stay there but they would go in to see Beth and Joseph for a cup of tea. Joseph's recovery was a slow one and he was emotionally drained by the loss of his best friend. Occasionally when their visits were in the evening cousin Joe would join them. Harriet found this very strange. The cousins were alike in so many ways that it was uncanny at times. Each visit Harriet would hope that Beth would have word from Edward and Beth would wish the same of Harriet. On the Wednesday and Saturday morning Harriet arose early to watch the *Courier* dock from her upstairs window. She walked up to the Butes where she could watch the passengers disembark. When the last passenger had left the ship and people began to alight for the return journey Harriet turned away, cold and disappointed. It was on that Saturday morning that cousin Joe was also walking past on his way back from taking a letter to the postmaster in order to catch the *Courier*. Harriet had given up writing by then. She reasoned that either Edward was on his way back to her or that he had already begun his adventure to travel the world. In her heart she believed the latter although she tried not to lose hope completely.

As Joe watched, Harriet turned to make her way to the schoolhouse.

'Good day to you Harriet,' said Joe. 'How are you?'

'As well as I can be,' replied Harriet as cheerfully as she could.

'May I walk with you to the school Harriet?' asked Joe.

'I do not believe I will be very good company, Joe,' replied Harriet.

Hoping to put Harriet at her ease Joe began to talk. 'I'll be starting work on Monday.' Seeing the fearful expression appear on Harriet's face he quickly added, 'No, Harriet. I know what you're thinking. I'm not going to work at the quarry. A man I spoke to at New Year is taking me on as an apprentice painter.'

Harriet looked visibly relieved at this.

'Will you be staying on the island for long Joe?' she asked.

'At least as long as it takes for my uncle to get back on his feet,' Joe replied. 'After that I am sure that this training will give me plenty of work on Sarnia. There are so many military establishments and forts being built over there too.'

'So you won't be painting people's homes?' Harriet asked.

'Oh no, Harriet. I'll be doing the elaborate work, the gold leaf ceilings and decorative finishes and so on. We have to travel over to France now and again for the special pigment to be used,' Joe explained proudly.

'You'll cope with the trip by sea,' teased Harriet, reminding Joe of his lack of sea legs.

'It's not so far, Harriet,' replied Joe, showing his embarrassment at his failure to enjoy the sea.

Sorry to have hurt his feelings Harriet quickly added, 'I'm sure that Aunt Beth and Uncle Joseph are very glad to have your company.' Harriet called them aunt and uncle even though they were not related.

'Would you be glad to have my company too do you think?' asked Joe, without thinking of the consequences of his question.

It was Harriet who was embarrassed and lost for words this time, though she was relieved that they had arrived at the school gates and she could say goodbye without answering.

'Goodbye Joe. I'm glad to hear about your job,' she said and soon had disappeared from view.

Joe turned a little red in the face. He had been pleased to have their first real conversation since his return to the island but was mortified that he had made Harriet feel uncomfortable. He decided to go for a long walk before returning to Platte Saline.

Chapter 25

EDWARD'S JOURNEY TO England had gone smoothly. He had spent only a few hours with Cousin Joe on Sarnia before catching the mail steamer to England. Joe had talked about his plans to return to Riduna and told Edward all about the opportunity of work that he had been offered in the New Year. Although Edward was pleased that his parents would have his cousin's support, and of course he was unaware at that time as to how much this would be needed, Edward felt uneasy about something. He still did not have the courage to confide in Joe about Harriet and was tempted to unburden Harriet's fears that she could be with child.

Time passed all too quickly and before he knew it he was a passenger on the steamer dreaming of the adventures ahead of him rather than what he had left behind. It was strange to be a passenger rather than one of the crew and he felt very much alone. He aimed to spend a couple of weeks in Southampton, sorting out his work papers and so on and signing up for work with The Royal Mail Company initially on the *Trent* when she came into dock. The ship would take him from Southampton to the West Indies. He had also heard that he could then sign up for steamers travelling between New York, Rio de

Janeiro and the West Indies. He could see the map he was shown at school in his mind's eye and it made him shiver with excitement.

Edward saw Bill on deck and arranged to meet him for a drink on the evening after they had arrived in Southampton. He tried not to worry about Harriet. Unfortunately the fear of having to return home immediately slightly dampened his excitement. However much he thought he loved Harriet he had little desire to settle down and start a family so soon. A fleeting thought of Marie flashed into his mind and he tried to dismiss it. He was determined to remain true to Harriet from now onwards.

That night he and Bill drank together in the Grapes Tavern until late in the night. Bill tried to persuade Edward to return to the alehouse of ill repute but Edward felt very virtuous returning to the Mission on his own. He was a little envious of Bill in that he had found his own lodgings and Edward vowed that one day he would have lodgings of his own, when Harriet could come and join him. Edward was resolute that he would keep Harriet's memory precious and he spent a while writing to her. He would send the letter as soon as he had word from her.

The days passed until finally the long awaited letter from Harriet arrived. Edward ripped it open and shouted for joy when he read it. He kissed the letter and then looked around him, glad that there were only a couple of strangers in the dormitory looking at him with some amusement. He lay back down on his bunk to complete his letter to Harriet.

My dearest Harriet,

I arrived in Southampton this evening and have just

returned to the Mission after having a drink with Bill. You are never far from my thoughts and I miss you already. A year will go quickly my love and then I promise that we will be together.

It's lonely here without Joe and now that Bill has sailed back to Sarnia I have to keep my own company. I have plenty to keep me occupied and when I am not busy I am thinking of you.

I have just received your letter and I jumped for joy at the news that I have not caused you the pain that we feared. It is not that I would not have loved to see you bearing our child but that I would never wish you to suffer any shame on my behalf. One day we shall have lots of children together. I hope that you are not offended by me talking in this way.

I wish to thank you from the depths of my heart because I realise that you are showing me a great amount of love by letting me go to follow my dreams for a while. I assure you that this selfless act only deepens my love for you.

In a year's time, God willing, I shall return to Riduna to claim you as my wife. I hope that the thought of this will keep you happy when you are lonely. I will have such adventures to share with you all and stories to tell our sons and daughters.

Lovingly yours
Edward

Once he had finished Edward needed a drink. All being well he would be sailing in two days' time. He would try to send letters home at each port of call but knew that it would be unlikely that he would hear from Harriet again until his return to Southampton. He went to the nearest tavern and sat on his own downing a few pints. He felt lonely without Joe or Bill for company and although he recognised a few men in the bar he had little desire to make conversation with them. He returned to his bunk a little worse for drink that night and had a fitful night dreaming.

His first dream took him back to Riduna. He could see Harriet waiting for him on the quayside waving to him. As he rushed into her arms he kissed her passionately, oblivious to the whistles from the men still on board and the tutting from the islanders standing on the quay. He picked her up to swing her round in joy, as he had done when she was a child but as he did so she seemed to vanish into thin air. He restlessly turned over and in his dream he was transported to Southampton. He was walking the streets, lost in a world of his own but every corner he turned he saw the familiar sight of the alehouse ahead of him. He tried to retrace his steps and return to the Mission but again he was faced with the same place, drawing him to it. He made one last attempt to find his way back to the docks when he met some familiar sailors. They persuaded him to join them for a drink and he was not in the least bit surprised when they took him back to the same tavern. He stood there at the door and watched the men walk in ahead of him. Then the door was closed in his face. He knew he had a choice but was unable to make that choice. After what seemed like an hour of standing at the door he was suddenly pushed from behind and ushered inside.

Edward woke up suddenly.

'Sorry mate,' apologised the chap from the top bunk who had slipped down on to the floor and accidentally knocked his arm and shoulder. 'I'm off early this morning. I'll leave you in peace.'

Edward tried to get back to sleep but although it was still dark, sleep eluded him. The memory of his dreams was still hovering in his state of consciousness and he tossed restlessly until he could stand it no more and he got up and tidied up his things. He wandered down to the dockside and watched the hustle and bustle of harbour life. The *Trent* was already docked and in the early light of day was beginning to unload its cargo. He would be embarking in twenty-four hours to make the ship ready for a lunchtime sailing. He watched the activity for a while before finding a café for breakfast. After the drinking of the night before he was surprised how hungry he was.

Edward's last day in Southampton seemed endless. He ambled about lost in thought in a more dreamlike state than his dreams. By evening he could stand it no longer. He decided that he would just call in to see Marie for some company. Surely there was no harm in buying the lass a drink and having a quiet talk before returning to the Mission for his final night on land for many weeks. Marie's eyes lit up as soon as she saw him walk through that all too familiar door. Her welcoming smile quickly overcame any nagging doubt or guilt he might have felt. With only a short pause at the bar to order a couple of drinks he followed her up the winding staircase. He was soon spending his last few moments ashore in the most pleasurable way with such lovely company so that, when he returned to the Mission that night, he slept soundly like a contented baby with a smile on its face.

Edward arose early the following morning and packed up his things. He was restless to be away now. He checked out of the Mission and wandered down to the dockside. As day broke he watched the mail steamer from Sarnia slip into port. He could see some familiar faces at work on deck and he waved at them. He watched the mail boy pull the trolley off the ship. Since he had both a letter of best wishes from his parents and a final letter from Harriet in his pocket, it did not cross his mind that the trolley might contain a letter for him. In fact, within an hour of his departure both letters arrived at the Mission and there they remained in the pigeonhole gathering dust until his return a year later.

Soon Edward was on board the *Trent*. He had little time to think of all he was leaving behind. It was not long before he glanced up from his work just in time to see the Isle of Wight disappear into the horizon. He took a deep breath. It was a cold and windy morning, but the waves and the rolling ship only added to his excitement. Suddenly he was filled with such a sense of peace that he knew he had found where he truly belonged.

Chapter 26

IT WAS THE following Wednesday that Harriet finally received word from Edward and his letter gave her some comfort. She thought lovingly of him and a wave of warm feelings swept over her. Harriet was lying on her bed in the small room she shared with her mama. Annie was resting in that half sleep which gave some rest but little consolation. Not wishing to disturb her and yet suddenly feeling claustrophobic, Harriet crept quietly into their second room. It was a cupboard of a place, which they had tried to make comfortable with a couple of armchairs beside the fireplace and a table by the window on which stood a lamp. There was hardly room for anything more and Harriet suddenly longed for the familiar sight of the range and large table in their cottage at Platte Saline. The fire was unlit. Annie and Harriet made a habit of retiring straight to their bedroom after supper, which they ate in the inn's large kitchen downstairs with her grandparents. It was cold and dark, despite the candle Harriet held in her hand.

She did not pause to sit down but blew out her candle, reached for her coat and crept down the back staircase and out into the night. With her grandparents busy and her mama asleep she thought wistfully of her papa. He would either have forbidden such stupidity or accompanied her on her walk, their arms linked as they strolled, talking and laughing as they went. Harriet desperately needed some space. The inn was strictly off limits to Harriet during opening hours so she strode boldly out into the lane and down towards Braye Bay. Although she was a little nervous at first, Harriet soon relaxed at the sight of the bay. It was a calm night and the sight of the inky sea, dappled in the moonlight, gave Harriet a rare moment of peace.

After the first occasion, Harriet looked forward to this moment of the day when she escaped for a while to be alone. On windy nights she would stand, holding her coat tightly around her, with her face into the wind and stare at the ocean. She would listen to the sound of the waves crashing over the breakwater in the distance. On the evenings when it was too wet to venture out Harriet was very restless. Those evenings seemed endless as she listened to her mama breathing quietly as she bent over her mending in the candlelight.

The first person she encountered on one of her nightly walks was Charlotte, who was out visiting her gran. Charlotte often paused to look over the bay before walking along the lane to her gran's cottage. It was on one of these occasions that she noticed the silhouette of Harriet half way along the bay. At first she was uncertain whether to approach her old friend but after watching Harriet for a few moments she walked towards her, calling her name softly. Harriet turned and at the sight of Charlotte she rushed to embrace her friend. Charlotte was so surprised by this spontaneous act of affection that she suggested Harriet walk with her. Since Charlotte came down to check up on her gran two evenings a week, they began to meet like this on a regular basis. Her gran had a cosy little room with a roaring fire and they would sit and talk for a while.

Sometimes, if it was one of those rare still nights, they would walk along the shore, sharing confidences that they could not mention in the presence of Gran and gradually a bridge of affection was rebuilt between them.

It was on one such occasion that Charlotte confided in Harriet about her feelings for John. Since the New Year's dance her feelings for him had changed.

'I don't wish to make a fool of myself again,' Charlotte explained, not daring to mention the fiasco with the letters for fear of ruining their rekindled friendship.

'Has he given you any indication that he has feelings for you too?' Harriet asked.

'I'm not sure,' Charlotte mused. 'Whenever I see him I am also with Michael, so it's difficult.'

'I'm sure that if you're patient something will happen, if it's meant to be,' reasoned Harriet.

'What will I do if he meets someone else on this foolish trip to Sarnia next month,' Charlotte agonised.

'Could you write him a note?' suggested Harriet.

'Letters get you into all sorts of trouble,' said Charlotte wryly. 'Anyway, what would I say?'

'Couldn't you tell him how you feel? After all we've all been friends for years,' continued Harriet.

'I'm not sure but what am I going to do Harriet?' Charlotte pleaded.

'We'll think of something,' Harriet assured Charlotte with a conviction that she did not feel. She did not have the slightest idea as to how they would go about it but she was nonetheless relieved that Charlotte's attentions had been completely diverted away from Edward. She could not help but wonder about the fickle nature of the human heart and with that thought her peace about Edward was unsettled a little more.

As Harriet walked each night she was totally unaware

that another friend was watching her. One evening as Joe was nearing the Braye Tavern for a drink he noticed her shadow creep out of the back of the building. On that occasion he hid himself in the porch unnoticed and watched Harriet as she walked along the lane. He was unable to call her name for fear of compromising her position but as she veered off on the path towards the shore he followed her at a distance. He watched her from the shadow of the cottage wall, longing to reach out to her and hold her tightly on her lonely vigil. On the nights when he noticed Charlotte appear he returned to have his drink before walking on back to Beth and Joseph's cottage but on the nights when Harriet remained alone, he stood watching her from afar. He took on the role of her Guardian Angel, knowing how protective her father would have been or Edward for that matter, if either had been there. Thinking of Edward made Joe jealous. He thought of the way in which they had grown up so closely together and wished that it had been him. It was not the first time that he wondered how close his cousin really was to this beautiful girl he was beginning to idolise. He dismissed any feelings of betrayal of his cousin by reasoning that, if Edward really cared for the girl, he should not have left her for so long.

Joe wondered if he should mention Harriet's nightly strolls to her grandparents but thought better of it. Surely one night he would have the courage or reason to approach her and that thought led him to dream of the future when he hoped she might look upon him with greater favour. He was also aware of Harriet's need for solitude and so he left her undisturbed. On the nights that she remained alone he waited until he knew that she was safely back inside the inn, before entering for a quick drink.

Young Joe had settled well into his life on the island. It had been a month now and he was pleased to be giving his uncle and aunt moral and financial support as well as keeping an eye on Harriet. On returning from the inn his uncle was usually in the mood for conversation.

'I wondered where you'd got to,' Joseph exclaimed one night as his nephew walked in, shutting out the cold and windy night.

'Come and sit by me and tell this old islander about Southampton, women and song eh,' said Joseph as he grinned at young Joe.

'Nothing unseemly mind,' scolded Beth. 'I don't believe that a decent lad like you could get up to anything untoward!'

'Get on with your chores woman, stop nagging and leave us to men's talk!' exclaimed Joseph teasingly as a small dry crust of bread was hurled across the room at him as Beth cleared the table. Joseph caught it and threw it playfully at Joe, who head-butted it back on to the table.

'You'll have to join the island football team,' chuckled Beth as she finished her task. She was glad to see her husband cheerful for a while despite his injuries.

'I'll leave you both in peace and retire early if you don't mind. I don't wish to hear any men's talk!'

She kissed her husband gently on the forehead and rearranged the pillows on his makeshift downstairs bed.

'I'll come down later, just before I go to sleep,' she said tenderly looking into her husband's eyes.

'No dirty talk under my roof do you hear. This isn't an inn!' she called down over her shoulder as she made her way up the stairs.

Beth knew that Joseph needed time to be a man. He missed his work, going out for a drink or two and conversation. Above all he missed his best friend Jack. She listened to the eerie quiet next door. All she could hear was the rumble of deep voices and occasional laughter from downstairs as Joe recounted tales of how he was not a good sailor and eventually confided in his uncle about the goings on in the Grapes Tavern.

It was the silence from next door that Beth found so deafeningly disturbing. She saw so little of Annie these days. Joseph took up virtually all of her waking hours and at first she was reluctant to leave him for more than a few moments. Even now, if she left him for more than an hour she would return to find him melancholy. Annie, on the other hand, having cleared out the little cottage as best as she could under the circumstances, rarely visited. Beth knew that she found it difficult. Just passing the cottage next door was a painful experience for all of them, especially for Annie. Jack was her rock over the years. God knows how she will cope without him, she mused.

Beth was so glad to have Joe staying with them for a few months. It helped to take the edge off the emptiness they felt and enabled them to have the occasional cheerful moment, despite missing Edward terribly and coping with the aftermath of the accident. She, too, had virtually given up hope of Edward returning soon. Beth was relieved that Joe had chosen not to work in the quarry in the circumstance. She was pleased that he was being trained in a skilled craft, which should be useful in the future but for now Joe was a godsend.

As she sat doing some mending by candlelight she resolved to visit Annie in the morning. She smiled as she heard yet more laughter from downstairs and then she paused as she listened to the sound of Joe making his way up to Edward's room. Beth went down once more to check that her husband was as comfortable as possible. She cleared away the two glasses and the half-empty bottle.

'Goodnight Joseph,' she said quietly since her husband's eyes were closed.

'Goodnight Beth my love,' she heard him whisper.

Joe had banked the fire for the night so she blew out the lamp and carefully carrying her candle before her, she returned to the bedroom to settle down to sleep.

Chapter 27

LIFE IN JANE'S household had changed completely since the wedding. Jane found herself increasingly alone and at a loose end. She no longer worked for her father, Mary having taken over the role of organising the surgery. The mood at home remained peaceful, despite the ebb and flow of patients and their needs and the occasional crisis. Jane had taken to help at the school, especially when Harriet stayed at home with her mother. Although this helped to pass the time of day, her heart wasn't in it. She was beginning to feel that it was time she moved on with her life and return to England to study for nursing.

Jane was pleased that her father and Mary were happy although their contentment made Jane more than a little jealous at times. She had a good relationship with Mary but she just did not feel needed anymore. Jane thought of Thomas. She remembered the last time that they had met before he had left for England last autumn. Thomas had finally got Jane to agree to meet on their own, assuring her that his motives were honourable but that he wanted to say goodbye. Jane had agreed to meet him near Fort Tourgis at the end of Platte Saline where they had first met. In fact Jane had an errand to deliver some more medicine to the old lady who lived further along the bay.

Thomas stood there waiting for her as she retraced her steps along the lonely lane from the old lady's isolated cottage. The sight of his smile dispelled any doubts she might have had at meeting him. He bowed, taking her hand to kiss it as they met. It seemed a little formal after their passion on the beach but Jane was relieved that Thomas was treating her with more respect. They walked along the track towards Fort Clonque, where the steep slopes of tangled undergrowth, occasionally broken by the hint of a narrow footpath, gave them some protection from the cold wind. It was a grey day and the sea looked angry as it crashed on the shore. Occasionally members from the military passed by, who bowed to Jane and a couple winked knowingly at Thomas as they returned from duty. Jane appreciated the character of these majestic buildings especially Fort Cloque, which towered at the end of the sweeping causeway ahead of them.

Thomas had talked about his impending return to England and his ambitions to rise in the ranks of military service. Although Jane admired him for this she could not help but fear its consequences and shivered as she imagined the possible conflicts that he might participate in. It was all very well serving in this quiet backwater. After all, although the island had been given the name of 'The Gibraltar of the English Channel', so far the defences had not been put to the test.

'I'm so glad that you agreed to see me Jane and that you trusted me today,' Thomas paused for a moment to look at her and then continued, 'I'm going to miss you.'

Jane wanted to reply that she would miss him too but took care to give a noncommittal response.

'I've enjoyed getting to know you too,' she replied at last, creating a tension between them of unspoken silences.

Thomas struggled to continue, never having been in a position before when he cared about what he said to a girl. 'I really feel that I have met someone very special on this island. She has made my stay here memorable. The only difficulty is that I don't think I will ever have the chance to return.'

'Who is that pray?' teased Jane, trying to ease the friction in the air and ignore the implications of his statement.

'Well, she's very beautiful and has a heart of gold. Mind you she's also very intelligent. Makes a man a bit fearful, don't you think?' replied Thomas warming to Jane's more light-hearted mood.

'I'm jealous,' retorted Jane and she darted to her left up a barely visible pathway that the islanders fondly called The Zigzag.

'Just you wait young lady,' called Thomas as he bounded after her.

Jane was a quick runner and was also more familiar with the path where they had often played as children. She scrambled above him and just as he was about to catch up the path veered to the left and she darted out of reach. They were nearing the next bend when Thomas caught up with her. He caught her trailing hand and pulled her towards him. Even then, though his instinct was to quieten her laughter with a kiss, he resisted the temptation and just held her close to him for a while, burying his face in her lovely hair.

'I may be coming to England in the next few months,' confided Jane bravely. 'I've not talked about it with my father as yet, but there's a possibility that I will be leaving Riduna soon.'

'I thought you loved this island,' exclaimed Thomas, not hiding his pleasure at the news or his surprise as he put her at arms' length so that he could see her face.

'I do love it here and it has been a wonderful place to grow up.'

'Your father will miss you!'

'Of course he'll miss me and I'll miss him but, now that he is going to be married again, I expect he'll not need me quite as much as he did,' explained Jane. 'Not only that but I need to find my own way in life.'

Jane refrained from explaining about her desire to become a nurse. If she had to make a choice she did not want to make it too soon.

'I don't wish you to flatter yourself that I am following you back to England, Thomas,' Jane said quietly as they continued to walk up the path, Jane following Thomas this time through the narrow cutting.

Thomas stopped again and faced her. He looked into her eyes and held both of her hands saying gently, 'Jane, don't make any decision hastily. Wait to see what it's like when your father is married. Talk with him about your thoughts. It is a big decision to make. Then, if you do decide it's right, have you decided where you will live?'

'With my brother's family in London,' Jane replied finding it difficult to hide the regret in her voice that Thomas didn't seem enthusiastic about her possible plans.

Realising the reason for the hesitancy in Jane's voice Thomas assured her, 'I'd love you to come to England, Jane. I just don't wish you to come for the wrong reason but will you write to me and tell me what you decide?'

'Will you write to me?' asked Jane, aware that the tension was returning to their conversation and longing to think of the right words to dispel it once more.

Thomas was reluctant to say the words that he felt Jane wanted so much to hear. He had never felt so moved by a girl before but there seemed so many obstacles in their path for them to see a future together. He was practised at the 'love you and leave you' type of relationship and was aware that he had already broken more than one heart in his short time in the forces. He felt that these feelings were different but how could he be sure that he would feel the same once he was back in England away from the Riduna magic. He stood looking out towards the sea while he was pondering his dilemma, but when he turned back to Jane he felt a sudden pain as he was aware that tears were silently falling down her cheeks. They were dignified tears, which only moved him to love Jane all the more. He took a handkerchief and gently wiped her cheeks.

'If I come to England will you still wish to be my friend,' asked Jane quietly.

Thomas could bear it no longer. He pulled Jane to him and lifted her chin so that she looked into his eyes. They stood there in silence for a few moments. It took all the will power he could muster to avoid their lips meeting once more and his actions helped to dispel Jane's inner fears.

She smiled. 'I must be getting back no.'

'Will I see you at the quay in the morning?' Thomas asked.

'Yes, of course,' replied Jane.

And so, on the following morning, almost before daylight, Jane stood on the quayside with several of the island girls to watch the men board the Courier at the end of their time on Riduna. Thomas turned to wave as he walked on to the ship. Within minutes he was ushered below deck by his captain and Jane saw him no more. She waited for a while to watch the ship sail out of the harbour but before it had reached the end of the breakwater she turned and walked quickly up the slopes towards the town. She reached the Butes just in time to see the Courier disappear from view.

Jane had received two letters from Thomas since he left in November, one at Christmas and another in January. In reply she wrote to tell him about the festivities on the island and the wedding followed by the New Year's ball. She was pleased that Thomas had been unable to hide an element of jealousy that she had danced with several men that night. Jane also described the horrific accident that had shaken the island to its core and she wept as she reread her words before sealing the envelope. She wrote a little of her loneliness in the evenings and the dreary winter days and he had responded with regret that he was not able to be with her and assured her that it was no less dreary in England.

By March, when spring flowers were beginning to show, she had almost made her decision. The only thing holding her back now was fear of talking to her father and Harriet. Her friend seemed to be a little less melancholy of late and spent a lot of time with Charlotte these days. Jane's greatest uncertainty was doubt about where her future lay. If she began her nursing training in earnest then there would be little room for Thomas in her future. Could she imagine the single life of a nurse, however interested she was in medicine and dedicated she might be? Her father would be angry with her if she began training and opted out half way through. There again, if she did not give the excuse of training in order for her father to agree to her returning to England then how would she ever find out if Thomas's affections were truly genuine? 'Was she being deceitful?' she wondered. She longed to have the chance to talk it over with Harriet and yet she dreaded that conversation almost as much as the one with her father. It was the last letter from Thomas that she now held in her hand that finally gave her the resolve to face the issue.

Dear Jane,

I still miss you and I can't believe that it's nearly four months since we parted. Unlike you, I had a very quiet Christmas with my parents and by New Year I was working again. Since leaving I have dared not ask you if you have come to a decision as yet and I am also reluctant to sway you by my words. Nevertheless I want you to know that I miss you.

You are rarely far from my thoughts during the day and sometimes I even dream of the moment I see you again. So you see Jane I can't even escape when I am asleep and I often wonder if you feel the same. I have thought of quitting at the end of my first term and returning to see you on Riduna, but I know in my heart that I could never settle to the quiet life on the island, however beautiful. I could never make you happy there. I am also sure though, come what may, my future lies in the forces.

I hope that I have not said too much and want to reassure you that whatever you decide, I will remain your friend.

Yours with affection
Thomas

Jane decided to talk to her father at the first possible opportunity. This presented itself that very evening when she was sitting with David and Mary by the fire. Her father was in his favourite armchair reading and Mary was sat beside him sewing. He was happy to be with the two most important women in his life and was unprepared for the conversation that followed.

'Father, I have been thinking about my future,' Jane ventured tentatively.

Alert now and looking quizzically at his daughter David suddenly was aware as to how selfish he had been not to concern himself with the feelings of his daughter. Since she seemed to have a good relationship with Mary he had thought no more about it.

'Yes my dear, and what have you been worrying your pretty head about,' he said, trying to keep the tone of his voice light but fearful that it was sounding patronising none the less.

'I'm considering returning to England,' replied Jane before she lost her confidence.

'I think that I would like to train to be a nurse Father, but I would like to spend a few months in England before making the final decision.'

David was not as slow at understanding the situation as Jane might have thought but he did not want to embarrass her. He knew that Jane had received a letter from Thomas that morning and was convinced that this letter was the driving force behind Jane's suggestion.

'Though I enjoy it here on Riduna, and I love being here with you and of course Mary,' she added smiling at Mary, 'but I feel that I need more of a purpose in my life.'

'Have you spoken to Harriet about this?' asked the doctor, wondering how her friend would cope with losing Jane's support.

'No Father. I felt that it was only right to speak with you first. Of course I would miss Harriet terribly. It would be like losing my left hand, but I will be no company for her if I am restless and unhappy.

'Time is ticking away, of course,' reasoned her father. 'If you are serious about nursing, the sooner you start the better. Leave it to me to make some enquiries Jane and meantime, I think you should have a long talk with Harriet. Perhaps in discussing it with her you'll be able to be honest with yourself about what you really want.'

'Do you mean to say that you are willing to let me go?' asked Jane tentatively.

'Jane, my dear, you are my only daughter and you know that I love to have you with me and there will always be a home here for you when you need it.' He smiled over to Mary again who nodded encouragingly; not feeling that it was her place to enter into the discussion.

'If your heart is set on leaving then, although we will miss you, we will send you with our blessing.' The doctor looked directly at his daughter when he added, 'Now that we can trust you to be sensible.'

Jane blushed and thanked him with a kiss on his forehead. She was about to retire to her room when Mary unexpectedly added, 'I think your father has some more news for you before you go.'

David looked surprised at first and then grinned up at his daughter and said, 'Oh yes. You will be having a baby brother or sister in the not too distant future my dear.'

Not knowing quite how to take the news, Jane responded with as much enthusiasm as she could muster, 'That's lovely news. Congratulations to you both!' With that she gave both Mary and her father a kiss on the cheek and left for the comfort and quiet of her own room where she was able to think.

Chapter 28

JOE HAD BEEN living on the island for nearly three months, continuing to take his nightly amble along to the Braye Tavern, an excuse for his real mission to keep a close eye on Harriet. Soon he would not have the protection of darkness to keep him hidden on his nightly vigil. One Friday evening in early March, when there was still a soft warm glimmer in the distance which lit the harbour and bay eerily in its wake, he watched Harriet on her lonely walk above the bay. The contrast of the starry deep blue-sky overhead and the faint glowing horizon gave the evening a romantic aura. Joe wished he had the courage to approach Harriet and offer to walk with her.

As he stood watching under the shadow of the cottage eaves at the end of the footpath he noticed that Harriet was walking further than her normal stroll. In fact she was nearing the quayside end of Braye Bay, almost out of sight. Joe was undecided. On the one hand he could try to close the space between them by walking back up the path to the lane and around to the harbour road. That way he would lose sight of her altogether for at least five minutes even at his fastest sprint. On the other hand he could follow Harriet along the grassy banks above the bay, by which time she would undoubtedly have spotted him. Relieved that Harriet had finally paused for thought at the cutting down to the bay, he held his breath as she stood gazing out to sea. In the next moment two figures appeared, walking along from the harbour. Although Joe was only guessing they appeared to be from the military, but they were too far away for him to be sure. In the dim light they seemed to hesitate on catching sight of Harriet and changed their course slightly to make their way towards her, unbeknown to Harriet since she had her back to them. They paused to talk to her. At first she seemed not unwilling to talk with them, which irritated Joe immensely, but then she appeared to be attempting to walk away. The men had effectively barred her escape route back up the cutting and so Harriet walked away from them down on to the beach. Though this would lead her back in Joe's direction there was no other obvious path down to the beach along that stretch and he knew that she would soon disappear from view behind the grassy slopes. The men appeared to laugh and after a moment's hesitation they looked quickly around them and followed her.

Joe waited no longer. He rushed along towards the cutting, anger mounting inside him, overshadowing any underlying fear. As he ran he saw that one of the men had already reached Harriet and had grabbed her arm. The other man took hold of her waist and was pushing her to the ground. Fortunately both had their backs to Joe and were so engrossed in their actions that neither noticed Joe approaching. He heard a ripping sound as he reached the man who stood leering over the writhing couple. Simultaneously he grabbed hold of the man's arm, turning him and landing a powerful punch on his chin. Catching the man unawares he kicked him leaving the man winded and bent over in agony.

Having effectively disarmed one target Joe wasted no

time. He grabbed the other man by the hair and dragged him away from the sobbing Harriet. One punch left him doubled up groaning on the sand. He took Harriet's hand pulling her to her feet and without looking back he ran along the shore, Harriet stumbling behind him, to the relative safety of the grassy slopes above. Joe did not pause to rest until they had reached the path by the cottages. Once sheltered under their familiar eaves he stopped for Harriet to catch her breath and was surprised that she fell sobbing into his willing arms. They stood there for many moments and despite the fearful event that Joe had just prevented, he could not help but treasure this moment. Up until then he had only experienced Harriet in his arms in his favourite dreams, so unlike the present nightmare.

It was a while before Harriet's body stopped shaking and the breathless sobs ceased. Joe reluctantly put Harriet at arm's length so that he could look into her face and talk with her. The light of the moon caught Harriet's tearful features, but it was the silver locket, which caught Joe's eye first. He recognised it instantly and the sight of it saddened him and simultaneously filled him with anger. Surely if his cousin had true feelings for this lovely girl he would not be so selfish as to leave her for so long. Now was not the moment to ponder on this matter and so Joe snapped his attention away from the locket and his disturbing thoughts and back to the present.

'Let's get you home,' he said firmly. He did not wait for a reply but wrapped Harriet's cloak firmly back around her shivering body and gently taking her hand he led her back along the dark path towards her grandparents' inn. As they reached the lane both hesitated at first, fearing that the men may have found their way to the inn via the lanes. Fortunately all was clear but before Joe allowed Harriet to emerge from the shadows to leave him he paused. He looked down at Harriet, who was obviously still badly shaken by her ordeal.

'I will tell no-one of tonight if you wish it that way Harriet,' he promised. 'I don't feel that complaining to the authorities will be in your best interests. I believe that it would only tarnish your reputation.'

Harriet nodded silently.

'Nevertheless you must promise me that you'll never be so foolish again, Harriet,' said Joe as he lifted her chin up so that she looked into his eyes and not down at her hands.

'Oh Joe,' she whispered, 'how can I ever thank you for what you did tonight?'

'Only by never walking alone at night again but go inside now,' Joe added firmly. 'I'll call on you tomorrow if I may.'

Harriet just nodded her head before stepping out into the lane. She crossed it quickly and, only looking over her shoulder once more, she entered the back door of the inn. She could just make out the shadowy figure of Joe, virtually hidden from view as she crept inside. Joe waited until he was sure that she was safely inside and straightened his clothes before emerging and making his way into the inn where he ordered a welcome drink.

Harriet closed the door behind her and stood for a while feeling the protection of the solid door against her back. She took a deep breath and shuddered once more. There was no point in thinking 'What if?' She had not recognised the men. They were probably from the new platoon of militia, stationed on the island as a replacement for the men who returned to England last autumn including Thomas and Frederick. All Harriet knew was that she never wanted to set eyes on them again, possibly a tall order for life on a small island. How stupid she had been!

Her mama calling out to her brought her to her senses. Usually she returned from her walk long before her mama stirred from her rest after supper. Harriet called out reassuringly that she would be up in a moment as she quietly climbed the short flight of stairs to their rooms. How could she hide her ripped dress from her mama since they shared the same bedroom? She went into the spare room to take off her coat. She tidied her hair and smoothed down her dress. Fortunately it was no more than a small tear in the trim around her skirt which had caught under the man's shoe as he had pushed Harriet to the sand. She found a pin out of their sewing box and pinned it up carefully, hoping that her mama would not notice in the evening light. If she did, Harriet decided that she would claim that it had caught on a thorn bush earlier in the day.

'How are you feeling Mama,' she asked in as normal voice as she could muster as she walked into their bedroom.

'I was worried about you,' exclaimed Annie. 'Where have you been?'

Not wanting to lie Harriet replied truthfully, 'I've just been out for some fresh air.'

'Oh Harriet, you foolish girl! Whatever would your papa have said,' Annie scolded.

Harriet was tempted to say crossly, 'but he's not here is he!' but she controlled her temper and explained quietly, 'I know it was silly but I felt so claustrophobic up in this little room. I needed space to think.'

'Well Harriet, I forbid you to go out again at night-time on your own. You're lucky nothing unfortunate happened.'

'Yes Mama,' Harriet answered flatly. 'I'm quite tired tonight though. I think I will get ready for bed and read for a while before going to sleep.' With that she turned her back on her mama and changed into her nightgown. It was such a relief to slip under the cosy inviting bedclothes and Harriet was soon drifting into a fitful sleep, her book falling to the floor. Annie sat up in bed, for a while puzzled by Harriet's strange behaviour. She longed to have Jack by her side to talk and to share the responsibility. She resolved to discuss it with her own parents when the moment presented itself. It was not long before she felt ready to sleep again. She got up to blow out the candle, pausing to retrieve Harriet's book from the floor as she went. She looked down at her daughter for a few moments. Something was troubling her, that Annie was sure. She resolved to watch Harriet more carefully in the weeks ahead. She had been so wrapped up in her own grief that she had not noticed the pain that Harriet was going through. Thus Annie returned to bed with a heavy heart.

The following morning Harriet had a chill and Annie let her remain in bed until late. She walked up to pick up some bread from the bakery.

'G'morning Mrs Loveridge. Where's Harriet today?' asked Charlotte cheerfully as she served Annie.

'She went out for a walk last night and caught a chill,' replied Annie.

'Do you think she will be recovered by this evening?' asked Charlotte, not realising that Mrs Loveridge knew nothing of her regular meetings with Harriet.

'What do you mean?' asked Annie puzzled.

'We usually meet up to visit my grandma's,' replied Charlotte.

'We'll just have to see,' replied Annie as she bade a hasty farewell.

As Annie walked home she wondered crossly what her daughter was really up to in the evenings without her mama's knowledge. Harriet was up and dressed by the time she reached the place that they had made their home. Fortunately she had just finished mending her dress, which she quickly hung up as her mama entered the room.

'Sit down Mama and I'll go down and make us a cup of tea,' suggested Harriet as her mama walked in.

'No Harriet!' exclaimed her mama. 'Sit down this minute. We need to have a serious talk.'

Annie sat down in the chair opposite Harriet, a little breathless since she was not used to exerting herself so much in the mornings and certainly not accustomed to being so angry.

'I've just been talking to your friend Charlotte. It's not that I mind you visiting her grandma with her. What I do mind is the lies Harriet,' Annie said firmly but calmly now. 'How often do you go out without my knowledge?' she added.

'Every night,' Harriet replied quietly. 'I go for a walk when you are resting.'

'Never again,' Annie replied crossly. 'How could you be so deceitful? I am so disappointed in you.'

'I'm so sorry Mama,' replied Harriet quietly. 'Please calm down. I will never do it again. Please don't worry about that.'

Thinking that it was Annie's own cross words that had knocked some sense in her daughter she began to calm down a little.

'You can get that tea now,' she said more softly. 'In fact we will go downstairs together to have some breakfast since you seem to be better now.'

As they walked downstairs together Harriet shuddered to think how her mama would have reacted if she had known the whole truth about last night. She had never seen her mama so angry. Joe was right in suggesting that they tell no one of the ordeal though she did not think that she could keep the secret from Jane. She held no secrets from her best friend.

As she sat in the huge kitchen downstairs listening to her mama and grandma talk, Harriet was overwhelmed by a sense of unworldliness. She thought of Edward. 'If Edward had been here it would never have happened,' she thought. Then if Edward had been here more would have happened, of that Harriet was certain. She was aware of her face colouring at the thought of the romantic interludes with Edward that might have been. Harriet did not notice her mama making sidelong glances her way. She just stood up and making some weak excuse she escaped back up to their rooms. Fortunately there was a direct door from the kitchen so that she did not have to venture outside. Once she had left, Annie confided in her mother of her concerns about Harriet. She told her about the secret walks and the state that Harriet seemed in since last night.

'She says she has a chill Ma, but it is more than that,' Annie puzzled. 'I wish she would talk to me more but since Jack's death she has hardly said a word of importance.'

'Don't you go forgetting that it is not just her father that she's lost Annie,' her mother reasoned. 'The love of her life has gone gallivanting to God knows where, just when she needed him most.'

'That wasn't Edward's fault,' replied Annie in Edward's defence. 'He wasn't to know and almost certainly still doesn't. Otherwise I'm sure he would have come home by now. Do you really think it was that serious between them? Wasn't it just a hangover from a childhood crush?' Annie asked.

'Harriet has grown up so quickly Annie. Jack was right to keep a close eye on her!' Grandma continued, warming to this rare opportunity to have a gossip with her daughter and glad that Annie had come out of her own shell for a while, if only to worry about her daughter.

'I can't think ill of them!' exclaimed Annie. 'I trust Edward, even if Harriet is a bit wayward and stubborn at times.'

'Have it your own way Annie,' she paused.

'Do you think that you could help out this lunchtime Annie?' asked grandma, sensing it was diplomatic to change the subject. 'We're expecting the blacksmith's family following the christening service of their little grandson. In fact I must get a move on otherwise nothing will be ready in time.'

'Jane's coming to see Harriet this afternoon. I'm glad she will have company otherwise I would be loath to leave her today so yes, I'm happy to help out,' Annie agreed. 'I will just follow Harriet up to see if she needs anything and I'll be down to give you a hand,' she added as she headed to the door. As she reached for the handle she turned and hesitated, as if not sure whether to say what was on her mind.

'You might as well say it my dear,' suggested grandma. 'Otherwise it'll burn inside you and do more harm than good.'

Annie paused and took a deep breath. 'Oh Ma,' she said. 'It's just a thought that keeps me awake at night sometimes and last night more so than ever. If anything happened to me and God forbid that it will. But if it did,' she paused for a moment, 'I think that Harriet would be better going over to my sister's on Sarnia. An inn is no place for a girl of her age. It's bad enough with me here but if...'

'Say no more,' replied her ma softly. 'Come here.' She was a large homely woman and in hugging her daughter in one of those rare affectionate moments she seemed to swamp Annie. 'If you didn't nap so much in the evening, pet, you would sleep better at night and be able to keep an eye on that wayward daughter of yours.'

'Oh Ma, she's a good girl really. You know she is,' said Annie as reluctantly she stepped away.

Jane called to see Harriet just after lunch and since Annie

was busy they were able to spend the afternoon talking in confidence. Jane could see from Harriet's face that there was something bothering her and it was not long before Harriet was whispering the whole tragic episode to her.

'I've always felt so safe here,' moaned Harriet. 'I've never felt uncomfortable walking on my own, even at night. I was angry when my papa made such an issue about meeting me but now I know why.'

'You forget that we are not children now Harriet. You are a desirable young lady and your father just wanted to protect his only daughter. Don't forget that you usually had Edward looking after you, even when you were young.'

'I miss Edward so much,' said Harriet. 'Sometimes I feel guilty when I think of him rather than my father.'

'Don't be so foolish Harriet. It's only natural that you think of those you love. Just think of your father watching over you. He can even watch over Edward too from where he is, don't you think?'

'You always have such comforting things to say Jane. I'm so glad that you are my friend,' Harriet exclaimed. 'It's just that thinking of Edward and my papa makes me feel so alone sometimes.'

'I know, Harriet. Don't forget that I have experienced loss too. You must think yourself lucky that Joe was there to rescue you. It was a miracle that he was passing at just the right moment,' Jane continued.

'Yes; what a blessing that Joe was close by. He's such a kind and caring man. I've never in all my life been so pleased to see someone I trusted,' Harriet cried, feeling a deep sense of gratitude to Edward's cousin.

The girls were quiet for a few moments before Jane ventured, 'I have got something to share with you too, Harriet.'

Jane talked to Harriet of her turmoil. The surprise she felt that she missed Thomas so much and the emptiness she experienced living at home. She also reminded Harriet of her desire to become a nurse and how confused that made her feel. Harriet listened intently. However great her own problems were, she was always a good listener.

'Oh Jane! You know that I would miss you dearly if you left for England but you must never consider staying on my account. You must listen to your heart. After all, even though you express your love for this island of ours you are only an honourable islander. Now if it was me who had to leave Riduna, I shudder to think how I might feel. I believe that my very soul is rooted in the soil here!'

They laughed. Jane was pleased to see Harriet more relaxed and that she had taken the news so well.

'Maybe your roots are over in London after all?' suggested Harriet.

'I don't think that it's as simple as that,' Jane replied, 'but thank you for being so reassuring. I would come home at least once a year I expect, twice if the weather allowed it at Christmas too. Meanwhile, if I did return to England would you write to me?'

'Of course I will write Jane,' replied Harriet. 'I will have a long wait before I hear from Edward again, so it would be quite nice to have a reason to visit the post office regularly again.'

'I had better be going now,' said Jane. 'Will I see you in church tomorrow?'

The thought of venturing as far as the church made Harriet shudder but she knew she had to go for the sake of her mama.

'Yes. I will be there in the morning but I was wondering if you would mind standing in for me at the school for a week. I have been thinking that perhaps I returned too quickly after everything and it would be good to spend more time with my mama.'

Jane was astute enough to realise that the real reason for Harriet's request was a fear of venturing out on her own and so did not answer immediately. She looked at Harriet and said quietly, 'I understand that you will find it difficult to go out Harriet but you can't hide here all your life. By all means I will go in for you until Wednesday but on Thursday and Friday I will come down and collect you. I will come in the buggy if my father's not using it.'

Harriet was relieved that her friend was so understanding. They parted with a hug and Harriet had a while by herself before Annie called her down to have a cup of tea in the kitchen. Her mama and gran were exhausted and so Harriet helped the kitchen lad to clear away and wash up the dishes. She was glad to have something practical to do, in the safety of their home that is.

Harriet was just about to rejoin her mama in their small living room when there was another knock at the door. Joe called with the excuse that he was inviting Annie and Harriet for lunch the following day with Beth and Joseph. Although Annie was tired and longed to lie down for a while, she was even more determined not to leave the two young people alone together, so she ordered Harriet to fetch a stool from their bedroom so that he could join them in the cosy little room. Conversation between Harriet and Joe was a little stilted at first but soon Annie was falling asleep in her chair and they felt more at ease to talk, albeit in a whisper. She occasionally surprised them by lifting her head with a start and interjecting their talk with a meaningless question before drifting to sleep again, barely waiting for a reply. Thus the conversation between Harriet and Joe was like a series of coded messages, the secrecy of which had the effect of enhancing Joe's desire for her. Even Harriet, whose only thoughts of a romantic nature were still directed to his cousin Edward, felt warm and safe in Joe's company and could feel a bond between them grow.

Joe did not stay long, just enough to check that Harriet was recovering from her ordeal and to reassure her of his friendship. After he had left, both Annie and Harriet chose to retire early and neither stirred until early the next morning. As Harriet drifted off to sleep she dreamed that she was looking for Edward.

Harriet ran along cliff top paths and through woods. At first the landscape was familiar. She knew every turn and slope. She ran to all their special places, along to Corblets Bay, peering down on to the beach, only to find it empty. Then she followed the track around to Longy Bay, stopping to let her eyes sweep along the sandy shore. Next she found herself stumbling along their favourite path towards Lovers' Rock. She fell down exhausted and wept; the breathtaking view no comfort to her heartache. Refreshed a little by her rest she turned her back on the sea, refusing to turn back to ask it to reveal its secrets, before taking the path back to the village. Harriet hesitated at the barn and could feel a pull towards it like a magnet. It was empty. Sitting down in the hay, dejected and alone she lay down and fell asleep.

It was within this sleep world within her dream that she finally found Edward, or at least she thought it was him. She was standing in a dark and dusty place and could hear his voice. It seemed to echo around her intermingled with voices and the laughter of strangers. She turned around and strained to distinguish Edward's voice, but each time she moved towards it, the voice seemed to be lost or echo, yet again, from behind her. Dizzy and lost she cried out in frustration only to find Joe reaching out to offer her a hand to guide her.

Harriet opened her eyes to see her mama looking at her with worried puzzled eyes.

'Don't look so worried Mama,' Harriet soothed. 'I was only having a dream.'

'A nightmare more like, my girl! It's just as well your yell woke me up; otherwise we would have been late for church,' Annie retorted.

It was the first time that Harriet had ventured out since the incident. All the way to church she was looking over her shoulder fearing that she might see those men again. Even in church she avoided eye contact with the group of men from the Militia. She recognised none of them but could not face to greet them with her normal coy smiles. Through the service she was aware that her hands were trembling and the palms of her hands were moist.

Although she felt safe in the company of Beth, Joseph and Joe at lunchtime and was glad to see that Uncle Joseph was able to hobble about now with the aid of a stick, she was still relieved to be back at the inn. Neither she nor Annie found it easy to pass their old familiar home which still lay empty and desolate. None of the islanders wished to move there at present and there were no new families arriving until summer. Joe offered to walk them home. To help to lighten their mood he offered an arm to each of them and they strolled together all the way to the inn. Annie offered him tea, which he gratefully accepted and on leaving he asked if he could call the following day. Annie was so concerned about her daughter's strange mood that she was very pleased to agree to him calling.

From then onwards Joe visited Harriet each evening at about the time that she would have gone for her lonely night-time stroll. As the evenings became lighter, Harriet became more confident and Annie more trusting so that he was able to persuade Harriet to go out for a walk. They tended to walk to the town and look out from the Butes or to stroll towards Corblets or Longy but avoided Braye Beach and the harbour, although Joe was acutely aware that Harriet should face that fear and one day lay those ghosts to rest.

Chapter 29

IT WAS ON a Sunday morning just before Easter when Harriet woke up and felt as if the cloud was beginning to lift from her life. Maybe it was the reality of the clear blue sky and the first hint of warmth in the spring air that greeted her as she leaned out of the window.

'Close the window Harriet,' moaned Annie who had stirred and was feeling a little under the weather that day. She tried to snuggle back down under the covers to avoid the draught.

Harriet pulled the window firmly shut before fetching her mama's breakfast tray from the kitchen downstairs.

'Are you staying in this morning?' she enquired as she fussed around Annie's bed straightening the covers.

'No love. I promised Beth that I would make the effort to join you all at church today and for lunch. It's Uncle Joseph's birthday, remember,' Annie replied.

Remembering Joe's ambition to persuade his uncle to take his first walk down to the harbour and Braye Bay on his birthday made Harriet shudder.

'There you are. It's chilly even though it looks bright,' reasoned Annie, mistaking Harriet's shudder for a shiver.

'Let's have that smile back on your face rather than the scowl,' she continued, noticing the change in Harriet's expression. 'Can you take this away now please?' she added. 'I'm getting dressed now.'

'Are you sure you're well enough Mama,' asked Harriet, looking at her mother's pale face.

'Don't fuss so, I'm fine,' exclaimed Annie in frustration as she struggled to get herself ready.

After church Annie and Harriet visited Jack's grave. They were pleased to see that the primroses were in bud now that the snowdrops were over. Soon the area would be a mass of colour. They stood there in silence, each deep in their own thoughts and memories.

Harriet put her arm around her mama's delicate shoulders.

'Come on Mama,' she said quietly. 'They are waiting.'

Beth and Joe stood at a discreet distance by the church door. As they met she reached out to give her best friend a spontaneous hug. Harriet and Joe stood there a little embarrassed. On the one hand Harriet longed to feel comforting arms around her but on the other Joe just longed to hold Harriet in his arms. Annie and Harriet made every effort to be more cheerful for Joseph's birthday lunch after which both were very tired and wished for the comfort and protection of their rooms at the inn.

Harriet was aware that the dreaded moment had arrived. Joseph was excited about his first walk down to the harbour and Joe was determined that Harriet would join them, despite her protests. He was sure that having familiar friends and family with her would help to dissolve her fear. Harriet dreaded the moment and could feel her hands shaking again as they neared Braye Beach, the sight of which used to give her an overwhelming sense of pleasure. She was so wrapped up in her own thoughts that she barely noticed that her mama, who had summoned all the energy she could muster to be sociable that afternoon, looked both tired and drained of strength. Beth was fussing around her husband, taking his free arm while he supported himself on a stick with the other. Joe offered each of his arms to Annie and Harriet, as he had become accustomed to do in the past.

As they neared Braye Beach Harriet took a long deep breath. She was determined to be brave and as she let her breath out slowly she imagined all her fears floating away with it. She stood on the sand and began to feel some sort of a peace at last. Gazing out to sea she felt Edward's encouraging presence and she could not help but smile. Joe, believing that she was smiling at him, beamed at her as he listened to the unfamiliar sound of his uncle laughing with pleasure at being out at last. It was only as Annie slipped from his grasp that he was aware that something was wrong. He was too slow to prevent her from sliding down on to the sand. Harriet came too from her daydream with a start. She and Joe fell simultaneously to their knees either side of Annie, Joe ripping his coat off and draping it over Annie's shoulders. He carefully rested her head on his lap and as she came to her senses and groaned Joseph passed his nephew a small flask deep from his pocket. He encouraged Annie to take a few sips and she coughed and spluttered as the warmth hit the back of her throat.

'Take Uncle Joseph home,' Joe ordered Beth. 'I'll see that Annie and Harriet are home safely and then I'll run up and fetch the doctor. Beth did not argue as she watched Joe lift the feather light figure of Annie into his arms. Her arms hung limply around his neck and her eyes drifted open occasionally as Joe hurried towards the Braye Tavern, Harriet racing by his side.

'Shall I go for the doctor?' she asked breathlessly.

'No Harriet. You should stay with your mother,' he answered firmly.

Without the strength to argue Harriet stumbled on. She followed Joe in through the back door of the inn and up the stairs, pausing briefly to call to her gran as she passed the kitchen door.

Joe lay the shivering form of Annie on her bed.

'I'll be as quick as I can,' he assured Harriet as he rushed from the room.

Harriet undressed her mama and with the help of her gran they got Annie into bed. As soon as her head hit the pillow she was asleep and Harriet sat on the stool by her bed helplessly watching her mother as she tossed and turned fitfully.

It did not seem many minutes before Harriet was aware of the sound of horse's hooves on the lane outside. The doctor was soon by Annie's side, checking her pulse and feeling her damp, hot brow. Harriet felt her gran guide her gently downstairs to the kitchen. They sat in silence drinking weak tea, Harriet too stunned to feel anything. She jumped when she felt the firm hand of the doctor on her shoulder. He sat down beside her and gratefully accepted the steaming mug offered to him.

'I'm afraid that your mother has acute pneumonia, Harriet. She's extremely ill but I'm sure that she has the strength to pull through, given rest, warmth and a great deal of loving care.' The doctor did not add that he was not sure whether Annie had the will to pull through.

'There's little more I can do for her tonight, but I'll call again first thing in the morning. Meanwhile you must get some rest too.'

In a daze Harriet bade the doctor farewell. 'I expect Jane will call tomorrow after school,' he added as he turned his buggy and set off back up towards the town.

Harriet continued to sit by her mama, gently mopping her brow and offering her water when she had the strength.

Joe visited Harriet early that evening and Harriet's gran sat by Annie while they talked. It grieved him to see Harriet's face so torn with pain and fear yet again. Even though they were alone he still refrained from giving Harriet any physical comfort. Joe was afraid that it would be easy to destroy the fragile trust she had in him. He was also held back by the ever present silver locket around Harriet's neck.

Damn the man, Joe thought as he walked back to Crabby with a heavy heart, not stopping for his usual drink at the inn.

It was on the Wednesday night that Annie passed away. Harriet was not at all surprised. In a strange sort of way she was relieved, believing that her mama was now at peace, reunited with her papa in heaven.

It was with a calm quiet dignity, showing maturity beyond her nineteen short years that she sat in church for her mother's funeral. It was the emptiness in the weeks that followed that she found hardest to bear. Mary had long since abandoned hope that she could persuade Harriet to return to her work in the school. Since Harriet had lost her fear of walking alone around the island, at least during the day that is, she spent most of the time wandering aimlessly.

Her friends, Jane, Charlotte and Joe visited her regularly but were unable to penetrate the invisible barrier that she had built around herself. People would see her out on her lonely walks, shake their heads and sigh. She refused company on these walks, no longer caring where she went as long as she was left alone. Her gran was dismayed at the responsibility Harriet's presence imposed on her. She knew that she must tell Harriet of Annie's wishes and yet there was never the right moment.

Even Charlotte and John's wedding at the beginning of May did little to lift Harriet's spirits. Jane had made plans to leave the island at the beginning of June but as yet had not had the courage to tell Harriet. Her best friend seemed a shadow of her former self. Joe was also planning to return to Sarnia soon. His uncle would soon be returning to work and Joe had been offered further work on his island home, which would give him the opportunity to continue the training in work he was beginning to enjoy.

That left Harriet. The situation came to a head one evening when Harriet returned from one of her long walks. It was later than usual, since she had spent some time sitting on the Lovers' Rock gazing out to sea. Fortunately the thought of following the example of the lovers in the local legend and leaping to her death did not cross her mind. Nevertheless she was foolish to be returning as darkness fell and she was relieved to reach the back door of the inn.

As she began to open the door she felt, to her horror, a hand reaching out of the gloom and cover her mouth and another grab her free arm behind her back. She could not see her assailant but could feel his breath on the back of her neck.

'So you are the beauty that got away, are you?' he whispered slyly in her ear. 'I've watched you wandering all over the island on your own. Asking for it you are and I'm going to see that you get it!' He dragged her deeper into the shadows behind the inn and Harriet tried to struggle free, but his grip was firm. Harriet was petrified. With his hand clasped tightly over her mouth she could not scream, only let out a silent prayer in her fear. Just as she was being pushed to the ground she felt his hand loosen and she let out a spontaneous yell which was echoed by a cry of pain from her attacker. She realised that he had been dragged away from her by his hair and in the shadows she could make out the figure of Joe fighting with the man.

Her gran was the first to appear at the sound of her

scream. She immediately misinterpreted the situation and tutted, 'Fancy a young lady like you having men fight over you. You should be ashamed my girl. Whatever would your mother have thought? It's high time you and I had a serious talk about your future.'

With that, despite Harriet's protests of innocence, her gran bundled her inside, just as the big hulk of her grandpa was striding past them. Harriet was just able to see him pick the two writhing men up by the scruff of their necks and give them both a dressing down before her gran pushed her inside the inn and into the kitchen.

'I've sent them both packing!' he yelled angrily through the kitchen door before returning to his customers, half of whom had come outside to witness the commotion.

'It's not what you are thinking Gran,' protested Harriet. 'Joe was trying to rescue me from that stranger!' she exclaimed in frustration.

'Sit down there and be quiet!' ordered her gran. 'Now you listen to me young lady and you listen carefully. This is no place to bring up a girl of your age and I am too busy to keep an eye on you.'

Harriet was just about to protest but the expression on her gran's face silenced her.

Her gran poured them both a drink and despite protests, coughing and spluttering Harriet was encouraged to drink it. The warm liquid calmed her a little and seemed to take the harsh edge off her gran's voice as she continued. 'I've left you to grieve in your own time. I know it's been hard for you but don't forget I've lost my daughter too. Your grandpa and I have been so worried about you and, my word, it's not as if we haven't got enough to worry about with the business and all at our age.'

'I've not been much help, have I?' acknowledged Harriet wistfully.

'Don't worry your head about that. It's just that we've been thinking as to what's best for you Harriet and after tonight we have to make a decision,' her gran continued.

'But…' protested Harriet.

'No buts,' interrupted Gran. 'You hear me out first young lady.' She took another sip of her drink to calm her down again and Harriet did likewise.

'Just before your mama died she made me promise that if anything should happen to her and you were left alone then I should send word to your aunt in Sarnia and ask her to take you in.'

Stunned, Harriet made to speak.

'Listen, I said,' exclaimed Gran crossly. 'I've already written to your mother's sister informing her of the sad events here and I received a reply from her yesterday. I didn't say anything because I felt that you needed time to yourself for a while. Perhaps after tonight I shouldn't have hesitated for so long. In a funny sort of way I selfishly wanted you to stay here for company and to help out, but I can see I was wrong to do so now. I think that it's time for you to prepare yourself to go as soon as possible. I know it's a shock,' she said responding to the agonised look on Harriet's face, 'but I'm sure that, when you get used to the idea, you'll realise that it's for the best.'

Harriet froze. Never in a million years would she imagine Mama inflicting such a punishment on her. Surely her parents could not wish for her to leave Riduna for good. It was unthinkable.

Her gran, misreading her granddaughter's silence as a form of agreement rather than the defiant protest she had feared continued, 'That's settled then. I'll write and tell your aunt to expect you in the middle of June giving you two weeks to get your things sorted out.'

Harriet pulled herself together. She must not be angry

with her gran, although she was furious with life in general. Just a few months ago she had everything she ever wanted from life and now; it did not bear thinking about. In a dazed dreamlike state she got up and, remembering to kiss her gran on the forehead, made her way up to her room.

'I am so tired, Gran,' she excused herself as she closed the kitchen door behind her.

Left alone her gran sighed with relief. Harriet had taken the news far better than the stormy tantrums she had half expected. The sooner Harriet was out of the influence of that young Joe the better as far as she was concerned. Rachael, her other daughter, would keep a close eye on the lass on Sarnia, she was sure of that. With that she reluctantly returned to her husband's side to attend to the last few customers before closing for the night. This was one occasion when she just longed to follow Harriet and have an early night.

'The young don't know how lucky they are,' she remarked to their cat, which was curled up by the range.

Although Harriet changed into her nightgown she did not climb into bed immediately. For a while she sat at the window and gazed out at the starry night.

'Why?' was all she could utter, as if asking an unknown power beyond her reach.

Chapter 30

STRANGELY ENOUGH THE one good consequence of the shattering news for Harriet was that it opened her eyes once more to life on the island. It was almost as if a doctor had told her that she only had two weeks to live. Instead of hiding further into the shell that she had built around her, it had the effect of shattering that shell. Her grandparents were relieved that she began to live each moment, visiting friends, being extremely helpful at the inn and maintaining a cheerful countenance. They were so surprised by this that when she asked if she could go to an island's dance for the last time they reluctantly agreed for her to go, especially when Jane's father offered to pick her up in his buggy and bring her home. At least that would deter Joe a little.

At the dance Jane shared the news that she too would be leaving the island soon, maybe on the same ship.

'I'm sorry that I've not had the courage to tell you earlier but I was so worried about how you would take the news,' Jane explained.

'Don't worry Jane,' Harriet replied. 'I knew that you were thinking seriously about going but it was just one more reality I couldn't face at the time.'

'Maybe you could write to your aunt and ask if I could stay with you on Sarnia for a week or two before travelling on to England. It would give you company and we could explore a little together,' Jane suggested.

'Oh Jane, you're a really good friend,' and the ladies embraced.

At that moment Joe appeared and asked Harriet if she would dance and she gratefully accepted; glad to be able to do so out of her grandparents' gaze.

'How are you Harriet?' he asked as he marvelled as to how gracefully she danced.

'Glad to be here,' replied Harriet, despite the disapproving frowns from some of the older generation present, who thought it disrespectful to see Harriet dancing so soon after her mother's death. Harriet wore her black mourning dress, which contrasted with her pale skin giving her an ethereal, unworldly quality as she spun weightlessly around the dance floor in Joe's arms. 'My grandparents still haven't forgiven you for fighting over me,' she teased.

'Surely they understand that you're telling them the truth,' exclaimed Joe a little crossly.

'I think that they were glad to have an excuse to send me away. They'll hear no more of the matter,' Harriet replied, 'but I suggest you keep clear of my grandparents' tavern, even when I'm gone.'

They danced in silence for a little while and then Joe said, 'as it happens I will be returning to Sarnia soon too.'

Harriet couldn't disguise the true pleasure that this news gave her. She beamed at him and he in turn melted in her presence.

'I've been offered to continue my apprenticeship on Sarnia and since Uncle Joseph will be returning to work soon I felt that I could not refuse such a good opportunity,' Joe explained.

The music was about to come to an end and although

Joe wished to continue this conversation he knew that he should return Harriet to Jane. He bowed politely and reluctantly left them, wondering when he would next have the opportunity to talk to her.

As Harriet sat in her room that night gazing at the same starry sky, it was as if she had been given an answer. Like any momentous question or prayer sent in anguish, Harriet knew that you were rarely blessed with the answer you expected or would dearly like but nevertheless, with both Jane's and Joe's news that night, she felt she had been given a glimmer of hope for the future. At least leaving Riduna might be a little easier to bear.

Only Beth saw through Harriet's façade and came close to understanding the anguish buried deep beneath. They met one day at the baker's and chose to walk some way together even though this meant a detour for Harriet. Beth suggested that they sit on the Butes for a while to talk and Harriet gratefully agreed. Beth noticed that Harriet wore her silver locket constantly now and despite Harriet's silence on the matter, and Joe's for that matter, was puzzled by the attention her nephew was giving Harriet.

'It's so hard that we've not heard from Edward isn't it?' she asked tentatively.

'Oh Beth! It's difficult not to be angry with him for going away when we needed him so much,' Harriet replied, involuntarily grasping her locket as if it were her only remaining link with the man she loved. 'It was one thing to miss him when we could write to him and receive letters in reply. It's the silence that I find so hard.'

'What shall I say to him when he eventually comes home?' Beth enquired gently.

'I really don't know any more, Beth. Sometimes I believe that, if he were here now, we would get married and I would never have to leave,' Harriet groaned.

They sat in silence for a while. The view soothed their anguished minds.

'I'm sure that Edward would do the honourable thing and marry you, too,' replied Beth with a knowing look, which made Harriet blush. 'But then what would he do?'

Harriet knew Edward too well to realise that Beth did not expect a reply. She knew the real question on Beth's lips was 'could Harriet imagine letting Edward go time and time again throughout their married lives?'

'Don't wait for Edward forever if it's going to make you unhappy, Harriet,' Beth painfully advised. 'Despite the fact that I long to witness you walking together down the aisle, and in many ways I think you were destined for each other from the moment you were born, but you mustn't lose sight of yourself and your own needs.'

'It seems a lifetime away that we were together Aunt Beth,' replied Harriet. 'Although I long to be with him again, I don't seem to be able to imagine it happening anymore. The dream seems to have faded with all the pain. Does that sound heartless?' Harriet pleaded.

'No my dear,' replied Beth, relieved that Harriet was facing up to the truth so maturely. 'If you're meant to be together, it will all work out. What I am sure of though, is that you need some happiness in your life young lady. So my advice is, don't turn away a chance of joy in the present for the sake of some distant dream.'

Both had tears brimming in their eyes by this time so they gave each other an affectionate hug. They understood in their hearts that the man both of them loved so much would never be content to settle for long, but would always be causing pain by disappearing into the blue beyond. Nevertheless that moment was very special for Harriet and Beth. They felt the invisible thread that tied them to him and to each other as strong and enduring as any ship's cable dropping anchor.

They parted then, Beth inviting Harriet to join them on her last evening on the island. She promised to visit Harriet's gran to try and soften their feelings towards Joe before the Friday night. Harriet returned to the inn to prepare for her voyage, wishing with all her heart and soul that she could drop anchor somehow and remain on the island, but feeling the relentless pull of the tide dragging her away against her will. The only consolation in her misery was that she was not drowning, but she was determined to make every minute of her last week special.

By Friday she had walked a circuit of Riduna, taking a different route north, south, east or west each day until on Friday she ambled around the island's heart, the town of St Anne's. There she said farewell to many of the shopkeepers, called in on Charlotte and John, who were now living together at the Rose and Crown and she had lunch with Jane, Mary and David. Michael had remained on Sarnia where he had allegedly fallen in love. In order to woo his intended, he had found himself a job in a bakery on Sarnia, much to the dismay of his parents, who were trying to cope without the help of either Charlotte or Michael. He had vowed to stay over the water until he could persuade the girl to marry him and come back to live on Riduna. It was the second part of the bargain that was causing the delay. Nevertheless it gave the islanders something amusing to gossip about. Harriet was comforted by the thought that she would see another familiar face in her new life.

Friday night finally arrived. Although her gran and grandpa had reluctantly agreed for Harriet to go to Beth and Joseph's, they refused the invitation themselves. They had the excuse of the business of course, but Harriet knew that their real reason was their deep-rooted distrust of Joe, despite Beth's protests of his innocence. This saddened Harriet because she had never met a more thoughtful and kind man. He always seemed to be there when she so desperately needed someone.

Beth hoped that the evening would be a cheerful one, echoing the ghosts of past celebrations. Even Joe felt the presence of unseen guests that night. In fact it was Joe and his uncle who maintained the light hearted joviality with their teasing and banter. It was only at the end of the evening that the conversation became a little emotional. Beth and Joseph would miss their nephew and at the end of the evening Beth was determined to express her gratitude.

'It's been lovely to have you with us Joe,' she exclaimed.

'It's been a pleasure to be here Aunt Beth, and if you continue to feed me like you have tonight I will be pining to return. I hope that I have come some way in filling the gap left by that wayward cousin of mine,' Joe joked.

'You've done more than that lad. You seem to have the knack of being here just when we need you,' said Joseph. Harriet blushed. Joseph sensitively glanced in Harriet's direction. 'I think I'm speaking for all of us,' he added.

Harriet looked as if she was fighting back tears. 'I don't know what I would have done without you,' she said quietly, smiling at Joe through watery eyes.

Joe melted at the sight of her smile. 'Just as well I will be able to continue to keep an eye on you over on Sarnia,' he answered gruffly. 'You do want us to keep in touch, don't you?' he asked, unable to disguise the plea in his voice.

Beth and Joseph glanced at each other and Joseph shrugged his shoulders as if to answer Beth's unspoken question with the unspoken answer, what will be, will be!

'Like father like son,' thought Beth, wondering if they were about to lose Harriet as a potential daughter-in-law. She had always imagined the joy she would have had with

Harriet and their grandchildren, wherever their son might have wandered.

Harriet pulled herself together with as much cheerfulness as she could muster. She did not answer Joe directly, fearful of giving misleading encouragement. She embraced Beth and Joseph, 'I'll miss you both so much, but I promise I will never forget you.' A knowing look passed between her and Beth.

Joe took Harriet's cue to move as it was taken for granted that he would walk Harriet back to the inn and he relished the thought of being alone with her for a short while. He held Harriet's cloak out for her and helped her to put it on.

'I promise I'll write,' Harriet called over her shoulder as they set off down the lane, leaving Joseph and Beth standing at their gate.

Harriet and Joe walked in silence at first. It was Joe who finally broke the stillness and spoke first.

'Sarnia is not as strange as you might imagine, Harriet. It's just a bit bigger and busier than Riduna, but it still has a charm of its own. Its coastline has many tiny coves and lovely coastal paths. You'll get accustomed to it and you may even learn to love it in time,' he encouraged.

'It's hard to explain Joe and I'm so grateful for you trying to understand, but I feel that on leaving Riduna, I am losing nearly everything in the world I have held dear to me since I was born,' Harriet explained reaching momentarily to her locket. 'Riduna is my life,' she continued. 'It's so much a part of me but I'm also comforted by the thought that I've also been a small part of it so I feel as if I'm losing myself, Joe.' Harriet attempted to express her deepest thoughts and fears but in a way she knew that she was really talking to herself, trying to make some sense of it all.

Without thinking, Joe placed a sympathetic arm over Harriet's shoulder and gently pulled her to him. Comforted by the feeling of warmth and security it gave her, Harriet rested her head amiably against him as they walked side by side. Harriet was past caring as to what people thought of her. Beth's words went through her mind and for the first time in weeks Harriet felt a tiny grain of peace seeping through her.

As they reached the inn Joe let go of Harriet as she opened the back door. She looked up at him and he longed to kiss her but he dared not break the spell of the moment. He noticed the locket glimmering in the moonlight and stood back and bowed.

'I'll see you on the ship in the morning, Harriet. Try to get some sleep and not to worry. Maybe you will come back one day.' He paused to check that she was safely inside.

'Goodnight Joe and thank you for everything,' exclaimed Harriet as she closed the door quietly behind her. She avoided the kitchen door as she crept straight upstairs to her room. It was sad that her grandparents misunderstood Joe. If only they knew what he was really like.

Once in her room, the one that she had shared with her mama, she placed the last few items in her bags and closed them tightly. She looked around the bare room. It was almost back as it was a few months earlier when they first arrived. She would not be as sorry to leave it as she was at leaving their cottage in Platte Saline.

If Harriet was to describe her feelings as she attempted to search for that illusive sleep it was of a resigned numb emptiness. She listened to the sounds from the inn below. Initially it was just a faint mumble of people talking, interspersed with an occasional burst of laughter. Finally she heard the bang of the bolt barring the door to the last inebriated customer who sang as he staggered down the street. She thought of her life here and her mind drifted to the lonely cottage next door to Beth and Joseph and the life and laughter it had held until only a few months before. The sound of her gran's heavy footsteps on the stair disturbed her thoughts.

'You're back safely then,' her gran said as she put her head around the door. 'We were beginning to worry about you.'

'I'm fine Gran. I had a nice evening,'

'Goodnight then Hetty,' said Gran as she came over to give Harriet a peck on the forehead, using a nickname Harriet had not heard in years.

'Goodnight Gran,' Harriet replied. 'I'm fine, really I am. I just wish you would not be so hard on Joe.'

'You're too trusting for your own good, young lady,' Gran retorted and with that last remark she closed the door.

In the stillness of the night Harriet tried to picture Edward and instinctively her hand grasped her locket yet again. She finally drifted off to sleep as she caught a glimpse of his face. Then she noticed that he was standing on a cliff top waving goodbye and it was she who was drifting slowly out to sea.

Chapter 31

June 1883

THE FOLLOWING MORNING Harriet slipped out early and walked up the cutting and through to St Anne's churchyard to visit her parents' grave one last time. She knelt beside it and touched the names of her father and mother written on the tombstone.

'Goodbye Mama. Goodbye Papa,' she whispered.

She remained there, breathing in the stillness of the moment and allowing herself the luxury of a few silent tears. On her way back she made a detour to one of her favourite places, the Butes. There she stood staring out to sea, the June morning mist clearing with the gentle sea breeze, promising a fine day. She listened to the occasional sounds of the town stirring to life behind her and in the wind she could imagine the distant echo of the sea on Braye Beach far below. Military personnel were already gathering at Fort Grosnez down by the harbour and another band was on their ant-like march emerging from the imposing battlements of Fort Albert along the bay.

On the horizon Harriet could just make out a speck appearing on the clear blue sea as she strained her eyes beyond the breakwater. As the unmistakable shape of the

Courier grew before her she stole her gaze away to let her eyes sweep along the bay one last time. She would have liked to make a promise that she would return one day, as she stood breathing in the familiar sight. She was amazed that the enduring view before her was as changeable as it was constant. Each season, in fact each moment in time, gave it a unique quality.

Harriet returned to the inn. She gathered her possessions together before joining her grandparents for breakfast in their large kitchen.

'Where've you been to this early in the morning?' her gran asked.

'To say goodbye to Mama and Papa,' Harriet replied matter of factly.

'Your aunt will have none of this wandering off on your own, my girl,' her gran added, but stopped from saying more when Harriet's grandpa gave her a warning look across the table.

'I'm glad you found time to pay your respects,' he remarked and was thanked by one of Harriet's grateful smiles.

After breakfast they set off towards the harbour, Harriet's grandpa carrying the small bags. Charlotte and her gran stood at the door of her little cottage and waved as she went by. Down at the harbour Harriet was relieved as well as nervous to see so many familiar faces. She had never imagined in all the times she had come down to watch the *Courier* set sail that one day people would be watching her leave. Mary and David were standing with Jane and Beth and Joseph were saying farewell to Joe. Harriet promised to write to her gran and to Beth and gave everyone a hug before walking up the gangway for the first time in her life. Her legs were shaking and she was relieved that Joe was being the perfect gentleman and had offered to carry their bags. He stood holding out his hand to Jane and Harriet as they stepped on to the deck.

The moment had arrived and the island began to slip away from the ship's side. Inside Harriet wanted to cry out in protest and she gripped Jane's hand tightly by her side. It was only when Beth caught her eye that her resistance began to crumble and her eyes began to water again. As they waved it was as if Harriet's whole world were slipping from beneath her feet.

She stood there transfixed, just as Edward had done all those months ago and she watched as they slipped past the breakwater and Riduna slowly became the horizon. As the sea engulfed the island making it thumbnail size and finally a mere smudge in the far distance, Harriet let go of Jane's hand and gripped the rails of the ship as the ship turned and it disappeared from her view altogether.

The sailing was uneventful and the sea was calm. Joe was attentive to the ladies' needs, fetching them tea and a sandwich and introducing them to the occasional inquisitive crew member, who happened to pass. It was late afternoon when they were finally nearing Sarnia. Joe suggested that they return to the deck to watch the island approach. As Harriet climbed the short ladder-like steps, which led outside, she stumbled. Jane, who had climbed up before her, held out a hand to steady Harriet, as she regained her footing and climbed out on to the deck but as Joe followed from behind something shiny caught his eye through the steps. He reached down and, realising it was Harriet's locket, he was about to call out after her but he paused. Instead he slipped the locket into his pocket and continued to climb out on to the deck. Jane was checking that Harriet was not hurt and Harriet was brushing down her black dress when he stepped out to join them. He gazed at Harriet musing that since he had known her she had rarely worn anything but black and wondered how she would look in other colours. Jane's puzzled look brought him to his senses and since Harriet protested that she was unhurt, he led them to the side of the ship to admire the view.

As they neared Sarnia, the harbour, vast in Harriet's opinion, was full to the brim with boats and ships. The higgledy-piggledy roofs of the buildings in front of them seemed to stretch on forever, as they meandered up the steep slopes of the town which swept around the harbour. As they neared the quayside Harriet found the noise of people, horses and carriages quite daunting. Nervously she stepped on to the quayside after Jane, Joe following behind them passing their luggage to a young boy waiting at the harbour's edge.

Soon Harriet was relieved to notice the unmistakable face of her aunt in the crowds. Her Aunt Rachael was so like her mama only more plump and homely. Her aunt waved frantically over the top of people's heads from the other side of the street and they made their way towards her, trying to avoid barrow boys rushing past with the mail, and carriages, already full of passengers, which sped away from the harbour. Once safely across the street, which was no mean task for Harriet, her aunt welcomed them all with open arms and bundled them on to the waiting buggy. Joe lifted their luggage on to the back and uncertain what to do or say he stood a moment while the ladies shared their welcomes and pleasantries about the journey. It was Harriet who noticed Joe standing there quietly.

'Thank you Joe. Aunt Rachael, this is our friend Joe. He is Edward's cousin and he lives on Sarnia and he has been looking after us during the journey.'

Her aunt held out her hand and Joe, ever the gentleman, took her hand and bowed.

'Pleased to meet you,' Aunt Rachael responded. 'Any friend of Harriet's will be welcome to call. Good day to you sir,' she added as the horse began to lead them out on to the busy street.

Harriet and Jane turned to wave to Joe, who stood and watched them until they were out of sight.

'Thank you so much for agreeing to give me a home for two weeks,' Jane said as she turned to watch where they were going.

'My pleasure,' replied Aunt Rachael, with such genuine warmth in her voice that both Harriet and Jane felt at ease with her immediately.

Jane smiled at Harriet and gave her friend's hand a squeeze of affection, which seemed to say 'everything is going to be alright.'

Once settled into their little room in the eaves of her aunt's terraced cottage Harriet and Jane joined Aunt Rachael in the kitchen for a light supper of soup and bread. They listened to Harriet's aunt talk about life on Sarnia and what they must see in the short time that Jane would be staying with them. Eventually she noticed how tired they both were and they were grateful when she suggested that they make their way to bed. Her last words to Harriet as she went out of the door were, 'You must not think of this as an end rather as a new beginning.'

It was only when Harriet was getting undressed that her hand inadvertently reached to unclasp her locket. She searched through all her belongings, trying hard not to disturb Jane who was already asleep. When at last she got into bed and admitted that it was lost a feeling of emptiness overwhelmed her yet again. Her loss seemed complete.

Chapter 32

AUNT RACHAEL LIVED in a little terraced cottage in an area overlooking St Peter Port called Les Canichers, narrow lanes of dwellings interlinked with steep flights of steps and dark passages. Harriet and Jane found the area quite claustrophobic at first. The girls woke up to the sound of the community stirring for an ever busy day. Harriet's Uncle Thomas, who had been out for his usual drink at the Britannia on their arrival the previous night, had left the house for work in the post office. He had a good and respectable job and the family were comfortably off compared to some, especially now Harriet's cousins Florence and Luke were contributing to the household. Aunt Rachael and Cousin Florence did sewing for the Moores Hotel, which was collected and delivered by a matronly lady, Mrs Pike, each Friday morning. It was her bustling departure which stirred Harriet and Jane to arise and face the new day.

Cousin Flo and Aunt Rachael were sitting by the narrow window busily sewing.

'Help yourselves to some bread and tea from the pot,' Aunt Rachael greeted them cheerily, 'excuse us while we work.'

'Good morning aunt and dear cousin,' replied Harriet politely, 'thank you kindly.'

'I have asked Mrs Pike,' said Aunt Rachael nodding to the recently closed door, 'to leave an extra batch for you next week Harriet, because it's best to keep busy and I'm sure you wish to earn your keep.'

'Yes aunt, I would be only too willing to work with you.' Inwardly Harriet's heart sighed at the pile of sewing before her. She had always been willing to do what was necessary at home but it was not an occupation she relished. In fact it was one job her mama could do, even when her health was not at its best. She had been so fortunate on Riduna that Mary had seen her potential and encouraged her. A pain of regret mixed with sadness brought a frown to Harriet's countenance which only Jane noticed.

'We are so fortunate to have this time together Harriet,' she said, catching Harriet's eye. 'Maybe if we both helped you for a few hours each day then Florence could accompany us in the afternoons,' Jane continued diplomatically.

'I would truly like that,' exclaimed Flo with a shy enthusiasm which Harriet found touching. She had a feeling that she would soon warm to her young cousin. A smile passed between them.

'Have it as you wish,' replied Aunt Rachael, who was inwardly relieved, since she expected a difficult time with her niece, so distraught with grief.

Jane and Harriet put on their cloaks and bonnets and left the security of the little cottage, which was now to be Harriet's home. They walked in a companionable silence, returning the smiles and acknowledgements of strangers as they passed by as best they could. Harriet walked in a daze but Jane took time to observe the fashion. All seemed to dress well, both rich and poor alike were wearing shoes. Jane made a mental note that she would need to improve her wardrobe when she reached London.

They made their way, gingerly at first, down the steep steps and on to the High Street below. They avoided the few carriages and traps by stepping to the edge of the still narrow street, but were surprised that it was not nearly as noisy as the harbour below them. Harriet found the multitude of shops bewildering but Jane found the French-like market town quite quaint compared to her memories of London.

At the end of the street they reached St Peter's Church, the imposing landmark which they recognised from their approach into the harbour the previous day. It was here that the crowds built up.

'This must be the famous market,' exclaimed Jane, holding on to her friend's arm tightly. She was charmed by the ladies' tall black hats and decorative costumes as they sold their wares of flowers, fruit and homemade cake, the locals called Gâche.

'Would you like to continue and explore Harriet or would you like to return to your Aunt Rachael?' she asked. Jane was very sensitive that Harriet might find the newness a bit daunting, never having left Riduna in her life. She was also aware that her friend's grief, although cloaked in the excitement of the moment, was never far away.

'Let's go back now,' Harriet replied nervously. 'I wonder which bakery Michael works in,' she continued, trying to lighten her mood and longing for another familiar face.

It was just at that moment that they caught sight of Joe. He was absorbed in conversation with a very pretty girl in an elegant maroon gown, small black cape and bonnet, in a style which appeared to be the current fashion.

Harriet could not help but feel a touch of jealousy, an unfamiliar feeling which irritated her immensely. She knew that she liked Joe's company and would be eternally grateful to him for rescuing her from certain shame, not just once but on two fearful occasions back on Riduna. She was also aware that his presence reminded her of Edward. He shared a likeness to Edward, especially in his looks, but he was also kind, gentle and caring in a way which made her feel protected. What he lacked in Edward's humour, spirit of adventure and joy for life he gained in the respect of stability and reliability.

Her comparisons were fleeting and subconscious as she snapped herself back into the present. Joe noticed them and beamed with obvious pleasure at the unexpected meeting. He brought his friend over towards the young ladies.

'I was just this minute talking about you both,' he exclaimed. 'Please allow me to introduce you to Miss Sarah Mortland, daughter of Mr and Mrs Jonathan Mortland, close family friends.

'This is Miss Harriet Loveridge and this is Miss Jane Hanwell.'

'Welcome to Sarnia,' greeted Miss Mortland warmly. 'I hope that you will eventually find pleasure in living on our island,' she continued taking Harriet's hand in hers, 'and that you will enjoy your brief visit too.' She added this half turning to Jane and nodding, although seemingly reluctant to let go of Harriet's hand, as if to convey her sympathy in a way that words could not express.

'You're most kind,' thanked Jane while Harriet just smiled in agreement. 'We have certainly enjoyed our first morning Miss Mortland.'

'I was enquiring as to whether Sarah, Miss Mortland, thought that you could be invited to attend one of the island's dances in the Assembly Rooms. It's normally strictly for certain residents of the island but we do occasionally have invited, approved guests,' Joe explained.

'Please call me Sarah,' she exclaimed. 'I'm going to see if

I can obtain permission to offer an invitation,' added Sarah, smiling encouragingly at Harriet. 'I also hear that you were accustomed to working at your local school on Riduna. You must visit and tell me about it Harriet, when you are able. I will send you my card.'

'That's more than kind,' Harriet replied shyly. 'Yes, I enjoyed working with the younger girls. It gave me a sense of purpose, but my aunt has found me employment doing some sewing,' she responded, barely able to hide the glimmer of regret in her voice.

'I can offer no promises but that the governor of the local school is a family friend,' said Sarah, giving Joe a knowing look. 'I hope you enjoy the remainder of your stroll.'

As Sarah walked away Joe accompanied the ladies back to Les Canichers. It was on his way back to his parents' guesthouse, where he was living. On the way he explained about the customs surrounding the island's dances in the Assembly Rooms. He and his brothers were invited because of the family's well-established business and they were perceived to be high enough on the social scale. Unfortunately Harriet's aunt and family were not. Sarah Mortland came from a very wealthy and influential family, added to which she had a heart of gold. Their families had been close acquaintances for years, following a time when Joe's father had come to the rescue of her father in an incident long before Sarah was born. If anyone could have influence in the matter Sarah could, he reassured them.

Soon they reached the door to Harriet's aunt's modest cottage and Joe bade them farewell. The next day being Sunday, he offered to take them for a ride around the west coast of the island.

Harriet and Jane went inside to join Harriet's aunt and uncle for lunch, meeting Uncle Thomas and Cousin Luke for the first time. Uncle Thomas was a kindly, portly man who was jovial and welcoming but both young ladies took an instant dislike to Cousin Luke, who seemed to resent their presence from the start.

After lunch Jane and Harriet had a rest before taking another stroll, this time towards the harbour. The numerous colourful boats and schooners amazed Harriet. Nothing could match the natural beauty of Braye Beach in her eyes, but she had to agree with Jane that this too had its own charm. There was a quality almost as magical with Castle Cornet standing majestically to the right of the harbour inlet and the smaller islands of Sark and Herm silhouetted in the distance to the left, across a deep-blue sea. As they strolled along the promenade Jane was again made aware of the fashion of the ladies as they passed by. She looked down at her own attire and for a moment longed to be back in London where she could enjoy the pleasure of purchasing some new outfits. The momentary pleasure gave way to sadness that she would soon be leaving her best friend. Harriet barely noticed the other ladies and fortunately her sombre mourning attire gave rise to nods of a sympathetic nature rather than scorn. She glanced wistfully back towards the docks where a ferry was just departing.

'A penny for your thoughts,' Jane enquired as light-heartedly as she could muster.

'I was thinking that Edward may have left for England on that ferry and I was wondering where he might be now,' replied Harriet.

'I expect he is having the time of his life, wherever he may be,' returned Jane. 'Try to relax and enjoy your new life here and not to pine for Edward,' she continued gently.

As they turned, Harriet smiled at Jane.

'I think you are right Jane. This is a new beginning for

me and I know I must make the most of life here, however difficult it will be,' she replied.

For the remainder of her stay, to Jane's great relief, Harriet's mood seemed to lift. On the following day when they walked along the beautiful coastal path near Fermaine Bay, catching glimpses of the other islands through the trees as they paused to enjoy the breathtaking views, she seemed to Jane to be quite cheerful.

During the next week they saw Joe quite frequently. He was not beginning his new job straight away but had returned to supporting his parents in the guesthouse, meeting and greeting guests. On his free afternoons he enjoyed the pleasure of taking the three young ladies around the island.

Time passed all too quickly and the day arrived when Joe and Harriet were standing at the docks, waving goodbye to Jane. For the first time in a week Joe was observant enough to notice that Harriet's eyes were watery and her skin had turned pale. His heart went out to her but he was powerless to help her.

When the ship became neared the harbour's mouth Harriet was overwhelmed by emotion. Joe watched her as the last remaining colour drained from her face and he was just able to catch her as she fainted before him.

Two middle-aged women came rushing to her aid with smelling salts and fans. They ushered Joe aside as they encouraged Harriet to regain composure and then offered her transport home in their buggy.

One whispered to Harriet, 'You are not with child my dear, are you?' sending Joe a sidelong accusing glance as he gazed on helplessly.

'No, no! I'll be fine. It was just a shock,' protested Harriet as they bundled her into their trap. She was just able to give Joe a backward wave as they sped off towards the place she must from now onwards call her home.

Aunt Rachael was so concerned about her niece that she ordered a week of rest, remaining at home with no visitors. Although she liked Joe she was also aware of the harm gossip from those two ladies could do to Harriet's reputation and was at pains to protect her.

For the next forty-eight hours Harriet remained in bed, drifting in and out of a fitful sleep. She dreamed so many dreams.

At one time she was searching for her missing locket. She had checked again through all her belongings but in her dream she was drawn up a steep and winding staircase. At the top of the staircase was a ladder against the wall. She climbed the ladder, pushed a hatch aside and entered a dingy attic. In the dim light of the attic there was a large oak cupboard. When she opened the door of the cupboard she found an ancient trunk. Her dream led her, like a Russian doll she had once been entranced by on Riduna, to lift the lid of the trunk and find a small plain wooden box amongst an assortment of dusty papers and belongings. The box was locked. She scrabbled around through the various items in the trunk and in one corner she found a little key. Ignoring all but the box she turned the little key to release the catch, only to find a little leather pouch. It was carefully wrapped in a small piece of cloth but as she pulled out the cloth the unmistakeable locket fell into her waiting hand. She lifted it to her neck and felt Edward close to her once more. Tears fell gently down her cheeks as she gazed into the dusty old mirror on the back of the wardrobe door, at the shadow of a face that she barely recognised as her own.

Aunt Rachael gently called to her, disquieted by the sight of Harriet weeping in her sleep. As Harriet came to, her hand inadvertently moved to her neck to where the locket should have been and Aunt Rachael was moved by the pain of the disappointment etched on Harriet's face. She reached out to give Harriet a warm hug, a spontaneous act of affection that she was not accustomed to make as a rule. Harriet fell limp into her arms with tears streaming uncontrollably. So great was her loss now that Jane had also left her.

That moment was a turning point for Harriet. She slept for a few hours more before getting up to join her aunt and cousin in the front room. By the next day she was up early and made a good effort to help to reduce the pile of sewing, which to Harriet appeared to grow before them. It was not a task she enjoyed but at least it required little thinking and it was a time to get to know her aunt and cousin. Harriet had never been one to be lazy, even as a young child, especially when her mama was ill. She tried to put all thoughts of her family and friends, Riduna and the missing locket behind her. She believed in fate and from her dream was convinced that one day she would find it again.

Maybe it is a sign, she mused as she placed her thoughts locked in the depths of her mind.

By the end of the following week Harriet was able to venture out on errands for her aunt, sometimes with her cousin but more often she preferred to go on her own. She had found the bakery where Michael worked and passing the time of day with him, albeit briefly to avoid gossip, was her only link with her past life.

It was on one such occasion, when she was returning from the fish market that she occasioned to meet Sarah Mortland who recognised her instantly.

'How are you Harriet?' she enquired warmly. 'I have heard from Joe that you have not been well. He was very concerned about you when we spoke two days ago.'

'I'm much stronger now, thank you,' Harriet replied. 'It's kind of you to ask,' she added.

'I hope that you don't think it is premature of me but I have already enquired at the local school for you and was wondering if I could come to visit your aunt to discuss the possibility of you finding some employment there,' Sarah continued.

'That's most kind of you,' Harriet replied, finding it impossible to conceal the first glimmer of enthusiasm she had felt in a long while. Sarah noticed that Harriet's eyes were perceptibly more cheerful at the news.

'I'm at home with my aunt each morning, when we are sewing. I'm sure that it would be convenient for you to call late morning one day,' continued Harriet enthusiastically.

And so it was that on the Wednesday of the following week Sarah called to discuss a possible position for Harriet at the school. A reference was requested and quickly dispatched from Riduna, so that Harriet was able to take up the position a month later when the harvest was over and the new term began. Harriet worked with the young girls as she had on Riduna and the children began to give her joy and a purpose in her life at last.

Once another month had passed Harriet's life settled into such a routine that her former life on Riduna seemed to be a distant dream. She saw Joe occasionally as her aunt saw fit, but her aunt was careful that she was always chaperoned by either herself, Florence or both. On one occasion Harriet had met Joe by chance when out running an errand for her. Foolishly they had decided to take a stroll to the harbour together unaccompanied and Cousin Luke, who had observed them deep in conversation and was jealous of their close proximity, soon reported the incident to his mother. This caused unnecessary friction, to Harriet's mind, and after this time Harriet was rarely allowed out unaccompanied. She found the restrictions unbearable and she resented the loss of her freedom.

Nevertheless increasingly she would look forward to the times when Joe would take them for rides around the island or a stroll along the promenade. If it was wet Joe would be invited to join the family in the front room to take tea and they would enjoy pleasant conversation for an hour or so. Occasionally his family would invite both Harriet and her cousins over on a Sunday. This happened mid afternoon following the hectic preparations of lunch for their guests.

Harriet had only received one more letter from Edward. She returned to the cottage one day to be greeted by her aunt's outstretched hand holding a letter. The handwriting was so familiar and her heart began to race. She thanked her aunt and as she fingered the letter in her hands she noticed that they were trembling and the palms of her hands were clammy. She made an excuse and climbed the steps to the privacy of the room she shared with Florence. Thankful for the few moments' solitude she began to read the letter. It was obvious that he had left port and had no idea of her tragic news and the changes to her life. The letter was postmarked from some foreign sounding place called Rio, which Harriet later discovered was in a country she remembered Edward mentioning called Brazil. It had taken three months to reach her especially since it had been redirected from Riduna, its original destination.

My dearest Harriet

I hope this letter reaches you and that you and your family are well. I am so excited to tell you of an irresistible opportunity which presented itself to me once we had docked at Rio. You would never believe what I have seen on this journey and the interesting people I have met. To witness palm trees and people living in beach shacks with grass roofs, each community with a similar beach bar nearby. And the heat! It is amazing.

I digress.

While relaxing at a beach bar the other night, where we sat on a wooden veranda drinking and gazing out over the bright blue sea, I was introduced to Captain Reynolds. He offered me a position in his fleet of ships which travel between here and New York via the West Indies and then down the coast to South America. They pick up various cargoes including cotton and coffee and also passengers. The crew are mainly locals but he needs people he can trust from England. As a reward for my efforts, if I prove my worth, he is offering me the job of First Mate if I return after Christmas on his ship the Humber. Thus I am sending this letter from Rio, since I will not be returning to Southampton until just before Christmas time, when I will be home to see you all.

I hope that you will be excited for me also. I so look forward to my visit at Christmas especially seeing your lovely face.

Yours as ever
Edward

Harriet sat for a long while, reading the pages over and over again and then just staring out into space. She daydreamed fleetingly of her view out of her old bedroom window at Platte Saline over the bubbling Swinge as one by one she tried to reason the implications of his words.

Firstly she realised that Edward still knew nothing of her tragic loss. His decision not to return to Southampton meant it was pointless writing him a reply. On the other hand, since it was now late September, Christmas was only three months away and surely she would see him then, even though he would be returning to Riduna to see his parents. Suddenly the realisation that Edward had already planned to return to his life at sea in foreign parts after Christmas pierced her consciousness. She should try to be happy for him if she could only find the strength.

Chapter 33

AS EACH WEEK passed Harriet lost a little more of that painful longing for her past life. She heard from Jane frequently and each evening she would sit and write about her news to Jane. Unbeknown to her this acted as a powerful tool of healing, since it replaced the act of writing to Edward each night as she had done on Riduna.

One day there was great excitement in the household as an unexpected invitation for Florence and Harriet arrived and was displayed on their mantelpiece by Aunt Rachael, who showed it to friends and neighbours alike with great pride.

'It's such an honour,' she exclaimed.

The invitation was for the Harvest Dance at the Assembly Rooms. At first Harriet thought of refusing, but Florence was so excited by the prospect that she did not have the heart to disappoint her. The only person to be upset was Cousin Luke who had inadvertently been omitted from the invitation. Harriet was not sure if this was an unfortunate error or whether Sarah also held reservations as to the nature of her male cousin. Harriet had been given little reason to think this way but nevertheless always ensured that she was never alone with Luke.

Harriet had just begun to venture out in grey rather than

black, because it was over six months since the death of her mother, but Aunt Rachael was now keen that her pretty young niece should begin to wear more pleasing colours occasionally. She organised for fabric for new dresses to be delivered for both girls. The cottage took on a frenzied air of activity each afternoon for the next week as the women set to work producing the new garments, thus enhancing the air of expectation. On the day that both girls were able to try on their garments for the first real fitting, even Harriet was moved to excitement and anticipation.

Harriet loved dancing and was determined to enjoy the experience. The evening came at last and Joe brought over the horse and trap to escort the ladies for the short ride to the Assembly Rooms. He failed to notice a person lurking in the shadows as he led them into the hall and he hovered attentively, making formal introductions as people came forward. Very soon both Harriet and Florence had their cards full for dances promised through the evening, but as the music commenced it was Joe who claimed Harriet for the first dance. She danced like a feather, floating in her new soft blue dress causing many admiring glances in their direction. Joe was in a dream that night and set his mind to ask Harriet's hand in marriage as soon as it was decently possible. He realised that it was too soon for her to echo his feelings but was sure that no other woman could make him as happy as he felt that night. He had a nagging feeling that he should approach Harriet before Christmas and remembered the locket. For some reason he had not returned it to her but had hidden it at home at the bottom of his old trunk.

The Harvest Dance was to begin a period in Harriet's life when she regained a glimmer of that calm and positive nature, which Mary had warmed to as they had worked together on Riduna. Her life fell into a pattern, working at the school in the mornings and helping her aunt or running errands in the afternoon. The one task she loved most, after her work at school, was to visit the local bakery to deliver or to collect one of her aunt's meat pies, deliciously made at home but baked in the large bakery's bread oven, a service offered to local people for just a few pence. This sent a wonderful aroma along Les Canichers, which was matched by the cheerful demeanour of the baker, who was always able to put a smile on Harriet's face. At first there was also the incentive that Michael worked for the baker, but he had recently married his sweetheart, the baker's only daughter and she had finally agreed to return to Riduna with Michael. Charlotte, her parents and John came over to Sarnia for the wedding; in fact November proved to be a lovely month for Harriet, with precious time spent with her very dear friends who brought her all the news and greetings from Riduna.

Harriet also started looking forward to Joe's regular visits, but she was totally unprepared for their conversation as they walked back from the harbour on that chilly November day when the wedding party had departed for Riduna. Joe was secretly pleased with this opportunity to talk to Harriet alone. Realising this was a difficult time for her and full of admiration for the way in which she remained calm, he suggested a detour along to the end of the jetty to watch the *Courier* depart.

It was here, as they gazed out to sea after the disappearing vessel, that he ventured, 'My dear Harriet. You must be aware that I have great affection for you and long for you to be happy again. Do you think you could consider that I could look after you and make you happy?' Joe paused a moment, waiting for Harriet to focus on his words.

'What I'm trying to say in such a fumbling fashion is, do you think you could consider favourably the offer of my hand in marriage?' Joe finished his proposal trailing his words into the blustery November sea breeze.

Once Harriet had grasped Joe's intentions, she was at a loss for words. She looked up at this man who had been her rock over the last few months when all else was so unstable. She was afraid that, if her words were discouraging, even Joe would abandon her. To be without his cheerful company, especially nearing Christmas was more than she could bear.

How can I be so selfish and thoughtless? she asked herself. On the contrary, she valued his friendship greatly but wanted to avoid misleading him if there was no chance she could love him. What could she say to this man who was watching her so intently? As if to avoid his gaze she started to walk back along the jetty, suddenly needing to feel the comfort of other folk around her.

'Joe, I'm indebted to you for your support in the past few months. You have been my stability when all around me is flotsam and jetsam. Living without your friendship would be unthinkable,' she exclaimed.

Sensing her struggle and trying to withhold any disappointment in his voice Joe continued, 'Harriet, you must be aware of my feelings for you. I've been in love with you from the moment I set my eyes on you in Riduna. Yet I know for you this must be difficult to comprehend, as you are still coming to terms with your grief. I promise I will not mention this again for a while and I hope that we'll continue to be friends. One day I will have the courage to ask for your hand once more and I hope that, by then, you will look upon me with more favour.'

Neither Harriet nor Joe noticed a figure in the shadows who was listening intently to every word.

'You're too generous and kind Joe. I appreciate your patience in this matter, as I also value your friendship,' Harriet replied sincerely.

Since they had arrived at Harriet's aunt's home she quickly bade Joe farewell and trying to hide her turmoil as best she could Harriet let herself into the cottage, followed not long after by her Cousin Luke. She quickly took her leave and fled to the retreat of the room she shared with Florence and poured out all her thoughts in a letter to Jane, the only person who she knew would understand.

Unbeknown to her, Cousin Luke was recounting his tale of Harriet's secret unchaperoned tryst with Joe, including embellished snippets of their overheard conversation, so that when Harriet finally felt calm enough to descend the staircase to join her adoptive family it was to stony faces of both her aunt and uncle.

'Harriet, come and sit down,' her aunt began firmly. 'We've something important to discuss with you.'

Harriet sat down and waited quietly.

'Harriet,' her aunt continued, pausing to decide how best to proceed. 'We, your uncle and I, are dismayed that you should be so disobedient as to have a secret meeting with your friend Joe without a chaperone. You bring dishonour not only to yourself but also to our family.'

Harriet moved forward as if to defend herself.

'I've not yet finished young lady,' Aunt Rachael continued, showing anger in her voice which Harriet had not witnessed in her short stay. 'It has also come to my attention that he has asked your hand in marriage. I am unhappy that you have not informed us of this and that Joe did not see fit to approach my husband to ask prior permission. Nevertheless, with your tarnished reputation to consider, we think that you should accept his proposal.'

Aunt Rachael's words were like a landslide in Harriet's fragile world.

'We realise that you are still mourning your parents and therefore understand that it's hard for you to consider the future in this way. Because of this we intend to be lenient at this time and not press you to make a decision. Your uncle will have a quiet and discreet word with Joe to explain that we are in favour of the match, but that we feel it is not appropriate for any final decision to be made for another six months. Until then you are to resume to only meeting with our permission and only then when you have company. Do you understand all that I have said, Harriet?' Aunt Rachael asked, not expecting any debate in the matter.

'I understand aunt, and thank you,' Harriet replied in a voice that tried to convey her compliance but quell her inner turmoil.

As she sat there memories of Joe's proposal flooded into her mind. She felt that her fate was totally out of her control, and for the second time that day longed that her friend Jane was not so far away.

Chapter 34

IT WAS VERY strange for Harriet to be preparing for Christmas on Sarnia. She felt otherworldly and the only way she could cope with her loss was to imagine that she was a completely different person to the young girl she had left behind on Riduna. Jane continued to be encouraging in her letters and advised Harriet to follow the path which gave her greatest contentment. She also wished Harriet the courage to stand firm and not be swayed into making decisions in haste.

Joe continued to be as attentive as ever although Harriet was thankful that there was never an opportunity for them to be alone together. Aunt Rachael had taken for granted that they were a courting couple, although she was discreet enough not to boast of the fact, to Harriet's relief. Nevertheless Aunt Rachael felt comforted that Harriet had her life mapped out before her and was eager to shed the weight of the responsibility for her niece. She was relieved, since her expectations on receiving Harriet had been of a stubborn flighty young lady who would need to be watched closely.

Joe always acted the perfect gentleman and Harriet appeared to be a dutiful and polite niece, who worked hard and contributed well to the household both financially and in effort. Since that unfortunate incident, which Luke had brought to her attention, she could find no fault in Harriet at all. In fact Aunt Rachael finally admitted that Harriet was a pleasure to keep and a good influence on Florence.

As the girls prepared for the Christmas Dance, sewing the final touches on their dresses by candlelight, into the early hours of the morning before the dance, Aunt Rachael noticed a restlessness in Harriet. She attributed it to the anniversary of her father's death and did not question her niece. She was very proud of both girls as Joe helped them to alight the trap which he had brought to take them.

Joe was just enjoying the pleasure of holding Harriet in his arms during the first dance and seeing Harriet smile when he caught a glimpse of Edward watching them from the other side of the room.

Harriet's smile turned to confusion as she followed Joe's gaze. As the music came to an end she stood in a dream as Edward made his way to where she was standing with Joe. Their eyes met and locked questioningly for a few seconds before Edward's eyes softened as he saw that Harriet's were beginning to fill with tears.

Joe greeted his cousin warmly and noticing Harriet's face looked pale, led them over to where Harriet's Cousin Florence was seated. Harriet struggled to regain her composure as she introduced Edward to Florence, before gratefully accepting the seat which Joe was offering her. She felt a little faint and was vaguely aware that Joe and Edward were talking behind them. Florence was concerned for her cousin's health and attempted to distract her by cheerful dialogue about the evening, but Harriet sat as if in a dream.

Edward had arrived back from his travels in Southampton a week ago, only to be greeted by three letters waiting for him at the Seaman's Mission, two of which had remained there for nearly a year. He found the news devastating and although he was keen to see his parents, he decided to stay on Sarnia for a night in the hopes that he might see Harriet. On surprising his aunt and uncle by arriving at the guesthouse unannounced, they informed him of the Christmas Dance. He had attended many dances on the island in the past with his cousin Joe and had no doubt that he could find a suitable person to sponsor him.

Joe was sensitively aware that the two friends would have much to discuss and so asked Florence if she would care to dance, leaving Edward standing behind Harriet's chair. For the first time in his life Edward was lost for words. Here was the lady he loved and he had not been with her to support her during the worst time in her life. They remained silent for a few moments, Harriet attempting to keep composed and Edward aware that any words of comfort sounded so shallow. He was pricked by a guilty conscience. Finally he asked Harriet to dance and it was only as they glided together that Harriet began to relax. They danced with such grace that heads turned in admiration once again. Harriet and Edward were as one.

'You leave for Riduna in the morning Edward?' Harriet asked wistfully.

'Yes Harriet, I'm afraid I do. I'm so sorry. I didn't receive your news until I reached Southampton alongside the letter which said that you were now living on Sarnia,' he explained. 'It was such a shock. I'm so sorry,' he repeated as if searching for the right words.

'So little time, Edward,' continued Harriet, in a daze.

'Oh Harriet, I believed and dreamed that we would be sharing Christmas together on Riduna. I had no idea!' Edward exclaimed with genuine concern.

'You were not to know,' replied Harriet quietly concentrating to keep her emotions in check.

'It's so difficult to talk here,' she continued, 'and we have so little time.'

Edward led Harriet to a side room where they became oblivious to passers by. They were only together for a few minutes but Edward expressed his sadness at her loss, and talked a little of the wonders he had witnessed on his trip. He was about to express his constant feelings for her when Florence interrupted them.

'Oh there you are Harriet, I was concerned about you,' she exclaimed a little crossly.

She had no time to continue in her remonstrations because Joe came to claim Harriet for the next dance. Edward politely returned the favour and danced with Florence, thus halting any chance for Harriet to talk in private with Edward again that night. She glimpsed Edward and Florence dancing on the other side of the hall and realised that her cousin would soon be charmed by the light-hearted tales of her lifetime friend.

Harriet, Joe and Flo watched the *Courier* as it left for Riduna in the morning.

'I will be back for two days in the New Year,' Edward called as the boat slipped away from the jetty, hoping for one of Harriet's encouraging smiles.

'Give my love to Aunt Beth, Uncle Joseph and my grandparents,' she called back in reply.

Christmas came and went in a hazy fog, both in the weather and in Harriet's heart. Cousin Luke had tried to cause trouble yet again since a friend had gossiped about Harriet slipping away and sitting alone with a stranger at the dance. Harriet proclaimed her innocence, explaining that she had known Edward all her life. They had grown up together like brother and sister. Aunt Rachael was satisfied with this explanation, but nevertheless she prayed that it would not be long before Joe asked Harriet's hand in marriage yet again. In fact a speedy engagement would be in everyone's best interest, she reasoned.

Harriet saw little of Joe over Christmas. Although his painting work had ceased for the seasonal festivities, he was needed to help his parents during this busy time. On New Year's Day he had sent a formal invitation for the following evening, the day in fact that Edward arrived back from Riduna. The soiree was arranged in Edward's honour. Cousin Luke, Cousin Florence and their parents were invited, as was Sarah Mortland and her two brothers.

Harriet could feel her heart beating faster as they walked the short distance to Well Road, a perfect place for a guesthouse since the quiet street ran directly down to the harbour. Harriet knew that she would have no opportunity to talk privately to Edward but nevertheless to be in his company was enough to bring a glimmer to her eyes and a healthy rosy complexion to her cheeks.

Edward and Harriet only talked on a couple of occasions during the evening. He explained in greater detail his plans to travel for the next year but, since their conversation was overheard, it was formal and a little stilted.

'When do you intend to return to Sarnia, Edward?' Harriet had the courage to enquire tentatively as their moment together was drawing to an end.

'My contract for Captain Reynolds is for a year Harriet and then I will be free to visit Sarnia and Riduna,' Edward explained gazing at the pendant adorning Harriet's neck. He tried not to show his disappointment that Harriet was not wearing the locket he had given her.

Harriet was about to ask what he intended to do after a year but Sarah Mortland's younger brother joined their conversation. He was interested in hearing more details about Edward's travels in the hopes of persuading his parents to allow him to follow in Edward's footsteps, though they intended for him to join the navy where he was more likely to be promoted to officer fairly rapidly.

The evening flowed with cheerful conversation, interspersed with Florence singing and Sarah playing the piano. The latter gave rise to a slight irritation on Harriet's part as she watched Joe dutifully turn the pages for Sarah, a feeling Harriet quickly dismissed as meaningless.

As the evening was coming to a close Harriet agreed to walk to the harbour at midday on the following day to say farewell to Edward. Her sleep that night was restless and she worked, as if in a dream, the following morning. Florence met her outside the school gates and they were soon at the quay, searching through the gathering throng of people for the familiar faces of Edward and Joe. This was not difficult since the cousins were tall and handsome, half a head above the mass of people gathered to await the arrival of the steam ship which would take Edward to Southampton. The two men turned and waved simultaneously, both smiling at Harriet, and she felt her heart miss a beat as they seemed like twins rather than cousins. She smiled and waved back, instantly recognising Edward's face, more rugged and travel worn than Joe's, with eyes full of excitement for his adventures to come. On the other hand there was Joe, whose now familiar features showed a genuine care and concern for her and this in turn filled her with a sense of peace. She ignored the dilemma in her heart and rushed forward, allowing Edward to take her hands in his.

'I promise I'll write to you as soon as I reach Southampton,' he reassured her, aware that it was their only private way to communicate.

For a few moments only it was as if there was no one else in the world. Edward gazed into Harriet's eyes just long enough so that each was aware that their deep bond remained secure.

A week later Edward was true to his word and Harriet received the promised letter.

My dearest Harriet

It was wonderful to see you again although, due to circumstances beyond our control, our time together was all too short.

I realised that it must be difficult for you to think of me so much, with your life so totally changed by such sad circumstances. I still think of you often Harriet. You are to me like my right hand. I cannot imagine my world without you. I promise that I will return next year and, if your feelings for me remain unchanged, I will ask your hand in marriage.

Nevertheless I hope that you will understand my need to accept this wonderful opportunity and can be pleased for me. My journey to America begins the day after tomorrow and so unfortunately I will not receive a reply from you until my return next year. In fact Harriet, I ask you not to reply in writing. I would like to hear the words from your beautiful lips.

Yours as ever
Edward

Harriet read the letter many times in private before hiding it with her few precious items in a box at the bottom of the wardrobe she shared with Florence. She resolved not to dwell on the matter but to hold the memory deep within her, alongside her feelings for Edward. She would focus on being as positive about her present life as she was able.

Chapter 35

BY THE END of January Harriet experienced a feeling of peace in her life, working at the school, living with her aunt and enjoying Joe's occasional visits. Since Joe had not mentioned marriage again Harriet relaxed in his company and began to look forward to seeing him. It was only in the evenings that she would allow herself to dream about Edward and wonder where he was and what he might be doing. She never questioned that one day he would return for her. She began to find the island a delight especially in the springtime when the red and white Campion adorned the edges of the cliff top pathways and bluebells filled the woods.

Joe worked hard and had secured a position in charge of five men, two of whom were lads he was training, much like he had been a couple of years before. He resolved to wait until at least May before repeating his proposal of marriage. By that time he hoped to have saved enough money in order to afford to rent modest accommodation for them to live in. Also by then the anniversary of Annie's death would have passed a milestone for Harriet. He was certain that Harriet enjoyed his company and hoped that her feelings for him would gently develop to more than a genuine friendship.

Early in May an unexpected letter arrived from Riduna. Harriet had not heard from Beth since Christmas and felt a twinge of guilt that she had not written to her. She was so excited to hear the news from the island that she opened the letter in the parlour, with her aunt and cousins present.

Dear Harriet

I am saddened to have to send you this news, but felt I should write to you before you heard rumours from other people. We had a personal visit from Bill, the coxswain on the mail steamer from Sarnia to Southampton. He had travelled from Sarnia to see us in person.

When he was last in Southampton he was informed of the Humber. We were so proud when Edward first told us of his promoted position and aware of his excitement about sailing this schooner across the other side of the Atlantic.

I do not know how to say this and wish I was there at your side Harriet, but there has been news that the Humber was caught in a terrible storm, a tornado I think he called it. The Humber was shipwrecked and there was a report that sixty-six lives were lost. Edward's body has never been found. I am so sorry to tell you of this tragedy in a letter Harriet. As you can imagine Joseph and I are devastated and do not know quite how to understand our loss.

Take care Harriet and we hope and pray that you will overcome your grief and eventually find some happiness in the future. I know that Edward loved you, of that I have no doubt and I hope that this will be some comfort to you.

Yours with affection

Beth and Joseph

Harriet, her face white with shock, held its dignity as she placed the letter back in its envelope and quietly walked upstairs to place it with her other letters in her special box. She closed the lid tight shut and placed it in the far corner of her wardrobe. She was too numb to talk of her grief, speaking very little that day, not even able to write her thoughts to Jane.

On the following afternoon Joe called. She was aware that he was watching her closely as he chatted amiably to her aunt and cousin. Harriet said little. They only spoke briefly of the news. It was much too painful for her to discuss.

Harriet quietly and calmly continued with her routine, not even aware that she was being deprived of a funeral, a public expression of her grief. She wrote to Beth and Joseph, aware that their pain must be greater than hers, if that was possible.

Joe continued to be there for her in a sensitive and supportive manner. The anniversary of Annie's death was approaching and he made the suggestion that they travel to Riduna together. He would have liked to pay his respects to his aunt and uncle and he thought that Harriet might benefit from the trip. Harriet firmly declined, preferring to pick some posies of flowers, like the ones she had recently so admired, tie them with white ribbon and walk with them to the end of the quay. Joe and Florence remained at a respectful distance as she threw the posies one by one into the swirling waters, in the direction of Riduna. It was a poignant moment as she stood there, silently saying farewell to Mama, Papa and to Edward.

She returned to Florence and Joe and they walked in silence along the winding streets and up the steps to Les Canichers where Joe bade them farewell. Three flowers remained in Harriet's hand, a red and white Campion and a 'forget me not'. She was unable to write in her journal that night but instead lay her flowers carefully between the last empty pages and closed it tight shut, placing the book in her box. She tied the box securely with the remainder of the white ribbon and placed it back in the far corner of her wardrobe.

Chapter 36

HARRIET AND JOE were married at All Saints Church on 29th June 1884, just a year after Harriet's arrival on Sarnia. It was a quiet but pleasant wedding attended mainly by Joe's family and friends. Charlotte, John, Michael and his new wife Clara came over from Riduna, but Harriet's grandparents felt unable to make the journey. Jane journeyed all the way from London to be with her best friend and David and Mary joined her, enthusiastic to have a holiday and take time to explore Sarnia with Jane. Harriet was delighted to see their familiar faces.

As they stood at the altar Harriet nervously glanced at Joe, who smiled with such genuine love that she was overwhelmed with warmth and affection for this man by her side. She remembered the day she had agreed to marry Joe and realised that on any other occasion she might have been suspicious that Florence had left them alone together.

Harriet, Joe and Flo had been taking a stroll along the promenade at the harbour's edge when Florence unexpectedly made an excuse to leave them and take a cutting through to the High Street to make a purchase. With her emotions in such turmoil so very recently, Harriet had been staring out to sea dreamily when Joe turned to her and took her hands in his.

'Harriet, you know my feelings for you and you know that I will

look after you and protect you. Would you do me the honour of becoming my wife?' he asked.

Still in a daze Harriet looked up into those deep eyes and she felt otherworldly as she could hear her quiet voice answering, 'Yes Joe, I will.'

Joe was so excited that he could hardly contain his desire to tell the world. Florence reappeared and feigned surprise at the news, which she had secretly expected. Back at Les Canichers her aunt and uncle were delighted and before Harriet knew it a date was set for the following month. Everyone she met from that moment on congratulated her and wished her well. With so much to organise her feet hardly touched the ground in a whirlwind of letters to be written, arrangements to be made and a dress to be sewn.

After the wedding Joe and Harriet moved into their own place, a terraced town house on Cornet Street with glimpses of the harbour from the upstairs window. It was in a much lighter disposition than Les Canichers and was just a stone's throw from the bustling market. For the first time for as long as Harriet could remember she felt a surge of happiness. She loved her husband Joe, of that she had no doubt. It was a warm comfortable kind of love which filled her with a sense of belonging. She was also reassured that he was devoted to her and would be there for her whatever the future may hold.

By the first of August Harriet was sure that she was with child and the newly married couple looked forward to the event with excitement. She wrote to Joseph and Beth and also to Jane with the wonderful news, hoping that Beth could be pleased for her and she soon received reassurance that this was so.

Chapter 37

SOME WOULD SAY that it was a coincidence dealt by the hand of fate that it was on 29th June that Edward regained consciousness. He was aware that he must be in some kind of hospital, but since he recognised no one and could not understand the nurses, he drifted back to sleep as if in a dream. When he woke the following morning he was more alert. The attractive dark-skinned nurses who bustled around his bed spoke in a lilting accent which he recognised to be somewhere in the West Indies. He understood the occasional French word as he became accustomed to the singsong voices. He tried to move but immediately a shooting pain spread across his ribs and his head started to spin.

'Non, non, monsieur!' exclaimed the younger of the two administering angels looking over him, who broke into a lovely smile at seeing him wake up.

Edward attempted to relax but was aware that he was only able to take short breaths to avoid sharp stabs of pain. He realised that he must have broken some of his ribs at the very least. He was also aware that he had no feeling in one of his legs, but he could not move enough to investigate. He turned his head towards the other nurse who he assumed was her superior. As if understanding the question he was unable to speak, she gesticulated towards his ribs and his right leg and using her hands as she spoke, he was able to interpret that she was saying that he must stay still for at least sixty days. In fact since he spoke some French he was able to interpret her Patois if she spoke slowly. After that she left him in the capable hands of the nurse with the beautiful smile.

As predicted it was two months before Edward was able to move about enough with a stick to be discharged from the hospital, by which time he had learnt a little of his fate through the broken English of one of the nurses and his limited knowledge of French. He had been found unconscious and dehydrated, washed up on one of the beaches by a local fisherman, who at first glance was sure he was dead. The fisherman had kindly brought him to the hospital and had been his only irregular visitor since he arrived. Edward had lain unconscious for over two months.

His day of freedom finally arrived and the nurse with the endearing smile helped him to the door where the fisherman greeted him with enthusiasm. Edward hobbled towards the waiting cart, not sure where he was being taken, but grateful to breathe in fresh air at last, although the heat winded him at first. He sat up at the back of the cart with his leg out straight in front of him. Every bump on the track added to his discomfort although this was dampened by his enthusiasm to find out where he was.

The fisherman took him down to the harbour where he had been enquiring as to who the stranger might be. As it happened one of Captain Reynold's schooners has docked the previous evening and was still in the harbour. The fisherman took Edward to a bar which he guessed correctly the English captain would frequent. Edward recognised the fellow seaman instantly and thanked the fisherman profusely before becoming deeply engrossed in conversation with Captain Myers, who had dug deep into his pocket and handed a handful of notes to the fisherman as he backed through the door.

Myers was very surprised to hear of Edward's survival and he explained to Edward that when the *Humber* was wrecked in a flash storm off the coast of Antigua and dashed on to treacherous rocks a couple of miles off the coast of the island, the few survivors had been rescued heroically from the wreck or washed up on the shores of Antigua. Edward has been assumed drowned since he was not among the few survivors and word was duly sent to his next of kin.

'So where are we now?' Edward asked, wishing so make sense of the story.

'On the neighbouring island of St Barts,' stated Myers matter of factly. 'We call in with mail and to pick up supplies from time to time but it is not regular on our trips.

'It is fortunate I knew a bit of French,' exclaimed Edward.

Late into the evening when the jigsaw pieces of the tale had been reassembled and both men had drunk enough for their senses to be numbed for a while, Captain Myers paid for lodgings for Edward in one of the beach shacks rented out cheaply by the barman. He also arranged for similar rustic transport to bring him to join his crew at first light, when they would be leaving for Puerto Rico and then on to New York, where Edward could pick up a free passage home to England to see his family and recover fully from his ordeal.

Chapter 38

A YEAR HAD passed on Sarnia and Harriet and Joe were blessed with a fine son who filled their lives with joy. Joe had heard the rumour that Edward was alive but decided it was best not to breathe a word to Harriet. He saw no reason to unsettle his wife, who seemed calm and contented with her life on Sarnia.

It was at Joe's parents' house that Harriet discovered the truth about Edward. She had taken Ernest over to see his grandparents one afternoon and Joe's mother had just received a letter from her sister Beth with the great news, which she was excited to share with Harriet. Harriet's reaction was initially of numb shock which she masked for the sake of the child and her parents-in-law. Later that night, as she waited for Joe's late return, she sat dreaming for a while wondering what might have been. She looked in on her sleeping child, smiled at his beautiful face and pushed all thoughts of Edward to the depths of her mind.

By the end of the year Harriet and Joe were also blessed with twins, sons whom both parents doted on.

It was early in the year 1890 that Joe faced an unfortunate crisis. The specialist painting work had all but dried up now, with no new military establishments being built and too many skilled people chasing the few restoration and maintenance jobs available in this line of work. Joe found it difficult to find alternative employment in order to provide for himself and his growing family.

When Joe first broached the subject, which had been burning within him, of the possibility of moving to Southampton to find work, it was met by dismay and anger. He was saddened to see his kind and gentle wife affected this way. For a while he took any odd job he could find in order to bring home enough to feed his family and Harriet also reluctantly resolved to take on batches of sewing. This made her all the more disheartened since it was a task she had no liking for. Harriet did all she could to make ends meet and keep her family cheerful and well nourished. One form of suffering she had never experienced in her life before was hardship.

One Sunday they were taking a stroll along Fermaine Bay to ease the tension at home. Joe was deep in thought and Harriet was watching the children playing in the sand. She looked up at Joe and saw the worried expression on his face. Then she observed the children, oblivious to the dilemma facing the family and she realised how lucky she was to have such a man for a husband and a lovely family. She realised that she was being selfish and to Joe's relief agreed to go with him to Southampton, where he promised there was an abundance of opportunities. It was as if a cloud lifted from his countenance. The relief was so great that they smiled at each other and he reached out to take her hand in his.

'It does not matter where we are, Harriet, so long as our family is safe and well and remain together,' he reasoned.

'I know,' replied Harriet gently.

It was only a month later, after many more painful goodbyes that Joe, Harriet and their children were standing out on deck on their way to Southampton. They passed a large island and a colourful lighthouse which seemed to Harriet to be balanced on an iceberg of a rock with other sharp bright white 'icicles' protruding from the water.

'That island is called the Isle of Wight and those rocks are called the Needles,' explained Joe as he pointed to the landmarks.

'I can see why,' said Harriet. 'Though they look like icicles to me. The rocks are so white that they shine in the sunlight.'

'And there,' stated Joe dramatically, with a sweeping gesture towards the land on the other side of the Solent, 'is England!'

Harriet stood lips slightly open, gazing at the landmass in front of them. As Joe talked to the children about what they could see Harriet was silent. She felt a mixture of fear and excitement for such an unknown future. They sailed up Southampton water among a litter of little sailing boats, passing a smaller Royal Mail Steam Packet ship, which Joe explained went over to the Isle of Wight and one larger ship.

'Where's that going to Papa?' asked their eldest son Ernest.

'That one! Oh it is probably on its way to India or South Africa, son. Just like the one your Uncle Edward sails in.'

Harriet's heart seemed to miss a beat at the mention of Edward's name. Then she was cross with herself for feeling that way with her lovely family around her feet and Joe at her side.

She smiled up at him looking for some reassurance.

Joe, who misinterpreting her pained expression as fear for the future, gently whispered, 'We will be fine Harriet, once we are settled. You will see.'

'I am sure we will be,' Harriet replied and squeezed his hand for a moment.

'That is Southampton,' said Joe, pointing up the river.

Nothing had prepared Harriet for the next sight that came into view. Southampton seemed to grow before their very eyes until it stretched to the entirety of their vision. Harriet was filled with fear now and wanted to beg Joe to take her back on the next available ship. She realised that she could not make a scene in front of the children and so she helped to gather their belongings and look after the children who stood nervously close to her skirts. Joe continued to talk about where they would be living but Harriet heard nothing. She followed as they joined the milling foot passengers waiting to disembark. The crowds made her want to scream as they pushed around her and it took all her concentration to keep her two charges by her side while Joe held the hand of their eldest son. He bundled them into an awaiting horse and trap. This took them a short distance to join yet another queue waiting for a strange, flat looking boat which seemed to Harriet to be pulled across the water by chains. It looked so low in the water by this time that Harriet feared for their lives. Joe looked at his wife's tired face and smiled.

'Look over to the other side. There is a little hotel called the Cliff where we will take a cheap room for the night and then we will search for a place to rent when we are fresher in the morning. We will be fine. You will see,' Joe added the last comment a little too brightly, realising that he was repeating himself and sounding as if he was beginning to doubt it himself.

'We are all tired. It has been a very long journey,' he said with more conviction, since he was stating simple fact rather than conjecture.

'Is it safe on this flat contraption?' Harriet exclaimed.

'Of course it is. It is called a floating bridge and they float across the water here many times a day.'

She looked up at the approaching shoreline, at the rows

of small houses weaving through the trees on a sloping hillside. A thought struck her that it was not dissimilar to St Peter Port, although it was certainly less quaint, a thought which comforted her a little as she held on tightly to the hands of her youngest children.

Harriet tried to smile. 'What is the name of this place?' she asked, trying to show more of an interest.

'It is called Woolston to our right and to our left the village is called "Itchen Ferry" after the ferry which has been here for years. Woolston is only a small village and if you walk along to Weston Shore you can take a nice stroll along the water's edge.' Joe did not have time to say anymore. Soon they were walking up the hard, passing the awaiting carriages, towards the hotel. Harriet was secretly relieved to be safe on dry land again. In years to come Joe teased her many a time of her fear of the floating bridge.

It did not take long for Joe and Harriet and their family to settle into their small dwelling in Florence Road. There was an estate office just over the road from the hotel which had several properties to rent in the area and they chose one only a few minutes from the shore. Harriet could never be far away from water. It was a world apart from living on either of the islands but Harriet quickly got used to the little local shops. She did not venture far without Joe, no further than the shops near the floating bridge and the little corner shops.

Soon another child was on the way and Harriet had her hands full looking after them all. Joe found plenty of work and often worked late on in the evenings, but they were happy enough. His job was not as rewarding as the specialised work he had carried out on the island but he resigned himself to general painting work for private houses and local light industry. Harriet used her sewing skills to mend and darn where she could and sometimes needed to take in some sewing work to supplement their income. It did not take long for Harriet to get to know the neighbours, as she was never slow at giving a helping hand to others. She made a special point of being there for old Mrs Barnes next door who was so kind with the children. In fact she would sometimes offer to mind the children of an evening so that Joe could take Harriet for a stroll down to Weston Shore or sometimes over the bridge to Southampton. On her birthday he treated her to a ride in one of those waiting carriages to the pier and they walked along the Esplanade together. They stood and watched the many ships come and go. Harriet marvelled at the trams but it was many years before she was brave enough to venture on one.

'Joe is a good man,' Harriet thought to herself one day. It gave her such a warm feeling inside when she thought of their life together. 'I was lucky to find such a loving dependable man.'

Their home was a bit cramped with four growing children and it had taken a while to become accustomed to the area, but Harriet had needed to adapt many a time in her short life. On the whole she was quite content with life.

She would not allow herself to dwell on the past.

1892

The fact that in her heart she knew that one day Edward would visit now they were in Southampton did little to prepare her for the actual event. It was on a cold winter's day in December, not long after Sarah was born that he came for the first time. Harriet was baking in preparation for Christmas, her two younger boys were playing on the rag rug by the warm hearth and Sarah was sound asleep in a cot on the other side of the room when there was a knock at the door. Harriet had her hands full of flour so she was grateful that Joe had come in from the backyard where he was carefully cleaning his tools.

'Come in my old mate!' he exclaimed as he recognised the person at the door. 'It's so good to see you. My word you really look the part of a sea captain now, with your beard and cap. I hardly recognised you. Harriet love, Edward's here!'

'Hello Harriet,' were the first words from that all too familiar voice which Harriet heard. She was relieved that her back was to the door and that she could take a moment to compose herself while she washed her trembling hands, before she faced him. She could feel her heart racing and she gripped the edge of the bowl for a moment, to steady herself. 'What a surprise,' she exclaimed. 'I will be with you in just a moment.'

'How did you find us old man?' asked Joe, guiding their guest to a chair by the hearth.

'Let's have less of the old man please. I'm only a year older than you, after all. I heard that you were in England the last time our ship called in at Sarnia on a special delivery of tea and I visited your parents, Joe, to get your address. In fact I took some leave in order to call in on the folks in Riduna. My parents and Charlotte send their love,' Edward replied, gratefully accepting the offered seat.

Harriet took a deep breath before turning and saying in as normal voice as she could muster, 'Hello Edward, it has been a good few years has it not?' She blushed as he stood up briefly to take her hand.

'Still as lovely as ever I see. You must have to keep her under lock and key Joe,' Edward teased, taking the chance of looking into her eyes for just a moment.

It did not last long because Harriet was too quick

thinking and stepped to her husband's side. She pointed to her two sons who were sitting open mouthed on the rug and retorted, 'I have my hands full enough with the twins,' and she smiled reassuringly at Joe, 'and my husband. Let me introduce you to Tom and Jack.'

'Hello Tom and Jack,' said Edward. 'Let me see what I've got in my sack for my two favourite nephews.'

Like an early Father Christmas Edward reached into his sack and pulled out two little wooden boats, one red and one green. The boys came gingerly towards him at first but were soon won over and before long they were sitting on either of Edward's knees captivated by one of his tales of a trip to China.

Joe winked at his wife as they stood there watching the scene and he squeezed her hand. Harriet relaxed and the tension in the air seemed to evaporate.

She smiled at her husband and whispered, 'I will make some tea. You sit down too for a while, Joe.'

Joe told Edward of the events that led to their move over to the mainland. It was obvious to Edward that they were happy together and he knew that he had no right to disturb that peace. As he listened to them he thought about his feelings. It was true that Harriet's presence still stirred him and he could tell that she, too, was moved in some way by his visit. On reflection his cousin Joe made a far better husband for Harriet than he ever would and he tried to be happy for them. After all he loved them both in different ways. He stood up as if to take his leave of the little family just as Sarah, unnoticed by Edward until that moment, stirred in her cot and whimpered.

'Now who have we here?' he exclaimed walking over to the cot and scooping up the child as if she were his own. Harriet gulped at the sight.

'That's little Sarah,' said Joe proudly, 'our latest addition to our growing family. 'Isn't she lovely,' he added. 'Just like her mother,' he said smiling at his wife.

As Edward talked to the infant Sarah gurgled and Harriet thought it must be her imagination but she was sure that she saw Sarah give a glimmer of a smile to this strange bearded figure. In fact, from that moment on, Sarah was Uncle Edward's favourite. Whenever he chose to visit, Sarah would be the first to rush to greet him and he would lift her high in the air and swing her round until she would giggle with glee.

Over the next few years, as the children grew up Edward would appear unannounced about once a year. It would never be at the same time of year, so it would always be a surprise. The children would sit on his lap or on the floor with their heads resting against his knee while he talked of his adventures. It was always tempting to stroke his beard or tap his pipe. For effect he would occasionally pause at a dramatic moment and holding his pipe aloft he would blow the most perfect smoke rings in the air and the children would try to catch them.

Harriet would listen to his tales from a distance, fascinated by the strange people and places Edward described. Each visit brought stories more outlandish than the last and more than once Harriet wondered if they were true or a figment of Edward's imagination. On one occasion, when Joe was there, he winked at her as if to say he shared her doubt. Nevertheless the children were always mesmerised.

At each visit Harriet made every effort to replace the powerful yearning of their last days on Riduna together by the brotherly, sisterly friendship of their childhood. It helped that they rarely talked about the past.

Only once had they mentioned anything personal. It was on one occasion he had visited when Joe and his eldest son had taken a trip to Sarnia because his father was ill. They usually avoided talking about difficult subjects, always keeping their conversation light and cheerful. Harriet never asked Edward if there was a woman in his life and Edward never felt that it was right to talk about Marie.

On this occasion when he called the twins were nine by then, and felt adult enough to shake Uncle Edward's hand in greeting, unlike Sarah who still rushed to be thrust into the air by her favourite uncle, before he settled in Joe's armchair by the hearth.

After Edward had satisfied the children's appetite for more tales of his adventures he looked up at Harriet and remarked almost wistfully, 'You have such a lovely family, Harriet. You are so fortunate.'

'Yes, I truly am, Edward,' she smiled warmly. 'But you, too, have lived your dreams. We have both been blessed in different ways,' she continued.

Edward wanted to say that it might have been different, but he so respected this gentle lady before him and his absent cousin that he held his peace and added, 'Joe is a very lucky man!'

'Yes, I think he is,' replied Harriet with a laugh and they parted amicably, both relieved that the memories of their shared dreams of their young adulthood were left unspoken.

This was the one and only occasion that Harriet allowed herself to pour out the confusion in her heart in a letter to her dear friend Jane. Her friend showed great wisdom in her speedy reply.

My dearest Harriet

It sounds from your letter that you are blessed with such a lovely family. Joe is as attentive as ever to your every need and the children sound mischievous, but adorable. Oh how I long to visit you all one day.

Reading your letter makes me a trifle pained that I have set aside any hopes of happiness in that direction, but nevertheless rest assured that I am fulfilled in my joy in becoming a fully qualified nurse.

You ask of Thomas. When Thomas and I occasioned to meet here in London, I am sorry to say that the magic was lost. It is difficult to explain. London seemed too harsh and we walked about like strangers among strangers. At that moment I knew for certain that I should concentrate on making a success of my training.

You talk briefly of a visit from Edward. What a surprise that must have been! How wonderful to hear all his news of his travels. It sounds as if, not unlike my own situation, that Edward has chosen 'sailing the seas' to be the love of his life and he, too, has found contentment.

Please send him my regards on his next visit. I send my love to you Harriet, to Joe and all your family.

Yours truly
Jane

Chapter 39

JANE WAS CORRECT in many ways regarding Edward, but he also found contentment in a different fashion. Not long after his initial visit to the family on Florence Road he returned to Marie for much needed solace before his next trip. Their union was beautiful since Marie gave herself to Edward completely, unlike the many strangers whom she was forced to be with in his absence. In her eyes he was her first love and she his. They had never spoken of Harriet, there was no need. This time seemed different and Edward found it very difficult to say goodbye.

He returned to his waiting ship the next morning feeling empty, unsettled for the first time by Marie's other life. It was as if he had been set free and yet he longed for stability in his life at last. He resolved to find a place to make his own on his return to Southampton. Riduna held no power over him since Harriet had left and his parents were very frail. Using his ample savings he visited an estates office near the harbour and soon found a modest but clean dwelling just over the water. This was far enough away from Marie's former life since he knew he needed to tread very carefully to ensure that she was safe from the tyranny of her father.

He bribed the publican handsomely and promised a

regular retainer in order to keep Marie's father in the manner he had become accustomed, and the publican silenced. As luck would have it a travelling French gentleman had frequented the establishment regularly of late, who had dangerously flaunted his wealth to all he had met.

Edward and the publican devised a story that the French gentleman had taken a liking to Marie and had vowed not to return to France without her, whatever it cost him. Early one evening Marie was sent on an errand to take provisions to the Frenchman's carriage which waited at the end of a nearby narrow street. Edward, who had donned appropriate apparel and shaved off his beloved beard to complete the disguise, greeted Marie and ushered her into the waiting carriage, which sped off towards the harbour. They mingled amongst the crowd waiting to board the ship to France, but just at the last minute they slipped away unnoticed and took the nearby ferry to Hythe.

Marie was overjoyed to be Edward's housekeeper and to be free of her life at the inn. She soon made the little house a comfortable home for them. He stayed with her for a month to ensure that she was safe, by which time his beard had begun to return to those familiar features. Hythe was a quiet little backwater where Marie soon made friends and kept herself busy by taking in washing from the nearby manor.

Although Edward never settled for long, always yearning for the next adventure, Marie gave him the stability in his life that he had not felt in years and also a reason to live. Above all he now had a home to return to, which was cosy and welcoming, and he could say goodbye to his life of backstreet lodgings in Southampton forever. His greatest regret was that they never bore a family, which made his infrequent visits to Harriet and Joe all the more important.

Chapter 40

1910

HARRIET AND JOE were sitting at the kitchen table eating breakfast on the day after Sarah's wedding and Joe was suffering from a restless spirit. He was unsettled and pined for Sarnia. He had been over for visits on a couple of occasions when his parents had still been alive, taking his eldest son with him, but he longed to visit it once more.

'I cannot become accustomed to the quiet in this house, Harriet,' Joe exclaimed in frustration.

'I miss Sarah too, Joe, but we should enjoy the peace and quiet now. The house will soon be full of grandchildren as like as not!' Harriet exclaimed cheerfully.

There was quiet for a few moments before Joe enquired, 'You are looking thoughtful Harriet, my love. Tell me what is on your mind.'

Harriet reminded Joe of Sarah's idea to set up a guesthouse together. With her husband Anthony a corporal in the army he was away a great deal and Sarah thought the new direction could be beneficial to all of the family.

'I really don't think I have the energy to begin a new business Harriet,' exclaimed Joe.

Harriet looked up at her husband whose face looked tired and pale.

'Perhaps you need a rest Joe. You have been overdoing it of late,' she said gently.

Joe paused before asking the question which burned on his lips 'Would you like to take a trip to Sarnia with me Harriet?'

Harriet sighed. She had half expected this question and having carefully thought it over she replied, looking into Joe's eyes, 'Joe, you know how I love the islands and if I return to Sarnia I would need to go to Riduna also. I have thought about it often but feel that it is just too much for me.'

'We could visit Riduna if you wish. It would only take a few extra days,' Joe encouraged.

'Joe, look at me,' Harriet said gently. 'I have my memories and most of the ones I dwell on are of happy times. If I went back to Riduna then I would probably never be able to leave again. Our family may not need us now but they will presently, you will see. Our home is here now. We already have two grandchildren and soon the place will be forever full of children, so that we will long for peace and quiet again,' she reasoned.

'All the more reason to take the time to go now,' exclaimed Joe.

'No Joe. You go if you really need to, but I cannot come with you. Please try to understand,' she pleaded.

Joe came to bend over the chair where Harriet was sitting and kissed her on the lips, a gesture he had not made for years.

'You would not object to me going one last time then? I do not think I can settle unless I do and I think it would give me the peace I really crave,' he explained.

Harriet stood up and took her husband's hand.

'Go with my blessing Joe,' she reassured him.

Harriet reached up and kissed Joe on the lips, stirring

feelings they had not felt in a long while. He took her in his arms and they made their way to bed, Joe carrying the gas lamp ahead of them up the steep staircase.

In the next few days Harriet made sure that Joe's clothes were mended and presentable and on one of her daughter's occasional but pleasurable visits she asked Sarah to go up to the attic to bring down her father's old trunk.

Sarah dragged the trunk out from the back of a large dusty wardrobe and opened it. She rummaged with pleasure as she found some of her old and favourite toys, lovingly kept by her parents. Each seemed to hold a special memory. The more exotic toys reminded her of her Uncle Edward. He would turn up unexpectedly at Christmas time like a true to life Santa Claus, bearing gifts from far off places, each with a fascinating tale to tell. Her Uncle Edward was the best storyteller in the whole world. She would recognise his chuckle at the door instantly.

Sarah smiled as she put them one by one into an empty box, including several papers and items which belonged to her father. Right at the bottom of the trunk she came across a small leather pouch which she carefully opened. A pretty locket fell out into her hands. With curiosity she opened it with her fingernail, surprised to find some strands of hair carefully entwined inside. She snapped it shut as if to hold its secret secure and then lifted it to her neck and glanced up into the dark mirror on the back of the wardrobe door. Sarah stared back at her reflection and wondered.

'What are you doing Sarah?' Harriet called up to her from the bedroom below.

Sarah quickly returned the locket to its leather pouch and slipped it into the box with the other treasures and dragged the trunk to the top of the ladder. She passed it down to her mother, who was waiting beneath her.

'I was just clearing it out,' she explained. Something made

her refrain from mentioning the locket and she had soon forgotten it in the mixed feelings of emotions as she said farewell to her father.

Looking back at the sad faces of Harriet and Sarah on the dockside, he called from the ship, 'I will only be away for a few weeks.'

Chapter 41

JOE FELT OVERWHELMED by tiredness as he sought a place away from the draughty deck. Five hours later he woke up with a start and tried to get up. His whole body ached which he attributed to sleeping awkwardly. Slowly he found his way to purchase some refreshments and the remainder of the journey passed uneventfully, since it was a very calm day. He returned to the deck in time to see Sarnia appear on the horizon and, ignoring the aching in his chest and arms, he stood transfixed as the island of his birth grew before him.

He smiled as his feet touched the path at the harbour's edge. A young lad rushed to his aid and with only a nod of encouragement, put Joe's trunk in a waiting barrow. Memories of his own youth flooded back as he gratefully trudged beside the lad up Well Road to the familiar guesthouse, which his sister and husband now ran. He gave the lad a few pence as his sister rushed out to greet him.

'Joe, how pale you look, come in and rest!' she exclaimed as she ushered him into the cosy parlour at the back of the building.

'Don't fuss sis, I'm just tired,' he replied.

With a large cup of tea and exhausted by Pamela's endless questions, Joe drifted off to sleep in the armchair by the fire, dreaming fitfully of snapshots of his earlier life on the island. He awoke when it was already dark and he heard his sister welcoming a late arrival, who had travelled from one of the nearby islands, with warmth and enthusiasm. He smiled and tried to get up, but a pain seared through his chest and he groaned as he slumped back in the chair. Hearing Joe cry out, Pamela rushed to his side and realising the seriousness of his condition ordered the young lad, who was waiting patiently for his tip, to rush to fetch the doctor.

The next time Joe regained consciousness he was aware of being bundled into a trap and was jarred by the juddering of the cobbled streets as the cart strained up the hill. Joe had been taken by the doctor to the nunnery up the hill, where he was to be cared for in their small but clean hospital wing. Les Cothils was nearby and his sister was thankful that the nuns had an excellent reputation for their care of local patients.

In the next few hours Joe was occasionally aware of veiled faces over him with kindly eyes and more than once believed he might have passed away to the other world. He did not have the strength to wake up but felt totally at peace as he slipped into oblivion.

For the first couple of days on her own Harriet busied herself with the task of spring-cleaning to prepare the house for Joe's return. At night she sat by the cosy fire, her mind drifting to happy times with Joe and their family; The day they proudly pushed Sarah along the exciting new Royal Pier in her pram and the street celebrations as they welcomed in the new century. She could not help but think of Sarnia and their joy when Ernest was born and wondered if Joe was enjoying his visit.

The following morning she felt a pang of loneliness but attributed her sadness to working too hard she decided to sit down for a well earned break and her eyes had just settled on Joe's favourite armchair when she was surprised by a firm knock at the door. She struggled to her feet and opened the door.

Nothing had prepared her for the sight of the black-capped telegram boy who was holding his outstretched hand towards her. She could see the curtains twitch at the house opposite as her neighbours strained to see what was happening. She slowly grasped the paper in his outstretched hand and thanked the boy before retreating to the relative safety of her home. Harriet sat back heavily in her chair and with shaking fingers she broke the seal. As she read the words her eyes misted over and the colour drained from her complexion. She felt so alone in the world.

A few minutes later one of her neighbours had let herself into the kitchen and, guessing the news, put the kettle on the stove to make Harriet a cup of strong tea, adding a drop of brandy in the cup before handing it to the ashen faced Harriet. Mrs Groom sent her son to take messages to Sarah and Ernest and she sat on a stool next to Harriet resting her hand on hers and chattering unending words of comfort.

Harriet heard nothing but stared into the embers of the fire until Sarah, Ernest and the twins were by her side. They hugged her as they arrived and their presence filled the tiny parlour. They talked among themselves over Harriet's head, hurt that their father had chosen to go to Sarnia and arguing about arrangements to be made.

'We shall book a passage for us all on the morning packet steamer to Sarnia, Mama. I will help you to get packed,' exclaimed Sarah.

Harriet, who had hardly spoken since their arrival and heard little of their conversation focussed on her words at last.

'No Sarah. You go to Sarnia. I have no wish to come but I understand your wish to go. I have my precious memories of your father here with me. I have no need to go to a funeral to remember him dead. I need to remember him alive.'

Nothing any of her children could say would change Harriet's mind and so they prepared to travel without her.

Since her brothers had departed to make ready, Sarah looked thoughtfully at her mama and asked gently, 'Should we send word to Uncle Edward Mama?'

'No Sarah, I do not even know where he lives,' Harriet exclaimed, surprised to hear her daughter mention Edward's name.

'I know where he lives Mama,' Sarah replied. She explained, to her mother's confusion and dismay, that her father Joe had taken her to see Uncle Edward and Marie on several occasions over the years, taking the trip on the little ferry to Hythe. It had been their little secret. She had never questioned why they did not tell Harriet of their visits and as she got older and more worldly wise she wondered if it was that her mother would not approve that Edward and Marie had never married.

Harriet was stunned by this revelation but she was too emotional to dwell on the reasons for her husband's deception.

'Send word by all means,' she replied quietly.

Sarah sent word to Edward as they prepared to set sail the following morning.

It was a tearful parting as she reluctantly left her mother in Florence Street. Harriet had no wish to say farewell at the harbour preferring to remain in the security of her home alone with her thoughts.

Sarah had been reassured by Mrs Groom that she would keep a close eye on her mother and so she reluctantly departed to join her brothers who were waiting for the steamer.

On the day of the funeral Harriet arranged some flowers and placed them in a vase beside a picture of Joe on their mantelpiece above the hearth. She was staring dreamily at the flowers when a knock at the door brought her back to reality. Harriet was not surprised to see the tall rugged figure of Edward filling the doorway.

'Come for a stroll with me Harriet,' he suggested firmly, not wishing to enter and settle in Joe's armchair beside the fire. 'The fresh air will do you good,' he added.

'Yes I think that would be nice,' she replied gently. She fetched her shawl and picked a red rose from the vase, gently wrapping it in her handkerchief. Ignoring the twitching curtains of the neighbours as they passed by and oblivious to the tutting behind closed doors, they walked in silence along the path towards Weston Shore.

It was comforting to hear the sound of their feet on the gravelly beach and the waves lapping gently at the water's edge. Fisherman's Walk was visible since it was low tide and Edward followed Harriet along the sandy flats out into the water. She stopped and said a silent prayer of thanks for Joe and their life together as she threw the rose out into the water.

Edward waited at a respectful distance for many minutes but, aware of the dangers of the incoming tide, he walked up to her and gently put his hand on her shoulder to guide Harriet safely back to the beach.

They strolled further along the beach towards Netley Abbey where they rested on a fallen log on the edge of the tree line, watching the many ships and tiny boats pass by.

'There's the mail steamer to Sarnia,' stated Edward, breaking the long silence between them.

The familiar vessel floated gently past them up the river.

'I know,' Harriet replied in a whisper.

They sat in companionable silence, each deep in thought. Harriet's hands were resting at her sides on the log.

Without thinking, slowly Edward moved his hand and gently rested it on Harriet's.